Praise for the novels of Patricia Rice

Almost Perfect

"Brilliant and riveting, edgy and funny."

—MARY JO PUTNEY

Nobody's Angel

"Passion, betrayal, and churning emotions make *Nobody's Angel* a terrific way to spend your leisure hours."

—*Romantic Times*

Impossible Dreams

"Patricia Rice shows her diverse talent as a writer in *Impossible Dreams*. . . . [It] will leave readers with a smile on their faces."

—*Murray Ledger & Times* (KY)

Volcano

"Fast-paced . . . Great sexual tension."

—*All About Romance*

Blue Clouds

"Totally engrossing! Fast-moving, great characters, suspense, and love—a must-read!"

—*The Literary Times*

Also by Patricia Rice

IMPOSSIBLE DREAMS
NOBODY'S ANGEL
VOLCANO
GARDEN OF DREAMS
BLUE CLOUDS
ALMOST PERFECT

McCLOUD'S WOMAN

PATRICIA RICE

IVY BOOKS • NEW YORK

This book contains an excerpt from the forthcoming paperback edition of *Her Magic Touch* by Patricia Rice. This excerpt has been set for this edition only and may not reflect the final content of the forthcoming edition.

An Ivy Book
Published by The Ballantine Publishing Group

www.ballantinebooks.com

ISBN 0-8041-1982-1

Manufactured in the United States of America

First Edition: March 2003

10 9 8 7 6 5 4 3 2 1

To all survivors everywhere—always choose to live life to the fullest. You never know how much that choice affects the world around you.

ONE

Slamming down the phone and shoving a wayward strand of hair away from her face, the woman in a pristine lab coat glared at the man hunkered over a microscope at the far end of the worktable. "You don't get it, do you? You just don't get anything."

Not immediately responding to his assistant's outburst, Timothy John McCloud methodically jotted his observations in his notebook. Then, removing his reading glasses, he swung around on his stool to cock an eyebrow at her. A V-shaped scar over the bridge of his nose would have created a permanent scowl if it hadn't also nicked his eyebrow. The inquisitive arch that resulted lessened the impact of the frown.

"I just don't get what?" he asked cautiously.

"This!" Leona pointed an accusing finger at the stack of cardboard boxes against the wall of the tiny storefront office. "Burn them, and save yourself the grief."

Another of those persistent idiots in the Defense Department must have been on the phone, TJ concluded. Problem solved, he returned to his microscope.

At least Leona had learned to keep the bastards off his back. Tearing the phone off the wall the last time they'd hounded him hadn't been his finest hour, but it had apparently impressed his assistant enough so that she now screened his calls.

"What about *us*? Are those damned boxes more important than our future?" She ripped off her white lab coat and shook it at him to catch his attention.

Reaching for another slide, TJ hoped he'd misunderstood Leona's histrionics. "There is no us," he clarified, just in case. "You're an employee. I'm the company. If anything happens, I'm responsible." He chose the more generous interpretation of her declaration. Just because he was on the brink of self-destruction didn't mean he needed to drag any idealistic innocents down with him.

"What about last night?" she demanded. "How can you say there is no us?"

TJ rubbed his forehead. Taking Leona out for coffee a few times probably had been a mistake. He always misunderstood the direction of the female mind. He'd thought they had a strictly professional relationship. But the way he'd let her ramble on about her dreams of their nonexistent future might have led her to believe differently. And maybe he shouldn't have kissed her last night when she'd thrown her arms around him. In hindsight, that had been a stupid move on his part, although at the time it had been a satisfactory distraction.

Given his current state of repressed desperation, though, it was a miracle he hadn't jumped her bones and accepted the consequences later.

He'd had a lucky escape, and he wanted to keep it that way. On his best day he didn't have the correct attention span to suit women, nor the kind of settled lifestyle they expected. Now that his life had sunk to a new nadir, he didn't need the additional hassle of second-guessing a woman's wants.

TJ started to run his fingers through his hair and knocked his glasses askew in the process. Mentally cursing, he tried to refocus on the skeletal fragment on the slide in front of him.

"Are you even listening, TJ?" Leona shouted. "We could have a good thing here. Doesn't that matter to you? Just burn the damned boxes and get on with life."

An invisible noose constricted his breathing as TJ thought of the papers in those boxes—papers that should have been shredded months ago. If he believed media hys-

terics, those boxes had the power to erase all the good he and dozens of others had accomplished in these last few years.

He didn't want to believe the media accusations that the family friend who had launched his career had profited from the crimes of war criminals. He should trust Martin, shred the box contents as he'd been ordered to do, and let the hysteria die of its own accord. But destroying potential evidence went against everything for which he lived. On the other hand, opening those boxes meant passing judgment on his mentor. He'd done that once to a friend, with spectacularly disastrous results.

TJ liked his career. Forensic anthropology might not be an exciting vocation to some, but studying human remains for judicial evidence suited his methodical, detail-oriented mind-set, with the added benefit of fulfilling his craving for justice. He didn't want his career going down in flames for concealing a criminal, or for consorting with one.

TJ couldn't remember ever panicking during years of traipsing the war zones of Eastern Europe and Africa, but something dark and ugly had taken root the day he'd returned home to open the newspapers—and had realized what the notebooks in those boxes could contain.

"Look, just burn the junk, all right?" Angrily Leona wadded up her lab coat. "No more threatening phone calls. No more hiding out in this backwater to avoid journalists. You're a brilliant scientist with a staggering reputation. You can work anywhere, demand any price. Why destroy your career for a battle that's already lost?"

Excellent question. He never hired dumb assistants.

TJ carefully annotated his slide label and didn't look up. "I don't betray friends." He dropped the slide into its box and closed the cover. "I'm a private consultant, not an employee, so empty Defense Department threats can't intimidate me. Are you taking an early lunch?"

Leona flung her lab coat at him. Scarcely moving a

muscle, TJ let the coat slide off his shoulder and turned toward the next plastic specimen bag on the table.

"You're only a private consultant as long as someone will hire you," she yelled. "Who the hell will hire you if the entire world thinks you aided and abetted a criminal?"

A very real possibility, given the incendiary potential of the boxes. Of course, if he turned them over to the Defense Department, their contents could disappear and never be heard of again. The colonel's mission in the Balkans had been a sensitive one, and the military protected their own.

TJ had spent his career uncovering crimes of war. He didn't want to be party to a cover-up now.

He didn't want to turn the colonel over to rabid media hounds, either.

Dropping out of sight here in the middle of nowhere was a desperate attempt to salvage his mental health—before choosing between friendship and potential career suicide. Destroy the boxes or open them? He lost either way.

"I can pay your wages for the project regardless of my ultimate decision." Using tweezers, TJ removed a single golden hair from the specimen bag and arranged it on a fresh slide. He ignored the puddle of white cloth at his feet. His focus on his work to the exclusion of all else had incited worse reactions than flying lab coats. If she reached for the other microscope, he'd duck.

"It isn't my damned wages that concern me," she shouted. "My father could give us a whole lab if we liked. We could have a future together. Why can't you see that?"

"The only future I see right now is solving the mystery of these bones. That's what I hired you for."

Her lab notebook clipped him on the ear, bounced off his shoulder, and struck the human skeleton hanging on a stand behind him, rattling its bones. TJ sighed and caught the skeleton before it toppled.

"Take your damned bones to bed with you, then. That's the only relationship you'll ever know." Leona stalked out of the shabby inner office, disappearing into the even shabbier outer one.

TJ heard the front door slam behind her. With a sigh of regret, he rubbed at the tarnish on the brass canister he'd dug from the excavation site. He wished life could be as simple as it had been in the pre–Civil War days when the canister had been molded: no telephones, no computers, and women who believed men knew what they were doing.

As he leaned over to retrieve the scattered pages of the notebook, a gentle clapping broke the silence.

TJ's head jerked up, almost slamming into the counter. Bent over, he could only see a shapely ankle accented by red high-heeled mules. Straightening slowly, he absorbed the magnificent apparition in his doorway.

The high heels emphasized the curving perfection of long tanned legs, capped by a tight red miniskirt. Eyes popping, TJ looked higher, to a breathtaking figure that could have graced the pages of *Playboy*. Aware of his gaze, the genie posed seductively against the institutional green of his office door.

Damn, was he hallucinating? He should have heard her enter.

Hell, her looks should have screamed her entrance. That red spandex top revealed far more than it concealed, even with the silky transparent shirt thrown over it. Removing his glasses, TJ massaged the bridge of his nose.

He was surprised at himself—he never noticed what women wore. Had a covey of angels alighted, he might have noticed they wore a lot of white before returning to work. His ex-fiancée had pointed that out to him on numerous occasions.

TJ raised his gaze from that distracting body, only to be captured by something even more fascinating. Whipped-cream-and-lemon-pie-colored curls bobbed from an impossible heap atop a tan face of delicate angles. Slanted green eyes watched him with amusement as she crossed her arms under her bounteous bosom. Her taunting smile and turned-up nose alone could have halted a rampaging grizzly and morphed it into a drooling teddy bear. The rest of her could roll dead men in their graves and kill live ones in the sheer ecstasy of testosterone overdose.

Why did she look familiar? Startled at that reaction, TJ absently polished his glasses while applying his analytical mind to the puzzle.

"I applaud your ability to defy temptation," she purred, swiveling her hips as she moved toward him, watching him through eyes gleaming with interest.

Where had he seen her before? She was beautiful enough to be a movie starlet, but he didn't watch movies, so that couldn't be the answer. TJ couldn't picture her in the army fatigues worn by most of the women he'd met lately, and she didn't look as if she possessed the brains to be on any university staff he knew.

"I don't have time for this," he said aloud, returning his reading glasses to his nose. "Tourist information is down the street." TJ swung around on his stool, presenting her with his back.

"Did all that youthful energy bouncing out of here wear you out?" she asked with a hint of humor. This close, her subtle cologne drifted temptingly between the sharper odors of ammonia and formaldehyde.

Awareness crept across TJ's skin, irritating him far more than Leona's senseless departure. "This is a private office. I'll thank you to state your business or depart."

Common sense told him his libido had taken an inconvenient detour. If he didn't have the patience to figure out the wayward path of an intelligent female mind like Leona's, he'd never calculate the logic of the blond genie glittering behind him. Ergo, there was no point in carrying his annoying fascination any further.

"Timid Timothy," she teased. "That much hasn't changed."

She ran a fingernail down the back of his lab coat, and the part of him with no brain reacted instantly. He broke his pencil lead and cursed.

She laughed, a low, knowing chuckle. "Want a hint?

Or shall I just fling something at you and flounce out like the last one?"

"Flounce, please," he answered mildly. "Without throwing anything breakable, if you could arrange it."

The sexy vibration of her laugh shot straight to his groin.

"I see the years have taught you flattery and charm," she teased. "I suppose there have been so many women in your life, they all look alike to you these days."

The second statement was as much mockery as the first, although TJ wasn't certain she knew it. He was aware he was certifiably charmless, and the only women in his life threw things at him.

And pointed jabs at open wounds didn't improve his humor. "The women I know have more brains than boobs, so their appearance is irrelevant," he replied, reaching for another slide.

"Oh, I'll get even with you for that one, Tim, just see if I don't." Her velvet voice slid into a dangerous undertone.

He couldn't concentrate on the slide under his microscope while inhaling an exotic scent with more mind-bending effect than pure opium. Was there something familiar in that warning? "If you're done threatening me, close the door behind you as you leave."

The air almost buzzed with her reaction, but her reply was bright and cheerful. "Your wish is my command, TJ."

He sensed more than heard her quiet departure. He couldn't know her, he swore. He'd certainly remember anyone that stunningly sexy. "Stunning" and "sexy" were not words to describe the intense, intelligent women he'd dated these last years. He looked for brains in women so he could converse with them on an equal level.

He shouldn't have insulted her, though. Obviously his temper had reached the snapping point, and he'd better resolve his problems soon, before his mind snapped with it.

He very definitely didn't need any more complications cluttering his thoughts, hampering the decision he had to make.

He hadn't been called Timid Tim since grammar school, and only his brothers lived to tell of it. Who the hell was she?

Humiliation still scalded.

Platform heels slapping the hot sidewalk, Mara Simon sizzled down the picturesque oak-lined street of the coastal South Carolina town she'd just arrived in. She hadn't been this embarrassed since tenth grade, when she'd asked a boy to the movies while they were standing in the school office, only to discover that the office microphone had been left on. The whole school had heard him laugh at her, and she'd hidden at home for a week. Leave it to Tim to dismiss her as if she were still that unwanted teen. Her cheeks burned.

Timothy John. TJ, as she'd heard the angry twit call him. TJ McCloud. He had changed since high school, but she'd still have known him anywhere. Obviously, though, he didn't know her.

That ought to teach her humility, if she needed any more lessons. She'd spent years believing they'd once had a meaningful relationship—even if it had consisted mostly of long-distance telephone calls for a brief time when they were kids. Tim had obviously forgotten her the instant he'd walked out of her life.

Stopping to elevate her sagging self-esteem, Mara applied her practiced smile to her reflection in a storefront window. Sticking her chin out, she noticed how her red lipstick matched her shirt, and she offered silent thanks to that dress-for-success book. Red was definitely a power color. She still had it together, even if Tim had shattered a few illusions.

She hadn't always had it together. Shy, skinny geeks seldom did.

Admiring the jut of her breasts as she took a deep breath, she recalled Tim's boobs comment. She wanted to be angry about it, but it only made her feel as giddy as a schoolgirl that he'd actually noticed she had breasts.

She should be pleased Tim hadn't recognized her, she decided. She'd worked long and hard to become a new and better person, and his lack of recognition proved she'd succeeded.

But he hadn't appreciated what he'd seen. She scowled again.

The last time she'd seen Tim, she'd been a gawky, owl-eyed teenager, and he had towered over almost every boy at the university. All awkward arms and legs from an adolescent growth spurt, Tim had been almost as skinny as she. Remembering the muscular breadth of the big man in that office, she could honestly say he wasn't skinny any longer.

She was, but she'd learned to deal with catty charges of anorexia. If he didn't like the way she looked, he could lump it.

"Define lump," she muttered to herself, stopping on a street corner and waiting for the town's lone traffic light to change. TJ McCloud still had the power to yank her chain.

Sunlight poured down on her, and she could smell the sea air from here. After the smog of L.A., the fresh air should be invigorating, but the only thing she could focus on was the look on TJ's face when he'd seen her. She might as well have been a fly in his jam. Damn him for reminding her of how humiliation felt. She'd suffered enough of that for a lifetime.

Sauntering across the intersection with the light change, Mara winked at a teenage boy. Head swiveling to follow her, the poor thing nearly fell over his feet.

My, how things changed. Once upon a time, she couldn't attract the interest of the scrawniest nerd in class.

Other things hadn't changed, though. Even as a gawky teenage boy, Tim had possessed that same dangerously impassive facade he'd presented to her today. She had been the only one in high school to glimpse the cauldron of passion simmering behind the facade. He'd been fiercely loyal, unfailingly generous, and uncompromisingly protective of those he considered friends. For whatever odd reason, he'd considered her brother, Brad, a friend.

At the memory of Brad, Mara's smile faded. She'd have mascara streaking her cheeks if she followed that thought. Seeing Tim brought back the devastating event that had torn her tightly knit family to shreds. Why the devil had she bothered looking him up?

Approaching the quaint B&B where she'd taken a suite, she grabbed an enormous pair of sunglasses from her bag and shoved them on her nose. Mara Simon didn't cry, but Patsy Simonetti, the teenage girl inside, still wept sometimes.

Think good thoughts, dope. She remembered the time a football player had called Brad a fag, and Tim had calmly lifted the two-hundred-pound linebacker, slammed him against a locker, and left him hanging on a hook by the back of his shirt. The memory provoked a smile. Tim hadn't raised a fist, or even his voice, but the jocks had left Brad alone from that day on.

She'd worshiped at Tim's feet that summer. He hadn't even known she'd existed.

Still didn't, she thought with wry honesty, although there had been those few short weeks . . .

But that led back to unhappy memories again, and she didn't go there anymore. She had a glorious future at her fingertips—one she'd earned by surviving hell—and those teenage days were behind her. She would taunt Tim to get even for his insult, then move on, as they both had before.

She stepped past the overgrown gardenia bush outside the B&B, inhaling the fragrance of a late blossom and admiring the carpet of magenta crape myrtle petals beneath her feet. The driver of the studio's Lincoln Town Car looked up from his newspaper. At her gesture, he laid the paper aside and smoothly rolled the limo up beside her. She did so love the perks of this business. Pity she'd had to give up most of them when she divorced Sid.

"Where's Ian?" she inquired, sliding onto the soft leather

rear seat, cooled by the air conditioner. She checked her hair in the mirror and applied a fresh coat of Rogue Rouge as the car purred past the gate and into the street.

"Round the corner, ma'am. Said to stop for him when you're ready." He drove the car past an antebellum mansion shaded by drooping oaks and down a narrow, crowded alley of brick restaurants and taverns.

The limo rolled up in front of a bar called the Blue Monkey, and Mara wrinkled her nose. They could be at an oasis in the Sahara and Ian would find a bar. Her ex said Ian was the best producer in the business, but she'd already learned that meant Ian could connect with anybody, anywhere, over a drink. She buzzed his cell phone, and he swaggered out a few minutes later.

"Hiya, babe. Was it the old boyfriend?" He slid in beside her.

Short, suave, and sophisticated, Ian would never be so crude as to reek of beer, but his three-hundred-dollar-an-ounce cologne smelled worse. Mara rolled her eyes behind her dark glasses and picked up her notebook. "Jared's brother, yes," she snapped. She hadn't seen Jared McCloud in years, either, but he was on the outskirts of the film industry, and her screenwriters had mentioned he had a house near this coastal resort. She'd put two and two together the instant she'd seen Tim's name in the weekly newspaper. There couldn't be two forensic anthropologists of the same name living in the same town with Tim's brother.

It was a small town. She supposed they'd all bump into each other sooner or later. She didn't know why she'd hoped for a more enlightening reunion. Must be that damned Patsy part of her, still clinging to teenage dreams of parties and popularity. Still, this way she could derive some entertainment from wondering how long it would take for the elusive McCloud brothers to figure out who she was.

Ian gave the driver directions to the beach where they'd be filming, and she studied a map of the area. Sid's scouts had been out here last year, but she'd been in town only a few hours. Time to get to work. "How difficult will it be to haul equipment?" she demanded. "It looks pretty rural from this."

"Last time I was here, there was an unpaved access road a crazy lady had blocked with weird contraptions," Ian answered, "but the state film board says that's all been cleared up. We have use of the road, but we have to stay off her property."

Mara grimaced. She was operating with a horrendously tight budget, and lunatics could be expensive. "The beach is public, right? We don't need anything but the state permit?"

Ian idly flipped through the channels on the limo's tiny TV. "Yeah, but the guys in the bar said there's been a hurricane through here since then. Sid should have sent someone to check it out. If the damned beach has washed away, we'll end up hauling in sand."

Damn Sid. Her ex had a penchant for ignoring details. Mara swallowed a lump of panic. Ian got paid whether this film made a profit or not. He didn't care how much sand cost. But every penny over budget cut into her share, and she needed every cent of it to buy out Sid. If she couldn't buy him out, she'd have to move back to her mother's place in Brooklyn, right back where she started ten thousand years ago. . . .

Never. She would bring the film in under budget and then some. She'd own the best small independent studio in Hollywood, and then no one could stop her.

The limo rolled quietly over a two-lane causeway connecting the town to the island. Pelicans soared across the Carolina blue sky. Waves lapped against the concrete abutments. Only Georgia pines and oaks broke the horizon. She loved the sun. She could work on her tan while here. She could work on Tim at the same time. She was a free agent now. The divorce was final, even if the financial settlement was iffy.

Smiling wickedly at the thought of freedom, Mara watched out the smoky glass as the limo turned from the asphalt highway onto a sandy lane. A thicket of bushes and palmettos gave the appearance of a deserted jungle, but she could see the shimmering copper of a weather-vane above a widow's walk on some house in the distance. The crazy lady's? If so, Mara liked her taste. It would be heavenly to sit in that tower, sipping coffee, watching the tide roll in as the sun came up.

The limo slowed to a halt, and Mara slipped off her Ferragamos to wiggle her toes. She should have brought sandals for strolling on the beach.

"Can't get no farther, ma'am," the driver said apologetically.

Thick, spiky bushes and dwarf palms lined either side of the road. Erasing the frown wrinkling her forehead, Mara slid her shoes back on and swung her legs out when the driver opened the door.

"Oh, shit," Ian muttered from the other side of the long black car.

Mara stared in horror at the chain-link fence stretched across the road, blocking access to a towering barrier of sand and debris.

A giant sign shouting WARNING in red letters hung from the rail. Mara stepped closer and read: *This property protected by the federal government. For information, contact TJ McCloud Enterprises.*

TWO

The dig site blocked the access road to the beach house Cleo rented to him, so TJ usually parked at the dig and walked home over the dune. Tonight he considered driving past Cleo and Jared's place and doing that, but he knew it wasn't a healthy choice. The beach house had no food in the refrigerator, and he'd end up working half the night instead of eating.

Working half the night had more appeal than facing the abundant cheer of his brother's house, but despite his currently depressed state, he was only contemplating career suicide. Aside from the mental-health aspects of avoiding family, Cleo would no doubt kill him for ignoring her invitation. Or torment him mercilessly.

Thinking of his brother's odd marriage, TJ shook his head and parked his rented Taurus beside Jared's Jeep. How his effervescent younger brother had hooked up with a misanthropic piece of work like Cleo was beyond his ability to comprehend. It just proved TJ's cluelessness about relationships, though, because he'd never seen two people happier together.

A seven-year-old bundle of energy burst through the front doorway, leapt from the porch, and landed squarely in TJ's arms as he approached the house. *Eight years old,* he reminded himself. Matty had just celebrated a birthday last week. The boy smelled of lemonade and onions. With experience gained in this last month, TJ swung his nephew under his arm. "Hey, soldier. Your mama feeding you pure sugar again?"

Dealing with children was a new experience, but TJ adapted well. Pushing past the screen door, he yelled, "I found a stray monkey in the yard!" into the seemingly empty house. "Should I put him in the zoo?" The boy under his arm giggled, naively accepting his world as an unthreatening place. TJ wished he could recapture that kind of innocence.

"Nah. Jared thinks he can train him for the circus, but he's having a little trouble keeping a lid on him." Wearing a grease-stained man's work shirt and wiping her hands on a red rag, Cleo emerged from a back room.

Maybe he should look for a woman like Cleo. She asked for nothing and expected nothing. She did things in her own way, in her own time. Other women might greet dinner guests in flour-covered aprons or high heels and sexy dresses, but Cleo had obviously been working on another of her mechanical contraptions and had forgotten the time. Jared had seen past Cleo's dirt-smudged face and uncombed curls to the gem beneath. Maybe TJ ought to learn from his little brother and practice looking beyond the obvious.

Not that he was ever in one place long enough to try. His contracts with the Defense Department and the United Nations might put him in the company of the occasional military female for a few weeks, but he spent the better part of his time digging in graves and the rest examining bones—not the kind of date most women cherished.

TJ didn't know why he was thinking along those lines at all. He had carved out a unique career few men could step into. He had awards for humanitarian efforts in half a dozen war-torn countries. He had dedicated his life to truth and justice, and didn't regret his footloose lifestyle for a minute.

Or hadn't, until he'd met the ugly underside of his accomplishment.

"Jared ordering pizza?" TJ asked gravely, handing the wriggling boy to his mother.

"Nope, fixing tacos. I have a whole bottle of ipecac in the medicine chest should we need it. Go on back. I'll clean up and be with you in a minute."

Jared looked up from a frying pan of hamburger and onions when TJ entered. "Hey, old man, you're looking grimmer than usual. Those skeletons rattling back?"

"Why? Does Cleo want them dancing in the drive?" TJ picked a tortilla chip from the bowl and stuck it in the guacamole.

Jared grinned. "She'd love that. The first of the movie people arrived in town today, and she's already muttering dire imprecations. The mayor suggested she open a road around your excavation."

"Tell her there are federal laws about sand dunes and sea oats. The movie people will have to hire a boat."

"I don't know if that hurricane trash pile you're digging in qualifies as a sand dune, and I don't remember any sea oats—"

The back door flew open and a short, stocky teenage boy burst in. "Did you see the limo? Did you? Reckon it had movie stars in it?"

A tall, wraithlike girl followed Gene at a more leisurely pace. Eyes darting to ascertain the occupants of the room, Kismet smiled shyly, then silently drifted past the men to the front room.

After a month of living on this island, TJ had grown accustomed to the neighbor's eccentric children. Taking a chair at the table, he munched on the chips and let Jared field the boy's eager questions. Movie stars? He grimaced at the memory of the woman in red. Definitely movie star material. He wondered how the hell she knew his name. Surely Jared hadn't mentioned him in his brief forays into Hollywood life.

"I don't think the actors arrive until production starts," Jared told the boy. "I imagine you saw the director or producer or their assistants."

"Do assistants wear see-through blouses and skirts that barely cover their rear?" TJ mused aloud, reaching behind him to open the refrigerator, remembering too late that Cleo didn't keep beer in the house.

Both Jared and Gene turned to study him with interest. "See-through?" the teenager prompted eagerly.

Scrubbed free of grease, Cleo caught the refrigerator door and removed a can of Dr Pepper before TJ could shut it. "See-through?" she repeated innocently, glancing at her husband as she popped the top.

"Ask big brother, not me." Jared threw up his hands in self-defense. "I don't do Hollywood these days."

Kismet followed Cleo into the kitchen, as if she felt safe only in the presence of another female. Quietly she began setting the table while Cleo produced chopped vegetables and opened a bottle of salsa to go with the tacos.

"You didn't ever do Hollywood," TJ reminded him. "They tried to do you, and you balked."

"Creative differences." Jared set the frying pan of sizzling meat onto a trivet in the center of the table. "But I've kept my contacts. I know Sid Rosenthal owns the studio for this film. A friend of mine worked on the script."

"I don't suppose Sid wears see-through red?" Cleo widened her eyes in feigned innocence and reached for a tortilla. Today her T-shirt read ALLOW ME TO INTRODUCE MY SELVES.

Jared kissed her nape and slid into the seat beside her. "No, but Sid's wife might. She owns half the company. The pirate film is her idea."

Rosenthal. Nope, he didn't know any Rosenthals. Besides, TJ couldn't imagine that high-heeled chorus girl as a producer of anything but seductive smiles. He wished she'd get out of his head. He had other things far more important to think about. Starting with replacing Leona.

"I think my assistant quit," he said by way of taking part in the conversation.

No one seemed surprised by the odd direction of his thoughts.

"You *think?*" Cleo asked.

"Tim's assistants always quit," Jared explained, reaching for the salsa. "He ignores them until they either do something explosive to prove they exist, or decide they're invisible and disappear into the woodwork."

"I hire them to work, not become a part of my life," TJ growled.

"You have no life," Cleo said bluntly. "Most women just don't realize you like it that way."

Exactly, TJ thought in satisfaction. Finally, a woman who got it, to use Leona's memorable phrasing. He liked his life the way it was.

Which was why he was reluctant to ruin it.

"Sid, you should have known about this!" Mara shouted into her cell phone while scanning through the files of her personal digital assistant, looking for the names of local officials. "There's a damned archeological dig square in the middle of the road. We'll never get equipment out there."

Locating the mayor's name, she handed the computerized address book to Ian, accepted the drink he offered her, and glanced at the scenery passing outside the limo's window. "No, I haven't talked to the site foreman yet." She grimaced at her ex-husband's annoying habit of treating her like an idiot. But what else could she expect? She'd disguised her brains too long. "I didn't even know the dig existed until two minutes ago. There has to be another entrance to that beach."

Using his own cell phone, Ian left a message on the mayor's machine and began scanning her file for other numbers. Mara took a sip of her martini while Sid ranted, then set the drink back in the limo bar and reached for her notes. She should have followed her instincts and left Sid out of this, but she was terrified she'd wreck everything on her own. She'd made a career of wrecking things.

"Sid, those scenes require a boom. We can't get it in there without taking a bulldozer to that dune. Someone should have checked the location after the hurricane." She rifled through her notes until she found the map again. A rock jetty blocked the east end of the beach. The crazy lady's swamp blocked the west end. No access anywhere.

Visions of the whole production imploding danced across her mind. They'd already spent a quarter million. Glynis Everett would only be available for the next six months, and they needed three of those months at this location. Without the star, the film was dead in the water. A quarter million down the drain—along with her dreams of owning her own studio. She'd be under her family's thumb for the rest of her life.

They'd crush her into the lowly creature she'd once been. She couldn't let that happen. She'd go as crazy as her mother.

Now there was a topic best avoided. Tapping her gold pen against her notes, Mara half listened to Sid's curses and threats while she formulated another plan in the back of her mind.

She knew Tim, or had, a lifetime ago. He'd probably been the only shy athlete in the history of their exclusive Long Island private school. He'd even had time for the lonely four-eyed sister of his best friend. She'd suffered a bad case of hero worship until the day he'd turned traitor and walked out on her when she needed him most. He owed her for that.

He wouldn't see it that way.

No matter. They were on level playing ground now. She was no longer the humble scholarship student, and he wasn't the wealthy golden-boy athlete. This time he could work with her, or she'd play hardball.

Remembering the dangerous light in TJ's eyes when he'd ordered her out of his lab, Mara thought she'd prefer working with him than against him, but the choice would have to be his.

Hitting the phone's end button and cutting Sid off in mid-rant, she retrieved her address book from the PDA and pointed out a list of names to Ian. "Call all the city council members. They want this film, they'll have to earn it."

"Hire a secretary," he growled, refusing the device.

"Hire one for me," she countered. That's what she had enjoyed most about being Sid's wife—other people always did what she couldn't, or what she was afraid to try. All she'd ever had to do was look good.

Those days were over. Mara dropped the palm-sized computer in Ian's lap. "The council or a temp agency," she ordered, returning her attention to the maps and notes in her lap.

She'd mourned her thirty-third birthday months ago. Time was passing. If she couldn't stand on her own two feet now, she never would. She had to reverse a lifetime of habits in the next six months if she wanted to survive.

Having been humiliated the day before, Mara carefully chose her clothing the next morning. TJ had nearly dropped his teeth when he'd seen her yesterday. She wanted his attention today, but she preferred he focus it on their discussion and not her boobs. That caused something of a dilemma. She didn't have much else in the way of attention-getting assets.

She glanced down at the cleavage exposed by her padded lace Wonderbra, wrinkled her nose, and debated. Her life had taken a 180-degree turn the day she'd shed her dowdy chrysalis and emerged as a glamorous butterfly. She'd worked on her image ever since. As Sid's wife, she'd had a personal trainer, a makeup consultant, a hairdresser, and a wardrobe designer. After the divorce, she'd had to let all of them go but Constantina, the hairdresser the company paid. She'd had her own gym in Sid's mansion until she gambled her share of the house in exchange for his half of the studio. Beauty equated with power in her world.

She examined the wrinkles at the corners of her eyes and wondered if she ought to consider a face-lift. Shrugging, she reached for an electric blue silk shirt from the closet. With all her money tied up in the film, she was lucky to be able to afford a nail clipper. She was too old for the ingenue parts she had taken when she'd first arrived in Hollywood. Her fledgling career had died an early death when she'd married Sid. Everyone made their fair share of mistakes. Why did hers have to be of such catastrophic quality?

"Not the blue!" her hairdresser wailed, entering without knocking. "You'll look like Dolly Parton."

"I should be so lucky," Mara muttered, defiantly buttoning the shirt. She grabbed a pair of tailored jeans from the shelf. Once upon a time she'd lived in jeans. Maybe TJ would recognize her if she reverted to form.

"You're too old to wear those," Constantina declared ominously. "You might as well part your hair in the middle and let it hang down your back like a teenager."

Just what she didn't need to hear with the upcoming meeting with TJ fraying her nerves. Mara narrowed her eyes at the reflection of her plump Italian hairdresser in the full-length mirror. "Tell me I'm old one more time, and you're outta here. I ditched a rich husband for that." A rich husband who had taught her to take the offensive when challenged.

"You ditched Sid because you caught him humping starlets again," Constantina said dismissively, accustomed to arguing with her Hollywood clientele. "It's not your fault if he's a few years short of a pedophile. But it *is* your fault if you go around looking like a derelict."

"Derelicts don't wear three-hundred-dollar jeans." Mara wriggled the denim over her long legs. This wasn't Hollywood. She didn't have to impress anyone—except TJ.

She liked his new nickname. It suited that seething cauldron he disguised behind his mild-mannered Clark Kent routine.

Constantina sniffed. "I thought you had a meeting with the mayor. Believe me, the town council's wives don't wear jeans."

"That's because they're fat and I'm not."

"That's because you're the next best thing to anorexic."

"I eat like a horse," Mara shouted, tired of hearing about her faults. "I'm naturally thin. It goes with the height."

"That's why you're supposed to wear skirts." Constantina gestured angrily. "You make men nervous when you tower over them and wear pants. They hide your femininity."

"Spoken like a short person." Political correctness be damned. She didn't even know the wives of the town council, and she hated them already. Shoving her bare feet into a pair of high-heeled snakeskin mules, Mara grabbed her portfolio off the dresser and headed for the door. She'd spent over half her life worrying about her looks. She was damned well tired of it.

Constantina threw an Italian curse after her as Mara slammed the bedroom door. Nothing like a good fight to start the day—just like home.

Clattering down the stairs of the antebellum B&B, Mara waved at Katy Richards, the proprietress, and hurried out the front door before being forced to indulge in chitchat. She'd rented the entire establishment for her staff so they wouldn't have to run a gauntlet of sightseers every time they left their rooms.

Leaning against the limo door, her driver snapped to attention at the sight of her striding down the drive, but she waved him off.

"I'm walking, Jim. I'll call if I need you."

This wasn't Hollywood. She didn't need bodyguards. Striding briskly from beneath the elongated limbs of Spanish-moss-draped oaks, she donned her sunglasses and headed in the direction of TJ's lab on the quaint street of old storefronts and new boutiques leading down to the harbor. Surely they could reach some rational agreement. What were old friends for?

Might depend on the definition of friends, she admitted. Sid had always said that the Hollywood kind of friend was good for publicity or parties or stabbing a person in the back. In that vein, she supposed the Brooklyn kind could be considered good for resentment and prejudice. TJ was from Long Island, but that didn't mean he had a higher standard.

So all right, she didn't have any real friends. Maybe only stupid, naive people actually believed in friendship. She'd live. There were far worse things in the world than not having friends. Her mother was one of them.

Wow, why did she keep heading down that tangled path? Had running into Tim reminded her too much of home? She shivered at the picture of her future if she didn't make this film work.

Glancing in a darkened store window, Mara caught her blond reflection and let her mood swing upward again. For thirty-three, she looked damned good in jeans. Now it was time to see what her old teenage idol thought.

Whistling, she swung around—and slammed straight into TJ McCloud's impressive chest.

THREE

Catching the long-legged femme fatale felt as familiar as looking at her. A memory tugged at the back of his mind, but TJ didn't have time to pin it down. He had to conquer an armful of pliant female curves and a starving libido run amok.

Slanted, cat green eyes peered up at him, and for one dread moment he thought she purred.

"Well, hello, handsome. Imagine running into you like this." She didn't immediately step back, but lightly rested her long fingers on his shoulders and regained her balance with a little shimmy that brushed her breasts close enough to smoke his shirt buttons. Then she released him but didn't move away.

The fragrance of gardenias lingered. The women TJ knew tended to smell of chalk dust or musty books or, in Cleo's case, mechanic's grease. Overseas, in the pits of hell he'd lived in, they tended to smell of sweat or fear. Gardenias were as foreign to him as wedding bouquets.

"Excuse me," he said politely, stepping to one side. If nothing else, he'd learned the value of self-discipline.

"Excuse you for what? Living?" she teased, fluttering her lashes. "That's probably an unpardonable sin, but I'm willing to overlook it." She tilted her head, and a few silky curls fell from the stack. "Once upon a time, you had the vestige of a sense of humor. Did it all dry up?"

His brothers had always called TJ the professor and swore he never laughed. In these past years he'd learned that humor and human remains didn't mix well. If she wanted a comedian, he'd send her to Jared. Maybe his brother was the one she was remembering. Jared had a way with women.

TJ took another step away, diverting his gaze from tantalizing curves revealed by an open button on her blue shirt. "In my profession, humor tends toward the macabre, so if I was supposed to laugh, I apologize. If you would excuse me, I have to go to the office. I have no one answering the phone today."

"That's why God invented answering machines." She swung into step beside him.

Her height and stride fit comfortably beside his. Reaching his office door, TJ unlocked but didn't open it. "Are you applying for the job of my assistant?"

"Do you think I'd look good in a lab coat?" She patted her upswept blond hair and batted her long lashes outrageously. "What else is your assistant required to do?"

"Work independently and leave me alone," he answered gravely.

An imp of interest played havoc with TJ's restraint as she began whistling an inane song from an old television show while giving him an appraising once-over as if he were a centerfold of *Playgirl*. The song rang clarion warnings in his mind, but her admiring stare was messing with his head, and he didn't heed the alarm.

"Honey, you'd better hire yourself a man if you want to be left alone. I don't think you'd be safe even with a blind woman." Her hand did an imitation of pitter-patter above her right breast, then transferred to repeat the gesture on his shirt pocket.

TJ dodged her marauding fingers and shoved open the door. "If you're not applying for the job, then I'll leave you here. We're not open to the public." He couldn't—wouldn't—let her distract him.

She leaned against the frame and crossed her arms, preventing him from closing the door. "I didn't come out here for the pleasure of torturing you—although that holds a certain appeal. We need to talk."

Another piece of the puzzle popped from his memory. Patsy used to say that. Her worst arguments started with "We need to talk," accompanied by exactly the same body language. *Doo-wah-diddy-diddy,* that was how the song went. She used to wail it off-key at the top of her lungs when she followed him and Brad down the street.

Patsy? TJ squeezed his eyes shut and shook his head to free the cobwebs. Why in hell had he thought of that skinny child when faced with this full-grown blond bombshell? Patsy had brown braids, thick glasses, and lurked a hundred years in his past. She was probably a lawyer tackling the Supreme Court by now.

Resolutely, TJ opened his eyes, determined to dismiss the puzzle and start sorting through the evidence boxes as he should have done when they'd arrived a few days ago.

Green eyes stared back at him. Patsy had green eyes. They'd been her best feature, although no one had noticed them behind her cheap horn-rims.

"Timothy John, if you don't quit looking at me like I'm a Martian invader, I'll kick your shin."

Patsy. TJ closed his eyes again and shuddered. No way. Not now. Not here. Not looking like *this*. A voice from his past speaking through the luscious lips of a movie star had to be a hallucination. Maybe his crazed brain thought he needed a sharp jab in the eye to get him focused.

The apparition caught his elbow and steered him inside, letting the door snap closed behind them. She was tall, reaching past his shoulder. He'd always liked that about Patsy—her height made him feel less awkward. He inhaled gardenias again and rejected the image. The Patsy he remembered had smelled of Tootsie Pops and cheap mouthwash and looked at him with adoration.

Patsy had been sixteen the last time he'd seen her. She hadn't smelled of Tootsie Pops then.

"I'm really having fun with this charade, Tim, but I don't have time to play anymore. Do you really need me to tell you who I am?" Impatience tinged her voice.

With his eyes closed, he could hear his boyhood nemesis clearly enough. The New York accent had blurred over the years, but her clipped words defined it better than the sexy drawl she'd been using. Maybe if he kept his eyes closed . . .

He opened them to narrow slits and studied the stunning woman propping her hands on her hips and glaring at him. The hair wasn't Patsy's. Neither was the nose. He cocked his head thoughtfully. He was a trained anthropologist, knew bone structure inside and out, and could identify sex, race, and age of a skeleton with relative accuracy at a glance. He just had some difficulty seeing bones through creamy skin and tempting curves.

Right height, right limb proportions. Patsy had been as tall as her brother. She should have gone to a school with a women's basketball team, but her parents were fixated on sending Brad to an exclusive prep school that would prepare him for Harvard. They'd sent Patsy to the expensive school only because Brad had refused to go without her.

Brad. Why did he have to be reminded of that tragic failure in judgment at a time when he had to make a worse choice involving another friend? TJ winced at the searing memory.

"What the hell did you do to your hair?" With that gruff acceptance of the improbable, he stalked toward his lab, grabbing his white coat off a hook as he passed by. He'd never be able to concentrate now. He would have to do the mundane stuff, like answer unanswered phone calls.

Mara breathed a sigh of both relief and trepidation at TJ's recognition. So much for hoping for fond reminiscences. The arrogant jock still carried the burden of guilt.

"Bleached it, like any sensible female," she retorted, following him in. "Will you stop ignoring me and sit down and talk a minute?" she demanded when he reached for his box of slides and pulled his glasses out of his lab coat pocket. "Couldn't we at least have a cup of coffee and get reacquainted?"

"What do you want, Pats? I'm on a tight schedule and short an assistant, if you haven't noticed."

Pats. It had been seventeen years since anyone had called her that. Her first husband had called her lots of names, but none of them as friendly as Pats. She'd dropped the whole ugly Patricia thing when she'd taken the job at Bloomingdale's.

But she didn't do trips down memory lane. "My schedule is not only tighter, but more expensive," she answered angrily. "I have half a dozen high-priced, high-strung actors descending on this fair city in the next few weeks, and I need to get my scenes set."

The look he shot her from beneath those sexy eyebrows awakened every ounce of femininity in her. TJ McCloud had grown into a hunk with smoldering dark eyes and shoulders a linebacker would envy. Why in the name of heaven had she ever settled for a spineless worm like Irving and an aging roué like Sid when there were men like TJ available?

Because men like TJ McCloud were never available to the Patsy Simonettis of the world. In a huff of impatience at that thought, Mara blew a straying curl off her forehead.

"Then I advise you to go set scenes," TJ answered, turning his back on her again to pull his microscope from a cabinet.

Mara thumped the back of his head with the rolled-up newspaper she'd picked up at his door. "If you don't start behaving, Timothy John, I'll tell your mother on you!"

He snorted something remarkably like laughter before swinging the stool around and propping his elbows against the battered wood counter behind him while he studied her from head to toe. His buttoned shirt strained across his chest, and his too-knowing eyes stripped her of all disguise.

"What did you do to your nose?" TJ demanded.

"Cut it off," she replied tartly. "It got in my way."

"I'm sorry to hear your parents are dead."

"My parents aren't dead!" Damn, but he had her behaving just like the frustrated teenager she'd once been. She wanted to stamp her feet and pelt him with Milk Duds. "What in hell makes you think they are?"

"I figured if they weren't already rolling in their graves, they'd have dropped dead in shock when you came home like that."

Mara grabbed a book from the shelves behind her and started to fling it at his head. Something in TJ's expression stopped her. Carefully setting the book down on a desk, she studied him. He almost looked disappointed that she hadn't thrown it.

"Obnoxious bastard," she muttered. "You want to drive me away. That's what you did to that idiot who flounced out of here yesterday, isn't it? You got a thing against women, TJ?"

"Not if they stay out of my way. I have work to do. What do you want, Patsy?"

"It's Mara now. Mara Simon, now that I've got rid of the Rosenthal."

His crooked eyebrow raised. So he wasn't completely oblivious after all, she thought. He'd heard of Sid, at least.

She nodded at the assortment of bones and other relics scattered across the counter. "What are you working on?"

"Not pirate bones," he answered in satisfaction. "So if you want a PR break, you'll not find it here."

She'd hoped the rumor of pirate remains had been true. It would have been great publicity, but she could survive without it. She couldn't survive without that beach. "Unless you've uncovered one of the Lost Tribes, I hope you'll cut me some slack and let me take my equipment through that access road you're blocking."

"It's private property, and I have federal permission to

dig. I'll be done in a few months. Come back then." He remained immovable.

Not totally immovable. She was aware of the way he studied her over the top of his half glasses. When his gaze dropped to her shirt, she realized she'd have to break the bad habit of leaving that extra button open. This wasn't L.A., and she didn't need his attention on her breasts right now. "The weather won't be as cooperative later. I have six months to complete this film, and I have to shoot these scenes now. We won't disturb your excavations. We just need to take trucks past your fence."

"I can't allow that dune to be destroyed by heavy vehicles any more than I can let you tear up the excavation until I've located all the remains. There are dead bodies buried there. You don't drive through cemeteries in semis."

"I have a state permit to film there!" she shouted. "I can do anything I damned well want."

"Try it and see what happens," he said calmly.

They were replaying adolescent roles. But Mara knew the futility of arguing with Tim. He'd only fling her out. "I have a permit," she repeated in the same calm tones. "If we can't work together, then I'll go to a higher authority. Your choice."

"Pats, it isn't going to work. I'm not Brad or whomever else you've learned to manipulate with that treacherous mind of yours. You can't threaten me. I have a federal grant for this site, and I'm not budging until I'm finished. Find another beach."

"There's a reason pirates used these beaches and not all the others." Throwing things would be so much simpler than reasoning with a hardheaded rhino like Tim, but at least he remembered she had brains. "I've spent a fortune scouting this location. It's too late to change."

"That's ridiculous. The Carolina coast is littered with beaches. Or you can ship your stuff to the island. Be creative. I have to get back to work." He stood up, apparently prepared to shove her out the door.

"You can't fight this," she warned. "The town wants my money. They're on my side."

"In your dreams. If I could make things happen simply by believing them, I'd wish for world peace. Out, Pats." He took a threatening step in her direction.

He was broader and taller, and she didn't have a chance against him physically. Mentally, however, they were evenly matched. Smiling, Mara didn't retreat but traced a long, polished fingernail down his shirt front. "I can make things happen, big boy. Want me to make them happen for you?"

He waited implacably.

"Loser," she taunted in retaliation. "Don't forget, I offered you a chance for old times' sake." Holding a finger to her lips, she kissed it, then pressed the print against TJ's cheek, leaving a slight smudge of red. "Toodle-oo, babe. I'll see you in court."

She sauntered out, swinging her hips. She didn't think it was just hostility that had raised the temperature in there.

Giving up on getting any work done, TJ eyed the boxes stacked along the wall and surrendered to the inevitable. Lifting the top one to his work counter, he slit open the sealing tape, sat down, and pulled out the top notebook. A moment later he reached for a pen and paper.

Combing through the notebook of Balkan testimonies translated from the original, he noted a page number and a description and flipped to the next statement. His gut churned at the entry. He'd known this would be painful, but he had to know the truth. If he'd been covering up for a traitor instead of protecting his country and a friend, as he'd assumed, he needed to know.

The truth could cripple him instead of setting him free. The newspapers were saying Martin had released war criminals that TJ's forensics team had indicted. Allegations of black-market racketeering, Mafia-like protection scams, and bribery had mushroomed from there. TJ had been traveling, mostly in Africa, and unaware of any of this until he'd returned to the States. He had assumed his written testimony had been sufficient for courts to indict the criminals his evidence had uncovered. He'd worked with Martin in Eastern Europe for years. If his team was dirty, TJ should have known.

He'd known the criminals weren't always arrested. He'd assumed there were military and political reasons for that. He'd trusted Martin, dammit.

If he had any sense at all, he'd burn these boxes as Leona had told him to do. Get rid of them and get on with his life. The motive wouldn't even be selfish. He was good at what he did. He'd documented enough evidence to put half a dozen war criminals that he knew of behind bars. He'd prevented wars between African tribes by identifying murderers. He fought for justice and truth. Being accused of something of which he knew nothing would be taking out one of the good guys.

The phone shrieked, and he let the machine answer it. The Defense Department had located him down here. TJ figured they couldn't know about the boxes but were on a fishing expedition to see how much he knew or how much he'd tell. But Colonel Martin hadn't tried to reach him yet. Until now, TJ had assumed that meant Martin wasn't worried about the media outcry.

The colonel had been the military leader and family friend who'd respected TJ's research and requested his services, a courageous man TJ had followed into war zones. He had never doubted Martin when he'd told him these boxes should be destroyed to protect national security.

The phone quit ringing, and TJ flung the notebook back in the box, his stomach too queasy to continue. He couldn't even pin down a single source for his discomfort. The reading material contained enough atrocities to make a strong man heave. But suspecting a trusted friend of protecting the criminals was beyond credibility. The likelihood that he could be accused of guilt by association—

TJ sealed the box and shoved it back in a closet. He needed to find a better hiding place. What were the chances anyone knew of their existence?

He prayed that the media wouldn't remember his connection with Martin before he'd had time to read all the material and make a decision. There'd been press with them through a lot of the earlier years. He'd come to know several reporters well over bars in foreign lands. How long before they remembered him and tracked him down?

Removing his lab coat, TJ caught a whiff of gardenias. The image of the new Patsy—Mara—had wormed its way into his thoughts so thoroughly that it popped up every time he let his defenses down. What the hell had she done to herself? And why?

He didn't want to think about that on top of everything else. He slammed out of the office, carefully locking the deadbolt behind him. The town didn't have much in the way of office buildings, so he'd rented an empty storefront, figuring security wasn't a problem. That had been before he'd started reading the notebooks.

He just needed a little time to decide what to do. Could he be objective in judging the material after he'd read it? Was it even his responsibility to deal with it?

He needed to hire an assistant. If he could get the grunt work off his back, he could be out of here faster. Patsy—Mara—would appreciate that.

Damn, but he couldn't believe what she'd done to herself. He'd thought she would have gone on to Harvard in Brad's place and be a doctor or a lawyer by now. But a movie producer?

Preferring to think of those high school and college days rather than his current predicament, TJ smiled at his memory of the teenage Patsy Amara Simonetti. He'd rather liked the way she'd looked back then. At least it had been honest and real. So she'd been a little on the skinny side. She'd filled out just fine. He'd liked her brown hair. She'd worn it long, and he could wrap his fingers in it when he kissed her.

He hadn't kissed her much. There hadn't been enough time. He'd always admired her spunk and wit, but he hadn't discovered she could be more than Brad's kid sister until a Christmas party when she'd indulged in too much punch she hadn't known was spiked. At sixteen, with her hair up and high heels on, she'd pulled him out of the doldrums with her laughter. He'd walked her home, and she'd thrown herself in his arms, and he'd discovered kisses made in heaven. Then he'd gone back to Harvard, and they'd only seen each other those few weekends he could make it home.

Damn. He'd done his best to forget those insane, testosterone-driven weeks of his sophomore year in college. He'd survived hell since then. His brain ought to relent and let it go.

"Dr. McCloud!" A booming voice of authority hailed him from across the street.

TJ grimaced at the title, but the mayor took pleasure in titles. Southerners didn't like surrendering any form of aristocracy. Checking the nearly empty street, he crossed in the middle. "Mayor Bridgeton," he acknowledged with a nod. "What can I do for you?"

"Let the pretty lady drive her trucks to the beach, of course." At five-ten, the mayor stood more than half a foot shorter than TJ, and the older man hid his discomfort by striding as briskly toward town as his portly frame would allow. "The bones of dead pirates won't mind a little disrespect."

TJ had known this was coming, but his worry over Martin hadn't left him the concentration to prepare a defense. Patsy hadn't wasted any time. Mara. He had to remember to call her Mara. She definitely didn't look like sweet, shy Patsy any longer.

If he was shooting down careers, he might as well take out a few hopes and illusions with him. "Even pirates deserve respect, sir," he began peacefully enough, before dropping the bomb on the community's claim to fame, "but those bones have been buried no more than sixty or seventy years, give or take a few."

"What!" The mayor stopped to glare at him. "I've never heard of any cemeteries on the island. That's ridiculous. Might have been a few Gullahs out there farming, but they didn't bury their dead there."

"The bones are Caucasian." TJ resumed walking. He was starved and the restaurants were down by the harbor. "I've not located any skulls, but I believe I have the remains of at least two white males."

The mayor uttered a profanity that reflected TJ's thoughts on the matter.

The town most likely had a seventy-year-old murder case on its hands.

FOUR

"Just a little party, punch and hors d'oeuvres." Stalking through the lobby of the B&B, Mara closed the "address book" icon on her PDA and flung a restaurant menu at Ian in the same motion. "You know the routine. We'll invite a few state and local officials, knock their socks off with glamour, yadda yadda. McCloud doesn't stand a chance."

"If the feds have the upper hand with that dunes law—"

"It's not a dune," Mara said decisively. "The hurricane just piled up a bunch of sand and debris. Those bones are probably scattered all up and down the beach or washed out to sea. He has no case."

"Then I should start bringing in the equipment?" Ian jotted his notes the old-fashioned way, into a notebook.

"Wait until after the party. I'd like to have some guarantees so we can sue later if the production schedule is delayed."

She could do this. She'd watched Sid for years. Take the offense and stay there. Never lose sight of the bottom line. She'd needed those lessons, or she would have spent her entire life as a doormat.

Of course, she was still relying entirely too much on others, but she'd work herself to death if she didn't. Ian could talk to city and state officials far better than she could. She'd done a damned poor job talking to the one person she'd had confidence in reasoning with. Maybe she should stick to planning and organization.

She left Ian in the sitting room talking into two phones

at once. She needed to walk the beach and verify there was no other access. Maybe her maps were wrong. Maybe the hurricane had changed things. Maybe she was fighting a lost cause.

A chill shivered her spine. *Please, Lord, let me do just this one thing right.* She had too many responsibilities to drop the ball now. If she didn't buy out Sid's company, it would be a hollow shell in a few years, and a lot of decent people would be out of jobs. It might be small, but the studio had a damned good director and a reputation for quality films that allowed it to survive in this megalopoly world, only Sid had lost interest years ago. People depended on her, ironic as that might be.

Her mother depended on her, but that was nothing new. Ever since Brad's death and her divorce from Mara's father, she'd been deteriorating. The doctors had claimed she'd been declining all along, but Mara had been too young to notice until the later stages. Brad's death still felt like the dividing line between childhood stability and a world gone insane.

After climbing into her waiting limo and giving directions, Mara gazed at the town passing by, for once not trying to do two things at once. She'd never lived in a small town, had no desire to do so, but she could admire the picturesque brick buildings and spreading oaks with their mossy beards for the past they represented—and the stories they might tell. It was peaceful here, a slower pace that gave a person time to think.

So why was the internationally renowned Dr. TJ McCloud playing in this backwater? She'd seen the newspapers—the man had won prestigious awards for his work, had shaken the hands of the president and half the governing powers of the world. Why would he bother with a grant for a hole in the middle of nowhere?

It wasn't any of her concern. She'd written him off her hero list the day he'd walked out on Brad's funeral.

The limo purred to a halt in front of the chain-link

fence bearing TJ's warning sign. She saw no car parked nearby, so she assumed he was still at the office.

Mara took her driver's helping hand and found her footing on the uneven sand. She'd come better prepared this time, having replaced her expensive snakeskin mules with a pair of Nikes.

"Stay with the car, Jim. I'll just cruise the beach, pace off a few sets. You're within screaming distance if I need you."

The remains of the original access road ran straight into the mountain of debris washed up by the hurricane. The fence didn't enclose the entire dune, just the highest part. By digging her toes into the slope, it could be scaled—on foot. They'd need a bulldozer to plow through the palmettos and wax myrtle at the base if they wanted to bring in trucks.

A bulldozer would require the owner's permission. Maybe it would be easier to tackle the local crazy lady.

She shook sand out of her shoes and trudged onward.

She was a city person. She'd learned the names of the local flora and fauna to check the authenticity of the script, but she had no idea what to expect from this jungle of exotic shrubbery smacking her legs. She only hoped it didn't contain snakes. Beaches didn't have snakes, did they? She knew how to mace a mugger, but a snake—

A wild animal shrieked from the bushes ahead, and Mara almost jumped out of her Nikes. Panicked squawks followed shrill shrieks, and she froze in her tracks. Behind her, Jim called out, asking if she was all right.

"So far," she shouted back. "What in hell is that?"

Like he'd know. Jim was a creature of L.A. They didn't have zoos in L.A. In the bad old days of her youth, she'd practically lived in New York's Central Park Zoo for a few weeks, but she still didn't recognize the noise. Mara heard her driver scrambling up the hill behind her—gun in hand, most likely. Jim liked guns.

Just as he arrived, the creature screeched again, bushes

rustled, and a stately procession of iridescent blue-green feathers emerged in her path.

"Peacocks!" She almost melted in relief, and gave her driver a deprecating grin. "I don't think I'm in danger of being pecked to death by glorified turkeys."

He shouldered his pistol, glared at the strutting birds, and slid back down the embankment.

"Make note to hire zookeeper instead of bodyguard," she muttered to herself, cautiously approaching the guard birds.

The big one shrieked again and spread his tail feathers. Had to be a male, she figured—all noise and no action. Feeling on familiar ground, she boldly walked past him, and the bird flopped its tail out of her path.

The sand sloped downward on this side, and she slid her way past the remaining shrubbery onto the wide expanse of beach her scouts had photographed last year. Perfect. Absolutely perfect. A natural harbor of gentle waves, deep enough for a galleon, hidden enough for protection from weather and the pirates' enemies. The artificial jetty to the east could be disguised as a natural barrier easily enough. Most viewers wouldn't realize that South Carolina beaches were made up of sand and not rocks. And even the ones who knew better would suspend disbelief when she was through disguising it.

Okay, so her talents were more in setting than production. That's what she had Ian for. She was good at disguising things. Ian got things done.

The ocean breeze wreaked havoc with the elaborate curls Constantina had fashioned, but Mara figured she didn't have to impress screaming peacocks or pelicans. Pulling her camera from her shoulder bag, she framed a few shots, catching the angle of the sun, noting the time of day in her PDA. The buried-treasure scene would take place at night. With the northern exposure, the camera crew shouldn't have to filter too much to get the right effect. They'd had to search hard to find a good beach with that kind of exposure. She made another note to fly her director in a day early. A lot of the trees she had counted on for shade on the south side hadn't survived the storm, and their graying carcasses formed an ugly backdrop to the beach.

Sid had taught her that flunkies worried over details, but she had control issues. This was her project, from beginning to end. She'd chosen the book and the screenwriter, had ordered the rewrites, and had conferred with the director on every page. If she was to support herself for the first time in her life, she had to quit relying on others.

Okay, so she was a Gemini and flip-flopped on every issue, but that was just seeing both sides of every question. If one more person told her she couldn't have her cake and eat it, too, she'd shove the icing up their nose.

Rounding a jungle of fallen palms and bleached driftwood, kicking sand and shells as she went, she stopped short at the sight of a trio racing across the beach, flying the strangest kite she'd ever seen.

She squinted and decided the kite might be Sir Lancelot with a Superman cape, but the sun was too bright and her interest was diverted by the people trespassing on the territory she'd thought of as her own. She'd have to hire more security for the filming. She'd thought there was only one access road and that the site would be clear of curious bystanders.

The teenager spotted her first, yelling over the lapping waves and wind to catch the attention of the other two. Hell, she'd hoped to have a few hours to herself. Now she'd have to don the prima donna role again, in jeans and Nikes and with her hair tumbling down.

The trio stopped running to stare as she approached. What would they do if she turned and walked away?

She didn't do the introvert thing anymore.

"Hi, I'm Mara Simon." Mara held out her hand to the woman watching her warily. Average height, more stocky than slim, auburn curls that looked hacked by kitchen scissors, short cutoffs, and midriff-baring tie-dye shirt that belonged on a teenager. The woman was a mess but didn't seem to care. She returned Mara's look with a frank, open stare.

"Cleo McCloud." She shook Mara's hand briefly before gesturing at the two boys hanging out behind her. "My son, Matty, and my good friend and neighbor, Gene Watkins. You must be the film producer Jared told us about."

McCloud. Jared—Tim's brother. The names clicked in place, and it took all Mara could do not to exclaim in incredulity. This eccentric creature had captured Jared McCloud? Tim's brother had been a womanizer since birth. After earning riches and recognition as a comic-strip artist and screenwriter, he would have had women crawling all over him. He'd settled for a sunburned—

Click—another piece fell into place. Cleo's Hardware. Jim had bought a bag of batteries with that logo on it. Maybe she'd better not underestimate a woman who could boldly tread on all-male territory by running a hardware store. If this was the crazy lady Ian had told her about, she'd like to be that kind of crazy. Far better than the alternative.

Not wanting to contemplate varieties of insanity, Mara offered her blinding starlet smile to the trio. "I'm happy to meet you." The teenager grinned in delight and puffed up his chest. Cleo crossed her arms and waited. Definitely a smart woman.

"Did Jared tell you I knew him when he was ten and bugged his big brother's bedroom with walkie-talkies?"

A hint of a grin curved Cleo's mouth, and Mara liked her instantly.

"He didn't happen to mention that, no," Cleo admitted. "Actually, he said he knew of you but had never met you."

"Well, the name may have fooled him. We were seldom in the same classes, and he probably only knew me as

Patsy. I dropped the diminutive from my family name for professional purposes, so I'm Simon now, not Simonetti. He didn't put the two together. Besides, I knew TJ better than Jared." Because TJ had the brains and Jared had the charm. Back then she'd been terrified by charm and could only deal with the male of the species on an intellectual level. Figured she'd end up in an industry that survived on charm and looks. Must be payback time from another reincarnation.

"TJ didn't mention that, but then," Cleo said, "he keeps a lot to himself. Katy says you'll begin filming soon."

Katy. Katy—the overly eager B&B proprietress. Knowing people was everything in this business. Mara brushed a straying curl from her eyes. "Not unless I can find a way through TJ's roadblock back there. Film crews require a lot of equipment that can't be hand-carried. Got any suggestions on how to persuade him?"

Mischief twinkled in Cleo's eyes as she considered the problem, but she answered without a hint of humor. "I don't think anyone knows TJ well, but I have a suspicion it would take a bulldozer to move him."

"I was seriously contemplating that. Do you think the feds would throw me in jail if I plowed up those bones? I mean, if TJ would only declare them pirate bones, I wouldn't be so ticked, but he's being nasty about that, too."

Cleo shrugged and watched as the boys, bored with the conversation, ran off with the kite. "I'm avoiding confrontation these days. If I were you, though, I'd be careful around TJ. From what I can tell, he's gnawing on something that doesn't digest well. He's likely to explode on contact."

Before Mara could translate any part of this, Cleo ran off to rescue the plunging kite. Definitely not Miss Congeniality, Mara concluded without rancor, kicking a shell on her way back to the road. It would be nice to know someone who didn't want or expect anything from her. She ought to get out and meet real people more often.

Of course, if people got any more real than TJ, she'd have to carry a gun and start shooting. That would take care of his little "digestion" problem.

What in hell had Cleo been talking about?

She'd have a digestion problem of her own if she couldn't move him out of the path of her trucks. Maybe a little media attention would twist his arm.

FIVE

"Saw it with my own eyes, right out there off the island where you're at now. Them German subs had their searchlights on, bold as brass." Wrapping both hands around the whiskey glass he was nursing, the wiry old man spoke earnestly on his favorite topic.

TJ popped another fried clam into his mouth. He'd already learned that Ed could talk for hours on the subject. He didn't have to say a word. A good bar like this one could keep a man entertained for a long time—or at least keep him from thinking too hard.

"Whales got searchlights?" another old man at the bar taunted. "Remember when old Hickock up on Bulls Island thought he saw a U-boat? Had the whole island up in arms, running around like chickens with their heads off, shooting everything that moved. Turned out to be nothing but beached whales."

"At least them people up at Bulls patrolled like they was supposed to," Ed replied indignantly. "We didn't have nobody hardly out there. Hickock even had a radio he could talk in. What did I have? I tell you—"

"They rode horses," another old-timer intruded. "We didn't have no horses and couldn't get them out to the island if we did. Wasn't no roads back in them days."

TJ forked the last clam, wiped his fingers on a bar napkin, and reached for his wallet. He rather enjoyed the muted argument over old wars instead of the rabid hostility over current depredations, but he'd heard this one a few times already. "My knowledge is limited to bones, gentlemen. I'll leave World War Two with you. I'll keep an eye out for whales, though. These days they might come knocking on my front door."

Laughter followed him out. They'd already hit him with every form of joke about sea creatures on his doorstep. Apparently the last hurricane had washed away his beach house's front yard. Jared and Cleo spent a lot of time pondering how to save it, but no solution had occurred to them as yet. It would be a shame to lose that piece of the past, but he didn't know how to save houses, either.

If he thought about it, his occupation was singularly useless. Once people were dead, did it really matter how they died? Justice wouldn't miraculously return them to life. He should have been something more constructive, like a doctor. Brad would have been saving thousands of lives by now, discovering a cure for AIDS or the like.

But Brad was dead, and it was TJ's fault.

He knew better than to go down that crooked path again, but the warm summer night with ocean breezes rippling through the leaves raised specters of the past. Walking under old oaks and catching the sweet perfume of a late magnolia blossom, he could almost imagine ghosts drifting from some of these old mansions.

Passing the gardenia bush outside the B&B, he heard laughter and music pouring from the lighted front rooms and wide porch, and he shoved his hands into his pockets and picked up speed. Patsy was having a party tonight. No, not Patsy, but Mara. She was definitely a Mara these days.

He'd stopped thinking of her as Brad's little sister a long time ago, but she was the reason he was wandering the melancholy alleys of his mind now.

He'd started college as a jock with no profession but basketball in mind. Sports had provided an acceptable outlet for the dangerous mix of testosterone and untapped emotion he'd been back then. His best friend had dedicated his life to becoming a doctor. Brad had been the keeper of the flame, the shining light of genius who would rescue the once-proud Simonettis from obscurity and save the world.

Brad's death had destroyed the Simonettis as completely as it had destroyed the car Brad had been driving. TJ's car. He might as well have handed Brad a loaded gun when he'd handed him the keys. If he'd been paying attention . . . but he hadn't.

TJ walked down to the waterfront and watched the yachts and fishing boats bobbing in the water. Some days he'd simply like to hop aboard one and sail away.

Other days his damned ingrained sense of responsibility demanded he get off his ass and do what had to be done.

Except doing what had to be done meant betraying still another friend, destroying him as finally as Brad had destroyed himself, and quite possibly taking down the colonel's family in the same way Brad's death had destroyed the Simonettis.

He'd lost one good friend tragically. He wouldn't give up on this one yet. He would finish reading through the notebooks and talk with the colonel. There could have been national security reasons involved that he didn't understand. Martin was the army insider. McCloud Enterprises just had government contracts. TJ didn't know anything about how the war crimes cases were handled after he turned over the evidence. He simply appeared at the trials when called upon.

He hadn't been called upon in the Balkan trials as often as he'd expected.

TJ turned his back on the harbor and headed for his car.

He had to walk past the B&B again to get there. The thick night air carried Mara's laughter clearly, and he couldn't resist glancing toward the old converted mansion.

A tall, slender figure in flowing white adorned the wide veranda, accompanied by a pair of business-suited men. She was gesticulating gracefully in the manner that for one brief spring had held TJ enthralled, so he knew the effect on her companions. She'd always possessed an enthusiasm and a joie de vivre that no other person of his acquaintance could equal once she got past her shyness.

"Oh, *People* magazine, definitely." Her voice carried as he passed the drive. "The town will be flooded with tourists. Are you certain you're prepared?"

The thick hedge obscured any reply as TJ walked on. His teeth clenched at the mention of the press. Damn it, he didn't need journalists here poking around. He just hoped the entertainment press wouldn't recognize his name.

Mara was promising the town council the moon, probably with no chance of delivering. Tamping down his irritation, he made a mental note to expect a deputation of city fathers in the morning, complaining that the dig site interfered with tourism.

He hadn't visited the excavation all day. He'd best go out and pull his records into order. The scraps of evidence he had extricated from the gravesite so far wouldn't interest the local police any more than archeologists. But he had a feeling that by the time he was done, the police would definitely be interested.

That hadn't been his original intention when he'd obtained the grant. Cleo would kill him.

With a wry grin, TJ concluded that would certainly solve a few problems.

"Offering to haul in new trees and shrubs was a stroke of genius." Ian returned the folded newspaper to the breakfast table the next morning. The headline, HOLLYWOOD PRODUCER PROMISES PARK, landed faceup.

"A park won't happen unless the state comes up with the funds to buy the adjoining land." Mara buttered her toast and glanced out the bay window to the lush lawn and gardens of the B&B. "I have a feeling it isn't TJ who will come gunning after me, though. His sister-in-law struck me as the type to dice me into little bits if I invade her island hideaway against her wishes."

Still watching the window, Mara smiled as one of the subjects in question stormed past the gardenia and down the drive, brandishing a fresh newspaper in his fist. TJ. His expression was so grim, she fully expected steam would pour from his ears shortly.

Uneasiness raised its ugly head, but she blithely added jam to her toast while Ian checked the view to see what she was smiling at. He whistled and hurriedly stood up.

"He's all yours, babe. I have better things to do than be flattened before the day begins."

"Cluck, cluck," Mara mocked softly before taking a bite of her toast. She was a pro at confrontation, but she preferred not to engage in hostilities on an empty stomach.

TJ disappeared behind the enormous ferns on the wide veranda. The bell tinkling over the front door followed. *Here he comes . . .* she sang mentally, until she remembered the rest of the verse mentioned nervous breakdowns.

Her mother did those. Mara Simon wouldn't. Couldn't. Not until she could afford to pay the consequences.

Ian slithered out the back way as TJ stormed in the front. Since Mara was the only other one of her company up at this hour, TJ found her easily. She sighed in admiration at the way he filled out the short-sleeved black polo and jeans. All that muscle wasted on an egghead—pity. Must have been dig day instead of lab day, she surmised—no starched white shirt.

"What the hell do you think you're doing?" TJ shouted, slamming the folded newspaper with the headline about the state park on the table. The scar over his nose twitched furiously.

"Eating breakfast?" she inquired, flapping her artful lashes at him while taking another bite of toast. She really did enjoy throwing TJ McCloud for a loop.

He recovered quickly though, she noticed in disappointment. Other men melted when she played innocent. TJ froze up colder than an iceberg in Antarctica.

"You come out here for a few months, turn people's lives and an entire town upside-down with grandiose plans that can't possibly be accomplished, and plan on walking away as soon as all-out war ensues, don't you?"

"Want to add 'That isn't the Patsy I used to know' while you're at it?" she asked sweetly, reaching for her coffee. Once she might have burst into tears at his scorn. Now she girded her loins, so to speak, and prepared for the showdown.

"Oh, I can do better than that." He toned down his voice, but it still dripped with scorn. "Brad always put others first, but baby sister takes the opposite tack, doesn't she? What you want counts most, and to hell with everyone else."

"Brad put himself first that last time, though, didn't he?" she countered flatly.

He looked startled at that observation. *Good,* she thought. She'd had to live with the results of Brad's death for seventeen years. Slapping TJ with reality held a measure of satisfaction.

"Is that your excuse? You can ruin people's lives because of what happened to Brad? Grow up." He clenched his fists as if to keep from reaching for her. "We'll fight you, tooth and nail. Cleo and Jared are building something good out there. You have no intention of carrying through on these lies." He pointed at the newspaper article about the park she was promoting. "The entire town will be up in arms against Cleo and Jared if they oppose a fantasy that's never going to happen. I won't have you destroying their happiness for your own selfish purposes."

"Open the gate to the road and it will all die down," she purred. Always purr, no matter how badly rattled, she'd learned.

"Those gates will protect a murder investigation shortly," he growled back. "You might want to start considering which of your newfound friends might have an interest in seeing a state park cover up the evidence."

He didn't hang around to see how she would take that but strode off, completely unaware of Mara's admiring interest in his tight posterior. She figured the crack about a murder investigation was simply one of TJ's better attempts to unsettle her and dismissed it. TJ's rear end, however, was definitely a point to ponder. If she still wore glasses, steam would be obscuring her view about now.

Just entering the dining room, Constantina swiveled her head to follow TJ's progress.

"My, my," she said with a sigh of pleasure, plopping down in the chair Ian had vacated. "I don't suppose I can hope that's your new director, can I?"

Mara snickered at the thought. "Not unless you favor the Red Queen school of directing. 'Off with her head!' doesn't work well in Hollywood these days."

"Oh, well, it was a nice thought," Constantina said. "Men with hot tempers are equally hot in bed, you know."

Shrugging, Mara watched TJ stride up the driveway to the street. If Brad hadn't died, she might have discovered what it was like to have a hot man in her bed. Her libido did a shiver of ecstasy at just the image of TJ naked. But that bird had flown. She had more important things to worry about.

The gardenia bush blocked her view of TJ reaching the street, so she turned back to her table companion. "It's more important to make a lot of people happy than a few, isn't it?"

"In my experience, you can't make anybody happy, so don't bother trying." Constantina signaled the waitress for coffee, effectively ending useless speculation.

A park would make lots and lots of people happy, Mara concluded, choosing to ignore her friend's advice. The McClouds didn't deserve their own private island.

SIX

"Talk to Mara Simon? Are you out of your mind?" Jared asked in alarm as he flipped an antiquated rubber jar seal over the bony uplifted middle finger of the skeleton in the corner.

TJ hit the delete button on his answering machine, erasing the host of messages from VIPs demanding he return their calls. Colonel Martin wasn't among them, and he had a suspicion most of the others had to do with Mara's state park idea and his refusal to cooperate. He had half the Defense Department down his back asking for his Balkan notes. He didn't know if they realized he had the other boxes or not, and he didn't care. He was a private contractor, and his notes belonged to him. If the feds couldn't intimidate him, the local chamber of commerce didn't have a chance.

The call from the Charleston newspaper was reason for fear, though. He calculated no one read the local rag, but the big city papers were picked up by the national press. The national media hadn't caught on to his name yet, but if the colonel's story grew any bigger, one of them would recall TJ's connection to him. Time was running out.

"Cleo would have my scalp if I got near the woman," Jared continued. "Besides, if Mara rescues Sid's company, I could someday be working with her. Hollywood's a small town."

"Fine. Then I'll send back the grant money, pack my

things, and take that job in Mexico," TJ responded absently to Jared's complaint. "You can explain to Cleo why bulldozers are plowing through the dune and land developers are knocking on your door. Little Patsy wins by a forfeit."

Jared emitted a rude sound. His next throw missed the skeleton, bouncing off the wall behind it. "Little Patsy was a holy terror even in middle school. She always ruined the grade curve, and tattled to the teacher if we got even."

"That was two decades ago," TJ shouted in frustration. "And you probably set fire to her schoolbooks, if I remember your tactics correctly. I told her to tell the teacher."

Jared grinned, unconcerned about details. "Good thing they pushed her into advanced classes. The two of you had a lot in common back then. Wine her, dine her, woo her into our way of thinking, big brother. She used to think you walked on water. I'm just the pest who shot her with a water pistol."

Wine her, dine her. That was easy for Jared to say. His younger brother had charmed starlets and socialites for years, while TJ had buried himself in labs with assistants who had a striking resemblance to the Patsy he remembered, now that he thought about it—brainy intellectuals with their hair pulled back and no makeup.

"If you're not worried about a state park on your doorstep, why should I be?" TJ asked gruffly, glaring at the counter that served as his desk. Days' worth of mail hadn't been opened. Leona hadn't returned to open it.

Jared shrugged and gathered the rubber rings scattered over the aging linoleum. "It's all Hollywood hype. Nothing will come of it but a lot of media attention. Hire your own spin doctors and toss it back into her court."

"That'll solve all my problems," TJ grumbled, locating a letter opener and slicing open the envelope on top. "A PR person to claim I've uncovered the murder of the century. Do PR people answer mail?"

Jared dropped all the jar rings over the skeleton's finger and eyed his brother skeptically. "Something else eating you that you're not telling us about?"

TJ threw out an ad for an American Express platinum card and sliced open a handwritten envelope addressed to Dr. McCloud. An unsigned piece of school notebook paper fell out. Frowning, he glanced over the arthritic scrawl, then handed it to Jared. "You tell me."

His brother scanned the one-line note, whistled, then read it more carefully. "All right, I'll bite. Why should you watch your back?" He quirked an eyebrow. "And how? Wear a mirror?"

Propping his shoulders against the wall behind his stool and sprawling his legs out, TJ shrugged. "Better yet, is it a threat or a warning?" he asked. " 'Watch your back' is not a clarifying communication."

"Take it to the sheriff. Maybe he knows the local cranks who do this kind of thing." Jared tossed the cryptic message back on the counter. "We've got our share of wackos around here, but none of them strike me as dangerous."

The postmark was Charleston, but that didn't mean anything. The local post office sent all its mail to the city for sorting.

Surely it was from a local prankster wanting the film to progress as planned. TJ couldn't see how it would have any relation to the Martin case. After all, no one but Leona knew he had the evidence boxes.

Leaving the mail on his desk, TJ grabbed the keys to his excavation site and headed for the door. Digging was uncomplicated and vastly more interesting than anything in the office. The clavicle he'd uncovered yesterday had shown definite signs of bullet damage. It was the brass button he'd located earlier that fascinated him, though. It certainly looked like a Nazi insignia. He'd start checking the Internet tonight.

"Squirt Patsy with a water gun next time you see her," TJ advised as he shoved his brother out the door ahead of him. "See how much of the Hollywood facade washes off."

Jared chuckled. "Not on your life, bro. She'll tattle to Sid, and I'd be blackballed for life. You're the man. I'm just the class clown."

TJ was damned tired of being the man. That's why he'd taken this beach job in the first place—to take a vacation from the burden of responsibility for a while. Maybe Mexico wasn't such a bad idea after all.

As they exited the storefront, Mara waved gaily at them from across the street. In her high-heeled mules, she towered over the town mayor and the local reporter she held captive. Given the cleavage that was practically at their eye level, TJ figured they had no reason for complaint. For a small southern town where all the women dressed in Laura Ashley dresses and pearls, Mara in her tight red leather miniskirt and belly-baring top must be a sight the men would relish for years to come.

He ought to walk away. He really wanted to walk away. But that was Brad's little sister over there.

With a grumble of exasperation, TJ veered from his chosen course to cross in the middle of the street.

Behind him, Jared laughed knowingly, climbed in his Jeep, and gunned the engine, leaving the fray behind.

Mara thrilled a little at the fierce light in TJ's eyes as he approached, just as she had when an adolescent Tim switched into dragon-slayer mode. There was just something downright sexy about a man prepared to fight for what was right.

Of course, what she really ought to fear was that this time, she was the enemy, and he meant to pin *her* against the wall. Oddly, even that idea entertained her. She might not even fight back. She could mouth empty phrases about despising the McClouds, but bookish firebrands had always lit her candles.

"Mayor Bridgestone, Ralph." TJ nodded curtly at her

companions, acknowledging their presence before grabbing Mara's arm. "If you'll excuse us."

She practically fell out of her shoes trying to follow TJ's tug. She recovered gracefully and even managed to make it look as if she hadn't just been swept off her feet by a hormonal ox.

"Prince Charming!" she chirped. "From what am I being rescued? Were the mayor's eyeballs on fire already?"

He stopped so suddenly, she stumbled. Damn, she'd have to start wearing loafers if she hung around him much longer. To get even, she caught TJ's shoulder with one hand and kept her grip on his arm with the other so that they were practically waltzing on Main Street. A little music, maestro. A pity that life couldn't be directed like a film.

TJ caught his breath and glared down at her.

She fluttered her eyelashes. She loved pushing his buttons like that.

"You enjoy being an exhibitionist?" he asked incredulously. "You want those old goats drooling down your shirt?"

His tone took all the fun out of it. Mara reclaimed her hands and folded her arms beneath her breasts so that he was the one getting the free show. "They're breasts, TJ. I put a lot of effort into getting people to look at them. Do you have a problem with women ogling your pectorals? You want to hear my hairdresser's comments on your ass? Or is it only okay if you're the one getting the attention and not me?"

"Why the hell would you care if people look at your breasts? It's your brain that matters," he asked with frustration. "Did you take it out and have it shrink-wrapped when you had your nose done?"

"You want to know how far my brain got me, bozo?" She shoved a hand against TJ's chest, pushing him in the direction of a deserted storefront instead of arguing in full view of the entire town. "My brain got me a high school diploma and a license to marry the most eligible bachelor in Brooklyn." Derision slid off her tongue with ease.

Getting the message, TJ stepped backward into the alcove provided by empty display windows. "You could have had a scholarship to any college of your choice. That's where your brains should have taken you."

She thought she'd conquered years of frustration and fury, but the condescension in his voice breached dangerous barriers. "Who would have looked after my mother if I went away to school?" she demanded. "Brad's ghost? My father and his new teenage bride? Money has always cleared your path, hasn't it? You never had any responsibility to live up to."

"Your mother is an adult! She was supposed to look after you. Your father should have looked after you. Your whole damn family had a responsibility to see that you were taken care of."

"They did." She folded her arms again. "They found me the most eligible bachelor in all Brooklyn. You didn't think mousy Patsy Simonetti with all her brains could have done that, do you? No sirree Bob. My family's the old-fashioned kind. They believe women belong at home. So Aunt Judith and Aunt Miriam and Uncle David did their duty and steered the most eligible bachelor they could find into my path, showed him how I was so smart and would be such an asset to his damned clothing store that I'd make him rich beyond his wildest dreams. Get little Patsy married, and she'll be around to help out for life. That's the way it works in my part of town."

TJ looked so furious and rattled at the same time, Mara almost laughed out loud. She'd pushed the sex button and the masculine overprotection button at the same time, and he was about to blow a gasket. She'd always adored the way he looked after her, but she didn't need that kind of care these days.

Patting TJ's bronzed arm, Mara hooked her fingers around his elbow and steered him back to the street. He resisted for a moment, but even he could see the futility of this argument.

"You can't save the world, TJ," she admonished. "That marriage was the education in life that college would never have taught me. Don't give me any more lectures on how looks don't count. I'm living proof that they do. Shave your head and grow a beer gut and see if you experience life the same way you do now."

"That depends on what you call a life," he growled. "I've got friends and family who don't give a damn what I look like. Can you say the same?"

Mara offered a blinding smile to conceal the stab of pain and regret. "My family doesn't care what I look like, either, as long as I send them money. Welcome to my world."

She didn't want him looking at her with pity. Kissing his cheek, she released his arm and sauntered down the street, swinging her hips so he could appreciate the view instead of thinking about how much she'd revealed.

If men listened with only half their brains, it was because the other half was too busy processing the visual to acknowledge the verbal. One swing of the hips ought to jam all his circuits.

She didn't care what anyone said. Beauty was power.

TJ swatted another mosquito and leaned against his shovel to wipe the sweat from his brow. This wasn't an archeological dig like most, where professional sifting and sorting was required. He could have hired cheap labor to dig. He just preferred an orderly unearthing of the haphazard heap the elements had created. It satisfied him that he wasn't overlooking anything of importance in his impatience to uncover the mystery buried here.

The hurricane had injudiciously seized everything in its path and flung it into this mound. Uprooted palmettos, rotting seaweed, fish carcasses, and shells were tangled together to form a solid structure holding tons of sand. Old tires and driftwood had to be dug around with care lest the loose foundation cave in, taking him with it. Maybe Mara was right. He ought to bulldoze the whole thing.

But at least two people had died on this beach some sixty years ago, and their stories deserved to be told. It might be a little late for justice, but there still could be families out there, waiting and wondering.

When he'd offered to take on this project, he'd hoped for a more personally rewarding discovery, something that might give his life an interesting new direction. One of the Lost Tribes, misplaced settlers, even pirates would have provided intellectual stimulation and maybe a book or two. If he could only plan far enough in advance, he wouldn't be so wrung out over his decision about those evidence boxes. Writing academic tomes might establish the foundation of a new career if he sacrificed the military one.

Not that he knew anything about writing books. He loved a good mystery, but he couldn't write one.

Prying loose another crumpled beer can to add to a growing stack of trash, TJ dropped that train of thought. He looked at bodies to determine how and when they died, and who they were, if possible. He seldom failed because he was thorough in his investigation, observant, and able to put details together that others ignored. He doubted that he could put words together in the same way, so he'd rather stick with what he did best—but not at the cost of sacrificing the truth. Shit.

He heard the kids shouting and laughing down on the beach and tried not to remember what Mara had told him about her family. His younger brothers liked to complain about the dysfunctional McClouds, but TJ had seen a lot more of the world than they had. Given the bigger picture, he was grateful for his parents' wealth, even if their caregiving bordered on apathetic. He and his brothers might not understand much about loving relationships, but they'd always had the material assets to make their own lives.

Knowing the tightly knit Simonetti family, he'd not once worried about Patsy. Brad's father had been aggressive in pushing their education. He'd always taken an interest in Brad's studies, unlike TJ's father. And Mrs. Simonetti might have been a doormat, but through his teenage eyes TJ had seen a woman who cooked and took care of her family—a paragon of virtue. He'd known Brad and his father argued frequently, but what had he known about father-son relationships? Nothing. He had spent a lot of years regretting the teenage relationship that died on the vine, but he'd never doubted that Patsy's family would be there for her after he left. It had never occurred to him that death could cause a solid family to self-destruct.

He'd been nineteen years old when Brad died. Patsy hadn't spoken to him at the funeral and never answered his calls later. The tragic car accident had turned his entire life upside-down, and Patsy's refusal to talk with him had confirmed what he'd already feared—that she hated him for his part in Brad's death. He'd gone back to college struggling to survive the upheaval left by the absence of his best friend and the hole in his heart created by Patsy's rejection. Her family had sold their house and moved away shortly after. He'd gone on with his life thinking she had gone on with hers.

Her tale nagged him now, making him more irritable. He wanted to despise the person she had become, but he admired her too damned much. To take what she'd been given and turn tragedy into success took more than brains. It took determination and talent and ambition and a host of other things not too many people possessed.

He climbed out of the hole and grabbed a bottle of water from the ice chest. He could finish this job twice as fast if he hired help. No sense in holding Patsy's—Mara's—looks against her and delaying her project just because he was having an identity crisis.

The roar of a horde of all-terrain vehicles jerked his head up.

Carrying backpacks and gear, the three-wheeled ATVs bounced over the rough ground with impunity, screeching past the outside of his fence, churning up sand, struggling weeds, and tree seedlings.

A helmeted figure riding behind one of the drivers waved at him as they passed.

Mara. In a halter top and shorts.

Damn! His gut churned at the invasion, but his lust level shot sky high at the sight of her bouncing round hips speeding away.

What evil genie had set the one woman in the world who understood him into his path again—at a time when he had to make a life-altering decision?

SEVEN

"Espresso," Mara muttered, grimacing and avoiding the mirror. Espresso and the *Times*. God made Sunday a day of rest for a reason—to recover from Saturday nights.

Tim hadn't come to her preproduction party last night. She'd invited the whole town, and she thought the entire county had probably shown up, except for the McClouds. TJ hadn't spoken to her since her crew started using ATVs to carry setting materials out to the jetty. A stroke of genius on her part, if she did say so herself.

Drinking all the martinis people handed her last night hadn't been quite as bright.

Still, the Charleston and Columbia papers would have a nice spread on the film in this morning's edition. Support for the film and tourism would skyrocket, twisting the screws a little tighter on Dr. TJ McCloud.

Covering her unstyled hair with a broad-brimmed straw hat and slipping on a pair of sunglasses, she set out in search of espresso. She already knew the B&B didn't serve it.

There had to be a Starbucks around here somewhere.

She'd planned to spend the day checking the books, so she'd given Jim the day off. It wasn't as if she couldn't walk around this town twice over if she needed anything. She just needed caffeine first.

Striking out in the direction of the harbor, Mara attempted a positive attitude even though her head was pounding due to the heat by the time she reached the end of the drive. August in South Carolina was probably not the wisest time to film, but she had no choice. It was the only time her leading lady could fit it into her busy schedule. At least the ocean breeze made the humidity bearable.

Ignoring the perspiration forming on her bare arms, Mara stared incredulously down the line of swinging signs as she reached the town's version of restaurant row. Not a Starbucks in sight. The Jolly Roger and Blue Marlin didn't look promising. Maybe she could find a coffee shop tucked between some of the larger places.

No newspaper stand visible, either. She started down the quaint tabby walk, past restaurants promising to open at eleven for Sunday brunch, a gas station, a minimart boasting six-packs of Cokes, a travel agency, a dozen or more antique and souvenir shops—

All she wanted was a damned cup of espresso and a newspaper. She could even find them in freaking L.A., where you needed a car to travel from coffee shop to newsstand. Some days she actually missed New York. In a town this small, she should be able to walk—

From one end to the other. She stared in consternation at the tidy line of antebellum brick residences lining the rest of the shore road, then glanced at her watch. It had taken all of fifteen minutes, with no sign of civilization. What in hell did people do here on Sunday mornings? There wasn't a soul on the street.

In answer to her question, half a dozen church bells tolled the ten o'clock hour.

She wondered if churches served espresso with their donuts. But her mixed ethnic background didn't include white-bread Baptist.

Maybe the minimart would have newspapers.

Sailboats bobbed on the gently lapping water, a gull screamed overhead, and Mara tried to pretend she was on a beach vacation at the Jersey shore. But dammit, they had a Starbucks there.

The guy with Nascar tattoos and a chew of tobacco

in his cheek manning the counter of the minimart didn't faze her, but the lack of anything resembling a newsstand did. Racks of car and beauty magazines filled the one shelf allotted to reading material. Bubble gum, plastic junk food, and toiletries dominated the rest. Not an espresso machine in sight, although one counter boasted every soft drink and juice known to mankind, plus a Mr. Coffee. Not quite what she had in mind.

Krispy Kremes! She grabbed a box of the sticky doughnuts, unburied a week-old *People* magazine, and flung them on the counter.

"They're two days old," a male voice said behind her. TJ.

She whipped around at the crackle of fresh newsprint as much as at the sound of his voice. She enviously eyed the thick, crisp bundle under his arm. She could almost smell the *Times*. "Where did you get that?"

TJ shrugged and set his cup of steaming coffee down on the counter. "Bookstore around the corner orders it for me. They leave it in the box so I can pick it up if the store isn't open."

She must have eyed it so hungrily that even an obtuse male like TJ could read her expression.

Warily he offered her a peek at the front page. "Want to share?"

"I don't suppose you have an espresso machine?" she almost whimpered, ignoring the headlines and gazing longingly at the middle section of the paper with the books and entertainment news.

"Jared has one," he answered hesitantly.

Mara didn't know whether to beg like a puppy or do her starlet flirt to persuade him. She didn't feel like a starlet this morning. She felt like a curmudgeonly New Yorker deprived of her caffeine-and-newspaper fix.

She lifted a hopeful gaze to the full impact of TJ's smoky one and nearly forgot what it was she wanted from him. It was a miracle the man didn't explode from all the fire smoldering behind those thick lashes. The restraint excited her as much as the hidden emotions behind it. What would it take to unlock his chains?

Even thinking of undoing TJ McCloud was living dangerously.

He picked up the Styrofoam cup of steaming coffee and handed it to her. "Here, take the edge off while I pick up some milk and eggs for Cleo."

He'd understood! Coffee and newspapers—that's what she wanted. All she wanted.

Well, maybe she'd also like to have a man who understood her, but she wasn't in the market for a man right now. She had enough of them interfering in her life already.

She paid for her purchases and gratefully sipped the hot brew while TJ completed his errand. Her adolescent fantasies had always pictured her high school champion battling boa constrictors in the jungle or standing like a stalwart knight against her enemies. She'd never pictured him in a domestic scene with eggs and a sister-in-law. It was almost sexy watching an oversize, dangerous male prowling the shelves of a giant refrigerator.

Maybe she ought to be producing contemporary chick flicks instead of pirate fantasies.

Brooding over whether contemporary fantasies were as marketable as her pirate one, Mara silently followed TJ out to his car, drinking his coffee and generously handling the paper for him. She grimaced at the boring rental car he led her to but climbed in without comment when he opened the door for her. She'd give the McClouds credit for one thing—good manners.

Scooting the passenger seat back so she could stretch out, she caught TJ's surreptitious glance at her legs. Considerately, she didn't tweak his switches by crossing her knees. She just wanted to inhale coffee, newsprint, and TJ's familiar presence.

After all these years, she still felt comfortable enough with TJ to relax and be herself. She just wasn't entirely certain who that self was anymore.

Returning the coffee to TJ after he maneuvered the car

into the street, she began flipping through the sections of the paper in search of the ones she wanted.

Out of the corner of her eye, she noticed he drained the hot liquid in almost a single gulp.

Knowing she could still get under the skin of a full-grown TJ McCloud soothed her mood considerably. Crossing her ankles and pulling out the books section, she broke the silence. "You didn't come to my party. Hot time at the McCloud residence last night?"

"Matty was upchucking. Jared had promised to take the neighbor's kids to a school thing, but Cleo was beside herself." He shrugged. "I figured I'd be persona non grata at your place, so I took the kids so Jared could stay home."

Mara had to mentally snap her jaw shut. "You took a couple of kids to a school function instead of attending the bash of the year? Knowing if you played your cards right, you might even get lucky? Are you applying for the Mother Teresa award?"

"You're the one who lectured me on responsibility." He kept his voice even and his eyes on the road.

She was quite certain the steam level had just risen ten degrees. A man didn't ignore a reference to getting lucky without reason, particularly not in this case. They had a lot of unresolved issues simmering here.

She didn't want to settle them on a Sunday morning with a hangover.

"Just remember I'm a Gemini." She flipped open the book review section and began scanning the headlines, looking for items of interest. "You never know which me you're talking to."

"Multiple personality disorder," he diagnosed. "You didn't used to suffer that."

"Did, too," she retorted, hiding her uneasiness at the mention of mental illness. "I was shy, obedient Patsy at school, and blunt, honest me with you."

"You just imitated Brad and me." He swung the car

down the sandy lane toward Cleo's house and the beach. "You grew out of it."

"Yeah, boy, did I ever," she muttered, glancing up from a book review to dig for her PDA. But when she caught sight of the widow's walk through the windshield, she forgot the computer and squinted into the sunlight. "Is he sunbathing up there?"

"Reading comic books, most likely." Unperturbed by his brother's activities, TJ veered into the driveway and cut the engine.

Carrying the *Times*, Mara climbed out of the car before TJ could grab his groceries and open the door for her. The half-dressed man on the roof waved from his lounge chair, and she waved back. She'd lived in L.A. for nearly ten years. Eccentricity was required for residency. What she really needed to be doing was scouting the location for more ways around TJ's roadblock.

"Hey, Pats! Sorry we missed your bash last night," Jared called down as they approached the house.

"Your loss, clumsy. Tim says you hide the espresso here."

"Yeah, I don't mind trading New York's exhaust fumes for all this sunshine, but a guy's got limits."

TJ interrupted this exchange of pleasantries. "Where's Cleo? Did she put the espresso machine back together?"

"She's in Matty's room, egging videos. I think it's fixed. Go look."

"Egging videos?" Mara inquired.

"We do what we can for entertainment around here," Jared called back.

TJ put a hand to the small of her back and shoved her toward the door. "Shut up and read your funnies, Jared," he shouted at the roof without looking up.

"Jared inherited all the charm, right?" she asked wryly, stumbling up the stairs under his direction.

"Right. I got the muscles, Jared got the charm, and our baby brother got the brains."

"How's Tom doing these days?" she tried to question casually while TJ all but hauled her into a charming cottage of gleaming pine floors and spacious sunlit windows. Somewhere in the back of the house, childish laughter echoed in accompaniment to the murmur of a television.

She ignored the tug of envy at the homey surroundings and jerked out of TJ's rough hold. The man didn't know his own strength, but she knew how to handle muscle better than the loneliness this house stirred.

"He goes by Clay these days. We never appreciated our first names, especially after Jared made a point of using them to insult us." Now that TJ had her out of Jared's view, he stalked ahead of her, his broad shoulders nearly filling the narrow hall. "Clay's working on a new kind of three-D computer animation that will turn the film industry on its head. Surprised you haven't run into him."

Amusement curled her lips. "Contrary to popular opinion, I don't know every man in L.A." Entering the large kitchen, she spun around to examine the tiled counters and trestle table while he put the milk and eggs away. Catching sight of a fascinating assortment of pewter and ceramic gremlins leaning over and grimacing from the tops of the cabinets, she stood on tiptoe to stare back at them.

"Clay's too cynical to look at women, anyway." TJ found the coffee beans and began filling the machine.

"Yeah, I never met a McCloud who looked at women," a feminine voice mocked from the doorway.

Mara swung around to greet the compact woman with the short auburn curls she'd met on the beach. "I never met a McCloud who was content with just looking," she agreed cheerfully.

Cleo leaned a shoulder against the door frame, crossed her arms, and lifted a wry eyebrow at her brother-in-law. "Do tell. TJ doesn't."

"Go egg a video, Cleo," he countered. Affection tinged

his words, but he didn't tear his gaze from the machine's operation.

Slipping one hand from beneath her armpit, Cleo flung an egg-shaped object at his solid back. Mara jumped at the resulting splat, then giggled when the ball did no more than bounce off him. With excellent reflexes or a lot of practice, TJ turned, caught it before it hit the ground, and flung it back at Cleo in a single fluid movement. The ball bounced off her shoulder and emitted another convincing splat.

"We egg each other on," TJ said gravely, catching the ball in his fist with Cleo's return throw. It squished satisfactorily between his fingers before he flung it at Mara.

Grinning broadly, Mara caught it and examined what appeared to be a spongy rubber ball in the shape and color of an egg.

"I'm inventing one that leaves egg goo just for TJ," Cleo informed them without breaking a smile. "Did you get my milk?"

"In the fridge. Why invent what already exists?" He stuck a mug under the steaming flow from the machine.

Mara inhaled the rich aroma and decided she was knocking on heaven's door. Despite the sharp banter, she sensed the high degree of respect between TJ and Cleo. Could families really live together like this without killing each other? Not the ones she knew, but she basked in the comforting ambiance of this one. Or maybe it was just the smell of coffee.

"Don't want to waste a perfectly edible egg when a rubber one would do." Cleo grabbed the milk from the refrigerator and ambled toward the back door. "Don't let your people swim off those rocks," she called over her shoulder to Mara. "There's a dangerous current out there." The screen door slammed behind her.

Cleo was a fascinating enigma that made Mara's fingers itch to sketch out character notes for a screenplay nagging at the back of her mind. "Where's she taking the milk?" Ten dozen questions leaped to mind, but this one emerged first.

"To the menagerie. Do iguanas drink milk? Or maybe a cat had kittens. Hell if I know. She's always got some animal out there needing care." With the second cup filled, TJ jerked his head toward the back door. "This way is shorter since we can't drive over."

She didn't even bother asking shorter to where. Feeling as if she'd just stepped through the looking glass, and discovered Oz instead of Alice, Mara hefted the newspaper and followed, humming happily. It wasn't New York, but being with TJ felt like home.

Strolling down a boardwalk in the direction of the beach, Mara admired the shrubby wax myrtle, listened to the birds singing, watched a crane gliding, and sipped her espresso. She'd never sought peace, but right this minute, her fractured nerves settled. With enough exposure to this calm, they might even knit together again.

"Why the boardwalk?" she asked as they reached an octagonal resting place of weathered boards complete with benches overlooking the ocean. Beyond this point, a graying beach house waited at the end of a shell path. She wondered if that was where TJ lived, but she didn't wish to say anything that would upset their unspoken truce. "Wouldn't it be just as easy to walk through the grass?" Or drive, given a small bulldozer and—

"Beach erosion." TJ settled on the far end of the lookout and helped himself to the front page of the paper she had tossed down beside him. "Before the hurricane, the sand reached out as far as the jetty. Now it's at the front door." He nodded at the beach house sitting only yards from lapping waves. "Cleo and Jared figure that after another blow like the last one, the beach house will be wiped out and the main house will be left sitting on the water unless they do something to prevent it. They're hoping a dune will form if they don't disturb the undergrowth."

So much for bulldozing dunes. Taking a seat on the other end of the bench, Mara propped her feet up and sipped her espresso. "I got environmental approval for this job, if that's what you're getting at."

"You asked." He drank his coffee and didn't comment further.

Now Mara understood the purpose of Cleo's egg—the harmless venting of frustration against this taciturn giant. She'd definitely make it a point to buy the first egg off the production line. Maybe two or three. Grabbing the book section and shaking it out, she pulled her sunglasses down her nose to read.

"I'd better get you some suntan lotion. You'll burn." TJ set the newspaper aside and started to stand up.

Startled, Mara glanced at the big man who had disrupted his Sunday-morning quiet for Cleo and for her. Okay, maybe she wouldn't use a *gooey* egg on him.

She hadn't had a man stir himself for her sake in a long time—if ever. She'd prefer it if he offered her the access road and not lotion, but the thought counted. "Sit down. I'm already wearing lotion. Can't afford to look old in this business." She lifted a bronzed ankle and waved it idly in the air. "Unless, of course, you simply wish to apply more, in which case I accept."

TJ sat back down, carefully refraining from staring at her bare legs.

Deciding Sunday morning was no time to take out her frustrations on TJ, Mara read in companionable silence for a while, sipping coffee and occasionally jotting notes in her PDA.

But with a double jolt of caffeine chasing through her arteries, Mara's attention soon drifted to the fascinating man sprawling across the bench only a yard away. He'd not worn reading glasses in high school, but she thought the small dark-tinted spectacles he wore now an attractive contrast to his macho image.

He had his nose buried in a story about the military

and a Balkan crime cover-up. A pity, wasting all that studiousness on a man who could make movie stars pale in comparison.

He wore his hair shorter than he used to, but it was still black and thick with sexy waves just over his temples. The sun had added an attractive bronze hue to his jaw that couldn't disguise the dark stubble of his beard. She remembered TJ as always careful about his appearance, but the island's laid-back atmosphere had apparently gotten to him. He didn't precisely look relaxed, but he was far more casual in a short-sleeved blue shirt and jeans than in his usual white shirt and dress pants. She'd like to see him in a lot less. Even the shirt's loose fit couldn't disguise the bulge of his biceps or the hard ridge of muscles defining his chest.

"Let's swim."

With no further warning, Mara threw off her blouse, dropped her shorts, kicked off her sandals, and raced for the beach.

EIGHT

TJ froze as the hot-pink fabric encasing firm buttocks and high breasts flashed past his nose.

In any normal situation, his reflexes would have reacted quickly enough for him to have grabbed Mara before she reached the sand. But libido-inflaming curves weren't any kind of normal situation.

Mara hit the beach before his mind jerked back to reality, and he leapt to his feet. Easily catching up to her as she raced along the sand, TJ prayed that was a bikini and not the secrets Victoria ought to keep to herself. He grabbed her around the waist and hauled her from the hot sand before she could reach the water. Hot female flesh wriggled in his arms, and it took physical as well as mental strength not to kiss her until they both passed out.

"Jellyfish," he yelled, wanting to shake the fool woman but disturbingly aware of a waterfall of curls tumbling over his bare arms. She quit squirming, and he instantly pulled away from her, too late for his own comfort. He shoved his hands into his pockets to cover the surge of blood to his groin and glared at her.

Mara crossed her eyes, pursed her lips, and stuck out her tongue in a mocking fish face.

TJ almost buckled with laughter. He still wanted to kiss her until both their heads spun, but he grudgingly conceded the battle. "You win. Go join your sister fishies in the sea." She'd defused his instant hard-on, but he ached with the residual effect.

"Show me your dig site, then." She swiveled on her heel

and headed down the beach, bikini-clad hips swinging in tantalizing rhythm.

He knew she was doing this on purpose, but if he went back and grabbed something to cover her up, she'd win. Her comment earlier that he might have gotten lucky had he attended her party had simmered in his imagination for the past hour.

He might have gotten lucky a long time ago if Brad hadn't died.

That cooled his ardor. It was time to let that adolescent crush go. Teenage hormones had thrown them into a frenzy that spring, but it would have been a mistake if they'd actually acted upon them. They'd been way too young. Brad's death had proven the transitory nature of teenage crushes.

Given the uproar in this morning's paper about Martin and his team's release of Balkan prisoners, he'd better concentrate on current problems and not past ones.

Watching Mara stride toward the dig site, TJ wondered how she walked barefoot through the shells and pebbles, but they were her feet, he told himself. Only after she stepped on a half-buried pinecone and yelped did he circle her waist again and haul her up to the platform on top of the mound.

With a purr of appreciation, she wrapped her arms around his neck.

TJ distracted his screaming libido with the awareness that she was entirely too light for a woman of her height. When he set her down, he looked her over more carefully. He was trained in observing skeletons, but that didn't mean he couldn't see flesh. He thought if he unfastened that tempting little hook holding the bathing suit in place over her breasts, she might not be the C-cup size she seemed to be. That realization did nothing to quench his simmering lust.

She crossed her arms, pushing her breasts higher. "Want to see more?"

"Yeah. Do you ever eat?"

She blinked in surprise, and TJ thought her lashes looked a little shorter than they had the last time she'd tried vamping him. How did she do that?

"You said the doughnuts were stale." She swung away and gazed through the chain-link fence to the hole he'd dug. "What's in those boxes?"

"Things that aren't a natural part of the environment. A lot of it is just garbage people have strewn on the beach over the years, but some of it might be useful should I ever capture a clear picture of what I'm looking for."

"What are you looking for?"

"Evidence of who the bones belong to and what happened to them. Come on, let's go back to the house and fix you something to eat." The availability of all that golden bare skin taunted him, and TJ was terrified of what he would do if he touched her again.

To his relief, she only poked around a little more, apparently reluctant to discover any more buried pinecones with her bare toes. Her hair had come loose from her hat and spilled in blond ringlets over her tanned shoulders, but she seemed oblivious to the dishevelment while she danced back down the path they'd come. TJ wondered how those few hanks of curls could equal the enormous stack she'd been wearing every other time he'd seen her.

He could probably spend a lifetime uncovering the secrets of Mara Simon. Damn his fascination with mysteries.

"If you're not finding historical clues, what difference does it make who they were?" she called over her shoulder. "They're long dead and gone. Why not let them stay that way?"

Because it wars with my need for justice, but TJ didn't try to explain that. "There may be families who need to know what happened, lives built on false hopes or foundations. Aren't you even curious?"

She shrugged and kicked at a shell. "If they're sixty years old, who would still be alive to care? That's what, World War Two? Two drunks got in a fight and shot each other before they were supposed to ship out?"

She was quick, he'd give her that. Just like old times, her brain not only kept up with him but raced ahead to consider scenarios his limited imagination couldn't reach.

"I only have the evidence of one bullet wound, and it could have been prior to death. I need more artifacts before I can even begin forming a scenario. All I know is that what I've found so far belongs to two Caucasian males. The storm did so much damage that I can't even determine if the hairs I found on scraps of cloth belonged to them. I'll probably have to dig out the whole mound before I'm done."

"Do you think they were buried on the beach?" She stopped and threw a look over her shoulder, waiting for him to catch up.

He didn't want to catch up. He liked the view from where he was.

Slapping down his voyeurism, TJ fell into step. "It's too hard to tell. From what I've learned, the island was pretty much deserted sixty years ago. The causeway hadn't been built, and only boats could get out here. A few farmers built houses and raised cotton and goats. Cleo's living in one of those houses. I haven't found any record of a family cemetery, though."

She took his arm as if they were in evening dress and promenading through a ballroom. "You researched the site?"

Trying to think while the blood boiled through his brain, TJ managed a nod. "Somewhat. But my assistant quit, and I don't have enough hands to manage the day-to-day office stuff and the research as well as the dig."

"Well, if you know the skeletons are roughly sixty years old, couldn't you just skim newspaper files? Maybe they would make note of anyone of the right age and height who disappeared back then. Or if they'd died and been buried here, they'd have that, too."

"The local rag is a weekly. Some of it is stored on microfiche at the library, but I haven't had time to go through all of it. The machine isn't in the best of repair. I decided to look for more specific evidence before trying to pinpoint newspaper articles."

"I could do that," she offered abruptly.

"Why would you want to?" Reeling with just the possibility of Mara's formidable mind being applied to his project, TJ reacted defensively.

"Because you might move out faster if I found the answers for you."

"I thought you had a film to produce." TJ tried to keep his tone noncommittal. He was having a hard enough time equating little Patsy Simonetti with this blond seductress on his arm. Picturing her as a Hollywood film producer boggled the mind. Having her work with him far exceeded his fantasies.

She shot him a sly glance. "What's the matter, TJ? Don't think I can do it?"

He shook his head in denial. "Even as a sixteen-year-old, you could do anything you put your mind to. I'm not arguing the point. I just thought film producers stayed too busy for things like research."

She shrugged and stopped to examine a shell that caught her eye. "I own half the company. That doesn't make me a producer. The company pays the real guys who can round up the money men. My job is to persuade the tight-fisted to part with their cash."

TJ didn't have to ask how she did that. Dress her in gold lamé and add a little sultry perfume, and every man in her vicinity would be peeling banknotes off rolls to please her. A basic instinct inside him roared objection at this exploitation of a brilliant woman who had far more to offer than looks.

"You'll not find many moneylenders out here." He tried not to sound angry, but from her expression, he figured he'd failed.

"I dated a set designer before I met Sid," she answered, as if that related. "I like camouflaging flaws and creating magic out of nothing. I've got a really tight budget on this film, and the director would haul in seventy-five royal palms and landscape the whole jetty if I let him loose on his own. With a little film magic and some cheap plastic palms, I can do the same thing and save a lot of money."

Even though there hadn't been a cloud in the sky, TJ's day brightened. "Brains and creativity, too. I always knew you'd be a dangerous woman."

She beamed at him. "So, can I do your research?"

He narrowed his eyes at her in return. "I just said I know you're a dangerous woman. Why should I let you anywhere near my project?"

She shrugged and skipped off down the sand again. "Because you also know I'm an honest one."

He knew she *used* to be an honest one. But he didn't know this woman with the dyed hair and bobbed nose. He'd learned the hard way to suspect everyone and everything. If it looked too good to be true, it usually was.

But damn, he'd love to have her brilliance on his side.

Mara felt TJ stiffen beside her as they approached the beach cottage. She eyed the visitor lounging on the steps. He was tall and out of shape, with male-pattern baldness badly concealed by a crew cut. Not bad-looking in a nondescript sort of fashion. She smelled reporter a mile away.

A reporter TJ obviously knew and didn't want around. Her vivid imagination kicked into gear.

"Roger," TJ acknowledged. "What brings you to these parts?"

Mara tugged her shirt over her bathing suit when the man's gaze turned to her. She liked the media noticing her only when she wanted something from them.

"A story," the reporter responded laconically, returning his gaze to TJ, "although I may have been steered wrong, from the looks of things."

"Mara, this is Roger Curtis, special correspondent for the *Post*. We met on assignment in the Balkans a few years ago. Roger, Mara Simon."

She waited to see if the reporter recognized her name,

but apparently he didn't. Amused, she played her dumb-blonde role, batted her lashes, and smiled. The reporter raised his eyebrows and nodded, but it was obvious she wasn't the focus of his interest. Very odd.

"Guess I caught you at a bad time. I couldn't find a room around here, so I thought I'd just stop by." Roger reluctantly unfurled from the steps. "Maybe I can give you a call later, after I check in over in Charleston."

"You're wasting your time, Rog," TJ said enigmatically. "I'm here visiting my family and working a dig of personal interest. Nothing to write home about."

"Then we'll just catch up on old times over a drink. Talk to you later." He nodded appreciatively at Mara. "Good meeting you, Miss Simon." He strode off across the beaten path to the sandy road the hurricane had cut off.

"Should I have disappeared and left you with your friend?" Mara demanded when TJ didn't immediately enter the house.

He shook his head and stepped onto the porch. "Nope. Eggs and bacon?"

"Yogurt and bagels." She followed him inside. Tim's compulsive neatness spilled over into his home, it seemed. She couldn't find a sign of habitation anywhere. "Are you sure you live here?"

He looked at her in puzzlement, gazed around the almost empty room, and shrugged. "I sleep here. I don't require much."

Mara suspected that was an understatement. She'd spent these last years in a culture that acquired things faster than they could be produced. TJ apparently existed on whatever anyone handed him. She watched in amazement as he fried bacon in the same battered iron skillet in which he scrambled eggs—with a fork. He prepared toast by buttering bread and holding it over an electric burner.

He didn't give her yogurt or bagels.

It smelled so mouthwateringly good, she ate what he set in front of her.

"Do you even own your own home?" she asked in curiosity a little while later, shoveling up the last bit of egg with a crust.

Carefully smearing jam over his toast, TJ looked surprised at the question. "Nope. Wouldn't ever be there, so what's the point?"

"How can you live like this?" She couldn't even conceive of it. She needed her own space, a place for her things, a place where she could relax and be her own person. She'd carried her photographs and pillows and books with her to the B&B so she could pretend it was home. She'd rented the whole inn so she could call it hers. One of the biggest regrets of her divorce from Sid was losing the Beverly Hills house she'd personally decorated. "Don't you ever want your own space, where you can sleep in your own bed?"

"I don't know." He wrinkled his forehead in thought before carrying his empty dish to the sink and turning on the hot water. "I've thought about it, but there never seemed much reason."

"Are you planning on spending the rest of your life globetrotting?" she demanded incredulously, carrying her plate to the sink and shoving him aside with her hip. "You cooked, I wash."

He didn't argue but dug a towel from a drawer. "It's what I do."

Standing there domestically washing dishes together, feeling awareness rising between them, Mara thought it a damned shame to waste a man like TJ on a footloose lifestyle. But then, she supposed, men like him weren't sufficiently domesticated for her pampered existence. He might know how to wash dishes and cook his own meals, but if her instincts were correct, his mind was already on another continent. Did the man ever live in the here and now?

He didn't even make a pass at her after they finished the dishes. Feeling disembodied and dazed from all the hormones zinging around, Mara followed him back to his car and sat in disbelief as he drove her back to town.

He even let her keep the *Times*.

Something was definitely not right. The TJ she knew seethed and boiled beneath a thin veneer of civilization. This TJ had gone stone-cold dead, and she thought the reporter had something to do with it.

Out of curiosity, Mara didn't immediately climb out of the car when it rolled up in front of the inn. Just to see if the man she knew still existed, she leaned over and kissed his craggy cheek.

Wordlessly regarding her through deep-set eyes that scorched her to the bone, TJ caught her chin, captured her mouth with his, and set her blood afire with a kiss so deep and heated that she almost came right there. Not dead, then, but hot lava buried under cold stone.

He let her go, threw open the car door, and escorted her to the B&B, leaving her on the doorstep without a word.

Watching him drive off, Mara decided she most certainly did not need a volatile, inscrutable man like TJ McCloud in her life. She was a mess enough without him.

But she tingled in places she'd thought long dead, and her errant heart wept wistfully for the innocent love they'd once shared and could never share again.

Crying on the front porch wasn't a smart move, even if she wasn't wearing mascara.

She spun on her heel and stalked inside. If she didn't apply her mind to more important matters, she'd be as homeless as TJ in a few short months.

NINE

After dropping Mara off at the B&B, TJ drove to the office, his thoughts churning. Mara's kiss had steamed the few brain cells that had survived their morning together.

He'd spent these last years attempting to forget Patsy and rebuild the same kind of relationship with someone else, but that morning had shown him the impossibility of it. Only one spontaneous, brainy, intriguing female existed in this world for him, and right at the moment, she was no doubt lining up all that creativity against him.

Somehow he'd have to pry Mara out of his head and concentrate on outmaneuvering Roger.

Roger had been with him in the Balkans, was aware TJ and Martin had worked together there. TJ knew quite well the reporter was after a story, but he couldn't give it to him—wouldn't give it to him. They both owed Martin their lives. They'd never have escaped that sniper outburst in Kosovo if Martin hadn't risked his neck by careening in with his Jeep, Uzi blasting.

Roger might not believe he owed the colonel for that act, but TJ did. He was loyal enough not to act hastily or without careful thought. Journalists were sensationmongers these days. Selling newspapers was more important than accuracy. TJ refused to add fuel to the fire until he was certain the evidence was damning.

He detested even the need to continue going through the boxes stored in his office. He ought to trust the colonel's word and shred them, as he'd been told to do.

But his own integrity was now in question. If there was evidence of the colonel's corruption in those boxes, his sense of justice would never allow him to support a criminal, no matter how much he owed or respected him.

The warring factions of his psyche were tearing him apart.

Setting aside the box he'd already worked through, TJ methodically lined up the remaining cardboard boxes across the lab floor. Slitting the tape on the unopened ones, he scanned them for some order in the contents. Several contained files brimming with invoices and correspondence. A couple more contained steno notebooks of chicken scratch. He'd already skimmed through the typed transcripts of translations from interviews with Balkan residents. He found another with similar files. He didn't know who had gathered all the material or why, but his cursory glance at the notebooks had revealed incendiary accusations of a Mafia-like protection scam—exactly what the media was screaming. Somebody was guilty of releasing accused criminals without trials, undoubtedly in exchange for large sums of money.

He didn't want to believe it was Colonel Martin.

Flipping through files revealed nothing riveting. No piece of paper yelled in big black letters *Martin is guilty*. It could take weeks to filter through this stuff, and he might still never understand the implications. He wasn't a lawyer. He knew bones, not bits of paper.

He wasn't suited to be Martin's judge and jury. He ought to hand the boxes over to someone more objective. Or believe Martin and shred them. *Shit.*

If he quit working on his excavation to work on the boxes, Mara would lose her film.

He hated his life right now.

Figuring the transcript box would be easiest to study, he returned it to the closet where he could get at it easily, and locked the door. He resealed the others, deciding to store them somewhere safer than a flimsy closet. If Roger knew enough to question him about the colonel, it was only a matter of time before others would hunt him down—if the Defense Department didn't send spooks to search his rooms first.

He'd start a more thorough reading of the transcripts tonight. Somewhere in there should be the proof of Martin's innocence. Or guilt.

TJ carried the other boxes to the trunk and backseat of his Taurus. He'd find an anonymous storage unit and install a strong lock. That should be safe enough.

Returning to the office, he grimaced at the blinking answering machine light. Next, he needed to hire an assistant, or at the very least a secretary, or he could spend his nights answering mail and phone calls.

Sorting through the junk on his desk, he located a clean sheet of paper and a pen. He punched the machine's button and waited for the first message, pen poised.

"This is Senator—" TJ hit message delete and waited for the next call.

"Carlton here. Give me a call at—"

"This is Congressman Throckwaite's office. If you would—"

Damn Mara. He smacked the machine again. Maybe he ought to just fling it against the wall.

"This is A-and-E Rentals." The voice sounded almost apologetic. "We will not be able to renew the lease on your office after the first of the month."

If he wasn't already so furious, this would almost be funny. How many more irritants could Mara have stirred up? Before he hit the play button again, the phone rang. With morbid curiosity, TJ folded his arms and waited for the machine to take it.

"TJ? Are you there?" Mara. He didn't want to talk to her. Just the sound of her voice engorged his prick and shut down his brain functions. He couldn't believe he'd let her leave the cottage without taking her right there on the couch. He wasn't immune to her flirtatious glances. They had old issues, and she'd signaled loud and clear that she was ready to settle them.

But he wasn't in the mood for settling them with sex when he couldn't tell the difference between wanting to wring her neck and needing to jump her bones.

Doo-wah-diddy-diddy hummed through his head like a bee buzzing.

"Oh, well, if you pick this up before you go home, come over around seven. Glynis Everett just arrived, and we're having a small welcoming party." Her voice turned sultry. "Maybe we can make the world go away."

The machine beeped, signaling the end of the message.

He didn't give a flying fart about Glynis Everett, but the invitation in Mara's voice was unmistakable. What would it hurt? They'd get it out of their systems, have a few laughs. Work off a little hostility . . . right.

He punched the button to pick up the last message.

"I think you'd better leave town, Dr. McCloud," a quavering female voice announced. "There's going to be trouble if you don't."

Summoning every foul word in his vocabulary, TJ ripped the machine from the phone and hurled it against the concrete block wall across the room.

Leaving the pieces where they were, he stalked out.

Mara widened her eyes in surprise as TJ strolled into her intimate soiree on the back terrace of the B&B that evening. She hadn't expected him to accept her invitation. She'd been teasing him with that message. She'd enjoyed their interlude this morning, but she was fully aware that she and TJ still had major issues.

He'd thrown a khaki microfiber jacket over his blue shirt, and with one hand in his jeans pocket, he looked as elegant as any man in here, and more authoritative with that chiseled jaw. A wave of dark hair falling over his high forehead and the questioning crook of his thick, dark eyebrow added an aspect of condescension to his unsmiling demeanor. Only she could tell by the tic in his unshaven jaw that he was on the verge of explosion.

Between husbands, her leading lady was salivating already. Glynis had a penchant for rough-looking bad boys—and right now TJ looked far surlier and more interesting than Glynis's current young lover. Watching trouble brew as her star's immature partner glared and Glynis preened, Mara realized how much she'd come to detest the world to which she'd once aspired.

But she knew how to work a room with the best of them. No more shy Patsy.

Snagging a martini from the waiter, she glided across the B&B's terrace, winking and waving and adroitly avoiding conversation.

"You came." She handed TJ the martini, captured his elbow, and steered him away from her predatory leading lady. "I didn't think you would."

"Didn't you?" He slanted her one of those enigmatic looks that gave her cold chills and hot tremors at the same time. The connection that had always been between them hummed, pheromones sang, and a whole chorus of hormones erupted in hallelujahs.

Right there and then Mara realized she'd dived into the deep end without a life jacket. "I figured you'd written me off as hopelessly shallow and beneath your contempt." She mocked herself more than him with that comment.

TJ lifted one sexy eyebrow, but his gaze diverted to the see-through effect of her gown. Good. Keep him as off balance as she was.

"Always keep the enemy in your sights," he replied gravely.

She wanted to smack him, but Ian's shouted demands for her to entertain a reporter intruded. She bussed TJ's cheek to mark him as hers, then reluctantly plunged into the midst of the publicity crew.

"What the devil is he doing here?" Ian muttered as she sauntered up. "Isn't he the guy keeping our trucks from the beach?"

Mara flashed a smile at a reporter, accepted a martini

from her PR man, and whispered to Ian, "He's an old friend, okay? Leave him alone."

"Does Sid know he's an old friend?" her producer demanded. "Better yet, does Sid know your old friend is the reason production costs are gonna skyrocket?"

"It's none of Sid's damned business," she retorted, "and it's none of yours either. Lay off, Ian."

"Sid's talking about hiring a lawyer to move McCloud's fat ass out of there." Ian threw back a swig of scotch and scowled.

"Quit talking to Sid behind my back." With a hiss of distaste, Mara swung on her heel and awarded the reporter her biggest smile. This was her project. Her ex could just keep his bloody hands off it.

Out of the corner of her eye, Mara watched TJ throughout the evening. He didn't appear to bat an eye when Glynis practically assaulted him in the shadows of the jasmine-covered trellis. Looking as tailored and businesslike as the politicians and millionaires she courted, he accepted a fresh drink while the mayor berated him about the access problem. She prayed they'd come to terms, but the parade of businessmen and council members approaching him throughout the evening didn't bode well.

She knew from prior experience that once TJ decided something was right, nothing shook him from his designated path. The man could give concrete fence posts a lesson.

He appeared at ease, sipping his drinks, occasionally sketching something on a napkin, other times sticking a hand in his pocket and nodding thoughtfully while someone talked. He might be bored, but he didn't show it. He rewarded everyone with his undivided interest.

Even the women. They flocked around him, touching, flirting, doing their best to capture his attention.

He wasn't even good-looking, Mara told herself. He had that sharp jut of a nose and no dimple to speak of, unless one counted the dent in his square chin. He seldom smiled. He oozed no charm. He simply regarded everyone with dark-eyed intensity and had them lapping out of his hand.

She hated him for it. He'd had that effect even as a solemn, rather shy high school athlete. She'd always had to fight for every ounce of attention, but TJ just stood there, radiating power, and the world bowed at his feet.

Well, she wasn't a high school wallflower anymore. She could attract just as much interest as he could. She smiled at the young anchorman in front of her, and he brightened perceptibly. She drifted toward one of the film's investors and laid a hand on the sleeve of his Italian silk suit. He caught and squeezed her fingers, holding her there while he talked sports with her director.

Across the room, TJ offered a glass of champagne to one of the supporting cast members, a young actress barely out of her teens.

Mara smiled invitingly at the local banker, a distinguished silver-haired gentleman. He zoomed in and hovered.

TJ collected a long-haired local model and another member of the supporting cast, this one older than himself. He caught her look across the room and lifted his glass in salute.

She wanted to rip the skin off every woman in his vicinity. Did TJ feel the same about the men in hers? The thought added a thrill of anticipation to the game.

The evening grew late. The levels in the liquor bottles lowered.

She caught TJ edging toward the door. So did Glynis Everett.

Enough was enough. Zigzagging through the noisy crowd, Mara cut them off at the pass.

"Glynis, Tony is looking for you," she purred at Hollywood's top box-office draw. Deliberately turning her back on the sexy redhead, Mara took Tim's arm and guided him into the corridor. "I think the party can go on without me now. Why don't we find someplace quiet where we can talk?"

She'd wipe that inscrutable expression off his face one way or another.

"I'm not shutting down my excavation," he informed her grimly as they entered the lobby. "You can set the mayor and all the king's men on me, and I won't leave until I'm done."

So his evening hadn't been any more pleasant than hers. Fine. Served him right. "What if I set Glynis to persuade you? How soon would you cave?" She led him toward the staircase.

"Do you really think all that hair and the lipsticked smirk would turn my head?" he asked scornfully, following her up the stairs. "Give me plain honesty every time."

Mara quaked a little at that, but she didn't exactly consider herself dishonest. She just didn't think she knew what honesty was anymore. She lived in a Technicolor world with flashing lights and glittering gems, some of which might even be genuine. Black and white had disappeared along the way.

She'd find it again once she got this film in the can and the company in her name. She'd have time to look around and rediscover herself then.

She unlocked the door to her suite and led TJ in.

She'd never done anything this brave or this insane in her life. She'd been a virgin when she married Irving, her first husband. Yeah, she'd slept with Sid before they married, but she had his engagement ring on her finger at the time. This was different. This was temporary.

This was Tim.

She wasn't really thinking of going to bed with him, was she?

No. Definitely not. She just wanted to get even for all those miserable school years she'd watched him wander off with the cheerleaders and the country club girls, leaving Brad's kid sister behind. She'd been sixteen before Tim deigned to notice her as anything more than a pest. By then, he'd been off at college, and those few short months of telephone calls and hasty weekend visits weren't enough to make up for the prior years of longing.

"Is honesty all you require in a woman?" she asked with interest.

"That's a stupid question." He prowled her suite restlessly, like a caged tiger, picking up expensive antique accessories and putting them down without really looking at them. He didn't really look at her.

Cooled by a blast of air-conditioning, Mara draped an expensive Italian lace shawl over the thin straps of her gown. She toyed with the fringe of feathers on the shawl as TJ paced the room. If sexual tension could be bottled, they could supply the entire state of South Carolina tonight.

She'd parried TJ's insults enough in the past to know how to deal with his bluntness. "Thank you," she purred. "I've always thought stupidity one of my more attractive assets."

He turned and eyed her with suspicion. "We don't have anything sensible to say to each other. Why am I here?"

This wasn't the considerate man of this morning, but a hot-blooded, angry one. His controlled facade had definitely slipped. She longed to explore the secrets TJ McCloud hid beneath his stony exterior, but they had past issues to work through first.

He shrugged off his coat as if the room had become warm, and Mara shivered nervously at the sight of the powerful biceps she'd admired earlier that day. If she were casting this film, he'd be the sexy antihero who snarled and offed people without a qualm.

Now that she had garnered his full attention, Mara spilled the silk of her shawl through her fingers and considered his question. Why *had* she asked him here?

She understood the answer he anticipated when she felt his gaze drop to the red feathers teasing the black lace of her barely-there neckline.

Defiantly she shifted the shawl a little, letting the silk slide over her cleavage. She smiled when TJ practically growled at her teasing gesture. The simmering cauldron she remembered had reached boiling, and her blood raced just as it had when she'd been sixteen.

Neither of them was an inexperienced teenager any longer. They had no reason for restraint.

"If you don't know why I'm here, either, maybe I'd better leave." TJ reached for his coat. The threat in his voice rumbled with the tension of a summer storm.

My, unleashed tigers were sexy. Maybe it was time for her to get in touch with her primitive side. Daringly Mara slipped the shawl farther down her arms. "I think maybe you know why you're here better than I do," she taunted.

TJ's enigmatic mask slipped, exposing raw hunger in coal dark eyes as he stalked toward her. Too late she realized tigers were also dangerous.

He dropped his coat on a chair arm as he crossed the room. Mara took a step backward, but the needy little girl in her refused to run.

"All right, I'll tell you—this is why I'm here." He caught the edges of the shawl, wrapped them around her arms, and tied them behind her, effectively creating a silken straitjacket.

Nervously Mara tried to defuse what she'd set in motion. "TJ—"

His brawny arm curled around her waist and lifted her from her feet. An abrupt encounter with his solid torso cut off her warning.

His hard lips slanted across hers, silencing all protest. The demanding grasp of TJ's arms, the heated pressure of his mouth, made her feel as no man had—as if she were manna from heaven, expressly delivered for his salvation. Helpless to beat him off with her hands or hold him off with her sarcasm, Mara succumbed to the fantasy of being TJ McCloud's dream come true.

When she yielded to his kiss, TJ's tongue instantly took possession of her mouth, and fireworks exploded inside her head.

She thought she might have moaned. She knew she let him take her weight as his grip softened, and she slid down his body. She pressed her hips closer to his until he bent her backward over his arm and increased his demands on her greedy mouth.

He left her no choice but to respond in kind, to curl her tongue about his, kiss him deeply, and moan in ecstasy at her helplessness beneath the heat pouring through her bloodstream.

She should have shoved him away when she had the chance. He was mixing sex and anger, and she didn't want him taking out his frustration on her—

She wanted him any way she could have him. This was the closure she needed to her adolescent daydreams.

She shuddered with desire as TJ's tongue probed and caressed and his hand slid between them to crush her breast. It had been so long since anyone had touched her like this. . . .

There was good reason she didn't let anyone touch her like this.

Arms still bound by the shawl, Mara tried to wriggle away, but TJ lowered her against the bed's edge, positioning her between the yielding mattress and thighs as solid as tree trunks. His kisses slid across her cheek and into her hair, melting her synapses with fire and tenderness. Panting and operating on sheer animal instinct, she returned his kisses where she could, desperate to hold him and kiss him properly.

TJ's solidness crushed her into the mattress. His arousal pressed through the thin layers of their clothes. Unable to use her hands, Mara lifted her hips to meet his—even as she tried to form a reproach through lips bruised and aching from his kisses.

She understood now why mares in heat screamed when stallions trapped and covered them. The primitive instinct to resist submission warred with the sexual excitement of being dominated.

Animal lust won. Hands still trapped, she accepted TJ's ravishment with a shudder of desire.

His hand slid between their bodies, taking possession of her breast again. Aroused by his deceptive caress, drowning in his kiss, Mara's brain didn't kick into gear until he had the shawl and gown off her shoulders and the hook off her bra. Abruptly aware of her seminakedness as cool air blew across her breasts, she struggled briefly. Then, realizing he'd freed her from the confines of the shawl, she slid her hands behind his neck and tugged his head closer.

TJ took advantage of her lifted arms to caress her nipples. His kiss strayed from her mouth to her throat, and delicious anticipation followed wherever he touched. She arched upward, needing his mouth where his hand played.

TJ took her breast in his mouth. Crying out at the electrifying touch of his tongue, Mara grabbed his shirt so she didn't levitate to the ceiling.

"TJ!" She tried to protest again, but to her surprise, his name emerged more as a demand.

He obliged by switching to her other breast. Need sizzled as he pushed her farther back on the bed. Her gown slid to her waist with the aid of his big hand.

"We're adults now," he muttered, returning to kissing her throat while his hands covered her breasts, teased, then explored lower. "It's time we got this out of our systems."

She didn't want it out of her system. Not now. Not this way.

But she needed it. She needed it so badly she registered no complaint when he ripped off her expensive lace panties. She merely offered a high-pitched cry of satisfaction as he touched her between her legs.

She quit thinking entirely and gave herself up to the sensation of TJ McCloud stripping her naked—a fantasy she'd created in her mind a long, long time ago.

TEN

Mara's satin skin radiated an erotic perfume that shot straight to TJ's groin. Riding high on alcohol and lust, he didn't fight a driving urge he normally curbed and whose power he'd forgotten.

She was beyond breathtaking. Mile-long legs adorned in outrageous high-heeled sandals, a taut abdomen framed by sharp hip bones, a tiny waist swelling to creamy hills more the size of cupcakes than the overripe melons she displayed in public. When he caressed her breasts, she closed her eyes and hummed in pleasure, as if he were the only man in the world who could do this for her.

The effect was astonishing. Her slender hips arched into him, and he grew so hard he'd erupt if he didn't act soon.

When he'd been nineteen, one of his greatest fears had been that his size could overwhelm the virginal sixteen-year-old he'd adored too much to harm. They both had more experience now. No barrier stood in their way.

No barrier other than his trouser fly, and TJ unfastened that without a hitch, shoving his jeans to the floor.

Mara's hungry whimpers escalated as he caressed moistened curls, seeking access. TJ tried to slow down enough to appreciate the tanned curves of her small waist, the bikini line at her hips. He ached so deep inside that he couldn't slow down more than that. The day's infuriating events and the evening's tortured contest of wills had aroused a primitive need to win the woman who should have been his long ago.

He slid his hands beneath Mara's slim buttocks and lifted her hips. She tried to keep her grip on his shoulders, but he teased his fingers between her thighs, and she intuitively fell back against the mattress and wrapped her legs about his waist.

She opened her eyes then, and stared at his seminude body in such wide-eyed amazement that TJ felt like the eighth wonder of the world. If he took time to think—

He didn't want to think. Leaning over to catch her mouth with his, TJ entered her and with a single shove drove all the way inside, swallowing her scream with his kiss. Ecstasy and relief poured through him as her inner muscles stretched to sheathe him, and her scream became a moan of pleasure.

This time it was his turn to close his eyes and absorb sensation. He registered her first shock with his body, not through his eyes. They both held still for a moment, adjusting to the newness, savoring the experience. Liquid heat caressed and aroused, and he struggled to hold the moment.

Mara's inner muscles tightened, and a burst of light shattered TJ's reserve. He pulled back and drove deep again, matching his rhythm to her moans.

It had been too long, and he wanted too much. She was slender, and he tried to be gentle, but every time he held back, his body rebelled by demanding more. At first she writhed and fought the onslaught, but then she cried out and met him in the middle, surrendering to the rhythm he set, until joy pulsed through his blood and they moved as one, with only one purpose.

She exploded first, in small lightning movements that pumped him dry in a shattering ecstasy. Shaken by the intensity of his release, he instantly craved more. He hadn't had enough of her—might never have enough.

TJ lifted Mara's hips to his, and she rubbed against him in a bid for more. He stirred inside her, growing hard again, and she whimpered in pleasure. His mind was mush, but the part of him that mattered right now possessed a spine of steel.

Reluctantly releasing his position, TJ lifted her from the mattress and stripped back the covers. Pulling her gown over her head and tossing it, Mara eagerly slid between the sheets and watched as he ripped off his shirt. Her admiring gaze increased his driving need to painful intensity. She looked at him as if he were a man and not just a brain.

Her blond upsweep of curls had tumbled to her shoulders, revealing the hairpiece beneath, and TJ grinned at this glimpse of the Patsy he'd known. He'd wondered how Hollywood stars managed to have more hair than real women. Reaching over, he unclipped the piece and flung it to the bedside table.

She watched him warily.

"I don't make love to your hair." He climbed in on top of her, straddling her legs, and claiming her mouth with his. Joy filled his soul as her fingers slid over his bare back, and she accepted him without question, as if they were two parts merging into one. This was how it should have been all those years ago.

Except all those years ago, he'd had sense enough to carry condoms.

Cursing his alcohol-deluded mind, TJ propped himself up. "Birth control?"

She looked stunned. Her big green eyes regarded him from behind dark lashes that were longer and blacker than this morning's set. He'd smeared her mascara into dark rings, but the raccoon effect tugged at his heart. She looked almost as vulnerable as she had at sixteen, when he'd caught her crying behind the gym during a dance.

"No," she whispered.

He didn't want to consider consequences in one of life's rare moments of perfection.

He leaned over the side of the bed and fished for his trousers on the floor. If he was really lucky, he might find safety in his wallet. He'd despised the uncertainty of his teenage years, but she reduced him to the status of adolescent all over again. He'd never in his life had sex with a woman without protection, and she'd inflamed him so quickly, he hadn't given it a thought. He'd analyze that error later.

She sighed in relief when he produced the plastic package. "You're supposed to be the responsible one around here," she scolded lightly.

"Don't wave a red flag at a raging bull next time," he retorted, nipping her ear and filling his hand with her breast. Her perfume wafted through his head with more power than a drug, and her softness begged to be squeezed.

"I'm a city girl. Teach me about raging bulls," she whispered against his mouth.

He did, claiming her as he'd wanted to long ago. Desperate for the ease of oblivion, TJ immersed both body and soul in a woman—or in the promise of the girl he'd once trusted.

Mara hadn't thought anyone could ease the hunger in her, hadn't realized how starved she was until TJ filled her. Still insatiable, she clawed at his back, wrapped her legs around his waist, and bucked like a mindless animal. He tore open the scars on her psyche and flooded the open wounds, healing and soothing. Her womb ached with need, and she wept when they finally found a second release.

She didn't want him to leave her again, physically, emotionally, or in any other way.

He would, though, and probably not as gently as he pulled away now. The chill of the air-conditioning crossing her skin as he withdrew his warmth reminded her that they had nothing more between them than sweaty bodies.

But at least she'd had that much, she thought in satisfaction as TJ rolled off and lifted her to rest on the rounded muscle of his shoulder. She—Patsy Simonetti—

had driven the self-contained Tim McCloud out of control. She squirmed to a more comfortable position and tried to believe that was enough.

Damn the man for reducing her to the lonely child she'd once been. She refused to become that needy child ever again. He hadn't come back to rescue her all those years ago, and she wouldn't count on him helping her out now.

She punched TJ's hard abs and rolled back to the pillow to stare at the ceiling.

"I don't think I can talk right now," he muttered, with his eyes closed. "Can you save that thought until morning?"

Morning. She could have him again in the morning. Crossing her leg over his so he couldn't slip away, Mara nodded. He was probably already asleep and couldn't see her nod. That was okay, too. He meant to stay the night. The long string of lonely nights that were her past had been broken.

The riot of emotions welling up inside her were terrifying.

A large male body occupying three-quarters of Mara's queen-size bed presented several dilemmas the next morning. The most immediate was that of a daunting obstacle between her and the supersize aspirins in her nightstand drawer.

Bright Carolina sunshine poured in the windows—she'd not closed the shutters last night. She would definitely start drinking tonic water at those damned cocktail parties from now on.

Rather than crawl over that wide expanse of muscled flesh, she supposed she could crawl around the bed, but at the moment she couldn't even open her eyes. Stupid of her, insisting on a room overlooking the harbor. She hadn't grasped that she was on the East Coast and the sun came *up* over the water—at disconcertingly early hours.

She lifted one eyelid to admire the hurdle blocking her access to relief. TJ slept on his back, and bronzed, hard shoulders covered her lace-bedecked pillows. She sighed in admiration and closed her eye again. She could endure a headache with all that masculinity a hairbreadth away.

It amazed her that she could still feel the ache of desire. Once a week had been more than enough with her ex-husbands. Not once had it occurred to her to instigate their occasional couplings, but she was definitely considering running her fingers through TJ's chest hairs right now. She didn't know if it was possible—or even wise—to satiate a need this strong. She might be in danger of addiction.

TJ resolved her dilemma by rolling onto his side and trapping her legs beneath a heavy thigh. His erection hardened against her hip, and Mara smiled with pleasure, not opening her eyes again.

"I'm out of condoms," he muttered against her hair. "Shove me out of bed now."

The hungry desperation in his voice thrilled her to the marrow.

"What do you think I am, a weight lifter?" She snuggled closer.

He crushed her breast in his hand, and her nipple rose to his palm. Desire seeped directly from her breast to the place between her legs. She squirmed restlessly, thinking she'd better move now or regret the consequences later.

Too late. She'd teased the tiger. TJ angled his body over hers, covered her mouth with a mind-bending kiss, and settled in to caress her until she demanded more. With the same urgency as she felt, he parted her thighs and slid home.

She groaned with the startling force of the need sweeping through them. Never had she known it could be like this. She might as well have tried to tame a hurricane as to stop what was happening to her, to him, to both of them. She'd never dreamed such insanity existed, but she reveled in it, let him sweep her up in it, and became part of the maelstrom as much as a leaf driven by the wind.

His primitive shout of triumph erupted in her ears as they reached the heights together. Mara dug her fingernails into his powerful shoulders, arched to take all of him, and climaxed as he poured himself into her.

This was how it should be. This was what the love stories in movies promised. Hollywood had been a disappointing illusion until now.

Aware of his heaviness, TJ rolled back to the mattress, wrapping her in his arms to keep their connection. Mara sprawled across his torso, conscious of the heat of his skin, the perspiration sealing their flesh, the way his heart beat next to hers.

"I wonder what our lives would have been like if we'd done this back then instead of just thinking about it," she murmured sleepily.

Every muscle in TJ's body stiffened beneath her. "If we hadn't thought about it, Brad would be alive right now."

He tumbled her back to the bed and climbed out, heading straight for the shower.

Well, so much for reminiscing. Mara covered her eyes with her arm. The ugly memory of that night would haunt them for the rest of their lives. No wonder he'd never looked for her after her family moved away.

While she was lying here vibrating with life, her beautiful, honorable older brother lay cold in the ground, never having lived to fulfill the promise of his genius.

She'd wept those tears long ago. She wouldn't do it anymore. She might carry the guilt forever, but she couldn't stop living just because Brad had. She'd had counseling and had chosen to live life to its fullest rather than burying herself in grief.

She wondered about TJ, though. Had he buried himself in his work to assuage his pain? It was too much for her pounding head to analyze. She just knew he was leaving her far sooner than she liked.

TJ emerged from the bathroom tugging his shirt over

the rippling muscles of his shoulders and chest, and she experienced a pang of regret, wondering if she'd ever see him that way again.

He stopped beside the bed and gazed down at her dispassionately, which meant nothing at all. TJ had dispassionate down to a science. Only she knew the chaos roaring behind the mask. She'd tapped into it last night. She didn't know if she had the strength—or the courage—to do so again.

"I'll look for another assistant to speed up the job," he said calmly. "I wish it could be easier, but once I've uncovered everything in the mound, I'll move out."

"How long will that take?" she demanded, not bothering to draw the sheet over her breasts to hide her lack in that department. Sid had wanted her to have implants, but she'd never been brave enough or stupid enough to risk them. Padding and push-up bras worked well enough for clothes. She was tired of disguising her faults. If TJ didn't like what he saw, screw him.

His gaze lingered a little too long on her chest to believe he wasn't interested. Her nipples rose to inviting peaks.

"Two months, if I don't come up for air," he replied doggedly, tearing his gaze away to meet her eyes.

"I can't wait two months!" Mara shot up from the pillow, carrying the sheet with her. No more free rides for the monster. She needed that beach, and she needed it now.

"Your pirates will have to sail in." He picked up his jacket and walked out.

Mara screamed and heaved her travel alarm after him. She followed it with a martini glass and a guidebook—none of which shattered sufficiently to match the devastation in her heart as he smashed her foolish dreams all over again.

Choking on sobs of fury, she stumbled out of bed, determined to overcome still one more male obstacle thrown in her way. She had lots of experience in circumventing stone walls. Sometimes that was all that kept her going each day.

TJ debated driving straight home, but this was Monday, and if he meant to hire an assistant, he'd have to drag out his address book and begin making inquiries. The address book was in his office.

He'd rather think about anything than about how he'd spent last night. He didn't want to analyze his abysmal behavior as any more than stress relief and the by-product of alcohol. He definitely did not want to know Mara's motivation for taking him to her room. He'd just mark it up to her living in Hollywood too long.

Maybe he should move to Hollywood. He'd never even imagined that kind of erotic experience. He would spend the rest of his life dreaming of having it again. Just what he needed, two Simonettis haunting his head, one dead and one vibrantly alive.

Parking in the alley, TJ rounded the corner to discover Roger leaning against the storefront, waiting for him.

"Late night?" the reporter inquired as TJ stalked up and stuck his key in the door. "Some guys have all the luck. I just found out who Mara Simon is."

"Tad slow, aren't you?" Pushing the door open, TJ hit the light switch. His foot encountered a fallen chair before his brain registered the havoc strewn across the floor.

All his meticulously labeled slides and notes and the artifacts he'd been working on for weeks lay strewn across the cheap vinyl. He'd wanted something to drive last night out of his head. This hadn't been what he had in mind.

Spray-painted in red across the wall was the message YANKEE, GO HOME!

"Looks like someone doesn't like you, old boy." Roger pushed past a frozen TJ to examine the destruction.

"Don't," TJ commanded.

Roger halted where he was.

"You'll disturb the evidence." He thought he sounded calm, but rage roared in his head so loudly that his ears rang with it.

Roger shrugged and stepped back. "You're the man. Want me to call the police, or you want at it first?"

This time, TJ was glad he was the man. This was how he'd gained his reputation. No two-bit, fly-by-night vandal could escape a trained observer who'd caught war criminals with far more experience and blood on their hands than the pathetic jerk who'd trashed his office.

"Right," Roger said, as if TJ had actually answered his question. "I'll get out of your way."

TJ was already examining the size-twelve footprint in the dust beneath the overturned table. His expertise might be forensic anthropology, but his training had taught him to look far beyond bones.

"Do that," TJ answered gruffly.

"You know I'll be back," Roger warned. "The colonel's story is too big. I thought I could count on you to give me the truth. I didn't picture you as the sort to cover up for corrupt officials."

"Don't come back until you can prove Martin is anything other than the man who saved our lives and taught us how to survive out there." Searching for anything that looked out of place, TJ turned his back on the reporter. "Until then, go far, far away."

"What makes you so certain he didn't do this?" Roger responded, indicating the mayhem. "Maybe it's a warning to tell you to go back to Africa. Maybe someone thinks you know more than you do and wants you out of here."

TJ turned a scathing look on him. "Rog, you've got a nose for news but no understanding of human nature. A sniveling coward did this. You want to call Martin a sniveling coward?"

"You have some better explanation for this senseless destruction? Give me something, McCloud. Your pal is about to go up in flames and your office is trashed. I don't believe in coincidences."

TJ slid a piece of paper underneath a gray hair snagged on a torn piece of vinyl. "I can give you at least three explanations."

Roger waited.

Folding the paper and tucking it into his pocket, TJ stood up again. "Either Mara's movie crew got tired of waiting around, someone wants to cover up a sixty-year old murder, or someone just plain doesn't like me."

Or any combination of the above, but Roger could figure that out for himself.

Checking the once-locked closet in the back room, TJ cursed at the paper evidence strewn across the floor. Good thing he'd taken the rest of the boxes to storage.

ELEVEN

"The limo can't take me to the set?" Glynis Everett gasped in the same tones of horror she'd used in a B film at the beginning of her career.

Glynis might think she was the next Julia Roberts, but she was still a second-tier star and didn't rate maximum perks. Mara ticked off a note on her clipboard and ignored the dramatics. Once upon a time she'd been burdened with the need to make everyone happy. Scenes like this had burned out that need years ago. "If you can't walk to the beach, you can take an ATV. Surely you're not too old to enjoy the experience."

Okay, so that last remark was malicious spite in retaliation for Glynis trying to move in on TJ last night. Glynis's official age was six years younger than Mara's real age, and Mara would resent every year of that difference if she believed in official bios. She didn't. Hollywood worshiped youth, and Glynis catered to the media. Mara calculated her star had hit the big three-oh last year.

She could tell from Glynis's angry silence that the dig had hit home. Having won the battle, Mara graciously gestured at her limo driver and bodyguard. "Jim, take Miss Everett out to the island, would you? I have a few more things to do here. You can pick me up later."

Gratified at the offer of the best car available, Glynis slinked off without further argument. Checking the actress's footwear, Mara grinned. Glynis would have to ride the ATV or break her fool neck trying to cross the dune in those heels.

"Perhaps I ought to open a shoe-rental stand," a dry voice remarked.

Spinning around, Mara caught Cleo McCloud eyeing the departing actress with cynical interest. Enjoying being on the same wavelength with another woman for a change, Mara pocketed her cell phone and set aside her pen to welcome Tim's sister-in-law. "A shoe rental will work only if you persuade them to check their egos at the door."

A brief grin of appreciation flitted across Cleo's face. Shoving her hands into the pockets of her baggy camp shorts, she sauntered closer. "A moment ago I was thinking you might be better at scaring off tourists in my driveway than the mechanical witch I used to hang there, but maybe you're human after all."

The blunt honesty hit Mara's funny bone, and she laughed at what should have been an insult. "I operate on automatic once production starts. Snap and I snap harder, so watch out."

Cleo eyed her with curiosity. "Snap too hard and you break. Been there, done that. But I didn't come over here to hand out bad psychology. I'm looking for TJ. He didn't come home last night, and this morning he has police tape across his office door. I figure he's a big boy and can take care of himself, but Matty still gets upset when he sees police tape. I told him I'd make certain everything is all right."

Mara had the feeling that this was a long speech for Cleo, and that she had to care about TJ a great deal more than she let on. Living in a shallow world that didn't look beneath surfaces, Mara normally would have accepted Cleo's speech at face value.

Today, the idea of anything happening to TJ aroused irrational panic.

"TJ spent the night here." Mara tried to act calm while her imagination flew over all the things that might have happened. "He was fine when he left a few hours ago."

Unthinkingly, she looked for Jim to see if he'd heard anything on his scanner, but, cursing, she remembered her driver had left for the beach. Shoving the clipboard at one of the dozen assistants running around trying to get the crew off, Mara strode for the street. "Where's the police station?"

Running backward in front of her, Cleo spread her arms and blocked Mara's path. "Whoa, sister! No point in going off like a cocked pistol. If TJ was alive and well this morning, then he's terrorizing some poor official somewhere. You really don't want to face the sheriff after Tim's worked him over."

Her heart rate slowing to almost normal, Mara halted and tried to locate her equilibrium. She couldn't. Police tape and TJ stirred ancient, moldering fears. "How do we know TJ's murdered body isn't behind that tape?" she demanded.

Cleo snorted in a definitely unladylike manner. "This is a small town. If TJ had been murdered, my phone would be ringing off the hook. Silence means no one got hurt. That's all that's important. Sorry if I disturbed you, but I wanted to be able to tell the kid his uncle could still beat him up when he gets home."

Still not convinced, Mara restlessly continued pacing toward the street. "What about Jared? Wouldn't TJ have called him?"

Cleo laughed and fell into step with her. "Just exactly how well do you know the McCloud men? Walking testimonies to testosterone, the three of them. Men like that don't communicate, they compete."

Mara considered that and kept walking. She might want to beat the aggravating beast to a pulp, but nobody—no one, ever—had treated her as if she were the moon and stars all wrapped in precious silk, as TJ had last night. Yeah, he had a little temper-control problem when she pushed too hard, but given how that had turned out, he could lose control with her anytime he chose. "They can communicate if pressed," Mara replied. "TJ's likely to blame me or the crew if anything happened. Where's the sheriff's office?"

Cleo whistled and glanced up and down the street as they emerged from the inn yard. "Forget the sheriff. Let's try the café." Without waiting for agreement, she strode off in the direction of the harbor.

All right, so networking worked the same in small-town America as it did in Hollywood. You just needed to know where the in crowd hung. She could accept that. Glancing down at her clinging white knit jumpsuit, Mara felt the old self-consciousness return. "They're not going to talk with me around, are they? Maybe I should go back—"

Impatiently Cleo tugged open a glass door painted with dolphins. "Don't wimp out now. You want to look like an albino giraffe, make 'em accept albino giraffes."

Albino giraffe? Startled by this perspective on her carefully chosen designer outfit, Mara instinctively sought retaliation—until she encountered a roomful of expectant faces watching their entrance, and froze. She hadn't been so nervous before an audience since her first communion. Gingerly she trailed Cleo into the lion's den.

"Where's TJ?" Cleo demanded of no one in particular, weaving her way between tables to the counter. "Did he finally murder his assistant?"

"Someone trashed his office," a gum-chewing waitress responded laconically. "Gonna introduce us to your friend?"

"Why? So you can ask for an autograph? I don't think so." Cleo appropriated a stool at the counter and spun it to face the grizzled old man on her left. "Hey, Ed, thought you were going to keep an eye on those pirate bones of Tim's."

Mara smiled apologetically at the unperturbed waitress and ordered a coffee. Nearly six feet in her high heels and stacked curls, she towered over her audience. Lowering herself to the stool on Cleo's right, she attempted invisibility while waiting for a reply to Cleo's question.

She might as well have attempted to feel inconspicuous sitting on a mantel flapping angel wings before a choir of awestruck kids. All eyes focused on her.

"Ain't pirate bones," the old man scoffed, tipping the bill of his John Deere cap to Mara. "German, if anything. Bet he'll find their sub if he digs deep enough."

"You'll be the first to know if he does," Cleo assured him before turning back to the waitress. "All right, you win. This is Mara Simon, and she's running the show over at the inn. Now tell us where Jared's big brother is."

The lanky waitress set two steaming mugs of coffee in front of them. "Pleased to meetcha, Miss Simon. Don't mind Cleo's manners. She's equally rude to everyone."

So this was what it was like to suffer culture shock, Mara decided, sipping her coffee and wondering how to reply. No false smiles or kissy faces, no charming lies, Versace halter tops, or glass slippers. Maybe she'd been gone from Brooklyn too long. Had people been this upfront there? If so, she didn't remember it. She'd done a damned good job of forgetting her childhood.

She had the nervous feeling everyone in the room hung on her reply. Setting the cup down, she tried to adapt to her surroundings. "Not rude, but blunt, I'd say," she answered cautiously. "Cleo is blunt and concerned. Police tape means bad things where I come from." Bad line, she reprimanded herself. Next they'd be asking where she came from.

Cleo expertly diverted their attention. "Yeah, I'm concerned. No one else is crazy enough to rent my beach house in the middle of hurricane season. I'm in danger of losing money here. Has the sheriff locked him up?"

Laughter rippled through the room, and Mara relaxed. Always take a good guide into strange territory, she noted in her mental PDA. Hurricane season? She pushed that particular piece of panic aside.

"Nah, McCloud is threatening to call in the state cops if the sheriff don't get off his fat duff and find out who trashed his office," a baseball-capped man commented from a nearby table.

Mara breathed a little easier knowing TJ was up to his usual macho tactics and not harmed in any way.

"Thanks, Goober," Cleo called. "Does the sheriff need rescuing, or should I leave them alone?"

More laughter. No longer feeling as if she was the target of everyone's gaze, Mara relaxed. Getting into the scene, she tried a line of her own. "Let the sheriff call the cops," she said blithely, helping herself to a doughnut from the plastic case on the counter. "I'll add them to the cast. The role of pirate should come naturally."

Ed snickered, and even the laconic waitress cracked a smile. As she'd guessed from Cleo's comment, in this freebooting society where government in any form was regarded with suspicion, uniformed law enforcement served as a target of humor.

Cleo gave her a nod of approval and broke off a piece of the doughnut to sample. "Works for me."

Mara finished her half of the donut and laid a crumpled ten on the counter. It might have been a long time since she'd waited on tables, but she'd never lost the habit of tipping well. "Guess I'd better mosey on back, as they say in the westerns. Good meeting all of you. Cleo, tell TJ to holler if he needs help cleaning up. I've got a maintenance crew."

Cleo waved her off. Sucking in her stomach, holding her shoulders back, Mara navigated the sea of stares as she'd been taught—with a swagger and a sway. She'd been momentarily off balance, but habit restored her training.

Until she reached the sidewalk, alone and feeling as if she straddled two worlds. She needed to leave the reality of hometown America and return to the synthetic glitz she knew, where she had some modicum of power and control. With that decision, she strode briskly toward the B&B—and collided with the familiar solidity of TJ's broad chest as he emerged from the inn's garden gate.

"Damn," she muttered, digging her fingers into his black polo shirt and steadying her accelerated pulse. He hadn't been wearing that muscle-conforming shirt this morning or she'd never have let him out of the room. Tim's big hands clasping her waist to steady her didn't help. She'd had some weird idea that last night would have flushed this need for him out of her system.

"Going somewhere?" he asked in a tone laced with irony.

The tone should have warned her, but Mara glanced up anyway. It would be much simpler if she could rip out her silly sentimental core and act the part of the heartless mogul, but this was TJ. He'd held a piece of her heart for so long, she couldn't disguise it. "Cleo was worried. What happened?" she demanded. Realizing she was still clinging to his shirt, she pushed away and attempted to casually brush a fallen curl from her face.

He scowled and released her. "I'll call Cleo. I hope you're satisfied. You've got the kids around here believing I'm the only thing standing between them and Disneyland."

"Disneyland?" She honestly didn't know what he was talking about. Recognizing his impatient wave of dismissal for what it was, she smacked his hand—hard. "Don't patronize me, Timothy John! I'm all grown up now, and I can hear the truth. What the hell are you talking about?"

Mara propped her hands on her hips, and the action tugged the sleeveless knit top tight across her breasts.

TJ all but bit his tongue off. Knowing how those high, firm curves molded perfectly to his palms made his groin ache. If he thought about how she'd writhed beneath him, he'd be reduced to a whimpering idiot. Or, if pushed, to a Neanderthal who'd grab her hairpiece and drag her back to his lair.

"I've just been over at the sheriff's office. Vandals trashed my lab last night."

"I heard that. I can send my crew over to help clean up. Why are you mad at me?"

He was mad at the world, mad at himself, and mad for reasons he'd prefer not to define.

"You all but promised to turn this town into Cinderella's palace!" he shouted, letting temper rule. "Do you have any idea what it's like for kids who live here in the middle of nowhere, with no hope of seeing the world outside? To have someone come along and offer them every fantasy come true? They're desperate to believe it."

"I don't know what the hell you're talking about," she cried. "All I promised was a little landscaping. The beach is a wreck."

He shoved his hand through his hair and tried to get a grip. "You promised them a damned park! It only takes a small leap of imagination to conjure Myrtle Beach in the making."

She looked briefly bewildered, then shook her head. "They have paradise already. All I wanted to do was help the state preserve it. And where do you fit into the picture?"

Shit, TJ thought, she'd have him believing her in a minute. Before he could think of a suitable retort, the rotund mayor sallied across the street, a benign frown upon his cherubic features. "Dr. McCloud, we don't shout at ladies down here. Miss Simon, how do you do this lovely morning?"

TJ rolled his eyes heavenward as the mayor drooled over Mara and she simpered back. He'd had just about enough for one day.

Returning his gaze to Mara's fair cheeks, he noted the pink forming there. "Wear a hat," he ordered. "You'll burn your nose if you don't." He turned stiffly to the mayor, nodded farewell, and walked away. He didn't need this hassle.

He needed Patricia Amara Simonetti in his bed beneath him—or on top of him, or any way he could have her. Last night he'd thought that one time would be enough to get her out of his system . . . but he'd been wrong.

Swearing at that realization, TJ walked faster, almost mowing down Matty before stumbling to a halt. The boy joyfully threw himself at his knees, and TJ stooped to catch him, watching for the man who seldom let the boy out of his sight. He located Jared pushing off the brick wall of his office front.

"Cleo send out a posse?" TJ asked, shifting Matty to one arm. The kid trusted too readily, as if the whole world were a charmed place protected by family, but TJ knew Cleo's history and the fears hidden behind Matty's wide, bright eyes. He'd worried them. He wasn't used to people worrying over him.

"Cleo has a thing about cops." Jared verified TJ's thoughts. With a jerk of his thumb, he indicated the police tape. "What happened?"

One of Cleo's bad decisions had landed her in jail and separated her from her son. TJ should have known she'd panic. He just had a hard time remembering that his brother's idyllic world could be disturbed by something he considered annoying but not earth-shattering. He tickled Matty's tummy to keep the kid from thinking this was serious adult stuff.

"Some spoiled brat needed a new playpen," TJ answered casually. "I get a little ticked when people play with my things."

Matty nodded solemnly. "Alexa broke my crayons and I got mad."

The boy was speaking of his baby cousin, TJ knew, and he nodded sympathetically. "Yeah, we probably shouldn't get mad at babies because they don't know better, but it's hard." He handed Matty over to Jared, who still watched him with suspicion. "I gave the cops some suggestions," TJ continued, "but they're not real interested in chasing vandals."

Especially after he'd told them one of the vandals was overweight and gray-haired. They'd practically hooted him out of the office at the thought of fat old men running rampant through the streets like delinquent teenagers.

"Need some cleanup help?"

The husky feminine voice came from behind him. Cleo. Just what he needed, more overconcerned citizens. How had he lived his life before this? TJ waited to answer until Cleo stood beside Jared, arms crossed, waiting impatiently. "Thanks for the offer, but what I need most is an assistant. Unless you know someone experienced in forensic anthropology, there's nothing you can do to help. They tore up my address book, and it will take me a while to piece it together again."

"We can handle that." Blithely ripping the police tape from the doorway. Cleo thrust open his office door and entered. TJ heard her swear. He exchanged looks with Jared, and, shrugging, joined her in the destroyed front room.

"I can't believe anyone here would do this," Cleo exclaimed in an unusual display of anger.

TJ couldn't either, but the only other persons coming to mind ought to be in Washington, D.C., and the lone box he'd kept out of the storage unit had been dumped across the floor in the same disregard as the site material.

"Someone doesn't want you here, bro," Jared commented idly, poking an overturned chair with his toe.

Mara.

TJ didn't want to consider that. The Patsy he'd known all those years ago had been adamant about truth and justice. He wouldn't believe her guilty of this kind of senseless rampage.

But the world she moved in now didn't necessarily have the same values. He'd have to take a closer look at her production crew. Did any of them have gray hair?

TWELVE

"I've ordered sand-colored canvas, and the netting will hold sea oat plugs. With a few fake palmettos, the background will look just like the foreground," Mara argued, pointing at the sketch she'd made while balancing her cell phone on her shoulder, waiting for her set designer to take her off hold.

This past week of rehearsal had driven everyone to the edge of desperation. Tempers would be a real bitch after a month of roughing it like this, but she had no intention of letting TJ halt her film. They'd work around him until it came time to move in the heavy equipment. Glynis had a contract specifying a limo, dressing rooms, and catering. Mara figured she could hire a yacht and convince Glynis it was an upgrade.

"Impossible!" her director argued. "The camera tells all. We must have trees or leave it as rocks."

"Rocks aren't natural out here." Impatiently she threw down the sketchbook and grabbed up the cell phone when a real human finally spoke through it. "Lenny?" she shouted over the crashing of breakers on the beach. "Where is that canvas? We'll be filming in a few days, and I need it here now!"

Her director stalked off, fuming. Over the phone Lenny made excuses. On the set Glynis was throwing a tantrum because no one had thought to clear the beach of real live crabs. Ignoring the commotion on the set, two assistants and a photographer waited impatiently in line for their turn to bend her ear. Mara wondered what it would be like to become a hermit and live in a cave.

Shutting up Lenny with a curt order for an overnight package, she clicked off his call and took the script change from the first assistant. Maybe Sid had the right idea—stay in an air-conditioned office in Hollywood and give orders over the phone. Perspiration pooled between her breasts, and she hated the push-up harness constricting them. August in South Carolina was a mean bugger. Maybe she could stand in the surf and give orders.

Had she retained any of her earlier illusion that the movie industry was glamorous, today would have scrubbed the glitter right off. The actors had taken to screaming their lines at each other while the sound man tried to filter out the screech of gulls and crashing breakers. The surf was up due to a storm farther out at sea. She'd checked the weather station, and no hurricanes hovered on the horizon. Still, she'd have to find some way of reworking this scene from inside the ship. Then it could be done on the set back in L.A. Lesson learned—use beach sparingly, for action only, especially if they couldn't get the equipment trucks in here.

She still needed to get the boom in for night shots, and trucks were rumbling across the state right now carrying loads of make-believe pirate ship parts for the fight scene. If she couldn't have road access . . .

Her cell phone rang again. Scribbling her initials on the script change, she answered the phone and gestured for the next assistant. The ability to do three things at once provided a definite advantage in this business.

"Aunt Miriam?" Mara cringed at the familiar nasal whine on the other end of the line, and waved away the line of people waiting for her. Her aunt never called unless it was something dire, and usually something Mara couldn't do a thing about from this distance. Her relatives thought she could wave a magic wand and produce miracles—probably because she was the only one in the family who took action instead of complaining. Stupid of her. Maybe she should try whining back.

As her aunt outlined her mother's latest episode, Mara felt the familiar pall of helplessness creep over her. "What do you want me to do?" she exclaimed into the phone. "I can't be both there and here. I thought we'd hired nurses to watch her."

She rubbed her forehead and let her aunt ramble on. Intellectually she knew her aunt just needed an ear to bend, but emotionally she was reduced to a teenage child watching her frail mother break down into hysterical torrents of tears in the middle of the grocery store because her favorite peanut butter wasn't on the shelf. Every nerve in Mara's body quivered, tears formed in the corners of her eyes, and she thought she would shatter if someone so much as touched her.

She'd built a tough carapace to hide that quivering child, but seeing TJ again after all these years had cracked it. Stupidly, she wanted his calming strength here, holding her, while her aunt described her mother's latest psychotic episode.

The day after Brad's funeral, Mara's father had walked out, and her mother had plummeted from smiling saint to broken woman in a matter of months. She loved her mother, she truly did. She just didn't know how to deal with her bewildering breakdowns.

Or the terror that the same thing would happen to her.

"Okay, Aunt Miriam, I'll come up, I promise. Just as soon as we have a break in the schedule. Call the agency, tell them I'll pay more if that's what it takes to hire a more competent nurse."

Mara dug her fingers into her hair and scrunched her eyes closed as Miriam whined about the agency, the lack of good nurses, and her mother's manipulative ability to elude them. They both knew the alternative—an institution. Mara fought against placing her mother in such a cold, inhospitable environment, but her aunt's argument was valid—Mara wasn't the one who had to live with her.

"Could we talk about it when I get there?" she pleaded. "No, Aunt Miriam, don't send Irving! I'll get there when I can. There has to be something else we can do—"

Aunt Miriam obviously didn't agree. Sinking down on the sand, burying her face against her raised knees, Mara let her drone on. She couldn't cut her aunt off as if she were one of her employees.

A small hand patted her shoulder, startling Mara from her misery. Glancing up at the sympathetic face of Cleo's son, she hastily explained that she had to go, she'd call back later, and clicked the phone off. She couldn't have children on the set. The insurance liability would go through the sky.

"I got some Dr Pepper," the boy offered, handing her a sweaty bottle of pop.

He looked enormously worried, and Mara couldn't snap at him. Her entire cast and crew were busily doing their own things, ignoring her misery. Only this small boy had seen it and taken the time to offer his small token of aid. Tears formed all over again as she accepted the bottle and took a sip. She nearly gagged on the fizzy drink but managed a smile while wiping off her mouth with pretend satisfaction. She'd never been a great actress, but he was only a small boy.

"Thank you, sir," she said politely, searching her memory. "Matty, isn't it? You're a lifesaver."

"No, I'm not," he answered seriously. "But I've got some Lifesavers at home. Would you like some?"

This time her smile was genuine. "I might just take you up on that, sport. Where's your mama?"

"Working, but my dad's here. He's over there talking to that fat man." He pointed to the island of beach umbrellas that were serving as the refreshment area until they could bring in trailers.

The tall, dark-haired man wearing a garish Tommy Bahamas print shirt, with one hand in the pocket of his camp shorts and the other gesturing with a script as he talked to her screenwriter, could only be Jared. Even after seventeen years, she'd met no one who exuded happy-go-lucky charm like TJ's brother. All the McCloud brothers had personalities so distinctly different that she wondered how they came from the same parents, but there was no mistaking the similarity of their masculine looks.

"Well, let's go talk to your daddy." She was fairly certain she'd been told that Matty was Cleo's kid, and that Jared and Cleo had only recently met and married, but Matty used the term "dad" with such pride, it tickled her fancy.

Kids always tickled her fancy. They were the true innocents of the world, and she wanted to hug them all so she could bask in their freshness and originality. It angered her to see kids mistreated or neglected, but she'd come to uncomfortable terms with the fact that she'd never have kids of her own, and she couldn't adopt the world.

Matty looked neither mistreated nor neglected, but Jared needed a small reminder of his responsibility. "Lost a kid lately?" she asked with dry sarcasm, poking Jared in the back while gesturing at the chef in charge of concessions to indicate Matty was with her.

Jared looked up with that mischievous gleam she remembered entirely too well from the old days. It meant he'd been caught doing something he shouldn't and was looking for a way to charm someone out of fury.

"Matty, see that man in the white hat over there?" She crouched down to his height and pointed to the chef. "Tell him you want a super ice cream special with candy on top, and see what he has for you."

The boy's eyes lit with excitement, but he politely turned to Jared first. "Can I, please?"

"Sure thing, short stuff. Just don't tell your mama, or she'll blame me when you don't eat your lunch."

"I'll eat it, I promise!" Matty shot off toward the smiling chef.

Mara stood and realized she no longer towered over her teenage nemesis. Jared had gained a few inches since she'd last seen him. And a few muscles. "Some things don't change," she remarked, to remind him of his place.

Jared beamed broadly, looked her up and down in a manner terribly similar to his brother's, and didn't show an inch of shame for his behavior. Most screenwriters would be ingratiating to the owner of a movie studio. Mara knew better than to expect a McCloud to be anything other than assured of his value.

"Man, and some things change for the better!" He cocked his head and blatantly admired her nose. "Can't call you Olive Oyl anymore, can I?"

Mara appropriated his paper cup of soft drink and deliberately dumped the syrupy liquid over his thick hair. "I've always wanted to do that, McCloud. It's so nice to be in a position to do so now."

He shouted as ice slid down his neck and the soft drink soaked the collar of his expensive shirt. Laughter broke through Mara's misery. She'd suffered years of Jared's torment in grade school. She rather liked having the temerity to retaliate, especially with everyone around them tuned in on their encounter.

Doing a little dance to jiggle the cold cubes from his back before they slid down his shorts, he shot her an abashed grin and pulled his shirttails out. "Okay, score one for Olive Oyl. You still have a way to go before you can tie me."

"Why on earth hasn't Cleo killed you by now?" she asked with interest. Cleo seemed like a sensible person who wouldn't tolerate his nonsense.

"Because I'm sexy?" he suggested, hugging her waist and kissing her cheek.

She considered smacking him for old times' sake, until she saw Matty running up with his ice cream treat in hand, a worried expression twisting his gap-toothed smile. With the concern of a loving father, Jared had been reassuring his son with that hug. That didn't mean she had to let him manhandle her.

Pinching the sensitive skin beneath Jared's arm through

his shirt, Mara beamed at the boy and slipped away before Jared could do more than yelp. That ought to teach him she wasn't shy little Patsy any longer, and he couldn't intimidate her with his tactics.

"Is it good?" she asked Matty. "Want to get me and your daddy some more soda? You can put your dish there on the table. We won't let anyone take it."

"Not Dr Pepper," Jared yelled after the boy before turning to Mara and making a comical face. "I can't believe you stock that stuff."

"I can't believe I do, either." Taking a seat at the table with Matty's ice cream, she nibbled a chocolate candy from the top. "Blame it on the local supplier. It's a southern thing."

Accepting that as close to a truce as she'd offer, Jared took the seat across from her. "You look as if you need a break. Got any problems Uncle Jared can solve?"

Mara laughed out loud. The idea of bratty Jared McCloud doing anything other than causing trouble appealed to her. "Okay, I can see Cleo's problem. She couldn't get rid of you, right?"

Matty returned with a soft drink and the bottle of water Mara's concessionaire knew she preferred. Taking the drinks and placing them on the table, Jared lifted the boy onto his lap and beamed at her recognition of his peculiar talents. "That's about the sum of it. You ought to come over and spend some time with her. She has this brilliantly creative mind no one ever took the time to recognize. She's absolutely amazing. If you need to solve any kind of mechanical problem on the set, call on Cleo. She'd lend a hand just for the fun of it."

Jared's obvious pride in his wife awed and overwhelmed her. She'd had two husbands, and they'd done nothing but gripe and criticize from the get-go. She'd bent over backward trying to please them until ultimately one had broken her and the other had made her hopping mad enough to haul him into court. Why couldn't she find men who actually liked her? Or was she that unlikable?

She pretty much guessed the latter. Her many faults had been delineated in explicit detail by most of the people in her life. She'd learned to live with herself. "Thanks, I'll keep that in mind." She wouldn't, but it was nice of him to offer. Maybe Jared had grown up a little since she'd known him. "You adding comedy to my script while you're at it?" She nodded in the direction of the scriptwriter he'd been talking to.

"Nah, pirates and romance don't need comedy. Just catching up on old times. I might steal your writers away someday. You never know."

She recognized the impish grin and narrowed her eyes. "And you know what I'll cut off if you try, don't you?"

He whistled in appreciation. "Man, you and TJ would make a pair. Do you have any idea how many times he's threatened the same? What's with you people, anyway? Life's for enjoying. The two of you make it look like work."

"Said the grasshopper to the ant," she scoffed. "Some people have to earn a living. They weren't born with a silver comic in their mouths."

Jared shrugged off this reference to the comic strip that had provided him fame and fortune before he'd graduated from college. "Yeah, but you could find work that you like, and not a job that makes you grumpy. So, what was making you miserable back there? Anything any of us can do? Old friends ought to stick together."

"We were never friends, McCloud," she reminded him. She could see where Jared's thoughtfulness might win over some women, but charm didn't work with her. "You put a frog in my backpack the first day of freshman term, if I remember. The whole class rolled on the floor when it burped."

Matty looked at his stepfather wide-eyed, but his mouth was full of ice cream, and he couldn't talk. Jared grinned and rubbed his son's hair. "Let that be a lesson to you, Matt. Girls think frogs burp."

Mara giggled at Matty's look of awe and Jared's idiotic way of looking at things. Life was too senseless to hold grudges. "Your father burps and he's a frog," she told the kid. "So don't believe everything he tells you."

Jared regarded her with approval. "Come to dinner tomorrow night. Tinseltown can be tiresome after a while. You need a few real people occasionally."

She needed a shrink, a keeper, and a lover, probably in that order, but she didn't classify any of them as real people. She shrugged. "I've got to make some script and set changes before I can spare the time. Thanks, anyway."

"I'll tell TJ to pick you up at seven," he said as if she hadn't just told him no. "Bring the script, we'll brainstorm. I'll tell Cleo you're coming, so if you don't show, she'll probably sic her peacocks on you. I don't advise making Cleo mad."

Jared scooped up Matty and his ice cream dish and walked away before Mara could argue.

As maddening as ever, Jared McCloud should have been locked up for his own good years ago.

It had been nearly a week since she'd seen TJ. Talk about your one-night stand, without even a loving phone call promising more.

Did she really want more? They'd only end up arguing.

Maybe not. Pieces of her were ready to agree to anything he said just so they could get to the good part.

Maybe Cleo and Jared could referee. Or Cleo could lend her one of her squishable, splattable eggs to heave at both aggravating McClouds. As Jared had said, you found amusement wherever you could.

THIRTEEN

Dithering in front of her closet, still uncertain what to wear to dinner at Cleo's, Mara ignored the knocking at her door. She'd turned off her cell phone, let the inn answering service take the room phone, and threatened to behead Constantina if she suggested the rhinestone T-shirt one more time.

This wasn't a public appearance. She'd sent Constantina away half an hour ago but hadn't made a decision yet.

The pounding on the door became more demanding, intruding on her concentration. The Ralph Lauren chambray work shirt was too informal for a dinner, even one at Cleo's. The Versace silk was too revealing for a house with a little kid around. But TJ would be there and she wanted—

Dammit! she thought furiously as the door practically rattled from the force of the blows. "Go away, will ya? I'm busy," she shouted, reaching for a cotton shirt with a high collar in back, long sleeves, and tails that tied in front—a white dress shirt that revealed her navel.

"I can open it myself, but I thought I'd be polite," a gravelly voice answered with equanimity.

TJ! Just the sound of his voice made her shiver. Swearing beneath her breath, Mara jerked the shirt on over her padded Wonderbra, tied the shirttails, and opened the door. She refused to chase after an obstinate man, but she wouldn't turn one down if he knocked on her door—not when that man was TJ.

TJ stood stiffly on the other side, his taupe sport jacket now covering a ribbed charcoal knit shirt that accentuated his flat abdomen and would reveal every muscle if he moved. He wasn't obliging her yet, but from the look in his eye Mara figured it would only be a matter of moments before he burst into flames or motion. She would have copped a siren stance, but she hadn't fastened the buttons over her breasts, and she wasn't prepared for an instant replay of last week.

The sex had been so great, it had terrified her. From the sizzling look in his dark eyes, he hadn't entirely worked off all his steam.

From the response of her hormones, neither had she.

"I apologize," he said resolutely when she didn't invite him in. "If I promise to behave better, will you accept Cleo's invitation? She's actually cooking tonight."

Mara wasn't entirely certain which of his many insults he apologized for, but a man who knew how to grovel was a fascinating new experience. She tilted her head and studied the irritated tic in his jaw. "What's she cooking?" she demanded rudely, testing his limits.

TJ's eyes narrowed and his mouth thinned into a grim line, but he still stood there like an automaton. "Fried chicken and mashed potatoes."

Calorie city. She didn't think she'd eaten mashed potatoes since she'd left Brooklyn. She wasn't entirely certain she'd ever eaten fried chicken. "No tofu-and-broccoli casserole?" she asked in seeming disappointment. Yanking TJ's chain gave her more thrills than a roller-coaster ride, and she hid her smile as anger finally flared in his eyes.

"Are you coming or do I have to tell Cleo you're in bed with the mayor?" he retaliated, finally reverting to form.

Mara beamed in delight and opened the door sufficiently to let him in. "I'm just deciding what to wear. Is this shirt suitable for a dinner of fried chicken?" Under his scrutiny, she hastily fastened a few buttons.

TJ eyed her cleavage and took a deep breath. "Does it have any more buttons?"

Mara pushed another button through its hole and awaited his approval.

TJ tried to tear his gaze away from the tantalizing swells still revealed by her shirt, but he was back in her bedroom, where he'd done far more than stare, and his head wouldn't shift out of that particular gear.

He'd spent a week trying to forget she existed, to return to his usual routine, but he'd been lying to himself. Mara in all her flashy beauty and perverse provocativeness hadn't been out of his head for a second, but it was the Patsy behind the flash that gnawed at his heart and brought him here despite every incentive to stay away. He saw the vulnerability behind her need for approval and appreciated the courage it took for her to provoke him.

"Are the slacks okay or should I wear jeans?" she demanded, swiveling her hips to distract him from her cleavage.

Her stretchy slacks conformed to every curve of hip and thigh. TJ knew for a fact that she didn't pad an inch of those curves. He supposed some might consider her too thin, but he'd known her as a kid. This wasn't thin. This was heaven.

This was the woman he'd attacked as if starved. Even after a week of digging mounds of sand by day and reading notebooks of terminally boring transcripts at night, he couldn't get the appalling fact out of his head that he'd jumped her bones without a single thought to the consequences. He jerked his eyes back where they belonged—encountering the top of Patsy's artificial curls. "The slacks are fine. Are you ready to go?"

Her cat-eyed gaze made him nervous. He hadn't been nervous around a woman since high school. He was looking at a female who wore high heels and a hairpiece to the beach. Why should he care what she thought?

Because this was Patsy, and behind the deceptive glitter

lurked the brains of a computer and the tenacity of a pit bull. And a vulnerable woman who fell to pieces when he held her.

He had absolutely no clue how to deal with women who fell to pieces, or ones who concealed so many facets he could never discover them all in a lifetime of trying. He preferred coolly intellectual women who could discuss the latest theory of forensic science right after sex.

Liar. He loved a mystery, and Patsy Amara was every fascinating enigma he'd ever dreamed of.

If he wanted a mystery, he told himself harshly, he ought to stick with Colonel Martin's problem. He'd not found evidence of anyone's guilt in the transcripts he'd read through. He needed to go back to the storage unit and look for something more damning. Or revealing. Something had to pry this black cloud from his head.

"Shall I bring my shawl?" Mara asked dryly, hauling him back to solid ground again.

"Not the red one with feathers," TJ answered in what he hoped was a tone to match hers. He wanted to see those red feathers draped over her naked breasts.

Mara smiled in triumph and sauntered past him in her high heels, every move drawing his attention to breasts and hips until TJ thought he'd go up in smoke if he had to watch her all evening. Slamming the door behind him as they entered the hall, he focused on her bleached blond hair. "You don't need a hairpiece at Cleo's."

Glancing over her shoulder at him through overlong eyelashes, she retorted, "You don't need a sport jacket in this heat."

"It's proper informal dinner attire," he argued, taking his place at her side, grateful for something to distract him from the erotic scent of her perfume. He'd been taught etiquette with his ABC's. A woman in heels needed support. He offered his arm.

She glanced at his sleeve in surprise, smiled seductively, and reached for the stairway banister to show she didn't need his help. "Then so is my hair," she insisted. "I have an image to uphold."

"I trust that image will keep you from falling down the damned stairs." Okay, so etiquette fell by the wayside when it came to Patsy. He was back to behaving like a frustrated teenager. How did one look after a woman too stubborn—or too strong—to accept his aid?

"I'll have you know I took a year of modeling school to learn how to walk in these heels, and I could probably beat you to the car if I knew where it was." She teased him as she had as a child, her ridiculous claims challenging him to notice her.

He was mature enough not to accept challenges these days. Racing her in those heels guaranteed trouble. He diverted the argument. "Modeling school? I thought you got married out of high school."

They reached the front foyer and ignored the fascinated clerk at the desk as TJ appropriated her arm and Mara elbowed him. He grunted and dropped her arm but held the door open. She patted his cheek and sailed by as if he were a doorman.

He wanted to wring her neck, but that body part was too close to softer places he'd much rather get his hands on. Besides, he knew she was simply getting even with him for his neglect. He caught her arm going down the porch stairs and refused to release it. "Well?" he demanded. "Did you go to modeling school instead of college?"

"I went to modeling school when a buyer for Irving's store said we could sell more clothes if I looked more glamorous."

The ugly, jealous monster inside him didn't want to hear about Irving or any of the other men in her life, but his conscience needed to know how she'd gotten to where she was now. It was as if he'd betrayed Brad's trust by letting Patsy fall into bad hands. He'd wanted her to be happy.

"That's a crock," he countered, guiding her down the

porch stairs and in the direction of his car. "You were model thin at sixteen, and tall enough to wear anything. What was this clown Irving selling, granny dresses?"

"Lingerie," she answered dryly, "and Irving was my husband. He thought he'd upscale his father's candy-panties business and rival Victoria's Secret, but I was the only sales clerk he could afford."

"Candy panties?" As soon as the question was out of his mouth, TJ knew he shouldn't have asked.

She sent him a flirtatious smile. "Want to try some? I bet I could find a pair or two."

TJ thought he ought to shut up and forget he'd heard any of this, but curiosity had usurped his usual reserve. "Your husband let you model underwear, in *public*?"

She shrugged and waited for him to unlock his car door. "This was Brooklyn, remember. Once our neighbors saw our inventory turning a skinny nerd like me into a glamorous model, they bought anything I recommended."

TJ waited until he'd slid into the driver's seat and his anger had cooled a bit before replying. "He *used* you to sell scanty underwear?"

"It's no big deal," she said dismissively, watching out the passenger-side window as they drove into the late summer twilight. "I kept the books and knew that with the way the rent was rising, it would be only a matter of time before we were out on the street if we didn't do something. We tried hiring a good-looking kid with a figure, but she was dumb as stones and didn't understand why we wanted her to *wear* a bra instead of taking it off. So I started taking modeling classes. Then I broke my nose, and one thing led to another. . . ."

Her voice trailed off, and TJ was hit hard by the memory of teenage Patsy doing that same thing when she didn't want to tell him something. Sometimes her chattering got ahead of her thinking and she said entirely too much.

"*How* did you break your nose?" he demanded in what he thought to be a perfectly reasonable voice.

"None of your damned business," she shot back, turning to glare at him. "It's way too late to waste energy looking after me now."

He didn't want to know what that meant, but he did. He and Brad had always looked after her, hauling her out of street brawls, helping her with science projects, dragging guys over to dance with her when she showed up on prom night—alone. Who had looked after her after Brad died? No one, apparently. What the hell had happened?

"At least tell me you broke the other guy's nose or tore off his balls to justify it."

She uttered a noise that could have been a giggle or a sob or both. "Kicked him in the balls, anyway. I caught Irving doing more than ogling the clerk's braless wonders. I should have known better than to attack a man with his pants down. He reacted before he thought."

"*Irving* broke your nose?" TJ wanted to grab the bastard by the ear and smack him against a brick wall, face first. "Your *husband* broke your nose? What in hell is wrong with your family? *Irving* was the most eligible bachelor in Brooklyn?"

"Like I said, he reacted before he thought, or he'd have known it would cost him. I got a bloody nose and a good cosmetic surgeon out of the incident." She crossed her long legs and rubbed her sandaled toe down his trousers. "You and Brad taught me how to take care of myself, and maybe I'm a wee bit psycho, but I'm not dumb."

Years of observing war atrocities had petrified TJ's weaker emotions, but he wanted to weep at this tale. Patsy Simonetti had been shy around strangers, brilliant around friends, creative in her troublemaking, and loyal to a fault, not to mention a royal pest when she put her mind to it. But she'd never been dumb.

She'd been the girl he'd loved with all his teenage heart, and she'd married a stinking, rotten bastard of an underwear salesman. He could imagine the smarmy, balding twinkie mauling Patsy's teenage breasts, and he wanted to upchuck.

Shy Patsy punched his biceps—hard.

"Whatever you're thinking, don't," she ordered. "Irving was a hunk with unmortgaged assets and an entrepreneurial mind. I didn't complain about being married to him while it lasted. The nose job he paid for got me the modeling job that took me out of Brooklyn, provided me with enough money to take care of my mother, and has given me great satisfaction over the years. I'm a winner, and if you start calling me anything else, I'll beat you into a pulp. Might I mention that I have a black belt in karate?"

Okay, deep breath, rearrange priorities. "You're a winner," he agreed with honesty. "And a survivor. I'm just having a hard time dealing with your parents' roles in all this. They worshiped at Brad's feet, worked two jobs to pay for his education, sent the two of you to private school so you'd have the best teachers and facilities . . . I just don't get it."

"No one says you have to," she said with a sigh shadowed in sadness. "It just is, okay? Brad's death took something out of them. I was never more than a carbuncle on his ass, anyway. I was informed daily that girls get married and have kids and don't need jobs, so Brad was their future. Since I thought I was too ugly for a boy to ever marry, I was kind of confused by it all for a while. But after Brad's death, my life went on, and theirs didn't. It happens, all right? You once promised me a red teddy bear and didn't come through. I didn't die of disappointment."

"I bought the damned bear." TJ could have bitten off his tongue after he said it. He could almost hear her lift her eyebrows, and he finished grudgingly, "You moved."

"My father walked out on us. My mother didn't have a job, so we moved in with her family."

"I tried calling you." Okay, so this was ancient history, but he'd been torn into shreds with the loss of both his best friend and the girl he'd adored. He hoped she didn't hear the question and the pain he'd buried long ago.

TJ breathed a sigh of relief when she merely eyed him consideringly.

"My mother wasn't precisely rational at the time. I didn't know you called. I tried calling you once, but you weren't there. Then we moved and my aunt wouldn't let me make long-distance calls. With everything happening, I just figured you'd lost interest."

He heard what she didn't say—everyone else had lost interest in her, so she figured he had, too. TJ couldn't get his head around a lack of self-assurance that large, but he should have known. Teenage boys didn't think with their heads, though. He'd been too bent out of shape to discover she'd moved without a trace. "I thought you blamed me. I should have known better." One more guilt to add to his burden. He should have been there for her instead of licking his own wounds.

"We were too young. I needed to learn not to rely on people or promises. You would have used me as a doormat, just like Irving." She diverted the topic to a safer one. "Tell me about the vandals. Were you able to put your office together again? Your work is much more interesting than my life."

Not to him, not right now. TJ wanted to know more about the beautiful tigress she'd become and how she'd gotten that way. She was more fascinating than any set of bones he'd ever unearthed or any mystery he'd ever explored.

He didn't regret how he'd spent these last seventeen years, but he sure wished he'd made an effort to keep an enigma like Patsy in it.

"Earth to TJ. Come in, pal. No tripping allowed on my watch." Mara flipped the overhead light on, leaned against the car door, and crossed her arms beneath her breasts to grab his attention.

"You do that on purpose, don't you?" TJ asked, understanding her actions a little better. "You don't need to wave your mammary glands in my face to keep me interested."

She snorted but sat upright again. "Made you look," she said provokingly.

"I looked when you were sixteen and didn't have any breasts to speak of," he retorted, remembering that episode of his life with clarity. "You were the only girl around who didn't rub her breasts in my face or giggle when I walked by. You were straight with me. Wanna go back in time and try that again?"

She thought about it, then shook her curls. "Nope. You had all the power then. You were the one who got to call the shots. It's my turn now, and I like having that power. Get used to it."

"Did Irving have time to appreciate the monster he created before you crucified him?" he asked in warped fascination with the woman she'd become.

"Nope, but Sid did. Stupid man thought he'd married a pussycat. Why in the world would any sane man want to marry a bubblehead? Explain that to me."

"Because bubbles only show them their reflection?" He didn't know where that came from, but he'd seen it often enough. Jared had dated women like that for years, but he'd never been serious about any of them. There was a difference between casual dating and committing for a lifetime.

She chuckled. "Sid's so ugly, I can't imagine why he'd want to see his reflection, but I see what you mean. Irving married me for my brains, Sid married me for my looks, and I married both of them for security, so we all lost. I learned my lesson. I provide my own security these days. What about you? Where are you going with this bone-digging stuff?"

"Probably nowhere," TJ admitted, "but that's not your problem. We're almost at Cleo's. She doesn't entertain often, so this is a big deal for her. I'll try not to yell at you if you'll try not to insult me, okay?"

"I like Cleo, and if she'll provide me with a supply of

those squishy eggs, I'll be quite content egging you and Jared all evening. I shall be the model guest. Are you going to tell me after we leave why the bones aren't going anywhere?" she asked with interest.

"Probably not." He braked the car in Cleo's drive and turned off the ignition. The sun hadn't quite set, and TJ could see Mara's delicate chin stuck out in a stubborn pose he knew too well. "If you're still willing to help, I'm ready to start researching the island. I have a secretary starting next week, but she won't be any good at research."

The diversion worked as well as he'd hoped. She lit up like a light bulb—the Christmas-tree kind in sparkly colors. Patsy would never be so ordinary as to radiate plain white light.

"I *adore* research." She sighed with satisfaction. "I drove the scriptwriter insane by forcing him to stick to the facts I dug out, but details positively *make* the film. I'll check when the library opens tomorrow."

"Thank you." And he meant it. He also knew the diversionary tactic would last only long enough to get him through the evening. The Patsy he knew never let a subject of interest escape her for long. Before she gave up, she would dissect his evasion into tiny pieces.

How long before she dissected him? And could they do it in bed—without killing each other first?

FOURTEEN

Approaching the McClouds' front porch, Mara admired the twinkle of a swinging mechanical Tinkerbell—until Jared stepped out, looking grimmer than TJ at his worst. Her stomach plummeted to a place between her toes.

TJ stiffened but calmly guided her down the shell path to the house. She didn't bother arguing with his proprietary support this time. She'd had enough bad news thrown her way to know when it was time to dodge and when it was time to run like hell. TJ apparently was of the old school of taking it like a man.

Jared slipped him a folded packet of papers as they stepped up on the porch. "Sheriff was by earlier looking for you at the dig. Needless to say, Cleo wouldn't have been happy to see him. I made the intercept. Sorry."

Mara had been in Hollywood long enough to know legal papers when she saw them. Sid kept a whole raft of lawyers on retainer to field just this sort of thing.

Pulling out his reading glasses, TJ glanced at the first few paragraphs, swore, and shoved both glasses and documents into his inside coat pocket. Without another word, he swung on his heel and started for the stairs.

The strong, silent act might work in some circles, but not in hers. Mara grabbed his arm as he passed and jerked hard enough to stop him. "Where do you think you're going?"

"To call a lawyer," he spat out, glaring at her as if she

were a cockroach he meant to crush. "You're not getting away with this."

A tiny tendril of panic threaded its way into her system. "Get away with what?"

"As if you didn't know." TJ tugged his arm free and would have pressed forward, but Jared's voice halted him.

"Cleo's been working all day on this dinner. She has the name of a legal shark, but I'd suggest you stay and eat before you ask for it."

Mara could see TJ obviously wavering, torn between family loyalty and the lethal fury boiling inside him. She swallowed hard, hating to lose the bridges they'd started to rebuild this evening. Bracing her backbone with the knowledge that she was innocent for a change, she steered him in the right direction. "I don't know what you think I did, but can it for a few hours. Only ambulance chasers answer phones at this time of night." She was rattled by those papers, but she knew how to put on a show. He could learn to do the same.

TJ ripped the papers from his pocket and waved them in her face. "Look at these and tell me you don't know what you did."

She snatched the document and tried to read it in the bad light but couldn't. Laser surgery had corrected the worst of her vision problems, but she still needed reading glasses. She never wore them in public, didn't even carry them with her. "It's too dark," she said boldly. "Let's go in." She started for the door that Jared was blocking.

TJ tore the papers from her grip and returned them to his pocket. "It says I have to cease and desist blocking the access road. Now tell me again that you don't know what this is about."

Jared whistled. "Cleo's not going to like that. She likes our privacy, and they'll have reporters crawling all over this story."

Sid. Mara recognized her ex's grimy pawprints all over it. And Ian, no doubt. She'd have to fire her producer—once she owned the company. Dammit.

You could start filming the night scenes now, a wayward voice in the back of her head crowed. They could bring in the sound equipment, and concession trucks so the crew wouldn't quit en masse. And haul in dressing rooms so Glynis wouldn't call her agent and complain for the umpteenth time this week.

At the cost of losing the friendship of the McClouds. And TJ. Double damn. She'd dearly like to know how it felt to have real friends. Was that asking so much? Maybe asking to have TJ in her bed again was pushing her luck, but she couldn't let Sid hurt people who had done nothing to him.

She had an opportunity to start a fresh life, her own life, and already she was flubbing it because she wasn't greedy enough to choose her career over friendship. Some tycoon she was.

"Are the lot of you going to stand out there gossiping, or do you prefer your potatoes cold?" Wearing a dark green miniskirt and matching tank top, Cleo appeared in the screen door like an inquisitive leprechaun.

Mara had the feeling that Cleo had even more issues than she did, and that her hostess was capable of slamming the door in their faces and telling them all to go to hell if they carried their argument inside. Maybe the way Jared opened the door and chucked his wife under the chin with a reassuring smile gave her the impression of her hostess's vulnerability. Maybe she just liked believing there was one man in the world who loved his wife enough to protect her from harm, and she simply imagined Cleo's insecurities.

Either way, she didn't want this misunderstanding to interfere in the first evening she'd had off in what seemed like decades. She wanted to be herself for a little while, if she could just remember who that self was.

"TJ says I can't throw eggs at him," she told Cleo with her best actress pout. "Is he always such a spoilsport?"

Jared grinned approval and shot his brother a warning glare. "You have to ask? Big brother created the law, and we all bow before it. C'mon—I'll see if I can slip you an egg or two before the evening's over."

Eyeing them warily, Cleo didn't appear fooled, but she pushed the door open. "It's always more fun if he doesn't know when it's going to hit him."

"He plays brooding gloom so well, too," Mara chirped happily, grabbing TJ's arm and tugging him toward the door. "If I ever do a remake of *Jane Eyre*, will you try out for the part of Rochester?" She flapped her fake lashes at him.

"Only if the self-righteous Jane gets murdered in the end," he said dryly, hauling her into the house.

The evening worked its way from hostile to surreal in a matter of minutes. Jared and Cleo evidently thought nothing of entertaining in the kitchen, and the neighbor's children apparently treated the McClouds' kitchen as home. Mara knew how to handle the teenage boy's awe, but doing it with TJ glowering at her was awkward. Matty's excited chatter and Jared's humor eased the conversation, but the girl called Kismet strained it with her shyness.

Cleo managed the whole milieu without any sign of noticing her guests' difficulties. Mara admired the way she nudged Gene when he grabbed for the chicken without asking, reminding him without words to use his manners. She'd not spent much time with kids, but she could remember her father's scolding. She liked Cleo's method better.

TJ didn't look at her as he complimented Cleo on the chicken. She couldn't believe the bastard thought she was capable of Sid's kind of treachery. What in hell made him think she cared so little? Hadn't they just discussed the result of their earlier lack of communication?

She wouldn't be ignored or forgotten this time.

"Rubber eggs should have rubber chickens," Mara murmured thoughtfully, fingering the toy Cleo had sneaked into her hand.

TJ lowered his V-shaped scar into a scowl but didn't otherwise acknowledge her seemingly senseless remark.

"The Three Stooges had a rubber chicken," Gene suggested eagerly. "They're funny."

"Spoken like a true man," Cleo acknowledged with a knowing grin.

Ignoring the byplay, Mara grasped her weapon.

TJ reached for the bowl of mashed potatoes.

Splat.

Fluffy white spots riddled TJ's forehead and jacket sleeve. One particularly fine glob slithered into his crooked eyebrow. It was his own fault for not believing her.

Mara recognized the dangerous gleam in his eye as he set the bowl down. When she'd been very young, she'd run from that look. In later years, she'd learned how to work it to suit her purposes. TJ had been her very first male role model, and all the other men in her life had failed to live up to his standards. Had she fantasized the man she remembered?

"Oops." She smiled coyly.

All conversation stopped as TJ swirled the egg in the potato bowl with deadly calm. Mara propped her elbow on the table and set her chin in her palm while she admired his intimidating maneuver. "Uncool, McCloud. Gentlemen don't strike ladies. Whatever would your mama say?"

"That you're not a lady?" he suggested, fishing the potato-covered egg from the bowl.

"That people don't play with their food?" came from the surprising quarter of Kismet, whose brown eyes had widened with both interest and trepidation.

"Tim, if you throw that thing, I'll dump the bowl over your head," Cleo intruded firmly. "How am I supposed to teach the kids manners?"

Mara stuck her tongue out at TJ's black glare. "I dare you," she goaded him.

Splat.

Mara's golden hairpiece caught the blow, tilting precariously over one ear while a gob of mashed potato slowly rolled down her forehead.

"She started it," TJ said in a childish falsetto.

The table erupted in roars of laughter. Even Cleo was wiping her eyes and laughing too hard to carry out her threat as Mara carefully plucked the comb of the hairpiece from her matted curls.

Gravely she laid the once-lovely curls across the remains of TJ's fried chicken and string beans. "You win."

She turned to the wide-eyed, giggling children. "Let this be a lesson to you. Uncle Tim doesn't get mad, he gets even."

"Maybe Baby Patsy ought to heed her own advice," TJ responded, a warning hidden behind his gibe.

Wiping her forehead with her napkin and running her fingers through her natural curls to check for damage, Mara savored the triumph of jarring a reaction from his cold demeanor. She didn't know why she needed evidence that the Tim she knew still existed, but even with egg all over her face—or potato, to be perfectly correct—satisfaction licked deep inside her. "I'm not Sugar Dave. I don't back down."

Jared chuckled at her reference. When all eyes turned to him for explanation, Jared shrugged. "Dave was on the basketball team of our high school's biggest rival. He was the only guard large enough to block TJ on the court. He made the very bad mistake of calling our cheerleaders a rude name."

"Okay, I'll bite." Cleo handed Mara a clean washrag. "What did our favorite Scorpio do?" She tugged the back of TJ's jacket until he stood up and took it off so she could clean the potatoes off of it.

TJ calmly dumped Mara's two-hundred-dollar hairpiece into the trash and found a clean plate, obviously pretending the tale had nothing to do with him.

"Nothing the referees could call him on," Mara answered, playing to her eager audience. "But oddly enough,

Sugar ended up in the strangest places on the court that night—in the stands, on top of his coach, rear-ending his own team, falling over the floor announcer—until his coach finally pulled him from the game for clumsiness."

Jared snorted. "Our side howled because they knew it was Tim, the Intimidator. All he had to do was get in someone's face and snarl, and they fell all over their feet backing off. Sugar didn't have a chance."

"Wow!" Gene looked at TJ in awe as he returned to the table. "You played basketball?"

Mara chuckled. If that was all the boy got out of the story, fine. Maybe it was better that he didn't realize the dangerous depths of the outwardly bookish man he saw. Kids saw so much television, they willingly accepted real-life acts of courage or villainy as ordinary. They didn't understand the motivation or character that would drive their heroes to behave like steamrollers.

She did. She'd seen through TJ's outward composure from the first day they'd met.

Ignoring TJ as he spoke to Gene about high school sports, Mara turned her attention to Kismet, who was eyeing her hair speculatively. "Is it a total mess?"

Kismet shook her wild tawny mane. "No, ma'am. Your hair is beautiful even with potatoes in it."

Mara dabbed at it with her napkin, searching for traces of potato. Leave it to TJ to hit her in her vanity. "Thank you. I used to hate it. It's naturally curly and mousy and horrid. A good hairdresser is a miracle worker."

The girl bit her bottom lip and stared at her plate.

Uh-oh. Realizing no one else had caught the exchange, Mara worried over the appropriate response. If the kid had been an adult, she could have exchanged notes about hairdressers, but she had a feeling that teenagers demanded a little more sincerity.

It horrified her to realize she didn't know how to do that anymore.

All right, dig deeper. Mara tried to remember her own

teenage years. "Do you have someone to teach you how to fix your hair?" Start simple, she decided.

The girl glanced up with a flash of hope and shook her head. Then, embarrassed, she looked back at her plate. "Mama braids it."

"My mother pulled mine back in a ponytail. I looked like a total dork." Mara smiled gratefully at the steaming cup of espresso Cleo set before her. She could tell Cleo had caught on to the conversation by now but wisely stayed out of it. "I was too busy to figure out how to fix it on my own. You get out of your hair the amount of work you're willing to put into it."

"You could never look like a dork," Kismet whispered in awe.

"Don't let TJ or Jared hear that," Mara whispered back. "I'll show you my high school yearbook sometime if you want real yucks. How much time do you want to spend messing with your hair?"

Kismet gave that some thought, then shook her head. "Not much," she admitted. "I'll never be pretty. I just want to look . . . normal."

"Ah," Mara said in satisfaction, finding an edge she understood. "There's the hook. There is no normal. You're supposed to look like you, whoever you are inside. If you're a wild woman on the inside, then that's how you should look. If you're a meek little bunny rabbit, then cute is probably how you want to look. I'm five-ten and figured I was bigger and better than everyone else, and that's how I wanted to look, not like a dork or a mouse. So, who do you think you really are inside?"

Kismet frowned in concentration, apparently aware that identifying herself could be important. "I'm . . . different." She eyed Mara carefully. "Begging your pardon, but I don't want to be like you. I don't feel bigger and better, just *different*."

Cleo lifted Matty up and set him in her lap so she could sit next to Kismet and look across the table at

Mara. "Kismet is an artist. She sees things around her that no one else does, and draws them brilliantly."

Mara nodded in understanding. "Excellent. Then you should enhance your differences. You have spectacular cheekbones and great eyes. Flaunt them. Pull your hair back off your face as tight as you can—force the world to look at you and recognize you for who you are. Then let the natural exuberance of your hair spring out behind you. That's a great look for kids your age. Later, when you have more experience and confidence in yourself, you can go sophisticated, tie it into a knot, and decorate it. It's all about who you are right now. People change."

Kismet's eyes widened as she touched her cheekbones, but she only smiled shyly and nodded, not begging for more compliments as another might. Mara's heart wept, seeing the damage behind that gesture, and she glanced to Cleo for verification.

Cleo nodded, but in her typical nonverbal fashion, she acknowledged the advice by brushing Kismet's hair back from her high forehead and holding it so Mara could see how it would look.

"Yes, that's it exactly. I'll send over some of my elastic headbands. They should work." With a sigh of relief that she'd solved Kismet's problem, Mara glanced up at the sound of silence around her.

Jared merely watched her with interest. TJ scowled and sipped his coffee as if she were the shallowest specimen of worm in existence.

"You have potato on your nose," she said sweetly, then hit him with the egg she'd held in reserve.

If he was taking her down, she'd go in flames.

FIFTEEN

The legal papers crackled in TJ's pocket as he helped Mara into the car. It was nearly midnight. She and Cleo had found so many things to talk about that he hadn't been able to pry them apart until now. He couldn't believe a woman as perceptive as Cleo could actually like the lying, conniving piece of work that Patsy had become.

Or maybe he could. She was good, he'd grant her that. He couldn't believe she remembered that old incident from his basketball days, and spoke about it as if he were some frigging hero instead of the spoiled thug he'd been. Then she'd turned the charm on the kids, and she'd almost had him believing that she cared about Kismet's problems or that she'd even remember to send the hair gear she'd promised the girl. He supposed he'd have to go out and hunt down whatever in hell an elastic headband was so Kismet wouldn't think she'd been forgotten for the millionth time in her neglected life.

"You'll never get the grease stains out of your jacket. I'm sorry." Mara examined his sleeve in the overhead light when he opened the car door. "I didn't realize mashed potatoes were made with butter."

"Butter is better than blood," he said curtly before slamming her door and going around to the driver's side. She was at it again, making him believe she was something she wasn't, making him believe she could be the person he desperately needed her to be.

She crossed her arms and glared out the window as he

took his seat and snapped the buckle. That was fine with him. Now he wouldn't have to live with the illusion of the Patsy who understood when life got too complicated, listened when he wanted to talk, and didn't condemn him when he'd been a fool. He shifted the car into gear and backed out.

"I am *not* responsible for that cease-and-desist order," she said firmly. "I was handling the access road perfectly well on my own."

"Yeah, right." He hit the sandy lane at a speed higher than the tires could manage, and slowed down. She'd probably thought seducing him was "handling" the matter. He gritted his teeth. He should have known better than to think he could connect in any meaningful way with a blond bombshell, even if she had once been Patsy Simonetti.

"Screw you," she spat at him. Holding her head high, she didn't look at him the rest of the way back to the inn.

Just as well, he thought. He could get back to doing his own research. He'd retrieved another box of documents to read. The first box had made a good case for believing someone had allowed accused killers and rapists to go free, but just because the colonel was in charge of the unit assigned to Kosovo didn't mean he'd done it.

Not wishing to contemplate Martin right now, TJ stopped the car in front of the B&B.

Mara slammed out before he could turn off the ignition. He was tempted to just let her go, but he'd been brainwashed by good manners at an early age. Cutting off the engine, he climbed out and loped after her into the lobby.

Inside, Mara stood frozen before a distinguished man with a thick head of dark hair turning gray at the temples. Tall, slightly stoop-shouldered, wearing a black sport coat over a black T-shirt, the man had just started to speak when TJ barged in.

With her back turned toward the door, Mara didn't

even notice his entrance. "Irving!" she cried in disbelief. "I told Aunt Miriam not to send you!"

TJ barely heard anything beyond "Irving." He'd been looking for a fight all evening, and the bastard who'd broken Patsy's nose would do far better than any other opponent he could name. His rage finding a target, TJ grasped Mara's slender shoulders, set her aside, rolled up his fist, and plowed it into Irving's prominent proboscis.

The crunch that followed satisfied TJ far more than the spurt of blood.

Mara shrieked. The inn clerk reached for the telephone. And Irving crumpled to his knees with a howl of pain.

The fight was over before TJ had even begun.

Mara clapped a hand over her mouth and, wide-eyed, turned to stare at TJ. He shoved his bruised fist into his pocket, prepared to apologize, when he recognized the dancing light behind those cat-green eyes. She was laughing. And the admiration he remembered from their youth lit her from within.

Something impossibly light invaded his heart, and he couldn't prevent the slow smile relaxing his jaw. No other woman had looked at him as if he were her hero, as Mara did. He knew he wasn't any such thing. He knew he'd behaved like a testosterone-driven jerk. That didn't prevent his primitive response to her appreciative expression.

"Might as well go to jail for something I enjoyed doing," he muttered.

"I'll bail you out," she murmured, "and give you a halo. Want to be my bodyguard?"

TJ bit back a chuckle. Bashing a wimp wasn't anything to laugh about. He just hadn't realized Irving was a wimp until too late. "*Guarding* your body wouldn't be enough," he admitted. As long as he was throwing out all restraint, he might as well go all the way. "You'd best tend to your ex. You can tell the sheriff he'll find me at the dig, disobeying the cease-and-desist order."

"Wait, TJ—" She held out her hand to him.

Too wired to listen or even to think, he strode away before he did anything even more incredibly stupid, like haul Mara up the stairs and back to the room where she'd shown him heaven. Repeating that night was a fantasy he couldn't afford. It was easier to write the last time off as a result of the alcohol than to believe it could ever happen again.

Not that the sex wouldn't be great again, but his suspicious mind corrupted anything it came in contact with. If he could still suspect that she used sex as a ploy to wheedle him out of the dig, he didn't deserve to believe they could have a relationship. And with Patsy, he couldn't settle for anything less.

TJ left the car at the B&B and walked to let off steam. He'd never been driven by hormones. Well, almost never. He couldn't believe he'd made such a Neanderthal of himself. Jared would laugh his head off when he heard.

Still, TJ smiled grimly at the memory of crunching cartilage. Now Irving could buy his own nose job.

She'd married a damned movie star! He'd been picturing some weasely nerd with slimy hands and slavering fat lips who was so weak-kneed that he had to hit women. Why in hell hadn't he known better? Patricia Amara Simonetti wasn't the kind of woman who walked into something like marriage without a good head on her shoulders, no matter how young she'd been.

She'd probably thought she loved the bastard. A shy kid like Patsy would have been desperate for love and attention anywhere she could find it.

He kicked a clamshell, and it ricocheted off the Blue Monkey's plate-glass window. The noise and laughter from inside didn't cease. Maybe he ought to go in and have a few beers before the sheriff came looking for him.

Mara was probably hauling poor, broken Irving up to her room right now, making soothing noises and calling for cold compresses or whatever it was women did when their men were hurt. Not that he had any experience to draw on. Women who talked about cadavers in bed weren't inclined to be overly sympathetic in other areas.

Stepping into the smoke and noise of the bar, TJ found a seat beside Ed. There was always a seat beside Ed. On both sides. His submarine obsession was notorious.

TJ ordered a beer and listened with half an ear to Ed expounding upon his theories. The old guy had obviously done his research on U-boat activity on the East Coast, not that the subject mattered in the age of satellites. Given current events, TJ could understand the fascination with terrorists, but even the most fanatical wouldn't blow up a nearly deserted island. Pity Ed hadn't applied his time and effort to something more productive, like having a life.

TJ winced. Nothing like the pot calling the kettle black.

"Dr. McCloud?" A suave young man in *GQ* casual tapped TJ on the shoulder. In pressed slacks and designer camp shirt, he looked like a swan in a duck pond in this bar filled with drunken seamen in crumpled shorts and T-shirts.

TJ dismissed him with a glance and returned to his beer. He was waiting for the sheriff, not one of Mara's Hollywood leeches.

"I'm Paul Harris from *People* magazine. Is it true that you and Mara Simon are an item?"

TJ's insides froze at the mention of the magazine, but he didn't let that hold him back. "Afghanistan has been bombed into a hole in the ground," he said to his beer bottle. "Israel is on the brink of exploding. The population of much of the Third World is starving. And you write for a magazine that reveres shallow punks who do drugs because they're bored. Ask me another."

Beside him, Ed cackled with glee. One of Ed's cronies leaned closer to catch the joke.

"When was the last time you read the magazine?" the reporter asked dryly.

"The last time you did a story on my kid brother. Cute story. Missed the whole point." TJ drained his bottle and wondered if he ought to walk out now or drink himself into a stupor.

"The locals claim you and Miss Simon are an item, but my sources claim you're at loggerheads over the film location. Would you care to comment?"

"Loggerheads," TJ mused. "Interesting choice of word. Did you know a loggerhead is a subtropical carnivorous turtle? Which one of us do you think they mean is carnivorous?"

Ed and a few more members of his pack roared and smacked the bar in appreciation of his wit. Nothing beat an audience who had been drinking since sundown.

"Hey, TJ," one of the pack shouted, "you found any more of them pirate bones?"

"They're not pirates," Ed shouted back. "He done tole you that. It's Germans, dollars to doughnuts."

With a sigh, TJ stood up and placed his money on the bar. He'd sat through plenty of the barroom brawls that ensued when hostilities arose this late in a crowd of drunks, but the topic of this argument would only incite the reporter's imagination. Time to depart.

"I read the newspapers, McCloud," the reporter called after him. "I looked your name up in our files. Your work in the Balkans gave you an international reputation. You might prefer talking to me instead of the rabble that will be down here once I send in this story."

Yeah, right, like telling *People* magazine he and Mara were an item would happen any time in his universe. TJ stalked out into the humid August night and kept on walking as the noise in the bar escalated.

He might as well be a carrier of a violence virus, trailing havoc in his wake. Maybe he belonged in war zones, where violence was normal. Maybe he'd lived in war zones so long, he accepted violence as a normal way of life. Who the hell knew?

He just knew he was tired of it.

That was a realization it had taken a long time to reach. Shoving his hands into his pockets, TJ wandered the empty streets to the inn parking lot. He was tired of war. He was tired of living alone. He was tired of drifting homeless.

Damned good thing, he thought cynically, because he could be going to jail along with the colonel unless those boxes proved Martin's innocence. So far, they hadn't. If anything, they made it a virtual certainty that some of the criminals he'd fingered had never come to trial. Since TJ had worked with Martin, he could be accused of covering up the crimes as well, not to mention protecting Martin while he was at it. Concealing evidence was a crime in most states, but if he turned the boxes over to the authorities, he might be writing his own warrant. Damned if he did, damned if he didn't. So much for truth and justice.

The *People* reporter knew he'd worked with Martin. All hell could break loose soon.

Might as well begin saving what he could from the dig. Between the restraining order and nosy reporters, he wouldn't work on the site much longer anyway. He'd really wanted to solve the mystery of the bones, too. *Shit.*

He glanced up at the inn as he climbed into the Taurus, but the place wasn't swarming with police or ambulances. Instinct told him to find Mara, to be certain she was all right, but his people instincts were lousy. More likely he wanted to console himself. Mara had already proved she was strong and didn't need him.

Drained and empty, he drove back to the island, filling his head with the proper procedures for securing the site rather than examine the loneliness gnawing at him.

How had it come about that a man of near-genius IQ, with halfway decent looks—if not charm—from a perfectly normal, well-to-do family, had no life? He really ought to sit down and figure out where he'd gone wrong, but if he hadn't seen it when he'd done it, he'd not recognize his error now. He knew how to investigate a crime site, examine evidence, analyze details, and solve a decades-old murder, but he couldn't apply the same intelligence to his own life.

It was a little late for working it out now. With the refrain *Doo-wah-diddy-diddy* humming through his head, he turned down the sandy lane leading to Cleo's. TJ passed her house and drove as far as the lane took him.

A movement in the shadows of the dune below the dig site caught in his headlights. TJ's already simmering adrenaline boiled over.

Slamming on the brakes, hitting the ignition, TJ leapt from the car. With the ease of experience, he dodged through the wax myrtles to the nearest path up the hill. The mood he was in tonight, he'd single-handedly take out any fool mucking with his project. He didn't need any weapons but bare fists and fury.

He understood action far better than analyzing his life.

He heard rustling in the bushes on the far side of the hill. Without hesitation, he clattered across the board platform supporting his excavation, slid down the sandy path on the beach side, and tore off after the dark figure racing toward the ocean.

TJ had long legs and temper to carry him, but the intruder had supernatural powers—he disappeared into the shadows of the rock jetty.

Cursing, TJ stalked up and down the canvas-covered rock pile of Mara's movie set, looking for some sign of the culprit. Nothing. Had it been daylight, he might have examined footprints, but he had no flashlight, nothing but the moon's fading glow to guide him.

A motor roared to life just on the other side of the rocks. Tearing across the artificial turf, TJ made it to the top in time to see a headlight beaming out to sea. What in hell was going on here?

Scrambling down the rocks, he jogged back to check

the dig site. He'd fenced in the excavation and locked it, more to prevent curious teenagers from hurting themselves than to keep out thieves. A good hacksaw would take out the lock or the chain link.

Sure enough, the lock was off and the gate open.

TJ entered cautiously, not wanting to disturb more evidence than necessary but needing to know what the intruder had wanted. He had a flashlight in his toolbox, and he dug it out now. Normal thieves would have stolen the equipment he kept in the box. Flipping on the light, he thought the tools were more jumbled than he'd left them, but they all seemed to be there.

He widened the light's beam and slid it over the sand and boards where he'd worked this past month.

The boxes of artifacts had been dumped and scattered across the sand. He couldn't easily tell if any were missing. All human remains had been taken to his office in town, and a bolt of fury tore through him. Had they torn the office apart again?

They hadn't stolen anything last time.

What the devil was the thief looking for?

With a sigh of exasperation, TJ pulled his cheap plastic lounge chair across the gate and prepared to spend the night guarding the site.

At least this time he knew it wasn't Mara or her crew messing with his head. Now that they had legal permission, they'd be in first thing in the morning with bulldozers.

Unless he stopped them.

He'd let Mara spin his head backward tonight. The vandals had done him a favor and spun it back. Why should he go down without a fight?

Grimly, TJ pulled out his cell phone and the business card Cleo had given him for her legal shark and punched in the office number. He'd have a message waiting when the office doors opened.

Let *People* decide if slapping a federal court order on Mara's film company constituted being at loggerheads.

SIXTEEN

"Sid, I am not taking bulldozers out there, and that's final," Mara screamed into her cell phone as she paced the B&B's breakfast room. "That's a rat-fink thing to do. This is *my* film, and I'll handle it my way!"

She glared at Irving, who sat at a table, prodding cautiously at his bandaged nose. She smacked his hand away in passing. He returned to sipping his coffee without a word—passive-aggressive to the bone.

"Don't give me that guff, Rosenthal. I'll have my lawyer on the phone so fast, your lawyer's head will spin. It's my film and my career on the line. If it sinks, I lose, so keep your damned shysters to yourself."

Constantina offered her a biscuit—bagels weren't on the B&B's menu. Mara shook her head and continued pacing. Her stomach wouldn't accept food right now. She had Irving down here, and Sid and his lawyers were giving her hives. Who could eat?

"You have no idea who you're messing with here, Sid, and I do. Lay off, or you'll ruin the deal. *Capisce?*" She slammed the phone off, folded it, and slid it into her shorts pocket. Now she had to find TJ and make certain he didn't draw and quarter her.

She still got a hot thrill reliving TJ's vengeful punch at Irving's nose. She suspected half his fury had been at her, but once his temper had exploded, it had morphed rapidly into a different kind of heat. He'd looked at her as if she were the moon and stars. For that look, she'd work a little harder to find a compromise over the access road.

"Constantina, did you find those headbands?" she demanded, still pacing. If she could control the small things in life, maybe the big ones would fall into place.

"Gave them to Jim to take out to the island," her hairdresser told her. "They don't work on you, anyway."

Nothing worked on her, but that was beside the point. She didn't want Kismet thinking she'd been forgotten. Maybe one good deed balanced the sin of enjoying Irving's bashed nose.

"You belong at home, taking care of your mother," Irving said disapprovingly. "Let Sid fight with the lawyers and do his job."

She didn't have to hear this. She wasn't married to the whining jerk anymore. Ignoring the roll of Constantina's eyes, Mara propped her palms on the table and put her face up to his. "I'm only saying this once, Irving, old friend. I have a *life*. You don't. You stay out of my life, and I won't disturb your nonlife. Mess with me, and I'll cut off your *cojones*. And you can tell Aunt Miriam I told you so."

With the adrenaline high of pure fury, Mara slammed out of the dining room. She couldn't believe Aunt Miriam would send the stinking, lying, whoring bastard down here after her. Did her aunt think she'd forgive the creep, go home, and settle down like a nice Jewish-Italian girl in the old neighborhood?

Of course she did.

What was even more appalling was that Irving seemed to think the same thing. And wouldn't that be a feather in his cap—movie star and producer for a wife, showing off his lingerie inventory in high society? Delusional. Positively delusional.

Storming outside, Mara scowled at the heavy clouds overhead. They wouldn't get any filming done today. She would have to concentrate on completing the camouflage job on the jetty. It wouldn't show up as more than a small angle shot in the ship scenes, but she wanted the authenticity. Big, hulking gray rocks weren't authentic.

She was almost afraid to have Jim drive her out to the beach after last night. TJ's red-hot streak wouldn't have had time to cool off. She glanced at her watch—nearly noon. She'd wasted the entire morning waiting for a decent hour to call Sid in California. She should have roused him from bed. Actually, she had.

She rubbed her forehead, but that didn't stimulate any ideas on how to pacify TJ. She'd just have to tell him she wouldn't enforce the cease-and-desist order.

She *wanted* to enforce it.

Her future depended on pulling this film in under budget. With Glynis's name on it, they had major sales locked in. She could buy Sid out, turn the company around, buy her own house, and provide her mother a place of her own. She wouldn't have to look to any man to support her ever again—unless she'd inherited her mother's psychosis. But worrying about that now would definitely make her crazy.

Were TJ's old bones really worth losing her home and her career and any hope of independence?

Research! She'd promised TJ she would research the project. Maybe she could prove the bones belonged to some long-ago drowning victim and weren't worth his time and effort.

With a much jauntier step, she set off in search of the library. She'd once entertained thoughts of a career in law, doing legal research. The summer she'd spent working in a law office had cured her of that foolishness, but she still loved digging through musty old tomes. Her Gemini mind saw both sides of the story too easily for law, but TJ's problem didn't require making judgments or searching for loopholes.

The library was housed in one of the old antebellum mansions, and the wood frame was sagging beneath the weight of the books inside. Paint peeled off the gracious columns, but the bearded oaks and rampant azaleas disguised the decay. Mara asked the librarian for old newspapers first, and any books on the history of the area. The elderly lady behind the desk was thrilled to help.

Surrounded by cartons of microfiche film, dusty volumes of bound newsprint, and a few self-published pamphlets on the islands, she joyfully settled in to work. Thunder rolled and cracked overhead, but the patter of rain on the roof only settled her more thoroughly into her seat. If she could make a living sitting on her rear end in a library all day, she'd be in heaven. She could wear her glasses and blue jeans, tug her hair into a ponytail—become the nerdy teenager TJ had once respected. And left behind.

She didn't have to be what another man expected of her ever again. Repeating this mantra, she buckled down to scanning ancient dusty tomes and taking notes.

Her cell phone vibrated, and she ignored it. Voice mail could get it. A film crew trapped inside a hotel all day could cause all manner of havoc, and she wasn't interested.

It buzzed again two minutes later. Probably Irving. He could go back home where he belonged.

She shoved a pencil through her upswept hair and concentrated on a World War II–era news article about a group wanting to form a coast watch on the islands. The Germans were invading the Netherlands. Why the devil would locals think they'd land on an impoverished part of the South Carolina coast? Could those bones just be some misguided Boy Scout who starved to death waiting for an invasion that never came?

The phone buzzed again. Scowling, she shut it off.

"You want me to get a federal injunction issued for *that*?" The portly lawyer with a silvered ponytail gazed at the muddy excavation in disbelief.

"It's under the auspices of a federal grant," TJ responded impassively. "The discovery of an early American settlement here would give grounds for further historical exploration." As far as he could tell, nothing had been stolen last night, and he'd like to keep it that way. Mostly, though, he wanted his project out of the film company's clutches.

The lawyer's sharp gaze took him in. "What about pirates?"

TJ shrugged noncommittally. "Pirates, smugglers, or wreckers are a possibility, given the history of coastlines. Doesn't change the historical significance. How long will it take to obtain the injunction?"

The lawyer didn't look as if he bought this for a minute, but his gaze returned to the mud wallow left in the wake of the morning's storm. "Depends on the judge's schedule. Could be hours or days."

"If you can obtain an injunction to void the film company's order, I can post guards out here and prevent further invasion." *And keep out film crews,* but TJ refrained from mentioning anything so politically incorrect. He might be ambivalent about keeping out Mara, but if her second ex was as big an ass as the first, he'd meet him head on.

The lawyer remained skeptical. "It's a sand pit. Why would anyone want to break into it? Are they expecting buried treasure?"

TJ raised his eyebrows. "Interesting thought. Hadn't considered that." Not that it was going to happen, but who knew what thieves might believe. "Mostly I want to protect the site's integrity."

"All right, I'll bite, although knowing your sister-in-law's views, I can't imagine she'll appreciate posting armed guards out here."

"Not armed. And it's for her privacy I'm doing this." Sort of. He respected Jared and Cleo's need for peace, but between film crews, vandals, thieves, and security guards, chances of that happening were slim.

The lawyer nodded and reached for his cell phone.

"I'll get on it. Shouldn't be too difficult." He gave TJ another appraising look. "You're prepared for the public outcry if you halt this film?"

TJ crossed his arms and stared back. "What do you think?"

"That I'm damned glad I'm not the other guy." With more grace than a man his size should possess, the lawyer stalked down the wet sand, shouting orders into a phone smaller than his hand.

Standing stiff and straight, arms still crossed, TJ watched his last chance of seeing admiration in Mara's eyes go by. By this time tomorrow, the place would be swarming with reporters, Mara would be furious, he'd have blown his cover, and his career would be on a fast track downhill.

He could still save his career. He doubted if he could save Mara.

His gaze flickered over the muddy pit that his life had become, and he thought the analogy more than apt. Trapped at the bottom of that hole, he couldn't see a future until he climbed out. The time had come to dig the first step in the wall.

"Sid, it rains out here." Mara shoved a loose curl off her forehead and growled into her cell phone. Sitting in the limo's climate-controlled interior, she handed Ian her PDA, pointed at the name of the set designer she wanted to talk to, and plastered on a conspiratorial smile for the reporter sitting next to him. "It's not L.A. South Carolina has rains and hurricanes. You ought to try weather sometime. It would be a new experience."

She only half listened to her ex's complaints about time and budget. Her stomach clenched nervously as they approached the island. She'd forestalled Sid's demand to rent bulldozers, but she didn't know how long she could hold back. They needed to get those ship scenes before the days grew too short.

She hadn't heard from TJ, hadn't expected to. She

knew his capacity for systematic revenge and was terrified to consider what he might do in retaliation for the court order. She'd hoped yesterday's research would yield instant success to pacify him, but she'd found little more than a few names of hunters who used the island and a couple of landowners. She needed to dig deeper.

She didn't have time to dig deeper. Sid was screaming, Irving was whining, her aunt had left messages on every voice mail Mara owned, and Ian had invited *People* and *Entertainment Tonight* to the set. The film crew was right behind the limo, and her teeth would be chattering if she hadn't clamped her lips into a bright smile.

She didn't need to inherit her mother's psychosis to go insane. This business would drive her there. She shoved her phone into her purse.

"I understand you had to obtain a court order to gain access to the beach location." The reporter clicked on his recorder now that he had her attention.

She continued smiling and shrugged nonchalantly. "Dr. McCloud has a federal grant and had to protect the government's interest. It's just a legal formality. We'll preserve his artifacts."

"I hear that you and Dr. McCloud have a relationship. Are you aware that—"

"Friggin' sheep shit!" Ian shouted, glancing through the limo's windshield to see why the car had slowed. "The turd's hired guards!"

Jim pulled the limo to a smooth halt and awaited further instruction. In front of the car, Day-Glo orange barriers blocked the access road. A uniformed security guard manned the barricade.

The reporter scribbled furiously. Mara didn't have to look out the rear window to know the film crew would be spilling from their van, cameras in hand. Every ounce of acting she had learned these last years would have to fall into play if she was to pull this off with any semblance of grace and aplomb. Anything less, and she'd have investors pulling the plug faster than her ship could sink.

What she wanted to do was hunt down TJ McCloud and bash him over his thick head with his stupid security guard.

Or crawl into his strong arms and cry until he made the world go away.

Talk about conflicts—she ought to write a book. She'd definitely do a chick flick next, should she survive this encounter.

Still smiling through her Rogue Rouge, Mara let Jim open the car door. With extravagant care she smoothed down her screaming orange miniskirt, adjusted her long, tanned, silk-clad legs, swung her stacked heels gracefully to the sand, then with a benevolent expression accepted Jim's hand and exited the limo.

She could feel the reporter's smoldering gaze burning the backs of her knees. She shimmied her hips to adjust her skirt again and figured he was out for the count. Show time.

Thrusting out her elastic-enhanced chest, teasing a lock of synthetic hair back into its stack, drawing attention to her cleavage with the gesture, Mara licked her lips and batted her fake lashes.

The guard's mouth hung open. Cameras whirred.

"Hello, honey," she purred, walking up to him. "I'm Mara Simon, and this is my right-of-way. Could you move these pretty orange things over to the side of the road?"

"In about three months," a familiar dry voice answered from the wax myrtle thicket as it parted.

Controlling her temper, fighting the sick curl of desire that the voice engendered, Mara swung around to glare at Dr. TJ McCloud, her nemesis. "Says who?"

"Says the federal injunction posted on that gate." TJ nodded at the chain link on the hill down the road. "I told you this was a federal grant. Your city buddies can't help you here."

He looked so good in those dark shades and that jungle hat, she thought she might change teams, climb over the barrier, and glare at the reporters from his side.

Traitorous instincts, indeed. She had a movie to make, a career to launch, an ailing mother to care for, and a faltering studio to save. Too many people counted on her to back down now.

What if she failed?

Advancing so they stood toe to toe and no one else could hear them, Mara ran her fingertips up and down the black cotton stretched across TJ's impressive chest. "I didn't request that order, TJ McCloud, and you damned well know it. Can't we find a compromise?"

If TJ felt anywhere near as breathless as she did, they'd both expire of asphyxiation. She deliberately took a deep breath, and the heated hunger of his gaze knocked the air out of her lungs again.

"I don't think so, Pats," he said gravely. "I'm paid to do this job, and securing the site is my priority." He stepped backward, away from her prying fingers.

If she'd thought crying would help, she would have turned on the tears, but the TJ she knew had more respect for brains than weeping wimps. She lifted her gaze to trap his, damning him to hell without saying the words. "I'm paid to do my job, too, and I'll warn you now: I've had dragons far more intimidating than you in my face, and I've slain them all. Watch your throat, McCloud. I'm winning this one."

Sunglasses hid his eyes, but she read the admiring tug on his lips before she swung away, sashaying her hips slowly to make him crazy.

TJ McCloud admired her.

She threw the film crew a stunning, genuine smile that faltered as she climbed back into the car.

She may have won TJ's admiration, but she had lost the battle.

SEVENTEEN

"Didn't you watch the news last night?" Sid screamed through the receiver the day after the barricade disaster. "You looked like a damned ass out there flirting with that Indiana Jones character! You're off the film, kid. Ian's in charge."

Panic flooded through her. Mara dug her fingers into her unstyled curls, leaned her elbows on the table, and fought down the hysteria pounding for escape. "*ET* isn't news," she muttered, knowing her ex's penchant for entertainment news over anything more substantial. "There are kids starving in Angola, and my disagreement with McCloud hardly rates tempest-in-a-teapot status. This is *my* film, Sid. You can't take me off it."

"I still own the effing company, doll, and I'm not wasting any more money. Either Ian takes over or I'm offering Glynis another production. I've already talked to her agent."

She couldn't bear this. He'd *promised*. Not that Sid's promises meant more than she could hold him to at the point of a gun. "I'm the one with the most at stake here, Sid. I'm the one who gets a share of the profit. Ian doesn't care about bottom lines."

"Ian cares about getting his butt chewed if he doesn't come in under budget. Go back to your whining relatives and get out of my hair." He hung up.

Shivering, Mara clicked the phone off and contemplated the empty dining room. A chill crawled across her skin, and she couldn't blame it on the air-conditioning.

She could call her divorce lawyer. The film was part of the settlement. She didn't understand the legal terms, just the ramifications. She got to keep the profits from the pirate film; Sid got to keep the house. Sounded like Sid would get both if he could pull her off the job.

If the film didn't make a profit, she couldn't buy out his half of the company. If the settlement awarded her half the business, didn't she have some say in who worked the film? Probably not the way Sid had it set up.

She dialed her attorney anyway.

He confirmed her suspicions. Sid was head of the company until she legally owned it. He could fire her anytime he liked. All she was entitled to was the profit—and, knowing Sid's practices, she was pretty sure there wouldn't be any.

She should have realized he'd agreed too easily to her demands. Honesty wasn't a word Sid understood.

Mara's mind danced wildly over impossible solutions while her insides slowly shriveled and died. She was out in the cold again, with nowhere to turn and little in the bank to show for the years of her life wasted.

"Do you have time to talk now?" a nasal whine intruded.

Irving. She didn't need the hassle, the reminder of another failure while she was still being crushed beneath the weight of this one.

The bandage plastered across Irving's handsome face reminded her that he wasn't what he appeared. She shot him a glare and reached for the coffeepot. "Go home, Irving. I'm not interested in anything you have to say."

Her hand shook as she poured the coffee.

"I promised your aunt I would talk to you, Patsy."

She hated that name. So appropriate, too. She was a walking, talking patsy for every man who had ever trodden through her life.

Irving took the seat across the table and gazed at her with imploring brown eyes. The color might be similar to Tim's, but not the expression. Irving's eyes reminded her of a spaniel. TJ's changed from laughter to admiration to fury in a matter of seconds, revealing all those boiling emotions his chiseled countenance concealed. Oh, damn, why was she thinking of that monster now? This was all his fault.

"The store is doing nicely." Irving helped himself to the coffee, then grimaced when he sipped it. "It's cold."

"Don't drink it," she advised wittily, taking a swig of her own. She desperately needed a caffeine infusion.

"I'm thinking of opening two more stores, in better locations."

"Franchise them." Swell—she needed her nose rubbed in how well she could have been doing if she'd stayed with him.

She could never have stayed with him. Unconsciously, she rubbed the nose he had smashed and let the misery build. No matter how much she'd learned in the process, she'd failed at every damned thing she'd done.

At least this time, she recognized the breaking point, where desperation drove her to do something foolish—like running off to Hollywood. Only this time she had nowhere left to run.

Irving looked interested in her suggestion. "Franchising involves more than I can handle on my own. I need to hire more staff for the branches as it is. I've got to get back today. Why don't you come with me? Your family wants to see you."

"My family wants me to shoulder their burdens." Maybe she should just get up and walk away. It wasn't as if Irving could fire her.

Irving had the tenacity of poison ivy. He'd never leave until she heard him out.

"Your mother really needs to be institutionalized," he said soothingly. "They've found an excellent home where she can have her own apartment. She'll be fine. These places aren't like what you see in the movies."

She heard the disapproval in his voice. Irving never had liked going to the movies. There had been a time when she'd practically lived in them rather than go home at night.

"Unless Aunt Miriam or Uncle David intends to move in with her, Mom will be terrified." She squelched that hope with as much force as her shattered psyche could manage. "Besides, I can't afford it."

"I'm doing very well," Irving replied suggestively. "You were young and foolish, and I didn't handle things well. We could try again. With your connections—"

That did it. The frayed rubber band that kept her motor running snapped. Tires squealed. Mechanical parts flew. The engine cracked and spewed steam. Mara lifted the cold coffeepot and swung.

Black liquid splattered across Irving's smug face. Before he could react, Mara smacked the empty glass pot upside-down on his professionally styled and colored hair, shoved back her chair, and marched away.

She dared them to lock her in the psycho ward with her mother.

TJ wiped the sweat from his forehead, stuck his shovel in the pile of rain-sodden sand he'd dug out this morning, and dropped down to sit on the box he'd locked his tools in. "What now?" he demanded of the visitor he found waiting at the top of the pit.

Jared looked up from the collection of artifacts representing the morning's work. "Rib bones and Nazi insignia?" he asked in curiosity, holding up the gold buttons.

Despite his laid-back attitude, Jared worked as hard as he played, so TJ knew he hadn't come out here to poke through garbage. But at the moment, TJ wasn't in any humor to figure out what he wanted. They'd learned non-communication at their parents' knees.

The security guard had already notified TJ that three reporters had camped out on the road and several others were trespassing on Cleo's property, trying to circumvent the barriers. How many were actually interested in

Mara's story and which ones had sniffed out Colonel Martin's?

He'd retrieved another box from storage and opened it last night. This one contained account books that made no sense to him but showed odd expenditures an accountant might be able to follow. It was becoming increasingly obvious that he made a lousy judge and jury. He'd have to decide soon who should get the boxes.

Burning them would be easier.

Taking the gold button Jared held out, TJ turned it over in his palm. "Tell Cleo there may be more to Ed's tales of subs than we suspected."

"Nazi spies instead of pirates," Jared mused, shaking his head. "Guess I should have listened in history class. I didn't think the Germans ever touched American soil."

"Ed gave me a book on U-boats. Besides the subs with torpedoes, several carrying spies landed on the East Coast, but there's no record of any in the Carolinas. Spies needed metropolitan areas where the men could blend in with the population. They'd stand out like sore thumbs in a small town like this." TJ took a long gulp of cold water.

Jared shrugged, losing interest. He eyed TJ instead. "You look like hell. I thought you won this round."

"I did." Of course, he'd also lost any hope of ever meeting Mara on amicable grounds again, but that was just the beginning of the story. She was better off out of his life right now. He'd survived on his own for a long, long time. He'd do it again—once he forgot the awe in her eyes after he'd punched her ex. Or the look of amazement that night he'd lost it and driven them both out of their minds with pleasure. Or . . .

The picture wasn't pretty. He knew how to focus on the immediate. "Is Cleo going to throw me out?"

"She's pissed, but she hasn't started heaving your worldly goods out the window yet. She did dump Gene's black snakes on the driveway, and when I left she was muttering about gators. She doesn't have anything against reporters personally, but she resents anyone messing with family. You know how it is."

Yeah, TJ knew how it was. Good thing he believed in gun control or he'd be hauling iron by now, taking out a few of the nosy bastards. He dried his face on a towel and wondered if all this was worth it. "Tell Cleo I'll cut the line the instant she tells me to. This is her hideaway, and I know what it means to both of you."

Jared snorted. "The minute you're out of here, the film crew moves in, so you're safe enough. I won't say the same for the reporters."

TJ threw the towel down. "I'm sorry about that. Maybe they'll leave once they see there's no story." He knew better, but for a little while he could pretend this was just entertainment news and not the beginning of the end—for Cleo's sake. He had never left a job undone, but for Cleo and Jared and the safe world they'd built, he would walk away.

"You don't have to lie to me." Jared helped himself to a soft drink from the ice chest and dropped down on the rickety lounge chair. "I've seen how Hollywood operates. You forget, I'm part of the media."

TJ grimaced. "How could I forget?" Comic-strip artists weren't precisely reporters, but they were all in the business of attracting a mass audience.

Jared popped the can top and didn't immediately reply. TJ recognized that as a danger sign. His younger brother did surface charm well but had to work harder at real communication. Cleo's stormy nature had taught Jared a lot, but the people skills of the McCloud family left a lot to be desired.

"Cleo's pregnant."

Pow. That shook the stuffing out of him. TJ ran the cold water bottle over his forehead and tried to think how to respond. He was about to become an *uncle*. He'd never had an uncle. What did one do? Matty was big enough to talk to, but an infant?

Picturing his younger brother as the father of a baby staggered the imagination. Jared had been the middle brother whose zany antics as a child had irritated TJ's too-mature sensibilities, but without Jared, he might never have learned to laugh.

He respected what Jared had done with his life, but it didn't seem logical that of the three brothers, the clown was the first one to grow up, settle down, and have *children.*

"Congratulations," was the only reply immediately coming to mind as TJ struggled to rearrange his thinking.

Jared grinned at his confusion. "I've been told women do that occasionally, you know—pop out squealing little monsters to make our lives interesting."

TJ's mind drifted to Mara popping out little monsters, and his head spun with delirium. He obviously had far too many changes in his life to digest another easily.

But now that he'd had time to grasp this latest shift in his world, TJ was happy for his brother. "You've always had a way with kids. You're great with Matty. You'll make a good father."

Jared seemed to relax a little at TJ's approval. "Thanks. I'm hoping so. It's kind of scary to think about, so I try not to think about it too hard."

TJ grunted at this typical Jared reaction. If nothing else, this time on the shore had taught him to better appreciate his family. "You told me this for a reason?"

His brother returned to staring at his drink can. Not a good sign. TJ let his mind roam over the possibilities while Jared looked for words to explain. TJ knew that Cleo was a great mother, far better than their own despite the differences in their upbringing. Whatever Jared's shortcomings, Cleo would overcome them, and vice versa. Working together, they balanced each other out.

TJ wondered if he'd ever find someone who could balance the huge scale of his own faults.

"Cleo freaks out if anyone threatens her kid," Jared

said slowly, frowning as he tried to explain. "I mean, really freaks."

Recalling the memorable episode when Cleo had commandeered the courthouse roof to get her point across, TJ nodded in agreement. "That's what she's got you for," he reminded Jared. "You can stand between her and any perceived danger." *Perceived danger.* TJ's eyes narrowed. "What's she afraid of?"

Jared helplessly lifted his arms. "Authority. Hurricanes. Anything she can't handle. She needs to feel in control."

Well, TJ could relate to that. "So she can't control reporters?"

"She can't control authority. A Colonel Martin called asking for you. Since your contacts know how to reach your business phone, she thinks this is related to us. She's terrified we'll have a military outpost on the beach next." He looked apologetic. "I think it's hormones."

TJ barely registered that last nonsensical statement. Cleo had excellent people instincts. Colonel Martin and hurricanes had a lot in common. Why the devil had the colonel waited until now to call him? And why hadn't he used official channels? Did he think TJ's phone line had been tapped?

Damn. He had far too much on his plate right now. He didn't want to talk to Martin on top of everything else. He had reporters crawling up his ass. If he read any more of the material in those boxes, he'd have to act on it one way or the other. He hated lying—to the reporters or to the colonel. Maybe if he didn't talk to Martin and didn't read more of the material, he could safely say he knew nothing should a reporter be so perspicacious as to ask about his connection to Martin's mounting problems.

But deep down he knew not reading the material was the coward's way out.

What could the colonel want? Martin thought TJ had destroyed the boxes, so he couldn't be after them. Although Martin was an old family friend and had acted as

TJ's mentor, their business relationship was strictly professional. He seldom called unless they were on assignment, and then he used his work phone. If the colonel was innocent, surely he didn't need to influence TJ's testimony, should it come to that.

TJ dragged to his feet and swigged the last drop of water before giving Jared the reply he wanted. "The colonel's a friend of mine. Tell Cleo this has nothing to do with the dig site. She can rig maniacal witches in the roadway with a clear conscience."

Jared looked relieved. "She has some warped idea that you're harboring a problem you're not telling us about, and she was afraid the colonel might be it. She'll be relieved to hear she was wrong."

TJ crushed the plastic bottle and heaved it at the trash bin. It bounced off the rim and fell in.

That Mexico job he'd been offered was sounding more promising by the minute. "Take her on a vacation while you still can," he advised his younger brother, out of caution as well as concern. "Rugrats are cute, but they eat up all your privacy."

Jared bounded up from the chair, full of enthusiasm. "That's a great idea. We'll take Matty to Disney World." He halted and gave TJ a shrewd look. "You might want to go with us. Invite Pats. Cleo likes her. Maybe the two of you can settle your differences over the Mad Hatter's teacups."

TJ longed to do just such a commonplace thing as that. It sounded so simple, so normal, and TJ could hear Mara's laughter as the cups spun and fireworks blossomed. He wanted that someday. He wanted his own kids to shout with joy and surprise at the things he could show them. He wanted to be their hero.

"Carry a barf bag if you take Cleo on the cups," TJ admonished, grabbing his shovel and driving it into the hole. Maybe he could solve the mystery of the bones before the rest of his life tumbled in on him.

EIGHTEEN

She would lose everything.

After bolting from the B&B, Mara paced up a shaded back street, broad-brimmed straw hat and sunglasses firmly in place to hide the tears streaking her cheeks. There had to be some way out of this, but the child crying inside her just wanted to run and hide. Or find Tim.

She couldn't believe after all these years she was reverting to that anxiety-riddled adolescent who saw Tim and her big brother as the security she craved. She knew better. Brad was dead. And Tim wasn't really part of her life, no matter how much she'd like to pretend she was a film heroine and he was the hero riding out of the storm to save her. In his own stubborn, noncommunicative way, Tim was as much a pain in the ass as any film star, and she wanted him for far different reasons than security.

Sid had told her she needed a shrink. For a change, he might be right.

She hugged herself, hoping to hold it all in, but she thought she might burst from the power of her fury and terror. She couldn't do it; she couldn't lose it all. She would do anything, *anything,* to save her film. Her entire future rested on it.

Maybe if she defied the federal injunction, ignored Sid, and brought in dozers . . . ?

She couldn't go back to Brooklyn and live with her aunt and uncle. She couldn't go back to Irving. She didn't have enough experience for anyone else in Hollywood to hire her. She only had this job because she'd married the boss. She had no education, no career, no talent except for disguising herself—and that was wearing mighty thin.

The film was all she had.

A pretty sad state of affairs, if she did say so herself. Mara glanced up at the gracious old homes framed in ancient oaks and azaleas and wondered what it would have been like to have grown up here, in this oasis of stability in a world gone mad. Boring, probably, but boring wasn't necessarily bad.

Maybe her family was right. Maybe she was meant to be a boring housewife, helping her husband to move up in the world, raising beautiful babies. Children were the future, after all.

She shook her head. Not her future. Going there was even worse than contemplating bankruptcy.

She was her mother's future. Dammit. If she was her mother's future, then they were both lost.

A wry grin curled one corner of her mouth at that churlish prediction. At least her sense of humor hadn't deserted her.

Once upon a long time ago, she'd worshiped TJ, loved him with all her adolescent heart. He'd understood truth and justice with a basic honesty that had shone through in his every action. A teenage hunk who could be kind to a plain-Jane nerd had to have a special place in heaven reserved for him.

How could she destroy his work by bringing in bulldozers? Building her career on the ruins of his would turn her into a monster like Sid.

With her world crumbling around her, she needed to believe in TJ's honesty and sense of justice. He represented an island of sanity in her life.

She needed TJ on her side. She'd already lost everything—what else did she have to lose?

Turning down a street leading to TJ's storefront office, Mara knew what she had to lose, but she'd lost that a long time ago. Her stupid teenage heart had gone with TJ the day he'd walked away without looking back.

He could keep her damned heart. She'd lived without it this long. She just wanted her life back.

Cooled by the air-conditioned ride into town, TJ parked in the alley beside the office and climbed out of the car without glancing in the mirror to see what he looked like. He hadn't showered and he probably stank, but that certainly ought to give his new secretary food for thought. He'd hired an airheaded teenager to guard the door and open the mail, hoping the age difference would discourage any of the fanciful ideas Leona had harbored.

As long as Mara was in the vicinity, *he* certainly wouldn't be having ideas about other women. He'd forgotten how crazy she'd made him all those years ago. How could a woman drive him to the brink of murder and arousal at the same time? He alternately wanted to feed her and strangle her, depending on what tangent she'd taken that minute. He could spend the rest of his life spinning like a top with a woman like Mara around. He wouldn't need war zones.

Hefting the box of artifacts from the trunk, he slammed the lid and carried it to the front door.

TJ grimaced as he recognized Roger Curtis lounging against the brick wall outside his door. Bad omens everywhere. Must be a full moon tonight.

"I'm tired, hot, and irritable," he growled before the reporter could open his mouth. "Go find a bar and bother me some other time."

Roger eyed TJ's mud-streaked T-shirt and jeans. "I take it you won't be joining me in a cold one."

"I could, but I won't." He reached for the office door. He didn't have the patience for pleasantries right now. His gut ached with guilt, and his mind roiled in doubt. He couldn't remember ever being reduced to a state where his next action wasn't clear and straight. He hated this.

"The independent investigator's office this afternoon

recommended a court-martial," Roger said, undeterred. "Looks like Martin and his buddies are going on trial."

"I've got my problems, he's got his." Rudely, TJ shouldered past Roger and entered the office, slamming the door behind him.

The phone was ringing off the hook. He should have thrown it against the wall along with the answering machine. It wasn't as if he had more than two weeks left before the management company threw him out of this dump, anyway, so who needed phones?

Looking harried, his teenage secretary served coffee in Styrofoam cups to a couple of reporter types lounging on the cheap plastic chairs in his front office. From his laboratory, a radio blared a Gilbert and Sullivan opera. Just what he needed—musical accompaniment to his comic-opera life.

Cursing mentally, TJ ignored the men leaping to their feet, strode straight to the back room, and nearly dropped his box. Mara rose from his stool, wearing a white lab coat and her reading glasses and looking as if she belonged there. Behind her, his laptop slipped into a screen saver of a polar bear on ice.

He couldn't *do* this. He wanted to drop the box and run for his life. Instead, he stood there gaping at the wickedly deceptive image of a Hollywood star dressed as his assistant and looking like the kid he'd loved back in the stone age.

She'd pulled her riotous curls into a fluffy knot on top of her head. The small wire-rimmed glasses looked so natural that he could swear it was Patsy staring over the top of them—but a different Patsy, one who had strength and determination shining behind her cat eyes instead of pleading anxiety and hero worship.

He liked the strength. It looked good on her. And it took some of the burden off his shoulders. He could fight equally with this woman and not fear hurting her feelings.

"I just talked to a Colonel Martin," she informed him

before he could formulate a coherent sentence. She glanced at a phone slip in her hand. "He said it's urgent that you call him back."

Life had an unfortunate way of dumping truckloads of manure on his head all at one time, TJ decided. He heaved the box onto the counter, grabbed the slip from her hand, and shoved it into his jeans pocket. "What are you doing here?"

"Borrowing your computer, since the library doesn't have one. You said I could research your project. Considering I'm out of a job, I thought maybe you could use an assistant as well."

He could tell by the twinkle in her eye that she was tweaking him, but he could also tell she'd been crying. He'd seen Patsy cry far more than he cared to remember. Damn, but he'd been an unthinking fool back then, a hormonal unthinking fool, although he'd never been the one to make her cry.

"What's wrong?" he demanded. He refused to let guilt and tears drive him from finishing the excavation, if that's what the crack about a job meant.

"What do you think is wrong?" she shot back.

The kid she'd been would have burst into tears. This one looked daggers at him, probably rightly so, but he didn't have patience with the problems of her glitzy world. Let her take them to one of her rich ex-husbands. "Irving wanted a loan and pouted when you refused?" he suggested nastily.

Mara's chin shot up. Her lips tightened. And TJ thought for a second she'd throw her clipboard at him. He waited. She didn't respond as anticipated. She reached for a notebook on the counter and slammed it into his chest.

"Here. Look at this. See if you think it's feasible before I present it to Cleo."

He glanced at the opening page, recognized the drawing of the access road and dig site with modifications, and flung it back onto the counter. He was too rattled to think right now. "I've got to label those specimens, take a shower, and answer my messages. I'll look at it later."

Mara drew herself up to her full height, nearly pressed her nose to his, and stabbed his chest with her finger. "This is *me*, Timothy John, not one of your lovestruck assistants. I'm sitting right here until you take time to listen to me. I'll join you in the shower if I have to. You will *not* drive me off like you have every other female in your life."

Amid all the crap turning his life into a cesspool, Mara's blunt words pealed like heavenly bells of joy. He figured he'd gone insane, but something very like hope wormed through the barriers around his heart and opened a pinprick of light. Maybe he'd start with that shower offer.

The phone shrieked.

His secretary returned and burst into tears rather than answer it.

Both reporters appeared in the doorway at once.

Mara raised her eyebrows and waited expectantly.

"You're hired." Spinning on his heel, TJ shoved past the reporters and stalked out the door.

If it wasn't so funny, she'd cry. Mara bit back both tears and laughter, gathered the teenager in her arms and patted her back, and glared at the stunned journalists who—when faced with real human drama—didn't have the sense to follow TJ. "Out," she commanded them firmly. "Business hours are over. Go find Ian down at the bar and commiserate."

They shrugged and obeyed. The answering machine she'd just purchased at Cleo's Hardware picked up the call, and whoever it was hung up.

Mara listened to the girl's sobbing account of a bad day and a broken love affair and idly wondered if happy teenagers existed.

Remembering TJ's wild-eyed look as he stormed out, she smiled again. Men like TJ needed mystery and adventure in their lives but didn't have the sense to recognize it in the everyday world around them. She thought maybe she could teach him a thing or two.

He'd better learn fast. She needed him here rather than out beating up reporters.

"Look, honey," she soothed the miserable girl, "men aren't worth our tears. Cry over babies and invalids, but tell the men in your life to go to hell. It's the only language they understand."

The girl looked at her in disbelief, but something in Mara's expression must have made a believer out of her. She nodded and wiped her eyes on her sleeve.

"Go on home. I'll lock up here. I don't think Dr. McCloud will need you this evening."

Mara ushered the girl out the door, turned the key in the deadbolt, and with grim-lipped decision marched back to TJ's office and the box marked "Martin" that she'd found in the closet.

She hadn't just spent the last hours weeping in her beer. She'd been listening, reading, and catching up on news she'd ignored while involved in her own troubles. A man named Martin had played a significant part in current events lately. TJ had been in the Balkans. This box contained notebooks that mentioned both the colonel and TJ.

It looked to her as if TJ McCloud might be involved in something far larger and darker than his impassive facade revealed. Maybe if she explored further, this could be her chance to rescue him the way he used to rescue the teenage Patsy.

Showered and relatively more lucid, TJ drove across the causeway back to town. He would have to call Martin tonight.

First, he needed to see what Mara wanted. If she owned half the film company, surely she couldn't be out of a job. She was just being dramatic.

After the debacle at the dig site, he couldn't believe

she'd come to him unless something was far more wrong than she was letting on. She might infuriate him, she might enflame his hormones, but she was still Patsy Amara, the funny, sensitive girl he would protect with his life.

So he had overdeveloped Neanderthal tendencies. Probably went with his size and hardheadedness.

He'd intended to find Mara at the B&B, but, passing his office on the way, he saw a crack of light through the curtains. The idiot he'd hired should have turned them off and locked up at five. Surely she could manage that much.

Surely thieves didn't turn on lights.

Switching off his headlights and pulling to the curb a few doors away, TJ got out of the car and slipped back to the storefront. The curtains blocked any view inside.

Without hesitation, he stuck his key in the lock and opened the door.

Mara instantly appeared in the lab doorway. "I hoped you'd be back tonight."

She had dust smudges on her perky little nose, and he wanted to kiss them away. Her topknot was tumbling from its pins, and he thought her natural curls far more appealing than the elaborate hairpiece. She'd shed the lab coat, revealing her movie-star designer crop top and hip-huggers, but he rather liked that tanned expanse of taut tummy wedged between vibrant reds. He more than liked it.

Reluctantly tearing his gaze away from the distraction, he focused on familiar green eyes. They watched him warily but not out of fear as much as concern. He had the sneaking suspicion Patsy had been playing snoop again.

"Some things don't change, do they?" he asked wearily, repeating her favorite phrase, closing and locking the door behind him.

"Have you eaten? I ordered pizza." She swung around and marched back into the lab without hammering him with questions.

He remembered that about her with a degree of

pleasure—she didn't try to pry things out of him when he didn't want to talk. Unfortunately, she still possessed the audacity to apply her razor-sharp mind to discovering his secrets on her own.

The aroma of sausage-laden pizza made his stomach rumble, and he grabbed the Coke bottle on the counter before tackling whatever monumental catastrophe Mara was about to fling at him.

"The new answering machine has caller ID." She took one of the counter stools and swung around in slow circles, sipping her soft drink and not watching him. "The person with the Washington area code keeps slamming down the phone rather than leave messages. The last few times, it's come through as 'unknown caller.' Do you think that means he's on a cell phone now?"

He refused to think of Martin on an empty stomach. Reaching for a pizza slice, TJ shrugged and took the other stool. He really didn't want to talk. He'd much rather carry her to the couch and find better things to do. It was easier to see her naked in his mind than to think about boxes and loyalty and scandal. That skimpy top of hers wouldn't resist a determined tug. He wondered what kind of contraption she wore under it to disguise her cupcakes as melons.

"Until we solve this problem of ours, we're not going to bed," she told him firmly, popping his bubble.

TJ glared at her and ripped off a bite of pizza instead of answering. Patsy's honesty never had any limits.

She shoved her notepad across the counter to him. "Sid fired me. I've lost the film because of you. The rat fink promised I could use the profits from the film to buy out the company, but there won't be any profits if Sid and his creative bookkeeping take over. I gave up my share of the house Sid and I owned for this opportunity, and you've cost me a fortune. Normally I'd tear you into shreds and spit you out like bad meat, but I think you've got as many problems as I do."

He glanced down at her sketch and took a swig of

Coke. If he was reading the plan correctly, Cleo would hate having her big bushes ripped out. It could destroy the delicate ecological balance out there. On the other hand, it might work.

"Why save the film if you've been fired?" He slid the sketch back over to her.

"Because it's *my* film," she all but shouted.

He should have figured rationality wouldn't last. She still operated on nervous energy. She just covered it up better these days.

The phone rang.

Mara stared at him, waiting.

"You have to talk to him sometime," she said softly.

"What do you know?" he growled.

"The Intimidator I remember never backed down from a problem."

"I'm not backing down. I'm protecting a friend." If he talked to Martin, should he tell him about the boxes? Should he say he had read what was in them? Or promise to destroy them or turn them over to the authorities? If he didn't talk to Martin, he could ponder his choices a while longer.

"If he's your friend, then you ought to tell him so," she chided. "The question is, is he really your friend?"

Cursing rabidly, TJ grabbed the phone and, instead of ripping it off the wall, answered it.

NINETEEN

"McCloud?"

The gruff voice sounded as commanding as ever. Standing beside his desk, TJ relaxed his jaw enough to respond. "Colonel. I'm a little shorthanded down here, but my new assistant said you called." He ignored the wadded paper napkin Mara flung at him from the worktable.

"Your family told me where to find you. What in hell are you doing in that hole? I thought you were in Africa until I saw you on the news the other night."

Well, that explained why the colonel hadn't called until TJ's little contretemps with Mara hit the television news. Grimacing, TJ flung the napkin back. "A little R and R, visiting the family. Needed a little time off."

"Can't say I blame you. I'd like a little of the same if I could get these damned media hounds off my back. Saw you've got some movie set down there, so you must know what they're like. Anything for a story. They've been on my doorstep night and day."

Thc colonel was never this loquacious. TJ tensed again. "The film crew brings them in," he agreed cautiously.

"None of them bothering you about me, are they? I'd hate to see a friend dragged into this."

"Looks like you've got yourself a little mess," TJ answered evasively. "Anything I can do to help?"

"Not that I know of, boy. Stay out of it if you can. Go back to Africa, where they can't find you. It will all blow over soon."

"Right. I'm considering a Mexican contract, down in

Yucatán, so I'll be out of touch. Let me know if I can do anything before I leave."

TJ let the colonel hang up first, then slowly lowered the receiver. Concentrating on his thoughts, he almost jumped when Mara covered his hand with a warm palm.

"Is he still your friend?" she whispered anxiously.

TJ wrapped his callused fingers around her manicured ones, glad to have a real friend to help him through this. Mara might have changed physically, but he trusted her innate honesty. Perhaps he'd gone ballistic over the court order, but once he'd calmed down, he'd believed that it was her ex's fault, not hers.

Filling his lungs, he processed his conversation with the colonel a second time. Confirming what he'd thought the first round, he shook his head. "He was telling me to get out of town."

"That means he's protecting you, doesn't it?"

Even after all these years, she was still a cockeyed optimist. He didn't want her involved in this. But he'd never been less than honest with her, either. "No, that means he's protecting his ass. A few months ago he ordered me to destroy boxes that might contain evidence against him, and he doesn't want me testifying to that."

He'd trusted Martin, admired him, followed him into the hell of war zones. He still couldn't believe the man had been using the power of his position to rake money out of the pockets of rapists and murderers, but the possibility that criminals had gone free because of him had become one step closer to real.

He exhaled the air he'd taken in.

Mara's arms circled his waist, and her soft curls brushed his chin. "I'm sorry, TJ. It's my fault, isn't it? He saw that tiff we had in front of the TV reporters, didn't he?"

"Tiff?" He gathered her against him, luxuriating in the feel of supple curves and exotic scents and mindless arousal. He didn't let down his guard often, but Mara had a way of stealing under and around it.

She had a career of her own to save. He couldn't involve her. He hadn't fully read the material in all the boxes, but if the rest was as incendiary as what he'd read so far, he could go down in flames along with Martin once the press found out. If she was just starting a new career, she didn't need her name connected to him and the scandal. Reluctantly he set her aside and returned to the pizza box. "You said Sid fired you. Was that a tiff, too?"

She didn't protest but returned to her stool and her pizza—no clinging vine, Mara Simon. He'd do well to watch his back if he really ticked her off. TJ chomped into his pizza crust.

"Yeah, Sid and I tiffed ourselves right out of marriage," she said dryly. "I learned from Irving, but I take my lessons to extremes. After Irving, the passive-aggressive whiner who never argued, I thought my screaming fights with Sid were refreshing."

"All of which is avoiding the point. What happens if he's kicked you off the film?" Solving Mara's problems seemed immensely more appealing than solving his own.

"What happens if your colonel discovers you have that box?" she countered, nodding at the neat stacks of notebooks she'd evidently been reading before he entered.

"I can't get fired. If I talk Cleo into your plan"—TJ pointed at the sketch—"will you be hired again?"

"Probably not. If I know Sid, he's planned this all along. Ian's probably in his pocket. They'll pad the expenses, pocket the difference, and tell the investors we broke even. He's about bankrupted the company with those tactics. Baby girlfriends and his nose snort a lot of cash."

"Damn, Pats, you sure can pick 'em." TJ slammed his plastic cup down and tried not to picture her with some old Hollywood fart who snorted coke and fondled kids. He wanted to rub his eyes to erase the image.

"Yeah, and you can't pick *any*," she retorted. "At least I've lived. What have you got to show for all your genius?"

Had him there. Truth and justice were pretty ephemeral at the best of times. What good had all his work in the Balkans done if Martin was letting the criminals go after TJ identified them? "Okay, let's get back to the problem. How do we get your job back?"

She wrinkled her pert little nose, and TJ had to admit it was an attractive nose.

"Get Ian drunk and pour him on a ship to China?" she suggested.

"Works for me. You find the ship, I'll find the bar." A good stiff drink would do him good, but then he'd have to go home and decide what to do about those boxes. Planning the demise of an evil little producer appealed to his more primitive instincts.

"Would you do that for me, even though I sicced the media on you?"

She sounded wistful, tugging at strings he resented having tugged, but no matter how hard he resisted her, he always succumbed sooner or later. Denying Mara was akin to denying himself.

He knew that if he were wise, he would stay out of her vicinity, but when had he ever been wise? He walked minefields for a living.

Deciding the box of evidence was no longer safe in his custody, TJ tucked it under his arm, caught Mara's shoulder, and nudged her toward the door. *Minimal contact,* his superego screamed, while his libido conjured visions of showers and comforting arms and naked breasts. "C'mon. You can't spend the night here. Let's play Bounce Ian Against the Wall and see what happens."

"This isn't high school, TJ," she warned, falling into step with him as he left the office, waiting patiently while he locked up and stored the box in his trunk. "You can't bully Ian and Sid into behaving."

"They're bullying you, aren't they?" he asked matter-of-factly, without a trace of anger.

Mara watched as TJ pocketed his keys and strode confidently toward the inn, his broad shoulders and tight ass swinging in the easy momentum of a born athlete. He'd been crushed and distraught two minutes ago but had switched into warrior mode in the blink of an eye. That's what confidence did for a person, she decided.

She'd never have that kind of confidence, but she damned well wouldn't let him run her life for her. She ran after him to catch up. "You're not my big brother, TJ."

It wasn't quite dark yet, and she could see his scarred eyebrow arch in wry humor that had her squirming in embarrassment. She flushed and tried to wriggle out of it. "You know what I mean."

"Yeah, I'd better not be your big brother." He picked up his pace. "So, what am I?"

"What *are* you?" She skipped a step and caught his arm before he had her running out of her shoes. The warmth generated where she touched his bare arm and the heated look he slanted her clarified the question, and she descended from embarrassment to smoldering desire. "Not boring, for certain." She dropped his arm like a hot potato. They didn't need sex confusing the issue here. They weren't officially lovers, but she certainly didn't regard him as a *brother*.

"Right. Not your brother and not boring," he agreed, as if that settled an argument. "But a bully," he reminded her, soliciting her opinion with a facsimile of intellectual interest.

"Probably. But a *good* bully," she amended, uncertain where he was going with this. "You just think that because you're bigger, that you can take charge."

"Is that what I do? Take charge?" he asked without any hint of distress, as if merely acquiring evidential information and not steamrolling down the hill toward Ian.

"Yes, you do, you know you do." Hurriedly she tried to explain before he pitched Ian out a window. "This is my problem, and I have to solve it."

He seemed to mull that over for a while, and she

breathed easier. Stepping briskly, she started down the drive to the inn at his side.

"All right, you get first chance at him. Then it's my turn," he said in satisfaction, as if they had similar goals in mind.

"TJ, you can't—"

But he could. She caught and tugged his arm, but he stalked up the steps as if she weighed no more than a shopping bag. She skipped a step to keep up, dropped his arm, and hurried to get ahead of him. Politely, he opened the door for her.

Still frantically trying to avoid bloodshed, Mara tripped over a suitcase as she entered. Overcorrecting, she nearly staggered into another before TJ caught her arm and helped her regain her balance. His ominous silence warned her even before she realized that the suitcases belonged to *her*.

Digging her fingernails into TJ's supportive arm, she looked up.

Irving was trundling his overnight bag down the stairs, and Ian stood at the bottom, directing the placement of her pillows and boxes of photos. Somewhere overhead, Constantina screamed Italian curses.

Icy terror momentarily froze her lungs, but TJ's locked jaw made it clear that he'd already switched to battle mode, and he didn't even know what was happening here.

Neither did she. "We're moving locations?" she inquired casually.

Ian quit speaking into his cell phone, gestured for Jim to place her box of favorite books beside the photos, and stepped over her pillows to greet her. "Sorry, Mara. We need space. Now that you're off the job, I figured we could use your room. Irving offered to see your stuff back home. I need Jim and the car here."

Her stomach dissolved in terror. Here it was, the moment she'd dreaded. *Homeless.*

She didn't bother looking at her ex. Five years of living with him had taught her his underhanded tactics well.

Rat fink Ian was the one she wanted nailed to the wall. She thought fast and furiously, searching for the producer's vulnerabilities, refusing to sink into crisis mode yet.

"I'm not going anywhere," she said calmly enough. TJ would probably have scars where her nails dug into him. True to his word, he let her speak first and remained blessedly silent, although she sensed her ex darting him nervous looks. Good, keep him occupied. "This is my project, and I'm here to see it stays under budget."

Ian shrugged. "Talk to Sid. He's my boss. I just do what he tells me."

TJ's muscles tensed beneath her hand, but she dug her nails deeper. "Tell Sid I'm the one who got the financing. The investors are expecting me at the helm, and if I tell them I'm off it, they'll pull their backing so fast, Sid's pockets will explode from the vacuum."

TJ snorted quietly, but she was too tense to smile. She had no idea if she could pull off her threat, but money was always a producer's Achilles' heel.

Ian looked uneasy but determined. "You and Sid fight that battle. I've got a film to do and people coming in, and I need the space."

"And I've already called your aunt Miriam," Irving intruded, sensing victory. "I told her we'd rent a van and drive back. They're thrilled to have you."

Cold pizza churned in her stomach, and Mara thought she would spew it up here, on the antique Persian rug in the B&B's elegant foyer.

"I'll call the security office," TJ intruded with such solemn aplomb that every head in the room swerved in his direction.

Mara stared at him wide eyed, wondering what the devil he was talking about.

He picked up her box of framed photos and tucked it under one arm as if it were her pillow. "The chain link will go across the walkway tomorrow, and I'll have guards posted on the perimeters. I told Cleo I'd keep her property clear of trespassers. She doesn't think of Mara as a trespasser, but the rest of you . . ." He shrugged and gathered her luggage.

He was scaring the shit out of Ian without laying a hand on him.

"We've got permission to use that beach," Ian shouted frantically, punching numbers into his phone. "You can't keep us off. I'll call the mayor."

Mara smiled and tucked her favorite lace pillows under her arm. "TJ has a federal injunction closing the access road, and Cleo owns all the property around it. Sail the crew in. I'm sure Glynis will love the adventure. And by the way, I have all the phone numbers in my PDA. You and Sid don't even know who the investors are. I'll let them get a good night's sleep before I call them."

In Italian, Mara called up to Constantina, who replied with a stream of invectives and a reassurance that Glynis would hire her—once she reamed Ian's black heart into an anatomically impossible edifice.

Reassured that her last remaining employee wouldn't be stranded, Mara grabbed the handle of her overnight bag and rolled it toward the door. Only then did she remember she had no car waiting outside and no chauffeur to pick up the rest of her luggage. And no place to go. The bottom of her stomach fell out, but she gritted her teeth and forced the panic down. *One foot in front of the other. Get out before anyone sees you shatter.*

"Have a good evening, gentlemen," TJ intoned in a toneless voice. "Tell Aunt Miriam that Tim McCloud sends his regards."

Mara choked on mixed laughter and sobs as he caught up with her, carrying her two heaviest bags along with the photos.

"Aunt Miriam will wet her undies if Irving delivers that message. You know that, don't you?" The overnight bag's wheels bumped down the stairs. She'd taken such good care of these damned Vuittons, making Jim handle them for her, hauling them in the limo instead of airplanes, and now they were dragging them up a seashell drive while her life crumbled under her. There was a metaphor in there somewhere.

"I don't believe I was anything but excessively polite to all your family," he said in that same grave voice he'd used all evening. She had an odd hunch TJ retreated behind politeness when confronted with turmoil. Excellent survival skill. She ought to try it sometime.

The big suitcases rattled as they progressed up the drive. "You're not only an infidel, but in my aunt's way of thinking, you're the infidel who cost the family Brad's genius." Mara regretted the words the instant they popped from her mouth. "I'm sorry—I should never have said that."

"It's all right. It's not anything I haven't thought myself."

If his voice had been without inflection earlier, it was sepulchral now. Her panic took a detour. "TJ, you're a brilliant man. You know full well Brad did what he did to himself. You were not my brother's keeper."

"I could have prevented it." Self-disgust welled in his voice, more terrible for the calm voice that had preceded it. Although he was hauling the heavier pieces of luggage, he caught up and stalked ahead of her.

"How? Locked him in his room?" she shouted after him.

"If I hadn't been blinded by hormones, he'd be solving world hunger today," he reminded her coldly, slowing his pace so she didn't have to shout.

The tears Mara had been holding back poured down her cheeks. Hands full, she made no attempt to wipe them away. "No, TJ," she said insistently. "Brad brimmed with idealism, but he would never have been strong enough to carry anything to completion."

"He would have grown stronger." TJ heard her tears, but he was wrestling with his own demons and didn't want them spilling over on her. "Brad just thought he had to carry the weight of the world alone, and the burden was too heavy. I should never have let him drive while he was upset."

The scene from that night seared TJ's memory. As a know-it-all Harvard sophomore on spring break, he'd driven over to the Simonettis' to see Patsy. He wasn't much of a ladies' man, but over Christmas he'd finally recognized the budding woman in the intelligent little girl he'd known for years. He'd spent hours on the phone with her, and the hours in between thinking of how they could be together.

In that spring night etched in his memory, she'd stood there in tight shorts and a tailored shirt, her tan bare legs looking like a college kid's dream come true. Her solemn green eyes had watched him come up the walk as if he were not only a man but the only man in the world. He hadn't been able to take his eyes off her to acknowledge his best friend standing on the doorstep beside her.

"He won't listen to me!" Brad cried as TJ walked up the cracked sidewalk. "I can't do this anymore. I'm never going to be a doctor, no matter how hard he pushes."

TJ had heard the argument before. Brad's grades at Harvard had never been as high as he expected, but Brad had always wanted to be a doctor. TJ figured grades wouldn't stop Brad from doing whatever he wanted once he stopped worrying and applied his mind to his goal. But right now TJ wasn't in a humor for school or studies. He didn't want to waste a single precious minute with the girl watching him with shining eyes and a love that turned everything he believed inside out.

He was afraid if he took her out in the car the way he felt now, he'd be in her pants before the night ended. She was only sixteen and didn't understand the hormones careening through his besotted veins. He loved her too much to push her too fast. He had to be the responsible one here.

"Then don't be a doctor," TJ said unsympathetically. "Are you planning on chaperoning us for the evening?"

That had been cruel, but he wanted Patsy to himself. He could listen to Brad's harangues anytime.

"Not if you give me your car keys. I'll go get Ben and Jerry's."

That should have signaled Brad's state of desperation. Not only did Brad never waste money on frivolities, but he was a lousy driver and rarely drove alone. But Patsy broke into a broad smile, and the need for her kiss obliterated TJ's ability to reason. He threw Brad the keys to his BMW just to get rid of him.

Seconds later, Brad roared off, leaving TJ and Patsy to stroll the nighttime city streets. TJ didn't remember his best friend existed as he pulled Patsy into his embrace in the shadows between the streetlights. She wrapped her arms around his shoulders and kissed him with such soul-piercing joy that his heart rate escalated to explosive. He'd kissed plenty of girls before, but none had touched the empty places inside him as Patsy did.

His only fear was of his palms sweating as he slid his hands beneath her shirt and touched her braless breasts for the first time. Her muffled moan of surprise and excitement wreaked havoc with his plans for restraint.

And then the quiet rumble of distant traffic erupted in a squeal of tires and brakes, followed by the crash that shattered their universe.

Leaping apart, staring at each other in terror, they wordlessly broke into a run toward the road Brad would have taken. Racing into the unlighted intersection, TJ panicked at the sight of the familiar BMW smashed against the lamppost. Recklessly he ran across the road, dodging skidding traffic and slamming brakes.

Before he could reach the opposite corner, a spark from a downed electric wire caught in the gas spilling from the punctured tank, and the street exploded in flames. Brad never had a chance.

The anguish of that fatal scene still had the power to twist his heart in knots.

And here TJ was again, walking a dark street with Patsy,

contemplating kisses he didn't deserve from a woman who felt like his missing half.

"TJ."

He bumped into Mara before he realized she'd quit walking. She set down her pillows and touched a hand to his chest, forcing him to halt or plow over her. He didn't want to halt. He wanted to keep on walking, march right on out of here, head for Mexico and never look back.

"TJ, *nothing* you could have done would have saved him."

He wanted to believe that, wanted to forget that night and every other by burying himself in her welcoming arms and making the world go away. He couldn't tell if the exotic scent filling the night was from her or the magnolias, but it wrapped him in temptation.

"He's gone and I'm here," he answered doggedly, if illogically. He never talked about this, didn't want to talk about it now, not on top of everything else. A dam inside him strained on the edge of breaking, and talk would only unleash the flood. "It's too late to do anything now. Come on, let's get moving."

"TJ."

She dropped the handle of her suitcase, and it rolled off the walk and tumbled over. She didn't notice but put both her hands on his chest, where they burned through his shirt.

"He left a note, TJ." Tears still choked her voice, but she spoke firmly. "Before you came over, he'd told my dad that he wasn't good enough to be a doctor, that he hated Harvard, that he wanted to teach."

TJ tried to push her aside, but his muscles wouldn't work. Her quiet words were forcing the cracks in his hard shell wider. Brad had always wanted to be a doctor, for as long as TJ had known him. Throughout high school, that had been all Brad had ever talked about, the reason he'd studied constantly, the reason he could never fail, because he wanted to save the world. Something had changed in college, but TJ had been too busy with sports and studies and girls to listen.

"He would have made a fine teacher," he growled in defense of his friend.

"Yes, he would have been a great teacher," she said softly, "but my father wanted him to be a *doctor*. Brad tried to tell him he couldn't take the stress of Harvard, that he'd never handle medical school. They'd skirmished over this before. That night Dad told Brad he wouldn't pay his tuition unless he agreed to study medicine. Brad was panicking, as he always did when they fought. I was tired of the arguments and wanted you to make the world go away for a little while. So I let him go, just the same as you did."

Her sadness dropped like a pall over TJ. He'd known Brad was agitated, but he'd brushed it aside without thinking beyond the nuisance his friend was making of himself. He certainly hadn't imagined the tragic results.

Not knowing what else to do, TJ stood there, suitcases in hand, staring down at his teenage dream, who was trying to unlock the chains of guilt that shackled him by taking them on herself.

"Brad wrote a note before you arrived, TJ, although I didn't know that until later. He would have died that night whether you'd been there or not."

Suicide. TJ let that horrifying revelation sink in. Deliberate suicide and not just a tragic accident.

Closing his eyes against the stab of agony, TJ wrestled with a fear he'd known all along but had refused to accept. His best friend had killed himself, believing TJ had deserted him.

Relentlessly, Mara continued. "TJ, it's not your fault. Brad was distraught that night. If you loved him as much as I did, then you have to believe Brad didn't know the hell he condemned us to when he drove so recklessly."

She stroked his cheek while she caught her breath, and TJ shuddered beneath the tenderness of the touch he didn't deserve.

"I try to remember him as the loving brother who taught me the joy of books," she finished softly, "and who did what he could to look after me when our parents fell down on the job. But in no way can you ever share the blame in what he chose to do."

With a sigh that ripped his heart out, TJ hefted the suitcases and started walking again. "Stand forewarned, Patsy. I'm a lousy friend."

TWENTY

They walked to TJ's car in silence. He heaved one suitcase in the trunk of the Taurus with the evidence box and the other in the backseat, tucking her boxes and pillows around them. Mara didn't know where he was taking her and didn't want to know. She just wanted to subside into misery and wallow for a little while.

But TJ was just as miserable, and the part of her that had once adored him couldn't let him suffer any more than he already had. She wasn't much of a caretaker or nurturer, but TJ was a part of her she didn't want harmed.

"What will you do about the colonel?" she asked quietly as the car rolled smoothly through dark streets in the direction of the causeway.

He didn't answer immediately, and his silence worried her. "If he's guilty of covering up any of those things in those notebooks—" she began.

"It's not that simple," he answered curtly, staring ahead.

"Explain," she demanded. "It looks to me like you're covering up evidence. Hand it in and let someone else decide the truth."

"You're a fine one to preach about truth." His fingers tightened on the steering wheel, and the car picked up speed over the empty causeway.

"When have I ever lied to you?"

"What do you think that hairpiece is? The padded bras? The nose job and dyed hair and glue-on lashes? You've become so fake, I don't think you could see the truth if you walked into it."

Mara reeled with shock at this unanticipated attack from a man she'd trusted to defend her. "And that makes you perfect, I suppose?" she retaliated, seeking a means of returning the hurt. "You were born with looks, brains, and money," she continued in scorn, "so you never had to pretend or fudge the truth. You just walk away when things get tough."

In the back of her mind, a little voice screamed that she was on to something here, but she wasn't listening to little voices through the red rage of anguish.

"Money hasn't bought you happiness, has it?" TJ said coldly. "And what does beauty get you? Shallow friends? Or is that what money buys? All the money and looks in the world mean nothing without honesty. Where are your so-called friends now?"

"I thought I was sitting next to one." The pain hurt too badly for tears, and Mara whispered the reply. "Turn around and take me back. I'll sleep in Constantina's room." She stared out the window at the ghostly ocean lapping against the causeway and wished she were dead.

"I'm sorry. That was uncalled for," TJ admitted hoarsely. He didn't turn the car around but eased up on the speed as they reached the island.

"You have every right to say what you think." She wrapped her arms around her pillow and wouldn't look at him, although every pore of her body was aware of him and their destination. This was *Tim*. He wouldn't have said those things to her without reason. Was that how he saw her? As shallow? Had she turned into a female version of her exes?

"I hate seeing what they do to you," he growled. "I think you're too smart and too real to put up with that crap back there."

"You're a fine one to talk," she said, still hurting and not wanting to think about his accusations. "You're letting some trumped-up punk in uniform tell you what to do. Hell, for all I know, you let Brad's death break us up and steer your course all these years. You can't punish yourself for what either Brad or your damned colonel did. Accuse me of selfishness for surviving, if you like, but I always figured I can't do anyone good if I'm dead."

She'd chosen to celebrate life, and he'd chosen to study death. Nothing could cement their differences more.

The car jolted onto the sandy lane leading back to Cleo's house and the beach. Mara thought he meant to ignore her again, and burning resentment built inside her, but TJ spoke before she could formulate the words to express it.

The gentle lap of waves upon the distant beach and the hoot of an owl were the only other sounds besides TJ's quiet voice. "There's more at stake than the colonel's career."

She should have known. "Do I want to hear it?"

"No."

She was still bleeding from a dozen verbal wounds and internally hemorrhaging over psychological ones. She wanted to be held and loved and understood, but she didn't know if that would happen in her lifetime. TJ's curt reply jarred her out of her self-absorption, to recognize what her instincts had been trying to tell her.

The wretched oaf was driving her away again. He was waiting for her to throw things at him and walk out, to resolve his need to protect by leaving, so he didn't have to dump his fears on her.

Lifting her chin, Mara glared at the headlighted lane. She'd be damned if she'd repeat the performance of that ninny he'd called an assistant.

He slowed the car at the juncture of Cleo's drive and the access road. "I can take you to Cleo's, or you can go home with me. Your choice."

"Let's not wake the kid. I can sleep on your couch," she replied stubbornly.

He shot her a look and eased the car down the bumpy road. "I'm still working on that image of you following me into the shower. Be wary."

Something hungry and desperate in his voice matched

the gaping wounds in her, and Mara relaxed. "Comfort sex," she said bluntly. "I've done that. I've done a whole lot of things the brave and noble Boy Scout Tim wouldn't approve of."

"The Boy Scout is a figment of your overactive imagination—always was." He braked the car at the foot of the excavation. "I hope you have what you need in the overnight bag. I'm not carting those packing boxes you call suitcases over the dune."

Mara pondered the inferences of his not being a Boy Scout as they trudged through the sand carrying her overnight case and pillows. Did that mean he wanted to sleep with her? Expected to sleep with her? Would jump her bones the instant they walked through the door?

That idea shivered *her* bones nicely, but what did bones know? He'd just insulted everything about her for reasons known only to his inscrutable mind. Sleeping with a powder keg like TJ wouldn't be conducive to logical forethought or action. It would simply be a reaction to the day's disasters. She didn't do things like that.

She'd done it with him a little over a week ago.

He flipped on a light switch as they entered, illuminating the Spartan interior of futon and wicker chairs, without a personal item in sight. Switching on a lamp, Mara decorated the futon with her lace pillows and felt better.

"I've always thought you were beautiful."

Mara swung around to find TJ's broad shoulders still blocking the doorway. Suitcase in hand, he didn't appear drunk, didn't give her a steamy look or use a sexy voice. He simply looked at her as she was, in all her rumpled, tearstained mess, stated a truth, and shattered her fractured heart into ten million pieces.

"And now?" She hoped she kept the quiver from her voice.

"I prefer full-grown women to teenagers," he answered gravely. "You can have the room upstairs. I'll take this up." Without waiting for a reply, he hauled her bag up the stairs.

Damn the man. That was probably as close to flattery as she'd ever pry from him.

She didn't need flattery. She needed honesty. TJ was never less than honest. He'd thought skinny, plain, four-eyed Patsy was beautiful.

Of course, that didn't mean he liked her better now. He just liked *women* better.

The man would drive her insane.

She was Patricia Amara Simonetti, and she knew how to make his clock tick. She was perfectly capable of discovering why TJ McCloud had taken to driving women out of his life. Then she could return the favor and drive *him* insane.

"Your couch will do," she called after him. "I don't need to disturb your privacy." Clutching one pillow under her arm, she tucked trailing strands of hair behind her ear, and rubbed beneath her eyes to remove any smeared mascara.

"There's a cot the kids use in the spare bedroom." He turned right into the first doorway. "I'll be fine."

Mara followed him into the bedroom and fell in love. Floor-to-ceiling windows overlooked the ocean, letting in ocean breezes and lifting the gauzy draperies. "I could live in here," she murmured, drifting to the cushioned window seat, impervious to the tension vibrating between them. "The view is spectacular. How could you ever leave?"

"I've seen spectacular views," he answered gravely from behind her. "None of them had anything to hold me until now."

The eternal flicker of hope grew brighter as she stared over the moonlit sea and let his words seep in. She had no reason to believe he meant that she gave him reason to linger after he'd just done his best to drive her off. She wouldn't demand an explanation. She'd just let hope smooth its way through the many and varied hurts of the day to start the healing process.

"Could we lay Brad to rest and start all over?" she asked wistfully.

"I think you've got two too many husbands on the scene right now," he said bluntly. "Let's lay them to rest first."

A wry smile tugged at her lips at the image of whacking both Irving and Sid with a shovel and burying them in that big pit on the dune. "Is that a promise?"

A peacock shrieked through the resulting silence. She thought he wouldn't answer, but TJ set her suitcase down with a thump.

"I'm not in a position to promise anything, but I figure I can lay a few ghosts to rest. Get some sleep, and we'll talk it over in the morning."

Clinging to the windowsill, Mara let him walk away. She wanted to be strong. She wanted to handle things herself.

But she had an inkling of suspicion that she and TJ working together might be far more effective than either of them alone, and he might need her aid as much as she did his. That's what friends were for, right?

The idea of trusting the reins of her life to someone else's hands terrified her almost as much as risking her heart to the man who'd already broken it once.

"That old black magic that you do so well . . ." drifted up the stairs, belted out in a husky voice that raised every hair on his body and shot pure testosterone straight to TJ's morning arousal.

He groaned, tried to turn on his side, and almost fell out of the narrow cot. Floundering awake, he collapsed on his back, staring at the early morning light on the ceiling, nursing a straining erection, while he tried to stir his bloodless brain.

Mara. If his thoughts weren't so dislocated to the wrong part of his anatomy, he'd smile at the ancient lyrics pouring from his normally silent kitchen. He'd forgotten that about her—she had a lovely voice, even if the notes tended to miss more often than not. He could remember her tagging behind him and Brad, singing advertising jingles to make them laugh.

Remembering the good times eased some of last night's agony. Maybe if he listened to Mara long enough, the good memories would override the horrible ones. He'd like to believe that.

He wondered what the devil the woman was doing in his kitchen at this hour. Once the question took root, his curiosity grew. With Mara, anything was possible.

With Mara, every day could be a new puzzle to solve.

Grunting at that anarchic thought, TJ rolled out of bed and staggered for the shower. Life got too confusing when half of him wanted to explore the intricacies of a woman's mind and the other half hungered for mindless rutting.

Showered, shaved, and with a clearer vision of the day ahead, TJ followed the aroma of coffee and bacon down the stairs—and out the front door.

Figuring that made about as much sense as anything else in his life these days, he shoved open the screen to investigate.

Her natural curls springing exuberantly in a halo around her face, Mara looked up from her coffee with a blinding smile that would have knocked his socks off had he been wearing any.

"Got any more of that?" Feeling as if he'd been on a two-day binge, TJ collapsed in the wicker chair he could have sworn had been in the front room last night, and for the second time that morning he tried to orient himself.

Mara filled a second cup from his Mr. Coffee carafe. "I have a plan," she announced in satisfaction.

Sipping cautiously, eyeing the colorful tablecloth he hadn't known he possessed draped over a table he couldn't identify, TJ listened. The lapping of the waves against the shore a few yards away and the beautiful woman amazingly occupying his breakfast table lulled him into believing domesticity was worth considering.

"I'll start by calling the film backers here on the East Coast. I'll tell them Sid is destroying a delicate ecosystem in a manner that would give the film really bad PR, that I'm working with the locals to prevent harm, and that they need to twist Sid's arm to do the right thing."

She was so pleased with herself that TJ couldn't point out all the obvious flaws in her plan. Patsy never had grasped the venality of human nature. Match ecosystems against money, and nature lost every time. Her investors would follow the money and figure any publicity was good publicity. Sipping his coffee, TJ realized he didn't want her sunny openness to change, even if he could cheerfully throttle her when she applied it to her bloodsucking ex-husbands.

"That's a start," he agreed noncommittally.

She crunched a piece of bacon and poked at her PDA with the handle of her spoon. "While I'm doing that, you need to call up one of those reporters hanging around and tell him to pick up that box of military stuff."

He sat up straight, nearly spewing his coffee through his nose. "*Reporters?* You want me to hand a ticking bomb to reporters?"

She looked up with interest. "What kind of bomb?"

TJ ran his hand over his face and reached for his coffee. "A bomb that could explode the career of a good man and take down all his associates with him."

"That's not for you to decide," she said calmly, buttering her biscuit.

"It's for *reporters* to decide?"

"One of the balances of power in our country is freedom of the press. Why have you been stalling over giving that box to the authorities?"

Because Martin *was* the authority. Mara beamed at him as if she'd read his mind.

"I don't trust the Defense Department," he admitted grumpily.

"And you can't hand the evidence to the colonel if he's guilty. But if he's *not* guilty, maybe the press can uncover that faster than we can. We certainly won't have to worry about them covering it up."

Another of his concerns. If Martin was guilty, TJ wanted to know, no matter how much damage it inflicted to his own career.

"Something dire is likely to happen to that stuff if you leave it around too long," she continued, "or is that what you're hoping will happen? If the box conveniently disappears, you won't have to deal with it?"

TJ gulped more coffee. "There's more where that came from," he growled with surliness. Leave it to Patsy to reduce an issue to the lowest common denominator. For the first time in his life he'd been letting justice take a backseat to his doubts—doubts about Martin, about their friendship, about the consequences of uncovering the truth.

Helping himself to a freshly baked biscuit and liberally smearing it with jelly, TJ debated ignoring her admonition or acting upon it. The beeps as Mara dialed her cell phone and started all-out war clashed with the peace of the lapping surf.

"That box could cause a feeding frenzy," he pointed out when she hung up after the first call.

She perked right up at that thought. "Lots of reporters?"

He should have realized they operated on opposite wavelengths. "I'll have to hide in the jungle. Cleo and Jared will have to leave town." Of course, he'd already told them to do that. "The newspapers could frame Martin before he has a chance to build a case."

"Forget Martin," she ordered, stabbing a pencil into her hair to scratch her head. "Let justice take its course. From what I could tell of those notebooks, if you hand them over to the government, they'll bury them so deep they'll never see the light of day. That kind of criminal activity on the part of our military would be a political debacle. If you want the truth, give them to someone who'll see that they reach court."

"Reporters are sensationalist leeches." TJ tried not to shout.

Mara slammed down her cup of coffee and leaned over the tiny table so her nose practically poked his. "Defense Department lackeys are elitist assholes."

A smile quirked the corner of his mouth. He remembered this game. TJ leaned over until their noses touched. "The media feeds pablum to the masses."

"Are you going to kiss me now, or will I have to grab you by the ears?" she whispered against his mouth.

TJ grabbed her arms and hauled her across the table. Cups smashed and jam smeared, but he had her coffee-flavored mouth against his and the world went away.

TWENTY-ONE

A cough intruded. TJ ignored it. Why had he never realized coffee tasted far better on Mara's lips than in a cup? She kissed with the same passion she displayed in everything she did—full-speed ahead, no questions asked, and with the inventiveness of her Gemini mind. She had his shirt buttons unfastened before his thoughts had traveled past the rich silk of her hair and the wicked heat of her tongue.

"I really hate to intrude on this poignant moment, but there's a padlock on your office and a military notice declaring it off-limits, so I don't have anywhere else to wait."

Mara gave a little screech and jerked away. TJ growled and turned to glare at the reporter. "Roger, you're in serious danger of losing your head if you stay there."

Roger shrugged. "I'll take my chances. What's with the padlock?"

"Militaristic pigs," Mara whispered defiantly.

"Rumormongers," TJ retorted, but his heart wasn't in the game any longer. Pinching the bridge of his nose, he tried to steady his whirling brain.

"Justice," Mara reminded him in a whisper Roger couldn't hear. "It's not about Martin and it's not about you. It's about justice."

She was right. Betraying a friend or destroying his career were all about him and not about the truth he'd spent his life defending.

Time to wake up and smell the roses. The world didn't revolve around him.

TJ hated hurting his family, who thought he walked on water, but he couldn't stand in the way of justice if those boxes would convict a man who freed murderers. Maybe Martin had thought he was protecting national security or his counterparts in other armed forces. It wasn't up to him to decide. And it wasn't up to the military to bury.

Mara's uncomplicated outlook untangled the knot he'd been tied in.

"There's a key hanging on a hook by the back door." TJ bathed his weary soul in the pride gleaming in Mara's eyes, ignoring Roger's suddenly alert stance. "There's a tag on it for a storage unit up in Charleston. The contents may or may not be helpful. I'm relying on you to keep me out of this for as long as you can." The anonymous storage unit distanced his connection to the material, but the box in his car didn't. He'd figure out how to get that to Roger some other time.

"Far as I know, you're honeymooning with your Hollywood starlet," Roger answered. "I just stopped by to wish you well."

"Yeah, tell the creep from *People* that we're an item."

Mara's lips turned up in an engaging grin at his sarcastic tone, and TJ didn't resent his descent into rumormongering while basking in her approval.

Roger coughed again as they shut him out, and shuffled his feet in embarrassment. "Well, you kids have fun. I'm off to Charleston."

"Have a safe trip." TJ didn't watch him lope around the corner of the house but kept his attention focused on Mara's shining eyes. Her pride in him almost made decimating his career worth it. He wouldn't contemplate what would happen should Martin actually be guilty.

"You're doing the right thing," she murmured, her cheeks becoming pink beneath his stare.

"Yeah, I always wanted to be a beach bum," he agreed. At her startled look, he relented. No point in adding to her troubles by explaining he'd just burned his bridges, and the walls would come tumbling down shortly. "I better call Jared and tell him and Cleo to skedaddle. I have a feeling privacy will be in short supply."

Her eyes narrowed into a speculative look that TJ knew to be wary of. "What?" he demanded. He might want to carry her up the stairs and bang her brains out right now, but Mara's brains had a dangerous tenacity he respected.

"If we don't need to worry about Jared and Cleo's privacy . . ." She halted, still thinking furiously.

"Forget it, whatever you're planning. Stick to calling investors. Your ex and his cronies can find some other beach to fry."

He started to stand up, but Mara slammed the coffeepot on the table, startling him into sitting again.

"That's *my* film! Sid's just looking for an excuse to pull Glynis out from under me and stick her in one of his losers. That film is my one and only chance of getting the company out from under his thumb. I won't let it die. Too many people are depending on me. You could pull that injunction and let me take dozers in there."

Out of the corner of his eye, TJ could see Roger hurrying back down the path, key—and TJ's future—in hand. Forensic anthropology might not be glamorous, but his nomadic existence had allowed him to save a good deal of money. The market had been kind to him, and he'd found safe places for most of his assets. He wouldn't starve anytime soon, even after his career crumbled.

But all his funds put together wouldn't be enough to save Mara's film if her vicious ex meant to steal it from her.

She watched him with hope in her eyes, as if he could really be the star of her film. Well, he wouldn't have anything better to do shortly. TJ shoved back his chair. "Okay, let me talk to Jared and Cleo. There may be a thing or two we can try."

* * *

Oh, damn, she loved the man so much, she thought her heart would burst with it.

Sitting back, Mara stared out over the ocean as TJ disappeared inside. He'd listened to her. He'd respected her opinion enough to go against his own wishes by turning those boxes over to a reporter. No one had ever valued her opinion that highly before.

Mara sighed and toyed with her cold biscuit. Her head had just swelled with pride there for a moment. She'd revert to form shortly. Clinging to an ancient infatuation probably wasn't healthy for anyone concerned.

TJ returned carrying his cordless phone and two more coffee mugs to replace the ones he'd smashed. "Cleo heard about the padlock on the office. I had to explain about the colonel. She and Jared want to stay and help me fight whoever shows up next."

"What did you tell them?" Mara accepted a mug and poured cold coffee into it. She hadn't forgotten the head-spinning kiss earlier, but she figured it was safer not to encourage fantasies.

"Told them I'd taken care of it. With the boxes gone, Defense can search all they like. I have nothing to hide. Jared's eager for any excuse to pull Cleo and Matty out of here, so he's taking my word for it. He suggested bringing in Clay to help you, and he may have a point."

"Little Tommy?" she asked in incredulity, remembering a curly-haired little brat with an evil genius for destruction. Thomas Clayton McCloud—hadn't she heard that name recently?

Slopping coffee into his cup and leaning against the porch rail, TJ studied her. "Say what you will about him, but he can dissect a problem with razor-sharp accuracy. He's a computer whiz with access to things I don't even want to think about, and he thinks outside the box. We may be too close to the problem."

"You don't think my calling the investors will work," she stated for him.

"Nope. Their money is on Sid and Glynis. You're an unknown factor."

"I hate it when you're right." She grimaced at the coffee and flung the contents over the rail. "So where does that leave us? If I can't influence the investors to get my job back, how does Clay fit in?"

"I've got one or two ideas, but let's get Clay on this first. It's too early in California to give him a ring. Can your people be trusted to keep the film on schedule without you? Or will Ian start running up expenses? Should I hire more security and block them out?"

She did adore the way he treated her, as if she knew as much as he did and more. Why couldn't she have found a man like that the first time around?

She had, but he'd walked out on her. She'd better remember that for future reference.

"I've reconfigured the schedule to work around the dig for the next few days while we're waiting for the ship replica to arrive. I've got good people on this. They'll be all right if Ian doesn't interfere and my director doesn't decide to create his own island idyll out of the jetty. They really don't need me. I'm available to help you with your research, if you'd like."

TJ's smoldering gaze suddenly blazed like hot coals, and Mara thought she'd melt beneath the heat of it. She knew exactly where his thoughts had traveled the instant she'd said she was available. She quit breathing while her mind frantically sought excuses.

"We have a few hours while California time catches up with us," he said without inflection, not moving from his relaxed position against the rail. "How would you like to spend them?"

Butterflies flooded Mara's stomach. This was it, the moment of decision. Did she have the courage to take up the challenge? Could she risk her heart again? Court a third disaster?

What did she have to lose? Certainly not her self-respect.

Rising, she stepped so close that she pressed TJ back

against the rail. His khakis rubbed her capris, and her unharnessed breasts were crushed against his cotton polo. She ran manicured nails over his clenched jaw and triumphed in the instant press of his arousal against her belly. She drank in the sea scent of his subtle shaving lotion and absorbed the faint tingle of stubble beneath her fingers. "Let's spend the next hours as Scarlett and Rhett," she murmured, standing on tiptoe so she could reach his mouth.

"That almost makes sense." Without further quibble, TJ buried his fingers in her hair, lowered his mouth to hers, and set about devouring her.

The ocean breeze blew the gauzy curtains across the bed, cooling their perspiring bodies. Mara tried to clear her head and schedule the rest of the day, but the sensations TJ had created inside her wound her tighter than a coiled spring. The solid muscle of his thigh pressed against hers. Conscious that he was wide awake and breathing as hard as she was, she couldn't think of anything else but the perfection of his lovemaking.

He'd carried her up the damned stairs. She wasn't any petite lightweight, but he'd carried her up the stairs as if she truly were Scarlett and he Rhett.

And then he'd slowly made love to her as if they were the last two people on earth and had the rest of their lives to do it in. It made her realize Sid and Irving had always made love to her as if they'd penciled it into their day along with their vitamins and lunch.

She didn't think there was a place on her body that TJ hadn't touched or kissed. Just thinking of what he'd done made the juices run.

"Did I see a whole box of Trojans in that drawer?" she inquired, staring at the shadowed ceiling, afraid to gaze over the vast expanse of bronzed chest so close beside her she could feel his heat.

"Yeah, I wasn't taking any chances." He didn't turn either, but his thigh inched closer to hers.

Daringly Mara dropped her gaze to his groin area. "I think it will take a very *big* warrior to cover that."

"As long as it fits." TJ shifted abruptly, hauled her on top of his hard abdomen, and drank in the sight of her with a ravenous gaze.

Excitement pooled in the pit of Mara's belly as TJ curled reverent hands around her breasts and studied her otherwise skinny frame. She saw nothing but approval in his eyes, and desire bubbled through her blood.

Constantina had been right. It took a hot man to melt her cold reserve. She needed to feel desired before she could desire in return. TJ made her feel as if she really were the most beautiful woman in the world.

"I think I'll burn those harnesses you call bras," he said gravely, caressing her nipples into aching buds of need. "This is what I want to see when I look at you."

She'd happily burn the bras herself if it meant he'd keep touching her like that. "I can knot my hair, wear a lab coat, and not wear any underwear," she whispered wickedly, leaning over to nibble his lip.

"Promise?" he demanded, arching his hips so she could feel the brush of his erection against her buttocks.

"Oh, yeah." Fastening her mouth to his, Mara rose up on her knees and adjusted her position.

TJ swallowed her gasp as he caught her hips and thrust deep inside her again.

They'd waited seventeen years for this moment. There was no need to hurry.

The ringing of the phone echoed up from both the kitchen and the receiver they'd left outside.

"How long did it take for them to find this number?" Mara murmured sleepily into TJ's shoulder.

"It's unlisted, but the colonel found Jared's." TJ didn't want to think about the colonel or the rest of the world right now. He was busy having an out-of-body experience. Or maybe an out-of-mind experience. Whatever, he floated weightlessly on a river of satiation. "Maybe it's a wrong number."

Mara snuggled closer, and the sensation of her aroused nipples stroking his side ignited a nerve running straight to his groin.

"It's either Jared or Clay," he decided. "They have no respect."

She pressed a kiss to his nipple that had his hair standing on end again.

"Your stomach's rumbling," she murmured. "You'll have to get up and answer it just so you'll get fed."

"I can eat anytime."

"The corollary being we can't mate like bunnies anytime?"

TJ chuckled and rolled away from temptation to fish on the floor for his shorts.

And yelped when she nipped at his derriere.

"Bunnies must have teeth for some reason," she said innocently, rolling from the other side of the bed.

He was losing his head over a crazy woman.

But he'd killed his sane, logical career. Why not indulge in insanity for a while?

TWENTY-TWO

"This better be good," TJ growled into the receiver he'd grabbed from the porch and carried to the kitchen.

"Jared said this is my opportunity to watch the Intimidator in action."

"Clay." TJ halted Mara's teasing kisses at the back of his neck by catching her waist and lifting her to the kitchen counter. He retreated to the stove with the phone while she stuck out her tongue at him. Looking at Mara all tousled and wearing nothing but one of his shirts was not conducive to concentration. "What can I do for you, bro?"

His youngest brother made a rude noise. "Come off that cloud, big brother. While you've been saving the world, I've been taking care of myself. Right now I'm just bored and looking for some fun and games."

TJ ran his hand over the back of his neck while Mara watched him with eager, expectant eyes. He didn't know a damned thing about the film industry, but Clay did. He lived in L.A., worked on computer film animation, and knew everyone. "What do you know about Sid Rosenthal?" Mara's eyes widened, but TJ didn't answer the question in them.

Clay made another rude noise. "He digs young girls and blows his nose. Why?"

TJ grimaced, wishing he didn't have to do this with Mara listening. "It's a long story. How bored are you?"

"Bored enough to fly out there. Jared said he and Cleo

are doing the Disney thing, and I could crash in their place. Will that help?"

Clay had been more cynical than usual since the dot-com collapse had taken out his high-tech software business. Maybe he needed this distraction.

"It might," he grudgingly admitted. "Weather's fine. You can keep your tan in shape. Find out what you can on Rosenthal first."

"Can't ask for more. See you soon." Clay hung up with his usual lack of polite farewell.

Take care of Mara's problem first, TJ figured. The vultures wouldn't start circling until Roger had time to sort through the boxes. Having Clay at his side when the shit hit might not accomplish anything but family solidarity, but it sounded as if Clay could use a little of that, too.

"Well?" Mara leapt from the counter, bare legs flashing as TJ hung up the phone.

"He's bored and coming out to visit." TJ would worry about his genius brother's other agendas when he arrived.

"Why?"

"With Clay, it's hard to say. He doesn't like your ex, though." TJ watched her carefully. Intimacy didn't give him the ability to read her mind. She'd done a lot of living since he'd known her last. He had difficulty imagining the Patsy he'd known hooked up with mean-spirited assholes like her exes.

Mara shrugged and began filling the coffeemaker. "Sid has a brilliant mind. He's just snorted it down the drain. One of his films bombed a few years back, and rather than learning from the experience, he crashed and burned. Stupid me, I thought I could save him. That was before his baby starlet phase."

He heard the betrayal and disappointment in her voice. TJ's instant reflex was to smash Sid's face in, but he was learning that he wasn't the sole arbiter of justice in the world. "I've got to go into town and find out what's happening with my office. Want to come with me? Or stay here and call your money men?"

She eyed him with a speculation that made him aware she was wearing his shirt and he wasn't. Damn, but he'd never had a woman affect him like this one.

"I'll do some more research on the island and hope I can solve your mystery. I want to be able to move in my trucks as soon as I settle this fight with Sid."

"It's still a gravesite," he warned, glad to be back on familiar ground.

"No, it's not. It's a bunch of bones washed up by a hurricane," she countered, filling her cup and dancing off while he filled his. "I'm moving in my trucks, McCloud," she sang as she raced for the stairs.

He just might let her if she kept that up.

"Search the office," TJ offered blandly to the government lackey waiting for him in town. "Can't imagine what you think you'll find aside from old bones, but I have nothing to hide." He tried not to think of the box still in his trunk. He needed to get that to Roger when he had a chance. If the Defense Department was sending spooks down to collect material, things were looking far darker than he'd expected.

He didn't want to spend half his life in jail for concealing evidence or for aiding and abetting criminals. Career suicide was one thing, but with Mara in his life now, he was ready to fight for his freedom. With a possible enemy in sight, adrenaline shot through his bloodstream. He wouldn't let the colonel or anyone else take him down with them if he could help it.

"It's just routine," the man in the brown suit claimed as he shoved past the office door and scanned the dismal interior. "The colonel said he'd given you some national-security-related material to destroy, but we don't have a record that it went through normal channels."

"I left it with military staff, as instructed." TJ scanned the office rapidly, praying Mara hadn't left any notebooks lying about. "I've been in Africa and several other places since then. I'm certainly not sitting on anything." *Anymore,* he amended silently.

"McCloud!"

TJ turned to intercept the suave *People* reporter while Brown Suit poked through his boxes of reference material. Today, Paul Harris wore Tommy Hilfiger shorts and a Hawaiian print shirt.

"Any comment on your relationship with Mara Simon?"

"She's an old friend," TJ answered solemnly, crossing his arms and guarding the doorway.

"I heard Sid fired her from the film because of you." The reporter scribbled in a notebook and flipped a page for his list of questions.

"You heard wrong." TJ wasn't loquacious on his best days. He could be downright contrary on his worst.

"The production crew said she left with you. Where is she now?"

"Do you know where your significant other is right now?"

Harris grinned. "Tanning at poolside. Want to try again?"

"Nope. If you'll excuse me, I have company." TJ closed the door in the reporter's smirking face and followed Brown Suit back to the inner office.

"I trust you didn't frighten off my secretary." TJ scanned the floor, not finding anything out of order.

"I told her you'd call when you want her to come back in."

"She's a kid and not the world's most efficient receptionist, but I'm sure she can tell you that there's nothing in here but the work from my dig site." Knock on wood that Brown Suit wasn't interested in digging deep enough to know the kid had just started. If the spook started talking to Leona, he was in deep shit.

Actually, he was already in deep shit. He'd just be deeper.

"Yeah, well, you know the routine. Sorry to bother

you. That what you dug up?" He pointed at the skeleton hanging in the corner, one of its fingers raised.

"This is what I'm working on." TJ showed him the deteriorating gray bones in his workbox. "In the ground for maybe sixty years. Male, mid-twenties, Caucasian. Sound like anyone you know?"

"You tell all that from those bits of bone?" Impressed, Brown Suit shrugged and walked away. "Guess you got more to do than play cops and robbers with old files. Sorry about the inconvenience."

TJ had been itching for a confrontation, but he supposed keeping things quiet would be preferable—for a while. They'd be down on him like a ton of bricks once the story broke. What the hell monster had he let loose by trusting Roger with those boxes?

"No problem. Give my regards to the colonel." Letting the spook out, TJ breathed a sigh of relief. Alone now, he could plan his battle with Sid unhampered.

It took TJ the better part of the day to call Clay back and put his scheme in motion, but he'd done what he could by the time Mara returned to the office with a file of notes she'd taken at the library and excitement in her eyes. She must have found something in her research.

He figured he must have looked grim when she entered because she wrinkled her upturned nose at him, made her fish face, and kissed his cheek. She dodged when he reached for more.

"There are reporters with television cameras out there, and I'm not appearing in the street looking as if I've just climbed out of bed," she said in explanation when TJ raised his eyebrow at her.

She'd pulled her curls into a thick swirl at the back of her head, covered them with a wide-brimmed floppy hat, and donned a pair of overlarge sunglasses in classic movie-star-in-disguise manner. TJ contemplated pouty lips bereft of her usual red lipstick and lost the path of his thoughts. "You look as if you just got off the plane from Hollywood."

"I won't for long if I let you kiss me," she replied with impudence. "Breakfast is the only meal I cook. Where shall we eat?"

Under the stars, with no one else around. Realizing he was staring at her as if famished, TJ pulled back. The pulse in his temple accelerated, and his mouth dried. He was a man of few words, and all of them fled beneath her laughing gaze. How the devil did she do that?

Apparently reading the hunger in his eyes, she sidled closer and ran her fingers down his shirt. "Yeah, that's what I thought, too," she murmured teasingly, translating his thoughts without need of his saying them aloud. "But we're still on public display. Let's try to pretend we're not cats in heat for a little while. It will be a challenge."

Just getting her out of the building without digging his hands into her hair and kissing her until their heads spun would be a challenge. "Hands to yourself," he ordered, clasping her wrists and removing her marauding fingers from his shirtfront. "Tell me what you uncovered at the library today that has you dancing with mischief, and I may survive this."

"Blackbeard used the island," she informed him with satisfaction, "just like I told you."

"Those aren't Blackbeard's bones." Grasping her elbow, TJ steered her out of the office, flipping off lights and locking doors as he went.

A gaggle of reporters snapped pictures as they exited, but his head was already on overload, so he ignored them.

"Maybe other pirates used it," Mara continued as if a TV camera weren't rolling down the road in front of her. "The island wasn't accessible by road until the sixties. Mostly it was used for hunting. Cleo's house is probably some rich nabob's hunting lodge."

She wasn't even wearing perfume—now it was her jasmine-scented shampoo that was turning him on. If he spent much more time in Mara's company, he'd be a basket case.

Did he mean to spend more time in her company? How much more?

TJ stepped into the street in front of the town's one traffic light just before it changed, leaving the camera crew and their unwieldy equipment trapped on the corner.

"Any rich nabobs go missing back then?" he asked. The way stories were passed down around here, TJ figured he would have heard of missing nabobs by now, but he needed to concentrate on something besides Mara's scent.

"Not that I've been able to tell so far," Mara continued complacently. "Place was pretty poor back then, if the local weekly is any gauge. I started with the thirties. This was all farm country with some sea traffic at the harbor. I read tobacco prices and local wedding announcements until my eyes crossed."

"Here comes the mayor. Cross your eyes at him."

She shot him an amused look. "Ticks you off, does he? According to my research, his father was mayor back in the fifties. Good old southern family. Play nice."

"Miss Simon, Dr. McCloud. Pleasure to see you out and about," the mayor called jovially. "I understand you've resolved your differences and the film is fully under way."

"Miss Simon and I have come to an agreement," TJ answered gravely, without commenting on the film.

"Good, good! I've been in touch with the state about that land out there. The funding isn't in the budget for more parks, but they're looking into it. You need to get your people together with mine." The mayor rocked back on his heels with an approving smile.

"Oh, I'm not the one in charge anymore," Mara said sweetly. "You'll need to speak with Ian. I'm sure he'll be delighted to form a committee."

The mayor's smile vanished. "Has something gone

amiss? You are still planning on landscaping the beach, aren't you?"

Mara's fingers tightened around TJ's arm, but she spoke with blithe insouciance. "I'm sure Ian will see to it. It's good to see you, Mayor Bridgeton. Let me know if I can help in any way with the project."

She tugged TJ away from the stuttering mayor and all but raced down the street toward restaurant row.

"I think I might be enjoying this," she whispered, stopping to investigate the posted menu at the Blue Monkey. "No responsibility, no pressure . . ."

"It's only an interlude," TJ warned. It was a reminder to himself as well. "Eventually we have to return to our real lives."

"I like thinking that we'll uncover a magic genie with the power to grant all our wishes." She caught his arm and dragged him through the open glass door into the noisy bar. "I'll wish for my job back later. Right now I'm enjoying this chance to have you."

"You ought to be a writer," TJ replied dryly, holding up two fingers to the harried waitress and pointing out the booth he wanted. At her nod, he led Mara to a quiet corner.

"After I make my first million. A girl has to live on something while pursuing her dreams." Removing her hat, she slid into the seat and eagerly looked around.

"Hey, Miss Simon, is that you on the cover of *People*?" a local at the bar shouted over the uproar.

"They only put movie stars and supermodels on the cover," she called back, "but thank you anyway!"

She beamed as the waitress threw down menus and took their drink order. "No one ever thought I looked like a supermodel before," she whispered after the waitress departed. "I think I like it here."

"Hollywood is probably the only place in the world where they wouldn't mistake you for a model." TJ studied her thoughtfully. "You're tall, striking, and wear clothes with the same sort of . . ." He shrugged, searching for the word. "I don't know. Glamour? Distinction?"

Her eyes widened. "I'm not even wearing makeup, TJ! I look like a tall, skinny librarian with my hair like this."

He didn't know whether to roll on the floor with laughter or shake her. "No one would ever get past the front desk if you were a librarian. You could stick pencils in your bun and wear dowdy dresses to your ankles, and you'd still look like a supermodel. It's the way you hold yourself, the way you smile at the world, the confidence in your attitude—you scream 'I'm someone' with every move you make."

"Wow." She shook her head in wonder. "I must have boffed your brains out."

TJ couldn't help laughing at that. The laughter ought to hurt after all the years of disuse, but once he'd started, it simply exploded out of him. The whole bar turned to stare, and he nearly ruptured a blood vessel trying to control himself, but tears came to his eyes, and he rolled off on another gale when Mara crossed her eyes and stuck her tongue out at him.

"Enjoying ourselves, are we?" Ian appeared like an evil genie, watching them with mistrust.

"Yeah, we are, so crawl back under your rock and wait for Sid to join you," Mara ordered.

Wiping his eyes and composing himself, TJ tried to maintain a solemn face, but he kept sniggering. His career would be decimated within days, but he hadn't felt this good in years. "You might consider changing rocks, old man," he told Ian between chuckles. "The one you're under is about to be kicked over, and you don't want to be part of the slimy underside exposed."

Mara turned her stare on him, but TJ ignored the question in her eyes while Ian regarded him with suspicion.

"What the hell are you talking about?"

"I'm just saying corruption takes its toll, and sometimes it's far better to side with the good guys. They might not get as rich, but they live longer."

Ian opened his mouth, darted a look at Mara, and closed it again. With a wary glance, he eased back to the bar and pulled his cell phone out of his jacket pocket.

"He's calling Sid," Mara whispered excitedly. "What have you done today, TJ? Have you been a bad boy?"

"I'm not a bully anymore," he warned. "I'm not the man, and I'm not the Intimidator."

She leaned across the booth and shoved his head back with the heel of her hand. "And you accuse me of having image problems." She dropped back to her seat and scowled. "Anyone who stands up to a bully isn't a bully. Standing up for your rights isn't being a bully. Bullies *abuse* power, not use it for justice. If you intimidate cowards, it's because they're cowards."

She gave him power far beyond any right he had to claim it, but TJ accepted the burden rather than see the light of indignation leave her eyes.

Soon enough the magic genie would pop back in his bottle and life would go back to normal, but for the moment TJ would continue pretending he had the ability to change the world.

Or Mara's version of it.

TWENTY-THREE

"I've never seen such a diligent researcher in all my born days. Anytime you need a job, honey, you call on me."

Mara smiled affectionately at the elderly librarian who'd helped her dig through the stacks for the past week, researching TJ's skeletons. "You have an amazing amount of material here. I've collected enough for a book, although I think I fancy Blackbeard a little more than the modern stuff." Standing on the front steps of the library, she squinted past the stately oaks, automatically scanning the sky for the source of the helicopter noise. "The mayor's family makes for a fascinating history, but they lack the character of Blackbeard."

The librarian chuckled. "Well, they never curled their beards or anyone's toes, for certain. I can remember my mother calling them Krauts and speaking disrespectfully of the mayor's daddy buying up the town, but times change, and she wasn't one to change with them."

"There isn't a helicopter pad around here, is there?" The noise seemed to be coming closer. She was just getting used to the quiet sounds of birdcalls and neighbors yelling greetings instead of the fast-paced roar of motors. She didn't like the intrusion.

"No, not that I know of." The librarian scanned the sky as well, but the branches of the oaks blocked most of it. "Must be one of those helicopters from Parris Island. Sometimes the boys like to see what's happening at the beach, I guess."

"Well, I'd better be going. TJ will appreciate the information, Mrs. Lisle. It's not much to work on, but at least we know what not to expect."

"I hope he finishes up soon so you can go back to work on your film, dear." The librarian waved her off and returned to the shady interior.

These days she'd almost be happy not to have her film back, Mara mused, admiring the cloudless sky as she walked to TJ's car. The helicopter must have moved off; she didn't hear it anymore.

She rather enjoyed having the leisure to dig through the library, laze on the beach, and make love all night. Unfortunately, her savings were nearly nil, Aunt Miriam still wanted to institutionalize her mother, and the studio would definitely go down the drain—along with a lot of investor financing and all its employees—if Sid and Ian continued on their present course. She'd heard Ian had decided to unload the pirate ship replica at the harbor, load it on a barge, and ship it to Cleo's beach. More delays, more expense, and still no guarantee that they could haul in the boom for the night scenes if TJ didn't move his dig.

It was *her* film going down the drain. Telling herself it wasn't her problem didn't help. Spending this week waiting for Clay McCloud to arrive with a solution didn't feel right either, but she was fresh out of ideas. And enjoying the vacation entirely too much.

Heaving her notebooks and heavy shoulder bag into the back of the Taurus, Mara glanced in the direction of the B&B. She had time to steal a gossip session with Constantina. Now that Irving had given up and gone back to Brooklyn, it should be safe enough to visit.

TJ and the beach tugged harder.

Thinking about losing everything she'd worked for was too damned depressing. It was much easier to escape to TJ and pretend he'd make everything right. She didn't even mind his enigmatic, secretive nature. She really didn't *want* to know what he'd been plotting with his mysterious calls to Clay all week.

She wasn't relying on others again, she told herself. She'd called all the money men, warned them they'd lose their shirts. She figured if they weren't busy harassing Sid, then they deserved to lose their investment. She simply didn't possess the skill or clout to bash the necessary heads.

She needed a big stick, and TJ was as close to one as she could get.

Climbing in the Taurus, she stopped and picked up dinner at the café. The regulars greeted her with waves, and in jeans and a tank top, she didn't feel like an albino giraffe. Her career might be in a shambles, but personally, this week with TJ had been the most idyllic one of her life. She didn't have to be glamorous, no one expected her to save the world or her mother, and she had a man who treated her as if she were a gift from the gods. It was hard to imagine a scientist type like TJ being a creative lover, but once he loosened up—wow!

Hormones zinging, Mara sang along with the radio on the way to the island. The beach house needed a hot tub.

She squealed the car to a skidding halt as soon as she turned from the highway onto Cleo's sandy lane.

An adorable little blue and white helicopter blocked the road.

"It's got to be a McCloud thing," she muttered, climbing out to investigate. "McGod is more like it. One of these days, I'm gonna write a book."

"Talking to ourselves, are we?" a laconic voice inquired from the vicinity of the machine.

"It's allowed. What have you done with TJ?" She squinted to see under the belly of the thing, where she could discern movement.

"He's gone to see if Cleo has wrenches. Never thought to see the day Jared would hook up with someone who knew her way around tools. Wish I'd met her first."

A long, angular form wriggled from beneath the copter's belly. Garbed in an oil-covered jumpsuit, he would have looked like a garage mechanic if it weren't for the styled, sun-streaked locks and expensive sunglasses pushed up onto his head. Mara could recognize Hollywood from a mile away.

"Thomas Clayton." She crossed her arms and studied the tall man rising to his feet. The little boy she'd remembered had grown into another damned McCloud, all right. But this one had gaunt planes beneath high cheekbones that would film more cinematically than Garner, Eastwood, and Cruise all rolled into one. Not a pretty face, but a compelling one. "When TJ said you'd fly in, I didn't think he meant it this literally."

Clay shrugged and shifted his sunglasses to his nose in perfect Hollywood-idol mode. "I just rented this baby at the airport. I'm thinking that if I have to live in L.A. any longer, this is the way to travel." He turned to examine the machine with interest. "If we could just get past the fossil-fuel problem, flight would provide the vehicles of the future."

"Solving the noise problem would be beneficial," TJ intruded dryly, entering the clearing with toolbox in hand. "Here, I brought what I could find. Cleo tends to keep tools in kitchen drawers."

"Never know when a wrench can come in handy." Grabbing the box, Clay disappeared beneath the machine again, effectively destroying his cover-model image.

"Is he planning on parking this thing here?" Mara asked doubtfully. "Cleo and Jared may not need the road while they're in Florida, but it's a bit of a hike for us."

"Never asking what's on Clay's mind lowers the stress level. Want to wait until he's done or hike on back? I think you've still got crew on the beach who will try to pass by here any minute. Might make for good entertainment."

Mara grinned. "Especially if Glynis and Ian are in the limo. I've got dinner in the car. Should we pull up a table and wait?"

"Hey, you got enough for me?" Clay shouted from beneath the machine.

"You're supposed to call ahead if you want to get fed, Tommo. If you want a vacation, you've got to warn us in advance." TJ moseyed over to the car and Mara.

"Think I'd do the work and not have the fun?" Clay called back.

Not wanting to know what he meant by that, Mara admired TJ's shirtless chest. "I like your work clothes," she murmured, now that she knew his brother eavesdropped.

TJ glanced down at his sweaty chest and dirty jeans and shrugged. "It's hot out here. We could leave the food for Clay and hike back to the house to shower," he suggested with the hint of a leer in his crooked eyebrow.

"Don't tempt me, big boy." She ran her fingers across the washboard muscles of his abdomen. "I'd even forgo the show Ian will put on when he discovers the copter—that is, if I didn't figure his next move would be to tear the house down to get at us."

"There, I think I've got it now." Clay wriggled out from under the helicopter, feetfirst. "I hear a cavalcade coming. I take it this isn't Jared's private drive?"

TJ offered his brother a look of aggrieved disbelief. Mara tickled the furry line of hair disappearing beneath his belt buckle and was rewarded when he turned his attention on her rather than on slaying his brother.

"You could park the copter on the beach the film crew is using," she suggested mischievously. "There's more space there than in front of the house."

"Sand and wind. Not good for the long term. Saw a field past those trees. I'll try that. Come pick me up?"

Mara tickled TJ's belly to prevent the retort from forming on his tongue. She remembered the insults the McCloud brothers had thrown at each other as kids. McClouds had invented one-upmanship. "I'd send the limo, but you've got to get my job back first."

On the far side of the helicopter, the caravan of cars and buses began slamming to a halt.

Clay shrugged and climbed into the pilot's seat. "The

Intimidator's already got that covered," he shouted as the rotors began to spin. "I'm just here to collect the baggage."

"You know, I've been real polite and not questioned you, but I think that's gonna stop," Mara said thoughtfully as the helicopter began dancing over the sandy lane.

"My teachers always wrote me up for not sharing." Feet planted firmly apart, muscled arms crossed over his bare chest, looking for all the world like a colossus, TJ watched the copter rise.

"If the logistics didn't seem impossible, I'd say you planned this." Mara wished she had her floppy hat and sunglasses as the helicopter disappeared over the trees. She'd rather face a furious Ian with all her protective shields in place. She felt naked without them.

"Clay is lousy at keeping a schedule, but excellent at choosing his timing," TJ replied enigmatically.

The limo remained where it had halted, and Ian stalked toward them. Several of the technicians climbed from their trucks to better watch the confrontation.

"What the hell do you think you're doing, McCloud? Isn't it bad enough we have to scale that dune every day? Now you have to turn the road into a helipad?"

"Even though I've got an injunction that permits it, I didn't increase security or block your ATVs," TJ said evenly. "You should be grateful for the reprieve."

"You knew I'd have your ass fried if you tried." Slender and half a foot shorter than TJ, the producer kept his distance. "Now, if you'll get out of our way—"

"Actually, I stopped you for a reason. I have enough evidence to prove a World War Two–era murder may have been committed here, and I have permission to expand the dig past the access road. The feds are waiting for a phone call from me to set the process in motion."

Mara knew TJ had evidence of a crime. She wasn't so certain about the feds agreeing to expand the dig, but she'd never seen Ian shut up so fast. She was pretty flabbergasted as well. World War II? She eyed TJ skeptically.

He wouldn't do this to her, would he? What good would it do to get her film back if she couldn't reach the beach?

In TJ's eyes, it wasn't her film anymore, and he was perfectly capable of getting even . . . or of using the threat to get her job back. *That* was the TJ she knew.

Slowly her hope rose, and Mara fought back a triumphant expression as she watched a reporter climb out of the limo and another hand his beer to a techie so he could reach for his notebook. War crimes made great press.

"You're bluffing," Ian countered brashly, reaching for his ever-present cell phone. "I'll sic the attorneys on you."

TJ shrugged, wrapped his arm around Mara's shoulders, and eased her toward the edge of the road. "Just thought a friendly warning was in order. I fear you'll find the attorneys otherwise occupied. Spoke to Sid lately?"

Mara's stomach clenched at the threat in TJ's voice. What had he done this time?

Ian's fingers hovered over the cell phone buttons. He glanced uncertainly at Mara, then back to TJ. "Why?"

"Probably not my business to say if he hasn't called you to explain. Let's just say that you've placed your bets on the wrong partner."

Mara recognized the expression in Ian's eyes. He was weighing odds, choosing which bridges not to burn. People didn't survive in Hollywood without leaving escape routes open, and Ian was as much of a survivor as she was. Or better. She'd actually trusted Sid in the divorce agreement. Ian wouldn't have.

"I'm just taking orders from my employer," Ian countered carefully.

In a decidedly proprietary manner, TJ caressed Mara's earlobe. A shiver of pleasure shot down her spine, but she was too interested in the conversation to return the gesture. Crossing her arms and leaning into TJ, she waited for the explosion.

"You own half the company, don't you?" TJ asked her.

She wasn't certain she'd told him that, but it wasn't exactly private information. She nodded, and a curl of hair fell from her topknot across her cheek. She must look a mess, and bored journalists were snapping their cameras to record her lack of glamour. She considered easing behind TJ's big body to hide, but his arm provided all the shelter she needed.

"Sid has the controlling share." She resisted saying she was a flunky, even if that was what every man here was thinking. Except TJ, bless his righteous heart.

"I think, in view of Sid's legal problems, he may be willing to forfeit that control," TJ replied thoughtfully, looking at Ian rather than at her. "I bet if you pick up your voice mail, you have calls from a number of investors by now."

Mara fumbled for her cell phone in her shoulder bag, while Ian glanced nervously at the one in his hand.

"It's still early in L.A.," TJ pointed out helpfully.

Escaping from TJ's hold and retreating to the Taurus with a pounding heart and a vaguely sick taste in her mouth, Mara punched in the number for her voice mail. A dozen messages waited. With fascination and dread building, she listened to the first staticky call. And the second.

By the time she'd heard them all, the clearing had fallen completely silent. Ian shut off his phone and stared at her as if he feared his head would roll.

And TJ was nowhere in sight.

"I know a lawyer who can advise you," Ian offered cautiously. "Sid's gonna have his hands full for some months to come. You don't want the company to slip out of control in the meantime."

Mara watched the reporters in the back hastily checking their own voice mail or making frantic calls. Reception on the island was bad, and some of them were cursing and urging their drivers to pull around the barrier of cars in the lane.

Sid had been arrested on drug and sex charges. Justice

had finally been served, and she suspected the wielder of the gavel came in the form of one TJ McCloud, with perhaps a little help from a brother. Clay should have stuck around to watch the fun.

"I can give you a ride into town," Ian offered. "We need to start making plans."

She had her life back. And TJ had just absented himself from it.

Something visceral ripped in two at the thought of returning to her lonely bed and a life surrounded by sycophants who would bring her coffee at a snap of the fingers but wouldn't share their *New York Times* with her. A week ago, that sort of obedience had been all she wanted out of life. A week ago, not one person in that caravan of cars had lifted a finger to help when Ian had tossed her out. TJ had.

She glanced at the bushes he'd disappeared into, then back to the limo waiting to return her to the film that would make her career.

Dammit, she wouldn't let him do this to her again. She was a big girl now, and this time she wouldn't let him walk away without some answers.

Smiling grimly at the line of actors, journalists, and technicians, no longer caring if she looked like a skinny librarian, Mara waved to them as if she were queen of all she surveyed. "See y'all in the morning. I've got better things to do tonight."

Fury concealed behind her smile, she stalked down the path toward the dune, leaving Ian to figure out how they'd get around the Taurus she had left blocking the lane.

TWENTY-FOUR

TJ had just stepped from the shower into the bedroom when his door slammed open and Mara stalked in with all the fires of hell blazing in her eyes. Still dripping and rubbing his hair with a towel, he tried not to let his need for her overrule common sense. Even though she'd regressed to a tank top and jeans, she only vaguely resembled the teenager he'd once loved. He knew the woman she was now far better than the child she'd been, though, and he wanted her more than ever.

Diplomatically, he wrapped the towel around his waist to conceal the direction of his thoughts.

"I'm sick and tired of people telling me how to lead my life!" she shouted. "I'm sick and tired of others thinking they know what's best for me." Crossing the room, she smacked her palm against TJ's chest, shoving him backward—or attempting to.

Having no clue where her agile mind had taken her and with no ability to ponder anything while she stood inches from his rapidly rising ardor, TJ simply waited for an explanation. Women always yelled at him and walked out. He'd never had one stand up to him before. He was fascinated.

"Don't give me that enigmatic look, Timothy John!" She pounded him with her fist, forcing him to back up against the bed. "You walked away again. Don't you *ever* walk away from me like that. If you want to get rid of me, say it to my face."

"I only wanted a shower," he muttered, but deep inside, he knew what she meant. He just hadn't expected to be called on it. He'd expected her to climb into the limo with Ian and start planning the rest of her life.

"The *hell* you did!" She kicked off her mules and undulated out of her tank top.

TJ thought his eyes might pop out as her naked breasts brushed his chest, more tempting than any strip show he'd ever seen. The tips were taut and begging for plucking, and releasing the towel, he placed his hands behind him on the bed to prevent reaching for them. "I *didn't* want a shower?" he asked with some confusion. So much for his much-heralded mental processes.

"You expected me to walk away, didn't you?" She reached for the snap of her jeans and wriggled out of them in record time.

He supposed he had, if he thought about it, but right now his mind was otherwise occupied. She wore a scanty bikini panty made of snow white lace. It skimmed curving hips and taunted him with a shadow of invitation. What exactly was he supposed to do here?

"Well, it's not working, TJ. I'm not one of your nitwit assistants. I'm not disappearing into the woodwork or walking out. Just call me your albatross." She flung her arms around his shoulders, pressed her mouth to his, and he couldn't call her anything if he wanted to. His mouth was much too busy.

TJ toppled back on the bed, and Mara fell on top of him. Scrambling to her knees, she continued leaning over him, wrapping her hands in his hair, pressing hungry kisses across his jaw, tempting him with breasts he could no longer resist. When he cupped them, she ground her hips against his abdomen, and TJ lost any pretense of control.

He caught her head and held her still so he could plunder her mouth with his tongue. She wriggled down until his erection brushed the lace of her panties, and he lost his grip on her hair to tear at the obstacle in his way. She yelped as he ripped off the scrap of lace, then rose high on her knees and came down on him so swiftly, he almost erupted right then.

Sheathed in her moist heat, he quit worrying about anything. He held her hips and pumped deeper, but he craved the softness of her breasts against his mouth. She shrieked as he rolled her to her back, then wrapped her legs around his hips once he captured her nipple and sucked it deeply.

He knew in the back of his mind that they needed to stop, to gain control, to think, but his id had taken the reins and urged his body to a gallop, and nothing barred his way.

Mara had come after him. He'd given her what she wanted most, and she'd turned her back on it and come looking for him. Joy and triumph flowed through him, unhampered by logic. Giving into primal need, TJ drove high, inhaled her scream of ecstasy as she climaxed, and in gratitude poured his release deep within her.

The blare of a car horn intruded through the open window.

Mara wriggled, but TJ held her pinned. Winded, he didn't bother explaining.

"I'm not going anywhere, TJ," she countered with stubbornness. "We're going to work this out this time. I'll go to the doctor in the morning to get the pill."

The pill. TJ pressed his forehead to hers, then rolled over, taking her with him. The car horn quit blowing. He knew that was an ominous sign but he had other alarming things to consider. They hadn't used a condom. Again.

He was on the brink of one disaster and courting another. "We've got separate lives, Mara," he cautioned. "You're better off recognizing that now and getting out while you can."

Still holding him inside her, she circled her hips, catching his anatomy's attention again. "Tell me you want me to leave," she taunted.

"Keep that up, and you'll be sporting a bulging belly

beneath those crop tops," he warned. "How will you vamp your money men then?"

"Low blow, McCloud." She rolled off and glared at the ceiling.

Feeling like a heel, TJ turned on his side to caress her tumbling hair from her face. "I'm sorry. You have this incredible ability to turn me into my old protective teenage hulk. I want to pound any man looking at you into dust. Breaking Irving's nose wasn't an accident."

Mara smiled, and TJ's insides melted. He could dive into those laughing green pools and never come up again. The wretched imp had him tied in knots, and if she started singing *Doo-wah-diddy-diddy* anytime in the next thirty seconds, he'd never escape alive.

"Thank you for nailing Sid for me," she whispered, wearing the admiring expression that turned him inside out every time.

"I didn't do anything you wouldn't have done once you'd gotten past your niceness. You need to trust yourself more," he said gruffly. He had to make her see that she could stand on her own. He wouldn't always be there. She'd gain confidence once she had this film in the can. She'd go back to Hollywood, he'd go back to whatever career was left to him, and he would never see her again. He had to imprint that fact on his lust-riddled brain.

"I'll give you two minutes to get decent!" an irritatingly familiar voice echoed from below.

"Shit." TJ dropped back to the mattress, jarred from his black thoughts by the intrusion. "This isn't Jared's place, baby brother," he shouted at the ceiling, lacking the energy to do more.

"There's no food in Jared's place," Clay shouted back. "But I picked up today's newspaper from his box. The headlines should have Mom on the phone screaming shortly."

Just what he needed. Roger must have had an entire

team of reporters working through that material to get a story out this soon.

Beside him, Mara chuckled and leaned over to kiss his bristly jaw. "I remember your mother. Charming woman. Give her my regards. I'll go fetch dinner and shove it down Clay's throat."

He'd just destroyed her ex-husband and partner without warning her of what he was doing. She hadn't offered a word of objection to his high-handedness. Did she really understand that he'd done it for her? Had he really found a woman who got it?

It didn't seem possible, but TJ wanted—needed—to keep the lines of communication open between them. He didn't want to screw things up this time, no matter what the future held.

He caught Mara's waist and held her still. "I'm sorry if I hurt you with what we did to Sid."

Mara blew a raspberry and wrinkled her nose. "He had it coming. I tried to save him, but I was just enabling. You did him a favor. And me. Bless you." She kissed his cheek and wriggled out of his hold when TJ's hands began to roam. "I want to hear the story, though. Let me get dressed first."

"There isn't much of a story." Reluctantly TJ rolled from the bed and reached for a pair of cutoffs. "Clay tracked down his schedule for the week—and we won't ask how he did that. Then we had a private investigator follow him. Sid set himself up. Everyone knew where he was going and what he was doing. The PI just called the cops."

"The terrible waste of a good mind." Mara headed for the shower, carrying her clothes. "And I'm not talking about Sid. That brother of yours needs a life."

TJ chuckled as she disappeared behind closed doors. Life could be very interesting with a woman like her around.

He sobered as he trotted down the stairs to face Clay

holding a folded newspaper. If he read his brother's expression correctly, Roger's story must be a humdinger.

"Don't suppose that's news of Sid's arrest you're reading." Stoically, without reaching for the newspaper, TJ headed for the kitchen. The scent of fried chicken wafted through the small cottage, but what he needed was a drink.

"Nope. Looks like your old friend Martin is in a bit of hot water." Clay flung the paper on the table and accepted the beer that TJ handed him. "Seems evidence has revealed that Balkan war criminals have been released without benefit of trial, and there's rumor of favors and cash being exchanged. The colonel's name seems to be all over it. They're talking of locking him up."

"And this involves me how?" TJ took a long gulp of beer.

"It doesn't yet. But even you strong, silent types occasionally mention who you're working with. And an old family friend in the headlines tends to attract Mom's notice." Clay rattled through the paper bags from the café, removing Styrofoam cartons of the dinner Mara had intended for her and TJ.

"The man's not convicted yet." TJ wandered to the kitchen window, but his excavation site was too far away to tell if Clay had brought back the car along with their dinner. Cold winds wailed through the hollow of his heart as he listened for Mara's footsteps on the stairs. Instead of trusting his friend and mentor, he'd betrayed Martin to the press, thrown him to the jackals. Retribution would follow. He didn't expect anything as dramatic as Brad's death, but the result could be just as devastating to his family.

The phone rang. TJ didn't answer it.

Gnawing on a chicken leg, Clay watched him with interest.

Mara's happy footsteps danced down the stairs. TJ turned to watch her enter. Inquisitive green eyes darted from him to Clay to the telephone, but she ignored the ringing as well. "That's my chicken you're eating, Thomas Clayton McCloud. Did you steal the car, too?"

"Hot-wired it. If I'd known I'd still have to walk, I'd have left it there. Why would anyone live out here, where there isn't even a Starbucks?" Clay threw the chicken bone into the trash and reached for a paper towel to clean his hands.

The phone stopped shrieking. The cottage had no answering machine or voice mail. TJ rummaged in the sacks while Mara reached for the newspaper. She whistled at the headline, scanned the article rapidly, then threw the paper back onto the table.

To TJ's relief, she walked across the room and wrapped her arms around his waist. He folded her in his arms, and soothing warmth and energy seeped through him from every place they touched. He couldn't let her get involved in the train wreck heading his way, but for right this minute, he absorbed the comfort of what might have been.

"If he's innocent, the truth will set him free," she whispered against his skin. "If he's guilty, he needs to go down."

"If he's guilty, TJ's likely to go down with him," Clay added cynically, popping open a carton of mashed potatoes. "Guilt by association, if nothing else. TJ's a trained observer and worked closely with Martin. A good prosecutor can tear his reputation to shreds."

"No one will believe the Incredible Hulk would be involved in covering up war crimes." Kissing TJ's shoulder, Mara slipped away to find plates and silverware. "Have faith, little brother."

"She's lived in never-never land too long, hasn't she?" Clay inquired of the air.

Snorting in disbelief at both of them, TJ finished emptying the sacks. He opened a bottle of the water that Mara favored and found her a glass. "You're the one who flies up in helicopters expecting Starbucks at the seashore. Peter Pan has nothing on you."

TJ pulled back a chair for Mara. She rewarded him by sliding her cool fingers down his arm as she took the seat offered. Realizing he wasn't wearing a shirt, TJ returned to the front room to pick up a pullover he'd discarded the night before.

"It's the beach," Clay reminded him when TJ returned to the kitchen, still tugging the knit into place. "People don't have to wear shirts at the table here."

"I do." Pulling up a chair, he ignored his brother's ribbing. When life was cracking apart at the seams, sometimes it helped to hold things together with the glue of proper conduct.

"Tell me how you tracked Sid." Mara intruded on their argument. "Even when I was married to him, I never knew where he was."

Clay shrugged. "He keeps his appointment book online."

Mara waited. TJ helped himself to the rest of the potatoes.

Starting to squirm in the silence, Clay reached for his beer. "Computers are my business, okay?"

"You hacked his computer?"

"I told you not to ask." Ignoring his brother's discomfort, TJ poured more water into Mara's glass.

In obvious fascination, Mara leaned back in her chair, sipping her water. She'd donned a long-sleeved shirt, but the clinging silk did little to disguise the fact that she wore nothing under it. TJ debated whether he preferred knowing she did that for him or if he should jerk a heavy sweater over her shoulders to keep Clay's eyes in his head.

"Can you hack anyone's computer?" she asked with deceptive innocence.

"Hacking's illegal." Clay ripped off a huge bite of biscuit so he wouldn't have to say anything else.

"You wrote the software for Jared's cartoon animation, didn't you?" She started digging from a different angle.

Fascinated with this picture of how her mind worked, TJ sat back as Mara lured his cynical younger brother into her snare. He had never fully appreciated the range of her dangerous imagination.

Clay shrugged, finished chewing, and eyed her skeptically. "Yeah. That's what I do, write programs."

"For the film industry." She nudged a little further.

"Yeah, it's more entertaining than Wall Street."

"What can you do with the actual film? Or do you just write programs?"

Looking a little less uncomfortable now that they'd reached a safe topic of interest, Clay sat forward and leaned his elbows on the table. "I work with film. That's how I know how to write the programs. I not only can create animation, I can slice, splice, dice, and rearrange anything you can film."

Mara beamed happily. "Okay, if I give you tape of the deep blue sea and tape of a pirate ship, you can make the two work together . . . for how much?"

"If you want the ship to roll with the waves, it costs more."

"How much?"

The phone began to ring. Shaking his head at the full-scale negotiation war beginning at his dinner table, TJ reached for it.

"Timothy John McCloud," the voice on the other end said scathingly, "if you're involved in this . . . this *scandal*, I'll never forgive you. Never."

His mother.

The fun had just begun.

TWENTY-FIVE

"He's always been the fair-haired boy, the one who could do no wrong."

Mara heard the admiration behind Clay's cynicism, but her attention was focused on TJ. A cloud of gloom hung over his head. Had she done the wrong thing in encouraging him to turn over those evidence boxes? She hadn't realized the colonel was an old family friend, that the scandal had complications beyond her understanding. TJ had warned her, but she had blithely believed his world operated on the black-and-white rules that hers didn't. Silly her.

They'd finished their meal and retired to the front room, but TJ had scarcely uttered two words since his mother's phone call. A few moments ago, he'd retrieved the cordless and taken it out on the front porch, leaving Mara and Clay to entertain each other.

"Does he never let out any of those things churning in his gut?" she asked, not certain how to deal with stone walls. Irving had whined and Sid had thrown fits. Her family never stopped talking, usually in circles and all at one time. She didn't know how to cope with a man who thought he was a law unto himself.

"I didn't know anything churned TJ's gut. Growing up, I occasionally wondered if I had a robot for a brother. I rarely saw him laugh or cry or get angry. If someone hassled me, he'd pick them up by the shirt collar and toss them without saying a word, kind of like the cartoon heroes Jared admired on TV." Restlessly,

Clay paced the room, examining the few artifacts that had collected there over the years of Cleo's haphazard care.

Mara shook her head in disbelief. "Smoke practically pours from the man's ears. You didn't really think he earned the tag of Intimidator because he was cold and unfeeling?"

Clay fingered a childishly molded pottery vase and glanced at the window framing TJ talking into the phone. "Kids don't think like that. He's almost six years older than I am. I saw him as my big brother, the guy I admired when he fixed my broken toys and who made me angry when he yelled at me for playing with matches. He was in college before I went to high school. He was the one who got good grades, won awards, the one our parents and teachers expected Jared and me to emulate."

"So, of course, being McClouds, you did the exact opposite."

"Maybe. Sometimes. But mostly we thought Tim walked on water and that we'd never be that good."

Mara understood. Brad had been that person for her. She could have been resentful, but she'd seen the burden her parents' pressure had placed on her brother. He'd ultimately crumpled under it, while she had survived. If she ever had kids . . .

She couldn't ever have kids. She refused to inflict the horror of watching a loving mother's bewildering deterioration on any child of hers.

TJ punched a button on the phone and set it on the porch rail. Instead of returning inside, he stared at the incoming tide.

"Time you took yourself back to Jared's place," Mara said softly to Clay. "I need to adjust his steam regulator."

Clay chuckled. "Glad you know where to find it. I've been wondering if he would just explode."

Mara shivered, remembering a brother who had reached that dangerous point. She ought to run as far as she could before it was too late.

She watched as Clay and TJ exchanged quick farewells, waited for Clay to disappear down the boardwalk to the main house. When TJ still didn't return inside, she went to him.

"Talk, McCloud." She massaged his tense shoulders and leaned against him until he reached behind him and pulled her to his side. She'd dreamed of sharing moments like this with a man she loved. She didn't believe in dreams anymore, but she held on to every piece of one that came her way.

"Nothing to say. I left messages on Roger's machine and called the hotel where Jared and Cleo are staying to give them some warning. They're out having fun, so I just told them to give me a call when they had a chance."

"That ought to relieve their minds," she said wryly. "Do you really care what your parents think? Would it have been better to let a criminal go free to please them?"

"He was my friend." TJ rubbed her arm and continued staring over the water. "Whatever was in those boxes doesn't explain his motivation. I could have caused a national security breach by revealing those files."

"Judge and jury again," she reminded him. "This is why we're a democracy and not a dictatorship. If people are given too much power, they act on their own selfish beliefs rather than the beliefs of the people they represent. Martin's motivation doesn't excuse the result. Don't make the same mistake as he did and assume you know what's best for everyone."

"There are two sides to every issue," he agreed with resignation. "But no matter how logical you make it sound, I'm ruining a friend, a mentor, a man I trusted with my life."

"What about yourself?" she whispered, shivering at the despair she heard in his words. "Don't you count for something? If those reports in the paper are true, Martin used you and all those others who worked with him. I don't care if he did it for fun and profit or if he thought he was benefiting some grander scheme. He let murderers and rapists go *free*. That wasn't his call to make."

"I'd better take you back to the hotel. You can pitch Ian out of his suite." Dropping his arm from around her, TJ headed back inside.

He was throwing her out of his life—again.

Mara wrapped her arms around herself to keep from flying apart. Staring out to sea, she fought the rising nausea, the knowledge that she could never be good enough, that she would always be alone.

Was that what she feared? Being alone for the rest of her life?

That might be preferable to having still another man mess with her head.

She was a strong woman, and a smart one. She didn't have to be told twice that she wasn't wanted. If this was TJ's polite way of saying he only wanted sex from her, she could accept that—sometime in the next century.

Right now she preferred her own company. Swiping at a wayward tear, she swung around to gather her things.

The first sign that all was not well in their small world appeared as they walked over the dune to the parking lot where Clay had left the Taurus.

Mara had packed her bags while TJ disappeared into the nether regions of the house. Furious with him, raging at herself, she kept her lips sealed. Donning figure-hugging stretch slacks and a flowing, diaphanous shirt that didn't conceal her gold tank top and cleavage, she marched out of the house on high-heeled mules, carrying her smallest suitcase. TJ miraculously appeared with her larger ones a minute later.

He'd been watching for her. Mara felt the scalding heat of his gaze as they crossed the dune, but she refused to acknowledge it. The man wasn't dense. He knew what he was doing by throwing her away. So let him do it. She didn't need a man in her life anymore.

The stranger in a heated argument with Clay at the foot of the dune stopped speaking as soon as he saw them.

"Wait here." TJ passed her the handle of one of her suitcases, left the other to fall over in the sand, and stalked down the path.

Mara could smell a reporter from a mile off, but this wasn't one of the entertainment journalists that haunted the shadows of film sets, greedy for every crumb thrown their way. Mara dropped her suitcases and sauntered down the hill to eavesdrop.

"How could you not be aware of the colonel's activities?" the reporter demanded of TJ. "You worked together, out of the same camp. You reported to him. You had to wonder why criminals continued to run loose after you identified them."

So this was what TJ had known would happen once the story broke. Strangers who didn't know his integrity would condemn him without proof. Fingers would point. His reputation would suffer, all without a shred of evidence. She wanted to give the reporter a good shake and explain that TJ had been in Africa and who knew where else and couldn't keep track of every case—and, because he'd left a trusted colleague in charge, hadn't thought he'd needed to. Mara was sorry she'd encouraged TJ to open Pandora's box.

"The colonel is a friend." Crossing his arms, wearing his most impassive expression, TJ remained unmoved by the reporter's increasingly vehement arguments. "I won't convict him on the basis of a single newspaper report. This is private property, and you're trespassing."

"The government subsidizes your contracts. Are you covering up for Martin and turning your back on war crimes just to save a cash cow?" the reporter asked incredulously.

TJ remained calm at this insult, but Mara wanted to rip the man's eyes out. Before she could utter a word, Clay grabbed the stranger's shirt, lifted him from the ground, and shook him until his teeth rattled. TJ merely watched, as if to say the reporter had been warned, and he wasn't responsible for the consequences.

"Journalism isn't putting words in a man's mouth," Clay shouted. "Now get out of here and make up your stories elsewhere."

Mara didn't intervene. The impact of the reporter's observations had stunned her. People would believe *TJ* supported criminal activities? She couldn't quite wrap her mind around the enormity of the accusation. *TJ?* The man who thought truth and justice so important he'd given up his life to them? The man who had agonized over trust and national security and government cover-ups while attempting to preserve a man's reputation until he had evidence of a crime?

Since when did the good guys lose? Frozen in horror, Mara did nothing to stop Clay. Faced with odds of two against one, the reporter ripped Clay's fists from his shirt and backed off. "I suggest you start coming up with an explanation soon," he sneered. "There's no way you're coming out of this clean. Let me know when you're ready to talk."

A peacock screamed in the distance as the reporter strode away.

"Charming," Clay commented when the silence threatened to solidify. "Guilt by association. Wonder if he's covered any witchcraft trials lately."

TJ's expression was so blank, Mara's stomach turned upside-down. She wanted to hug him and tell him everything would be all right, but even she knew better. Everything wouldn't be all right for a long, long time. He could lose his job, his career, maybe even his family and friends. And she'd done this to him.

TJ trudged off to retrieve her suitcases, and Mara finally understood what he was doing—he was throwing her out for her own good.

Clay must have seen it, too. He crossed his arms and gave her that McCloud glare. "Deserting rats?" he inquired loftily.

"Deserting rats drown. I'm heading for the lifeboats. Keep his head above water until I find one." Turning on her heel, Mara marched back to pick up her carry-on.

She couldn't fight the world and the McClouds, too. She needed to sort all this out and figure out what to do.

She was used to TJ rescuing her, not the other way around. This would take some serious thinking.

She had lots of time to do it in. TJ didn't say a word all the way back to town.

"I've talked to all the investors, Mara," Ian yelled at her as she paced up and down the deserted dining room where he'd dragged her as soon as she and TJ had arrived at the B&B. "We can do this. If you fire me, you'll lose everything."

"No, she'll lose a two-faced scorpion," TJ interrupted from the dark corner he'd occupied instead of leaving as he ought.

"Shut up, TJ. This is my company and my problem. You won't let me touch your problems; I won't let you mess with mine."

Fair enough. TJ figured this was the point where he hauled her bags up the stairs and departed.

To his amazement, he couldn't do it. He'd meant to. Mara didn't deserve to be caught in the destruction of his career. But maybe there was time to hold her up until she found her feet.

He rested his shoulder against the wall, crossed his arms, and waited.

Ian scowled at him and returned to pleading with Mara. "I'm good, babe. I can keep this thing on schedule, keep the money flowing. I'll back out of your way, let you do your own thing. You've got vision. I know you can do it."

"I had vision last week and the week before," she informed him coldly. "But you preferred Sid lining your pockets. That's not happening with me in charge. I run a clean ship. I'm hiring new accountants and a team of auditors. I want someone in charge of the money who looks after it like it's their own. You don't qualify, Ian."

TJ admired her adamancy, although he thought kicking out a qualified professional in midstream might be a little extreme. "I'll give you a ride to the airport, old boy," he offered helpfully.

"Shut up, TJ." Mara threw him a dirty look.

Okay, so he was persona non grata everywhere. TJ still didn't leave. Sooner or later the showdown would end, and someone would have to carry out the bodies.

"I'll work with the accountants," Ian responded eagerly, grasping the opening. "Let them write the checks, keep the books, whatever. We're a team, babe. We can pull in the money, keep the film moving. Now that Sid's out of the way, there won't be any interference."

"I'm hiring a computer graphics guy to handle the ship scenes," Mara boldly declared. "We can float the replica in the harbor, and he'll punch in the beach film. We've got to rework the scenes to accommodate him."

TJ gave the little producer credit. He didn't blink an eye.

"It's your call, babe. Do we have samples of his work?"

"He'll bring in his stuff next week. We'll decide then. Throw your girlfriend out of my suite. I'm moving back in."

Ian turned red and puffed up his feathers, but Mara had already turned her back on him. TJ watched with interest as she stalked across the floor in his direction. He didn't harbor any hope that she would throw herself at him again, but he wouldn't mind it if she did. He'd never had a woman knock him back on the bed and have her way with him. He enjoyed new experiences.

He ought to get a real kick out of unemployment.

"You've not seen the last of me, Timothy John." She poked her finger into his chest. "You're judging me again, making my decisions for me, and I don't like it. Go home and sleep in your cold bed, and when you're ready to admit you're wrong, you just let me know. I'm counting on you having the amount of brains I think you do. Don't let testosterone poison them."

TJ's lip curled against his will. In her high heels, Mara stood nearly eye level with him, and he wanted to grab her and kiss her silly.

Remembering the reporter's accusations, and knowing that Mara's optimism wouldn't let her see the disaster looming ahead, TJ resisted. "I'll be working night and day to get my job done so I can get out of your way. Don't expect to see me around much."

She made a rude noise, stood on her toes, branded him with her lipstick-enhanced kiss, then spun around and marched off, shouting orders at the staff lurking outside the door.

TJ continued leaning against the wall while he pushed his heart back in his chest. She'd almost ripped it out there for a moment. He'd be more careful in the future.

TWENTY-SIX

TJ wiped at the sweat dripping off his nose, knowing he left a smear of dirt over half his face.

Nudging his hat back, he answered his screaming cell phone. He'd had call forwarding added to his business number in preparation for shutting down on the first of the month, when his landlord would be throwing him out. So far there had been a dearth of callers wanting to hire him. "McCloud Enterprises."

"Señor McCloud, please."

Well, he should have seen that coming. Leaning against his shovel, TJ scowled. "Speaking."

"Señor McCloud, I regret to inform you that we have filled the position in Yucatán. We will not be needing your services," the voice responded stiffly, as if reciting a memorized speech.

"Fine. Call me if you need me." He hung up without a polite farewell. If he'd had the energy for it, he would have growled.

Was this how Brad had felt those last days of his life—pressured beyond bearing, with nowhere to turn?

He needed a break. He could hear laughter floating up from the beach, knew the film crew had stopped working to eat. He could walk a few steps and be in their midst within minutes. Maybe he just needed company to relieve the burden of his conscience. He didn't know how Mara's crew would react to his presence, and he really didn't care. They'd dubbed him Indiana Jones and left him alone.

It was Mara's reaction that mattered, and he decided he didn't dare risk it. Ending up in bed together again wasn't the wisest course of action. This time common sense instead of hormones would prevail.

He reached for a bottle of water from the cooler. The sooner he got this done, the sooner he could be out of her hair.

"Found anything yet?"

TJ almost dropped the water bottle before looking behind him.

The rotund mayor stood just outside the chain link, studying the mounds of dirt with what appeared to be fascination. Carrying his suit coat over his shoulder, wearing his white dress shirt with the sleeves rolled up, he looked hotter than TJ felt.

TJ grabbed a rag and rubbed his face, trying to figure what the town mayor was doing all the way out here. He'd never expressed any interest in the site since TJ had warned him it didn't contain pirate bones.

"Haven't identified anyone, if that's what you're asking." The mayor would have been what—ten at most?—during World War II. He couldn't have been involved in whatever had happened here.

"Guess clues would have been buried with the hurricane," the mayor commented, dabbing a handkerchief to his forehead. "You about done yet?"

"Don't think I'll find much more without bulldozing the beach. Not certain anyone's interested in going that far." He could have interested lots of people in his Nazi theory a week ago. Not now. The grant people weren't taking his calls. The grim spiral downward had begun as soon as his name had appeared in the media connected with Martin's. Even the Defense Department had quit calling.

"Then we'll never know who was buried here?" the mayor inquired, shoving his handkerchief back in his pocket.

"Didn't say that."

"You know who they are?"

"Didn't say that, either." Just call him a sadistic bastard, but it was nice to watch someone else squirm for a change. TJ collapsed on his plastic lounge chair and took a swig from his bottle of water.

"Confound it! Either they're pirates or they're not. Either they were murdered or they weren't. Why is the government paying you all this money if you don't know anything?"

"They're paying me to be cautious. I'll write my report when I'm done. In the meantime, speculating is useless."

"I thought you were an honorable man, Dr. McCloud, but I'm beginning to think you're blocking progress for your own purposes. Looks as if the newspapers may be right." Clearly irate, the mayor slid down the dune in the direction of the beach and the film crew's laughter.

Might as well alienate the whole town while he was at it, TJ thought. He wasn't a sociable man, didn't need the approval of others. He had to live with himself, and that meant doing what he thought was right, regardless of consequences.

He just wished he knew what was right. Crucifying a friend sure didn't feel right.

TJ picked up the letter he'd received from Jared yesterday, pulled out the picture Matty had drawn of Mickey Mouse, and read the boy's uneven letters: "To Unca TJ, Yr Frnd, Matty." So he had one friend left.

He flipped through the photographs of Cleo and Matty riding blue elephants, Jared clowning with Goofy, and the neighbor kids, Kismet and Gene, standing in front of a pink castle. They were having a good time. Jared had called last night to promise he'd take the kids and Cleo to his Miami condo and shelter them from any fallout. Cleo had been yelling in the background that she'd come home and get rid of the reporters, but Jared must have convinced her that TJ could take care of himself.

He missed them. He'd been traveling for fifteen years without any such regrets, and now he was getting bleary-eyed, wishing he could be as happy and carefree as they seemed to be, wishing he could have what Jared had.

Jared, the goof-off, the one his parents figured would never amount to anything.

TJ leaned his head back against the chair and tried to rearrange his priorities to suit the situation, but he couldn't focus any longer. He needed Mara here to explain things to him. He wasn't much on this family stuff. His parents had practiced benign neglect and let their sons grow up on their own. He'd always secretly admired the way Brad's family had worked so hard together to achieve their goals.

Apparently, from Mara's viewpoint, there were disadvantages to that kind of single-minded support. Maybe people weren't meant to be happy.

He narrowed his eyes at the sight of still another reporter kicking up dust down the lane. His security guards had barricaded the turnoff from the public road to keep the jackals out. Mara's crew had kicked in half the fee to secure the film site. Her people could drive past, but uninvited reporters had to hoof it.

TJ relaxed as he recognized Roger Curtis. He'd pulled his tie loose and discarded his sport jacket before he'd even attempted the walk. He and Roger had shared beers and battles together, and he trusted the man.

As Roger reached the gate, TJ tossed him a cold bottle of beer.

Roger twisted off the cap as he nudged the gate open with his shoulder. "Why aren't you down at the beach with your girlfriend?"

"She's got her job, I've got mine." Girlfriend. TJ snorted at the schoolboy appellation. Mara was way past being a girl. He hoped she was still a friend, but he wouldn't call her on it right now. The week since he'd seen her last seemed like eternity. He wondered how long it would take before she became a distant memory.

He had a sneaking suspicion it wouldn't happen this time around. Even if he hated the outcome, these past weeks would be branded into his brain cells forever.

"How much longer have you got your job?" Roger asked with the cynicism of experience.

"You and Clay could be clones."

"Doubt if Pretty Boy would appreciate the comparison. He said I'd find you here."

TJ chuckled at the description. Clay had a gruff attitude that attracted women like flies. "I wouldn't call him pretty by a long shot, but I know what you mean. Maybe we should learn to snarl at women."

"Not worth the effort. Heard from Martin yet?"

That's why he liked Roger. He didn't mess around with small talk. "Nope. Don't figure the colonel's much on talking to me right about now."

"The evidence is pretty damning, but he's claiming innocence. I thought maybe you might have some insight. The two of you were close."

TJ shrugged. "He's an old family friend. He recruited me to the job. He supported my reports when his superiors wanted to ignore them. I want to believe he's innocent. Your articles paint a pretty grim picture against it."

"A lot of the transcripts could point to the operations of some kind of Balkan Mafia involving foreign military and not ours. The boxes could contain testimonies the colonel collected in an attempt to snuff them out. But we've uncovered clear-cut evidence that Martin let Turkosevic go free. The bastard was responsible for the rape of fifteen young women in an uprising a year after he got out. I have your reports enumerating the evidence against Turkosevic's superiors in the earlier massacre, and your forensic reports supporting the army's conclusion that men under Turkosevic raped and murdered those women whose bodies were uncovered later. Not one of those people has been brought to trial. It looks pretty damning to me."

TJ sipped his water and thought about it, then shook his head. "We can't judge until we've heard the colonel. Aren't reporters supposed to seek both sides?"

"His lawyer isn't letting him talk, so I can't report his side. A hearing has been scheduled, but he's not locked up. You might want to watch your back," Roger warned. "You're the only one who can connect Martin to those boxes. How did you get them?"

"So you can know and be called as a witness, too? It was just an army snafu, pure accident. I've got another in the trunk of the Taurus. You might as well have that one." TJ dug in his pocket for the car keys. "I trust you've turned the first batch over to the authorities?"

"After copying every page," Roger admitted. "I gave them to the FBI, not military. Best I could do."

"Better than I managed. Now that the story is out, no one can bury it. I owe you."

Roger shook his head. "That story made my career. I can have any assignment I ask for right now. It's you I'm worried about. If there's anything I can do . . ."

TJ shrugged. "You took care of a problem for me. Ask for an assignment to Honolulu and maybe I'll meet you there."

Roger laughed. "The only bodies there are mummified in suntan oil. That might be a pleasant change. I'll leave the keys under the seat."

Just like that, TJ thought, wishing for a beer as he watched Roger walk off—his career down the drain. It was so easy. Virtually painless—if it weren't for losing Mara. No numbness on earth could shield him from the agony of letting Mara slip away again.

Even if he had a career left, she had a life he couldn't share. He knew that. No point in prolonging the torture of teenage dreams. He'd finish up here and move on. She'd finish the film, start an illustrious career, and maybe she'd finally have the confidence she needed to stand on her own. She didn't need him.

But right this minute, he needed to hear *Doo-wah-diddy-diddy* humming behind him just one more time.

"You've put on weight," Constantina griped, pulling up the hidden zipper at the back of Mara's spandex gown.

"A month ago you told me I was too skinny. Now you tell me I'm fat." Ignoring her hairdresser's constant carping, Mara poked at her new hairpiece and grimaced. TJ was right—she looked phony in all this crap. Once she had the film canned and the power of the studio was really hers, she would ditch the artifice and come out of the closet as an intellectual harpy. Hollywood could use a good shock.

"Making love makes you hungry," Constantina concluded with approval. "You will need a whole new wardrobe if you stay with that man."

TJ hadn't called her since she'd left. If she kept busy enough, she wouldn't have time to fret over that. Call her Pollyanna, but she intended to keep her appointment with the doctor in the morning for birth control pills. TJ was still out there, and he wasn't picking up women in bars. She had her spies.

"Making love makes me fat—a whole new concept in weight consciousness." Mara jerked off the hairpiece and flung it on the bed. "I think I'll let my hair go natural."

Constantina snorted. "You don't remember what natural is. Men like blondes. And redheads. Why look dowdy when you don't have to?"

Okay, maybe she wouldn't go back to brown. She poked her reading glasses on her nose and peered at the mirror closer. Nope, she didn't like her glasses any better, either—at least not while wearing an evening gown.

She liked glasses in the library and while reading the Sunday papers with TJ. She was two damned different people.

"I'm not out to impress anyone tonight. I'll make it an early night. I have some material I want to go over before I go to bed." Ignoring Constantina's clucking as she rearranged her curls without the filler, Mara made mental notes of everything she needed to do between now and the time she hit the bed. She'd once thrived on being needed. Now the idea of so many senseless tasks exhausted her. When would she ever have a life of her own?

She did what she had to do. She'd persuaded Aunt Miriam to keep Mama out of the institution for a while longer. They'd hired two nurses to watch her. It stretched her budget, but she could be in only so many places at once. "That's fine, Con. I'll just flap my lashes, fill the rich guys with alcohol, and get the checks signed. Don't wait up."

Leaving Constantina muttering dire imprecations, Mara sashayed down the stairs. She'd debated between holding the party outside, where the humidity would curl the straightest hair, or inside, where the narrow dining room provided an intimacy she didn't want without TJ present. She'd opted for the terrace but regretted it as soon as the soggy air hit her.

Her guests were already mingling under the influence of the open bar. Taking a deep breath, she plunged into the glitzy milieu of Mara the party girl.

"Durwood, so good of you to come." She took the arm of one of her biggest investors. "Has Ian showed you the daily rushes? Aren't they stupendous? Glynis at her best. That sheer dress for the sea scene was sheer genius."

Durwood failed to notice her play on words or alliterative license, opting instead to look down her cleavage. "You're better off without Sid, kid. We should work together more often."

His suggestive tone opened pathways she once might have explored. Durwood was rich, currently single, and a power in this business.

With burgeoning confidence in her abilities, she chose to believe she didn't need a man to get her where she wanted to go these days. Smiling, she patted his arm. "That's a wonderful idea. I'll have Ian give you a call when we're ready to start the next project." She leaned closer to whisper, "I have a wonderful idea involving U-boats and a spy who falls in love with the enemy. What do you think?"

She didn't care what he thought, but Durwood liked giving advice. When he appeared ready to wind down, she located her next victim. Waving at the mayor, she kissed Durwood's cheek and drifted toward the little group of locals.

"Mayor Bridgeton! So good to see you."

"Fine party, Miss Simon. I understand filming is ahead of schedule. Do you have any idea when Dr. McCloud will be done with his project? I'm still working on the state, hoping to get that park."

She didn't have any idea when Dr. McCloud would do anything, and the knife in her heart dug a little deeper, but she smiled brilliantly. "We've worked out an agreement. He's brought in his brother to help. I've been doing a little research on my own. Did you know German U-boats used to patrol these waters?"

One of the men with the mayor laughed as if she'd just told a good joke. "You been talking to Ed? He swears he saw one land. Can you imagine some poor German wandering out there lost, eaten by mosquitoes and chased by wild boars? Maybe it's their bones McCloud is digging up."

The idea took root, and Mara glowed with the images it conjured. "Stranded in paradise. Stranger in a strange land. Or maybe a romantic comedy, if the daughter of a local fisherman finds them . . ."

The mayor coughed. "He's being facetious, Miss Simon. I'm sure those bones belong to some poor fisherman who stayed out too late, got drunk, and never came home."

"Oh, no. TJ says one was definitely shot, and there are two bodies out there. But I wouldn't end the movie that way. I prefer happy endings."

"Movie?" The mayor looked vaguely alarmed.

Mara patted his arm reassuringly. "It takes a long, long time to pull together a script and a film. We won't wreak havoc on your quiet town again for another few years."

She left him choking on his olive. She'd just had this marvelous idea for a story line. If she got upstairs in time, she could scribble it all down before it got away from her.

Let Ian handle the investors, media, and other assorted sharks.

TWENTY-SEVEN

Ignoring the fading *Southern Living* magazines scattered across the sixties-style laminated end table in the doctor's office, Mara scribbled notes into her PDA as fast as her stylus would allow.

"Make note to buy keyboard," she muttered. She'd read an article on a minicomputer that had enough memory for a hundred pages of manuscript. If it could fold up to fit in her purse—

"The doctor will see you now, Miss Simonetti."

Maybe she should have made the appointment under her married name. Maybe she should have gone into Charleston instead of the local office. She'd never given much thought to prescriptions for birth control before—probably because she'd been married or about to be. Leave it to TJ to reduce her to the status of embarrassed adolescent again. Was there any way of amputating her shyness gene?

She squirmed even more at the sight of the doctor. He was old enough to be her father, and she worried he was going to lecture her on the perils of immorality. He didn't hide behind a TV-doctor persona of silver, blow-dried hair and geniality, either. He looked at her from over old-fashioned bifocals, ordered her to undress, and ambled off to do whatever mysterious things doctors did.

Men ought to be put through this humiliating routine on a regular basis—it would deflate their egos to a manageable level, Mara thought grumpily, trying to keep the drafty hospital gown modest while the nurse put her through the usual series of tests. If she ever decided TJ wasn't worth the effort, she'd never put herself through this again. She could swear off men with a snap of the fingers.

She couldn't swear off TJ. She looked for him around every corner, stopped by the dig every day, but he managed to stay out of sight. Smart man. She might fling herself at him again and embarrass them both in public.

At some point she would have to quit pampering his screwed-up overprotective urges and call a showdown—but not until she had better control of this contraception thing. She'd learned her limits where TJ was concerned. She couldn't ever risk having a child.

She wondered if that would bother TJ, but it wasn't as if they were talking marriage. At best they could only manage a long-distance relationship. She could do that. She wasn't much good at the regular kind, anyway.

The thought of any kind of relationship with TJ lifted her spirits. It was far better than anything she'd dared hope a month ago. They could meet in romantic hideaways. He could fly to her locations between contracts. She could do the same. They'd once talked of seeing the world together; now they could.

The doctor entered, jotting notes in his chart and looking over his spectacles at her. Perfunctorily he ordered her to assume the position. Retreating to the world she was creating in her mind, Mara submitted to the examination, buoyed by new hope.

"You may get dressed now, Miss Simonetti. I'll see you in my office when you're ready."

Definitely old-fashioned, Mara concluded. Doctors never took time to talk to patients these days. Not that she wanted to talk. She wanted a prescription and out of here. And then she would hunt down TJ in his lair.

Dressed and feeling more confident, even though she'd donned her nondescript librarian's guise today, she sauntered into the doctor's consultation room, glancing at her watch. Not yet lunchtime. She could find TJ, wring his neck and other parts south, and still have time to get back to the set before the afternoon scenes. She could make this work.

"What was the date of your last menstrual period, Miss Simonetti?"

Annoyed at being asked to repeat what was right there on his chart, Mara returned to the moment. "Approximately the second week of July. I've never been regular when I'm off the pill." It was only the end of August.

The doctor made another note. "What means of protection have you been using during intercourse?"

"Condoms." She tapped her toe and glanced at her watch again.

"They're not always reliable, Miss Simonetti," the physician lectured.

"Tell me about it. That's why I'm here."

"Your records show you aren't married, Miss Simonetti. Engaged?"

She wasn't always this slow. The pointed question filtered into her brain, setting off alarms. "I'm a grown woman." She tried hard not to sound like a frightened teenager. "If there's something wrong, just tell me."

"Nothing abnormal, I assure you, just the usual consequences of unprotected intercourse. Urine tests aren't always accurate, but judging from all factors, I'd say you are roughly four weeks pregnant. It's a little late to prescribe birth control."

The doctor's drone as he recommended prenatal vitamins faded as Mara grasped the chair arms unbelievingly.

Four weeks pregnant. The words reverberated in her mind. *Too late for birth control.*

Oh, damn. Oh, shit. Oh, no.

Blankly, Mara took the piece of paper the doctor handed her, nodded when the talking paused, wrote a check when presented with an invoice, but dismay filled every synapse, preventing any coherent thought.

Four weeks pregnant. Too late for birth control.

This couldn't be happening. Not now. Not after all these years.

"The family will recover, TJ," Clay assured him, grabbing the beer the bartender shoved in his direction. "Mom brags about you all the time. It's not as if your name is in the headlines or anything."

"It doesn't need to be. The funding for the beach project got pulled today," TJ replied gloomily. "Good timing. Whoever wants me out of here had my office lease canceled as of September first. I have to pack it up tomorrow." He didn't know where he'd go after he did. For fifteen years he'd been on the run. Slamming into a wall now had knocked him out.

"They can't do that, can they?" Outraged, Clay smacked his bottle down. "A grant is a grant. They can't pull it midstream."

"I'm paid in increments. It wasn't much, anyway." TJ shrugged it off. He wouldn't starve anytime soon.

He had no excuse to stay and see Mara again.

"What did you mean about someone wanting you to leave?" Clay's always suspicious mind caught another thread.

"They seem to have given up lately. They trashed my office, the dig site, sent nasty little notes. I just figured they were behind the lease cancellation as well. Some local yokel thinks I'm standing in the way of progress." TJ sipped his beer, aware of the low murmur of conversation in several corners of the bar. It was too early for Ed and his cronies to take their places. Or maybe all the strangers had driven them to more comfortable environs. There was a new reporter here every night. TJ thought they ought to form a network and save themselves a lot of trouble.

"Have you heard from Martin?"

"The colonel wouldn't have anything to do with petty vandalism." TJ corrected Clay's path of thought. "If he's after my head, he'll arrive brandishing a sword."

"Some friend. You sure know how to pick 'em."

TJ didn't bother to interpret that remark.

"McCloud," a worried voice intruded.

Both TJ and Clay glanced over their shoulders.

The pretentious little producer from Mara's crew nervously tapped the cell phone in his hand as he looked from one unmistakable McCloud face to the other. "*Dr.* McCloud, sorry. Could I speak with you a moment?"

TJ debated telling him where to go, but his curiosity had always been his downfall. Shoving away from the bar, he followed Ian to an unoccupied corner. "What is it? I'll be closing the site shortly. You ought to be thrilled."

"It's Mara," Ian blurted with uncharacteristic emotion. "I think she's having a breakdown. She's always been clearheaded and on top of things when Sid lost it, but this time . . . If neither Sid nor Mara is in charge of the production—"

Ian choked as TJ grabbed his collar and dragged him toward the door.

"Who did what to her?" TJ demanded, physically heaving the smaller man into the street and following him out.

"No one. Nothing that I know of." Frantically following TJ's giant strides, Ian attempted to straighten his shirt. "She went out this morning, came back at noon and locked herself in, and she won't come out. She hasn't eaten, doesn't answer the phone, and every so often something crashes against the wall. Katy is concerned about the antiques in there."

"To hell with the damned antiques," TJ shouted, increasing his pace to a run. "What has Sid done this time?" His stride outstripped Ian's, and he didn't hear the reply.

Racing past the overgrown gardenia and down the drive to the B&B, TJ tried convincing himself that he didn't know Mara as well as he thought. Just because the teenager he'd once known was temperamentally unsuited to hysterical fits didn't mean the woman she was now wasn't capable of them.

Mara was capable of fits, all right, but only for a reason. What reason? Panic socked him in the stomach, and his feet pounded the wooden porch at warp speed. The old-fashioned wooden screen door slammed against the wall when he threw it open.

Katy, the anxious proprietor, stepped out of his way as TJ took the stairs two at a time. He didn't hear anything overhead, but in his present state of mind, even silence was ominous.

He rattled the knob without knocking. Finding it locked, TJ cursed and pounded the door panel. "Mara! I've got news. Open up." Her curiosity had always been stronger than his.

Something breakable shattered against the other side of the door. So much for curiosity.

"Throw things at me instead of the door," he shouted, frantically seeking some way of reaching her. There'd been a time when he'd ignored Brad's tantrums. He had to believe Mara was stronger than Brad. "Don't be such a wimp," he shouted, praying anger would drive her to throttle him.

A heavy object collided with the other side of the door, followed by something that sounded like a book. Experience had taught TJ how to control panic and seek solutions, but not when it came to Mara. Terror tore through him at the sound of breaking glass.

"She's slid the bolt," Katy whispered from behind him. "The door is solid oak."

"Windows?" TJ demanded. Mara couldn't be doing anything too drastic if she still had the strength to heave things.

"It's the second floor. We'd need a ladder. The glass is old and the panes are small," Katy warned.

"Bring me a toolbox." TJ eyed the old-fashioned backward door hinges, judging the level of difficulty.

While she ran to follow his orders, TJ pounded the

door again. "I'm not leaving until I talk to you. You've got to come out sometime."

Silence.

That was worse than breaking glass. Frantically TJ grabbed the hinge pin and tried to work it loose with his fingers. As he feared, it was thoroughly hammered in.

"I've got Godivas," he called, his mind racing while suppressing his alarm. "Let's find some espresso and talk about it."

Silence again. Then the lock clicked. Nearly collapsing in relief, TJ closed his eyes in a prayer of thanksgiving. The instant the door cracked open, he shouldered through the crack, slammed the solid oak panel closed behind him, and leaned against it to prevent escape. He stood in a war zone of broken glass and hurled objects.

"You lied." Glancing at his empty hands, Mara spun around and stalked to the window, presenting him with her back.

He'd seen enough with his first glance. She looked terrible. She looked wonderful. He wanted to scoop her up and carry her away and forget everything that had gone before this.

He knew better than to presume too much.

In these past few weeks, she'd turned everything he'd believed about himself inside out. His momentary panic over losing her permanently had drained him, and he needed time to recover. Letting the door hold him up, TJ watched her pace.

Multicolored tangles of bleached hair tumbled to her shoulders. She wore a white cotton bathrobe that revealed nothing of her figure but her height and slenderness. She wore no makeup, but TJ could tell she'd been crying. She finally stopped pacing and stood huddled in front of the window seat. He ached to reach for her, but after this past week, he really didn't have that right.

"I'll break into the drugstore and steal the Godivas," he offered helplessly. "We can go back to Jared's for the espresso."

"I'm pregnant."

Shock hit TJ's bloodstream like an injection, spreading slowly but insidiously until all his vital signs went bonkers and hammers pounded his brain.

"Pregnant?" he repeated cautiously, still using the door for support. It had only been a week—

His gaze fell on the red shawl wadded up on the floor, and the vivid image of that maddening evening—how long ago? a month?—filled his mind. They'd gone at each other like hungry animals. Half-sloshed, angry, and overheated, he'd responded to her taunts with his body instead of his head.

She was carrying his child. His mind felt as if it was exploding in fifteen different directions at once, but concern emerged first. "You've seen a doctor?"

"Don't worry. I'm not having it." She continued staring over the harbor, the robe wrapped tightly around her.

If the door hadn't been holding him up, he'd crumple to his knees. He'd never thought about babies, but his gut reaction was fascination at the idea of fatherhood and horror at the idea of losing a child. Trying to think rationally, TJ sought some reply. "We can get married." Propriety. Always fall back on prescribed behavior when all else failed. He began to feel a little better. "I would have asked you sooner—"

"I'm not having a baby. Save your proposals. I don't need you or any other man, now or ever."

She straightened her spine, clenched her fists at her side, and spoke with coldness, but TJ caught the tiny hitch in her voice. A little girl called Patsy still hid somewhere behind that sophisticated woman. Patsy couldn't swat a fly. She'd never harm a baby.

Gathering all the shattered bits of his courage, TJ crossed the room to stand behind her. He didn't trust himself to touch her yet. "We have time to think about this. Don't do anything rash. Come home with me, and we can talk."

He had a purpose again. He didn't dare explore his

feelings just yet, not while Mara was in this state. He just knew he needed to be with her. And she needed to be with him.

The starch seemed to drain out of her all at once. Her shoulders slumped, and she shook her head helplessly. "No, I don't want you to talk me out of this. If you're a real friend, you'll find a place that takes care of this kind of thing."

Her broken whisper tore TJ's heart into shreds. More terrified than he'd ever been in his life, he hesitated, afraid he'd drive her to something irrational if he came any closer.

But he couldn't *not* touch her. Gently TJ wrapped his arms around her waist. "Do you hate me that much? I'm sorry I didn't protect you. I was unforgivably reckless and had no excuse. But you can't take it out—"

She shook her head violently. "Stop it, TJ! You're only making things worse. Find a clinic. Don't ever come near me again, and this will all go away with time."

Maybe he was kidding himself, but he didn't think she meant that. There was more here than met the eye.

TJ refused to release her, and eventually she began to weep. He turned her in his arms, pressed her tears against his chest, and dug his fingers into her springy curls. "Explain in words that make me understand," he murmured as her sobs escalated and his own eyes burned. He never in his life wanted to hurt Patsy, but he seemed to do it repeatedly.

"I can't have a baby," she sobbed into his shoulder. "I just can't. I'll go crazy, just like my mother."

"Your mother isn't crazy. A little neurotic, but not crazy." He hadn't seen her mother in seventeen years. What did he know? But he'd say anything to calm her right now.

"She's mentally ill," Mara responded vehemently. "Certifiably. It runs in the family. It's a chemical imbalance." She slammed her fist into his shoulder, trying to get free, but TJ only hung on tighter. "Damn you, Tim! Let me go."

"No, not until I hear the whole story. Chemical imbalances can be treated. Give me more."

Mara shook her head and collapsed against Tim's muscled shoulder. He rubbed his hand up and down her spine, and his strength calmed her, but physical strength wouldn't solve her problems this time. Nor would his cleverness, his sense of justice, or his family connections.

"I don't know the technical terms. Her wiring is out of whack—the imbalance makes it worse. Some days medication is enough. Others it isn't. She can be gentle as a lamb or tear a room into shreds in a matter of minutes. She tried to kill me once. She didn't remember it the next day. It's hereditary, TJ. My mind can snap just like that. It did. I completely lost it after Irving hit me. I lived in the park for weeks with all the other homeless people. I refuse to pass this horrible degenerative thing on to another generation. I can't have this baby!"

His silence didn't tell her everything she wanted to hear, but it said enough. Carefully, feeling as if she held the shattered bits of herself together with frayed twine, Mara pried free of his hold and retreated across the room.

Her father had deserted her when she needed him most, even knowing her mother was ill. Irving had left her after the homeless incident. Brad—no point in rehashing old news. The men in her life didn't hang around. She had depended on them, but they'd never needed her. She wouldn't repeat past failures.

"It's okay, Tim. I can take care of myself." She could barely stand to watch the devastation written across his face, but it strengthened her resolve. "I just can't take care of anyone else. Aunt Miriam takes care of Mom. I send her money. That's the most I can manage."

He looked so sad, she wanted to weep for him, but she'd already shed all the tears she had for herself. Gripping her elbows, her arms wrapped around herself, she waited. If she had to find an abortion clinic on her own, she would. She just prayed TJ was the friend she needed.

"We need time," he said slowly, obviously hunting for

words. "I've got to know more." He studied her through grief-stricken dark eyes. "Please, give me time. I know it's your decision, and I won't stand in your way—but just wait and let me find some way of understanding."

His gaze never left her face, and Mara drew reassurance from that. She couldn't see what there was to understand, but relief flooded through her at his acceptance. She didn't want to do this alone.

Let him leave her after it was over.

TWENTY-EIGHT

Once she'd given him her promise, TJ held his finger to his lips, cocked his head, and narrowed his gaze at the door. "Throw something," he whispered.

Startled, Mara leapt to do as asked. He had that effect on her. Without giving it much thought, she flung a brass candlestick from the mantel.

TJ nodded. "More, and shout." Leaving her in front of the window, he eased toward the door.

Permission to throw a fit. Just what she needed. Full of pent-up misery, Mara flung pillows, shoes, and her damned PDA. She felt a certain sense of satisfaction as it exploded into a million bytes.

"Out, you miserable, rotten cur," she screamed at the top of her lungs. That felt so good, she threw herself into it with more enthusiasm. "I'll rip your tongue out, TJ McCloud! I'll dice your balls."

TJ arched a wry eyebrow as he reached for the doorknob, but Mara was in full gear now. "I'll slice your liver and serve it to the turkeys—"

TJ flung open the door, and half a dozen startled people nearly fell over each other as they tumbled into the room.

Unabashed, Ian righted himself and glared at TJ. Katy Richards took in the layer of shattered glass with dismay. Constantina rushed to hug Mara, murmuring Italian consolations and giving TJ the evil eye. Several of the crew hastily backed down the hall at the sight of TJ's threatening demeanor. And Clay waited, hands in pockets, taking in the whole scene with sardonic humor, apparently well acquainted with his brother's Machiavellian tactics.

Before anyone else could speak, TJ escalated into field commander mode. "Ian, find Godivas for the lady. Break into the drugstore if it's closed. Katy, find a good hot dinner."

TJ glanced over his shoulder, and Mara's frayed nerve endings quivered at his look of concern. Independence was fine when she was feeling strong, but when the world rolled over her and crushed her flat, it was heartbreakingly wonderful to have a wiser, stronger head in charge.

"What would you like to eat?" he asked in a voice that allowed no argument.

She was starving. Now that she knew she could rely on TJ a little longer, it was as if the weight of the world had temporarily lifted, and she could look around again. "Meatloaf," she stated decisively, "with lots of gravy and biscuits."

Constantina stared at her in horror. Ian looked confused. Mara simply didn't care. She beamed at them with good humor.

"Clay, take my car," TJ ordered. "Bring my duffel and shaving kit back in the morning. And Jared's espresso machine."

Mara liked the sound of espresso. She wasn't too certain about the rest, but TJ was doing what he did best, taking charge. Who was she to interfere?

Clay looked her up and down. Apparently deciding she wouldn't explode and take TJ with her, he grabbed the back of Ian's shirt. "C'mon. I'm good at breaking and entering. Show me the drugstore."

Sputtering, Ian backed out the door.

"Katy, we'll reimburse you for the breakage." Deciding she ought to be responsible for some of these orders, Mara turned to Constantina. "Con, find some cleaning equipment so I can clean up this mess. I'm fine, really I am." *Sort of. Someday.* Putting on a brave face was half the job.

Under TJ's not-so-gentle urging, their audience reluctantly departed. With a look of exhaustion, he closed the door and leaned against it. Arms rippling with muscle bespoke his strength, but his collapsed stance warned her that even TJ had his limits.

"I'm sorry," Mara murmured, not knowing what else to say.

"You don't have to apologize." He straightened, driving his hand through his hair. It had grown longer these last weeks and kept falling in his eyes. "If anyone's to blame here, I am."

"Well, yeah, if my producer gets arrested for stealing chocolate, I'll hold you responsible, but that wasn't what I meant." Uneasy now that the drama had ended, Mara wandered lost around the room, not knowing what to do with herself.

"I knew what you meant." TJ blocked the French windows overlooking the harbor, following her every move with his eyes. "I'm not Sid or Irving. I take responsibility for my actions. This is my fault."

"Oh, right, and I was just a chair in all this." She liked it that he didn't blame her, that he stood ready to shoulder his fair share and more. She just wasn't used to it. She took the seat at her vanity and began picking up the bottles and cosmetics she'd knocked to the floor in her earlier storm of raging fear. "You don't have to stay, TJ. I'll be okay."

"No, you won't. And neither will I. This is not something that will ever be *okay*." He glanced around, and finding the desk phone under a chair, pulled it out and started dialing.

Guilt stole through Mara, but she couldn't give in to it. Most men would be relieved that she wanted to get rid of this problem. Not TJ. She shouldn't have told him.

She couldn't have done anything less. That realization momentarily overwhelmed her. TJ was a part of her. She couldn't hide things from him, couldn't lie, couldn't pretend, couldn't even *think* about pretending. All these years since Brad's death, she'd gone through life alone. It had taken TJ less than a month to become an extension of herself, the part that understood even when she was most confused, the part that could be strong when she was weak.

She didn't know how she could go on without him, but after this disaster, there was no question of going on together. He would hate her for what she had to do. And she couldn't burden him with what she was.

She couldn't face the totality of the devastation just yet.

"Yeah, move the guys here," TJ said into the receiver. "The place is fenced, but it's not secured. We'll need two guards to patrol, and at least one on the drive. If there's any trouble, we may need to upgrade to two. Immediately. Right." TJ hung up the phone and started to dial again.

Mara caught the receiver and hung it up. "What are you doing?" They were too close. She instantly backed away as the intensity of TJ's stare burned into her like a laser beam.

"I'm reverting to Incredible Hulk mode," he said gravely. "You throw things. I put up barriers. I'm moving security here."

"You've been reading Jared's comics again, haven't you? What the devil do we need security for?"

"I'm not having this place crawling with reporters out to nail my hide to the wall." He punched buttons as curtly as he spoke. "We need time to talk, and we can't do it in the middle of a three-ring circus."

Not entirely certain that a circus wouldn't be the best solution, Mara answered a hesitant knock at the door and let Katy and Constantina in, wielding brooms and vacuums.

After that, the constant coming and going prevented serious conversation, just as he'd predicted. Ian returned with Godivas and wine and the next day's script changes.

One of Katy's staff arrived bearing meatloaf and french fries and an assortment of veggies smothered in butter.

Mara settled down to dig into the food but looked up in surprise when TJ appropriated her wine.

"Alcohol is bad for babies." He carried the bottle back to the desk and sipped from the glass he'd taken from her.

Half a dozen arguments leapt futilely to her lips, but she didn't utter any of them. He'd said he needed time to adjust. She'd give him a few days. That's all she could afford.

"I've spent fifteen years studying bones of dead people," he continued without any prompting from her. "I'm discovering a dismaying desire for life-affirming events. There's too much death in this world."

Oh, damn. Mara rubbed her forehead. "There's life all around us, TJ."

"I know. And I know that life doesn't have to be my baby. Babies are born all the time." He turned his back to her so she couldn't read the shadows of his face.

"Don't you think this would be easier if we didn't see each other?" *He wanted children.* She lost her appetite, but she picked at the food anyway. She wasn't eating for two. She would not kid herself into believing that.

"No. There's no 'easier' to it." Grimly he settled into the wing chair by the fireplace and drained the wineglass.

This time she bore the full brunt of his gaze. Damn, he was so strikingly large, so *male* sitting there like some arrogant prince weighing the woes of the world. If he weren't so darned full of integrity, she could almost resist him.

"Go back and visit my mother," Mara said dryly. "Don't get me wrong. I love her. She loved us and took care of us and stood up for us against all but my father. But the woman who brought me up is almost totally gone now."

He set the glass aside and rubbed his temples. "Your aunt isn't afflicted. Grandparents? Anyone else?"

"They think it's a recessive gene." Giving up on food, Mara sipped the coffee TJ had ordered for her. "My maternal grandparents died in the war, so we don't have a family history. The doctor said Brad's suicide could have been some form of it, but we'll never know now. Aunt Miriam says we come from a long line of eccentrics." She offered a deprecating grin. "My aunt speaks ill only of the living."

TJ started to speak, but Mara waved his words away. "Don't, TJ. I've already experienced one terrifying episode. I can't afford another, and I can't inflict on a child what my mother has inflicted on me. I refuse to pass on this trait to another generation. The buck stops here."

"Tell me about the homeless-in-the-park incident."

The change in direction jolted her, but TJ's inquiring mind needed feeding, and she was his current topic of interest. She tried not to revisit this particular subject if she could avoid it, but she supposed he ought to know all the parameters of the situation. "I was only twenty. Irving and I had our ups and downs, but I was raised to believe marriage was forever, so I was making the best of it. This was before my mother's symptoms were diagnosed."

TJ poured another glass of wine and stoically bit his tongue—she could tell by the way his jaw muscles clenched. She'd lived it. He could listen.

"Anyway, I arrived at the store early one day, and there was Irving in the back room, his pants down around his ankles, boffing the airhead clerk." Mara closed her eyes against the pain. "I'm not certain what I did—screamed, hit him with my pocketbook, who knows? I certainly caught him off guard, and he came up swinging. I think it was the gushing blood that prevented us from killing each other. We were all absurdly civilized, finding ice, cleaning up, taking me to the emergency room. The doctors patched me up, told me to come back for surgery, and I got up, got dressed, and left without looking for Irving. I didn't go home. I went away somewhere inside my head. The police returned me to Irving a few weeks later when they found me crying on a park bench. I remember very little of those weeks. End of story."

TJ nodded knowingly. "Depression. That's treatable."

"What Mama has isn't," she argued, knowing the subject well.

"You don't know that you have what she does."

"I'm not willing to take that risk." She bit her lip against a sob, praying he'd understand.

TJ leaned his head back against the chair. "I want to come over there and hold you right now, but I don't dare." His voice sounded strained, and his big hands gripped the chair arms until his knuckles turned white. "You cried all the way through Brad's funeral, and I didn't dare go to you then, either. Where you're concerned, my protective instincts are all screwed up with hormones. Back then, I figured you hated me and wouldn't want me touching you. Right now . . ." He gestured helplessly. "You have reason to hate me twice as much."

"The Incredible Hulk thinks with his prick," she said dryly. "Women understand that. We're really not as dumb as we look."

He sat up and cocked his eyebrow, challenging her. "All right, we'll take this one step at a time. Will you let me sleep with you, or shall I ask Katy for a cot?"

Sometimes his bluntness was hard to take. There was something to be said for padding honesty with warm fuzzies. But she wanted TJ in her lonely bed so much, she didn't care how the offer arrived. She submitted a perfunctory protest. "Do you think sleeping together is the smart thing to do?"

"I don't think intelligence has anything to do with where we are now." The dry tone of his voice made her wince.

"I'm winging it," he continued, staying firmly planted in the chair. "I want to sleep with you. That's not all I want to do," he admitted, "but I thought maybe this time, we could try talking about it first. Lend some token of rationality."

He still wanted to sleep with her. Mara let that pleasant thought comfort her. Despite everything she'd hit him with in these last few hours, he didn't want to run screaming for the hills. Every other man of her acquaintance would be running so hard by now, she wouldn't even see his dust. "You're the one who threw me out last time," she reminded him.

"For your own good. I've got a few problems you don't need to be burdened with."

Mara flung the coffee cup at his obtuse head. Fortunately for both of them, it was empty. TJ caught it with one hand and set it beside his glass.

Her breath caught as he rose from the chair. He was so damned magnificent. It terrified her to believe a man like that would want her.

Though she knew he was in as much turmoil as she, he looked calm and confident and gorgeous. Sturdy tanned hands reached out to help her from the chair. Muscled arms clasped her against a chest so powerful, she could feel the strength he restrained as he bent to kiss her cheek. In TJ's arms, even an ungraceful ostrich like her could feel cherished.

It couldn't hurt to feel loved for just a few days. Every soul needed the nourishment of love and gentleness to flourish and grow. Perhaps, if she was very careful, she could help TJ in the same way.

Standing on tiptoe, she clasped the sides of his head and brought his lips to hers. She would offer what little she could, and pray she wouldn't drive him away too soon.

TJ leaned his shoulder on the window frame and watched the dawn spread over the yachts bobbing in the harbor. After Mara's incredibly intense lovemaking last night, he should have slept like a dead man. He hadn't slept a wink.

The woman in the bed behind him had seeped inside some part of him he hadn't known existed. He wanted her. He'd always wanted her. That much he understood.

But even after they made love and physical desires had been momentarily satiated, there was a connection, and a hunger he couldn't resolve in any known fashion.

For one insane moment yesterday, wild hope had blossomed, and he had imagined marriage and babies and a house he could go home to at night where he could feel loved and wanted.

He hadn't even known he'd needed those things until Mara had said he couldn't have them—not with her. She was the only woman he knew who could make him contemplate domesticity—probably because Mara's idea of domesticity had him ducking for cover half the time.

He grinned briefly at the memory of some of their skirmishes, then rubbed his forehead again and tried not to turn to admire Mara's slenderness buried under the covers. He'd learned she liked the air-conditioning turned up so she could sleep with the blankets on. He thought he could spend a lifetime uncovering the secrets of her mind and never grow bored. He wanted a lifetime with Mara.

He wanted their child.

Tears prickled behind his eyelids, but he wasn't a man who cried easily. Pain simply welled and ate at his gut.

He had no right to demand anything of her. He'd already caused enough harm. But every time he thought about the child they'd created . . . He knew he was willing to take chances. Mara wasn't. She needed security. She needed hairdressers and limos and lace pillows and all those things his life didn't include.

She stirred and called sleepily. The seductive sound drew TJ like a siren song, reminding him of why he couldn't insist, couldn't argue, could do nothing to make this more difficult for her. He had to think of Mara first.

Trying to find that place inside himself where he retreated when he examined the bones of murdered children, TJ forced a smile and sat down on the bed. "I'll bring you some coffee," he promised, brushing a kiss across her brow.

"And shoot anyone who comes near us," she murmured, snuggling closer.

"That can be arranged." Smiling genuinely now, TJ smoothed the hair from her eyes.

He just needed to find the woman he knew and loved inside the shell of Mara Simon, glamorous movie producer. Shy Patsy had retreated into hiding, but once he persuaded her to come out, he could try reasoning with her fears.

She needed him. This time he wouldn't leave.

TWENTY-NINE

"You had a message from Dad and a rather erratic one from the colonel," Clay announced, entering the dining room where TJ and Mara sat sipping coffee and scanning newspapers. He set the espresso machine he carried on the counter where Katy indicated.

"The cottage doesn't have an answering machine," TJ replied curtly.

Aware of her crew gradually filling the other tables, Mara didn't interfere in the conversation between brothers, but she rather thought TJ was missing the point. Probably deliberately.

"Jared does." Clay plugged in the coffee machine and checked the dials.

TJ growled and set aside his newspaper. "How erratic?"

"Once I got past some of the most inventive swearing I've heard in a while, it sounded as if the colonel's blaming you for turning on him. I believe he accused you of lying, betrayal, and possibly the end of Christianity."

"He found out I gave the boxes to the media." TJ picked up the paper again.

Mara snatched it from his hands. "Call him, TJ. Explain what happened. If he's innocent, you owe him that."

He regarded her over the top of his cup. "I can only take care of so many innocents at one time. Martin can take care of himself."

She didn't want to read more into his words than was there. If he spoke of the child, she wouldn't listen.

But she knew he'd never forgiven himself for not listening to Brad. She didn't want to see him destroyed, didn't want to heap more guilt on his overworked conscience—as she was doing. Unable to consider that thought, she stuck out her hand. "Give me his number and I'll call."

Clay dropped the phone message into her palm. "Maybe you'll want to call Dad, too. This is the first time in my recollection that he's taken his nose out of a book long enough to pick up a phone."

"He called once from the hospital when you were born," TJ offered without inflection, grabbing the message from Mara's hand and tucking it into his pocket. "I didn't recognize his voice until he yelled at me for answering the phone improperly. You haven't missed much."

Clay laughed and crossed the room again to watch Katy feed coffee beans to the espresso machine, leaving them to their privacy.

"Okay, so wealthy doesn't mean functional." Mara interpreted TJ's meaning this time. "But your parents are at least minimally sane."

A smile cocked one corner of his mouth. "Define 'sane.' "

She was as much into avoidance as TJ this morning. "Not in this lifetime. Are you going to the dig? I want to see how the production is coming, then I thought I'd double-check the library to see if I missed anything and go back to the courthouse to look up the names of the landowners on the island. I hate giving up on your bones."

"I'm packing up the site and the office, shipping everything to the storage unit in Charleston until someone claims them. Stop by the dig and tell me when you leave for the courthouse, and I can join you if I'm done."

She loved talking about mundane daily tasks with TJ. It established a balance of order she could learn to enjoy. He didn't complain if she neglected him to follow her own pursuits. He even offered to *help*. For the first time in her life, a man made her feel important.

She was dreaming again. TJ would despise her once he understood she was serious about not having babies. *Keep this strictly professional, Patsy Amara.* "I thought I'd dig deeper into the mayor's family. Something the librarian said made me curious. I doubt there's any relationship, but—"

"You never could resist curiosity. Got it." TJ polished his reading glasses while watching from across the table. "Would you rather I stayed with you today?"

Mara fought back tears at his concern. "I'll be okay. Just don't remind me, all right?"

He pinched the bridge of his nose and nodded. "I'll try. Just keep talking to me. I need to know what's happening inside your head or I'll panic and pull a Hulk again."

She hated what she was doing to him. Underneath all that muscle was a man who genuinely cared and worried about her, but she couldn't help smiling at the image his words summoned. "You're not green, but I like the idea of you bursting out of your shirt. Instead of talking, can I tease you once in a while?"

"Not right now. I'm walking a wire so thin, I can't see it." Abruptly he stood and walked away from the table without a word of farewell or a kiss to ease the parting.

Mara understood. Sometimes this sharing business left the skin thin and tender to the touch. He'd already pierced her in a thousand places this morning without even trying.

She'd hate to see what damage he could wreak when he really worked at it.

"Did I show you pictures of my nephew, Miss Simon? He's only nine months old and already walking. My sister says he calls for auntie all the time." The young assistant librarian brought out a string of plastic-covered snapshots and spread them across the counter for Mara's perusal.

The precocious child in the pictures had black hair the color of TJ's.

Mara choked out some senseless sentiment, gathered up her papers, and fled the quiet library. So much for the peace of research.

She'd run away from the set when one of the locals brought his twin toddlers to the beach to show off. She'd escaped the B&B when friends of Katy's brought their children to play in the private pool. Everywhere she turned, adorable babies smiled and cooed at her, promising love and laughter and hope for the future.

She'd get her tubes tied. She was too old to change her ways or to endure this indecision any longer. She liked her freedom. For the first time in her life, she was on the brink of having her own life, supporting herself, and enjoying it. In a year or two perhaps she could have a house of her own, and her mother could stay with her. That ought to kill any annoying hormonal need to nurture.

She wouldn't think about the bundle of chromosomes growing inside her.

She stalked into the courthouse, and a curly-haired toddler beamed at her from behind a giant red lollipop. Instant anguish.

Get over it. Get on, get moving, keep busy. Don't stop now.

Biting back tears, cursing rampaging hormones, Mara located the property tax office and asked for deed listings. With a list of addresses in hand, she dug through aging deed books, spreading them out on the table provided. She loved research. Dead, lifeless tomes could reveal secrets of the living. How had the mayor's family acquired half the property in town? Were they really German, as the librarian had mentioned?

It was a fascinating puzzle that should have kept her occupied for hours, but she couldn't concentrate.

Dead, lifeless tomes were just that. Dead and lifeless.

Tears trickling down her cheeks, Mara abandoned the books, fled the courthouse, and ran directly into the object of her research.

Tired, dirty, and disgusted with himself and life in general, TJ trudged into the B&B in search of Mara. The film crew had said she'd left the beach early. She hadn't stopped at the dig, as she'd promised. He didn't want to think about why she hadn't. He didn't want to think about her wandering the streets of New York homeless, either, but she'd done it.

Did he really want to spend the rest of his life worrying if she'd gone off the deep end?

Even as irritated and world-weary as he was now, TJ knew the answer to that one. Mara was precious enough to protect until his last, dying breath. He'd take her any way he could have her. He needed to hear her singing *Doo-wah-diddy-diddy* for the rest of his life.

How could he trust himself to protect her? He'd done a damned lousy job of it so far.

Trudging upstairs, he found no sign that she'd returned to her room. No one claimed to have seen her. The library or courthouse, then.

He took a quick shower and changed into fresh clothes he'd brought from the cottage. He'd tried calling the number Clay had given him for the colonel, but he'd received no answer. He hated having Martin think of him as a traitor, but he had to remember this wasn't about him anymore. This was about truth and justice.

He was tired of truth and justice. He wanted home and Mara. And their child. He'd never once given thought to having children. They died as easily as adults in the war-torn zones he'd traveled. Tragedy had a way of blocking out life, numbing the senses. Dying seemed easy, living too hard.

But if Mara would only give him reason to live, he'd do whatever it took. The thought of Mara and a home opened up his life to endless possibilities.

He'd never tried out for the debate team, had no particular talent for words, but he would somehow persuade Mara to keep their child. Medicine had cures for everything on the horizon. He could handle the responsibility of whatever happened. But for them to live together, he would have to convince her to give up her career.

Right, like that was going to happen.

Leaving the inn to head for the library, TJ almost walked straight into Roger Curtis. The reporter caught his arm and prevented the crash.

"Have you seen Colonel Martin?" Roger demanded without preface.

TJ scowled. "Hardly. He left a scathing diatribe on my brother's machine, but I can't reach him."

"One of the guys swore he saw him at the airport in Charleston. I figured he was heading here. He has to know the evidence came from those boxes he told you to destroy. You might want to take that Mexican job."

At the moment TJ was glad he couldn't take the job. He wanted to stay with Mara and not dig up the bones of still another guerrilla massacre, or drug war—he couldn't remember which. "I'll talk to Martin if I see him. I can't believe the man is a violent criminal. You're getting paranoid in your old age, Rog."

The reporter shrugged. "I owe you a favor. I'm just trying to help out."

TJ had never stayed in one place long enough to make many friends. It was nice to know he had at least one. He pounded Roger on the back, causing the other man to wince. "I appreciate it. I'd buy you a drink, but I'm in search of an elusive butterfly. Some other time, maybe?"

"Your butterfly was flitting around the courthouse last time I saw her. She didn't look too happy being cornered by the mayor, so I stayed out of the way. Figured she could handle him better than I could."

TJ glanced at his watch. "Courthouse is closed. Maybe they went for drinks somewhere. I'll keep looking."

The mayor. He didn't know why, but TJ didn't like the idea of Mara hanging around the mayor. He didn't like jovial politicians, maybe. How could a man trust someone who smiled all the time?

He ran into Ian next. The town had more bars than coffee shops, and Ian knew every one of them. He'd give the little producer credit for knowing his limits, though. He didn't appear the least bit drunk as TJ stopped him in the street. "Have you seen Mara?"

"I thought she was with you. I need her to sign these liability releases for the bulldozer." Ian scowled, patted his pocket to make certain the papers were still there, and sidestepped TJ's looming form. "Tell her we'll be ready to open that road first thing in the morning if she'll sign these."

TJ hated the idea of bulldozing the dune, but it really wasn't a dune. Truth was, it was more of a public hazard than anything else. He supposed what he really hated was not solving the mystery. "I'll give the papers to her when I find her, if you want."

"Not on your life." Obviously not trusting him, Ian spun around and started back for the inn.

Well, he wouldn't trust himself, either, as things stood. Wishing for a good cold beer, TJ marched toward the courthouse. He needed Cleo here to tell him where the best places to hunt a mayor were.

On a weeknight, everything shut down early, especially away from the tourist part of town. The courthouse and all the small shops and restaurants that catered to a courthouse clientele had closed by the time TJ reached them. Daylight lingered, though long shadows crossed the street. He hoped Mara wasn't wandering out here alone. The town center was surrounded by quiet residential streets lined with fading mansions in various degrees of restoration. They seemed safe enough, but beautiful women ought to be wary of walking dark streets alone.

Not that the idiot thought she was beautiful, he

grumbled to himself. Mara had spent too much time looking at the outside and not enough looking on the inside. He supposed in places like Hollywood, appearance was all that counted. He wished he could persuade her to give up that life. She deserved better, but he figured that would be the same as asking him to give up forensics. Of course, with the military and the press reducing his career to shambles, that was a distinct possibility. Maybe he could move to Hollywood with her.

Exhaustion subsiding as worry increased, TJ stalked back to the inn. Where could she have gone?

He wouldn't think of Brad's death. Mara was strong. She wouldn't do that to herself. Or to him. The conviction that she would protect him from pain grew stronger with every passing step. Mara would never devastate him as Brad had.

He trusted Mara.

That was a revelation in itself. After Brad's death, he'd quit letting anyone get close to him, but he had to believe Mara knew how much it would hurt him if she hurt herself. Mara was the only person alive who understood he wasn't made of steel.

He'd almost decided he was an idiot for worrying when he encountered the mayor coming out of the B&B.

"Dr. McCloud!"

TJ refrained from rolling his eyes at the title. "Mayor. You'll be pleased to know the lane to the beach will be bulldozed in the morning."

The mayor beamed. "Good to hear that, sir. Very good to hear that. That's a load off my mind, I'll tell you. The little lady didn't seem certain about the schedule. Give her my apologies if I offended her, will you?"

Mara towered over the old goat, and he still called her "little." TJ would like to hear Mara's comments on the subject, but he'd have to find the damned woman first. "Did you speak with her?"

"Just came looking for her to extend my apologies. Saw her earlier and she seemed a mite distressed, so I thought

I'd try again. They say she's gone back to the island to set up some night scene."

Ian should have known that, the miserable bastard.

"Your brother is inside," the mayor continued. "Handy man, that. He's taking apart Katy's kitchen and putting it back together again better than new. Need to set him to fixing the courthouse clock."

Cleo had tried that once. TJ would rather not think about his younger brother up there on that roof. Shaking his head, he left the mayor to see what kind of damage Clay was creating now. He distinctly remembered a time when his brother had dismantled the kitchen gas stove, run a pipe to the backyard, and launched his own space missile.

Their father had patted Clay on the head and wandered back to his library. Their mother had thrown a benefit to appease the firefighters and policemen who'd spent the night calming the crowds and overseeing the gas-main repairs.

And Mara thought *her* family had problems?

He found Clay under the counter with the stove burners, or he found his brother's legs, anyway. His head was buried in the wiring inside the cabinet. Katy's cook was hacking raw vegetables so brutally, TJ feared a finger would fly.

"Did you tell the lady you'd have that done by mealtime?" TJ inquired without really wanting to hear the answer.

"Yeah, I'll be done in just a minute," echoed from beneath the counter.

The cook glanced significantly at the clock.

"Mealtime is here, little brother, and I believe it's written somewhere that meals need to be cooked before they can be served."

"Oh, right, microwaves aren't good enough." Clay inched out from under the counter, a smear of dirt across his nose. "It's connected. I need to buy some stronger wiring before I can do more."

The two-hundred-pound cook shoved TJ out of the way in her hurry to reach the stove. Clay she stepped over.

Scooting out of her way, Clay clambered up. Sun-bleached hair fell across his bronzed forehead as he wiped his hands on a rag. "Did you and the colonel resolve your differences?"

The colonel? Where? Here? The bottom fell out of TJ's stomach, but he struggled for calm. "I couldn't reach him on the phone." He prayed that was what Clay meant, but Roger's warning had set off his interior alarms. He'd just been too worried about Mara to listen.

Clay shoved the hair from his eyes and frowned. "You didn't see him? He was here, talking to Mara. I thought she sent him to you."

"She probably sent him to the dig. Did she say where she was going?" TJ had lived in dangerous situations for years, had developed a sixth sense for trouble. He could feel the storm clouds forming even without Clay's answer, and he wanted to fly after Mara and take her to shelter. He just didn't know in which direction to fly.

"I only saw them through the window," Clay answered, watching him with growing concern. "His family knows ours. They would have said something if he was dangerous, wouldn't they?"

He must be giving off bad vibrations if even the oblivious genius picked up on them. TJ sought calm in logic, but logic failed when it came to Mara. "Did she go with him?"

"She'd have to, to show him the dig, wouldn't she? I haven't seen her around since."

TJ was out the door before the last words emerged from Clay's mouth.

THIRTY

TJ found Mara's chauffeur in the drive, waxing the limo. If she didn't have her car, she must have gone in the colonel's. Was the woman crazy?

He grimaced and vowed to sever that word from his vocabulary before Mara heard him use it. "Jim, did you see where Mara went?"

"Said she needed to check on something at the set, and she was leading some friend of yours down to the island. Your keys were in the Taurus, so she took it." The chauffeur's tone gave away his opinion of her choice of vehicle.

TJ would kill Clay for leaving the keys in the car, but he refused to let paranoia get the best of him. "She does know how to drive?" he asked stoically, revealing only one of his many fears.

Jim shrugged. "In theory. The road to the island should be safe enough this time of day."

Mara had his car—he couldn't follow her. Shit. Clay had a damned *helicopter*. No wonder he was idling about, tinkering with the kitchen. He couldn't leave until the car returned.

TJ couldn't stand it. He had to go after Mara. "Give me the keys." He stuck out his hand to the chauffeur, expecting his command to be obeyed.

The driver merely looked at his upturned palm with incredulity. "No way, man. You want to go after her, I'll take you."

"Not unless you know how to do ninety in sand."

"Better than you can." Throwing aside his rag, Jim jumped into the driver's seat and ignited the engine.

To hell with riding in the back. TJ took the front passenger side and snapped his seat belt in place. "Move it."

The powerful car surged forward, taking the turn out of the drive with a squeal. It wasn't exactly the fastest vehicle on the road, but the Lincoln had been built for power as well as luxury. It flew right over potholes.

"I'm supposed to be her bodyguard, but she said she didn't need me," Jim complained. "Is she in trouble?"

"Mara's always in trouble. It's knowing when she needs help that's the problem." TJ hated sitting still. He needed his foot on the gas and his hands on the wheel. His pent-up frustration threatened to explode as the car glided onto the causeway and the beam from the lighthouse struck through the open sky ahead. Night had arrived, and Mara was out there alone with a man who killed for a living.

That was unfair. Martin had been in the Balkans on a peacekeeping mission. He would never harm Mara.

But then, TJ reflected, it was conceivable that Martin had profited from the crimes of others. Maybe he didn't really know the colonel as well as he believed he did.

"I thought she knew the guy," Jim intruded, as if reading TJ's mind.

"If she trusted him, she would have let him drive instead of taking my only transportation." Give her credit for some sense, TJ told himself. Mara wasn't a fool.

"He dangerous?" the driver asked warily.

"Yeah, but it's me he wants. He has no argument with Mara." Martin didn't even know what Mara was to him, TJ told himself. She should be fine. He was worrying needlessly.

But he knew that wasn't true. Martin wouldn't have traveled to a Podunk town at a time like this if he wasn't desperate.

The limo slid around the curve from the main highway into Cleo's sandy lane. The long rear of the car didn't respond well to the lack of traction and fishtailed halfway down the drive.

TJ spotted a strange vehicle in front of Cleo's garage and ordered Jim to halt.

"That's his car," Jim verified.

"Go in, tell them you're security, verify his identity. If it's Colonel Martin, tell him I'll be with him in a minute. I'm going to check the beach in case Mara went there."

This time Jim responded to orders. TJ breathed a sigh of relief, let himself out, and slipped into the shrubbery leading toward the dune.

He should have brought a flashlight. He'd had a lantern at the dig, but he'd packed his gear and hauled it to Cleo's garage. The well-worn path beneath his feet crunched with dead branches and old clamshells. He couldn't arrive quietly if he tried.

He wasn't trying. The colonel was back at the house, and TJ was racing after Mara.

The mayor had said she was upset. How upset? Had she reconsidered since they'd talked this morning? He'd never believed she would harm a child, but then he'd never believed Brad would kill himself. He was lousy at predicting what people he loved would do.

People he *loved*. He should have told Mara how he felt. What was the matter with him? Why couldn't his damned intellectual brain grasp that women needed words? If he'd just given her the right words—

"That you, TJ?"

The unexpected sound of a male voice ringing from the direction of the dune stopped TJ in his tracks. The colonel was supposed to be back at the house waiting for him. Where was Mara? Fear blossomed into panic, but TJ clenched his teeth and quelled it, groping for an adequate response.

"I just want to talk, McCloud. You never gave me a chance to explain. Why didn't you call before you threw me to the wolves?"

Feeling as if Martin had shredded his soul with that plea, TJ walked out of the bushes to the bottom of the hill.

He could see the glowing tip of the colonel's cigarette at the top of the dune, where Martin was apparently examining the abandoned excavation. TJ had removed the fence and ripped off the board supports in preparation for the bulldozer's arrival. It wasn't the most stable place to stand, but that was a minor argument next to the major one. "I didn't want to be judge and jury," he called, letting Martin know where he was.

He remembered cold winter nights with the colonel standing much as he was now, cigarette in hand, staring into the distance as some Balkan city in the countryside echoed with artillery fire. They'd talked of politics and peace, holidays and home. Now that he might become a father, TJ truly understood how much those nights had meant to him. The colonel had filled the place of father that TJ's own parent had vacated. Should he have a son, he wanted to be there for the boy as the colonel had been there for him.

Reminded that he might never have the chance to know his child, TJ tried to find some sign of Mara, to verify she was all right, but it was dark. She was supposed to be at the set, taking night shots.

"You played judge and jury when you didn't destroy the boxes as I asked," Martin pointed out with inexorable logic.

Guilt froze TJ's tongue. He hadn't listened to the colonel, as he hadn't listened to Brad. He could have cost the colonel his career, as he'd cost Brad his life. He'd chosen to do things his own way, instead of doing as his friend had expected him to do—as his friend had needed him to do. Had he been acting as judge and jury by handing the boxes to an objective third party?

"Your incompetent staff disobeyed TJ's order to destroy the boxes."

Mara. TJ cursed and ran his hand through his hair in disbelief at her angry defense.

"Your staff shipped the boxes back with TJ's gear. He knew nothing about it until he returned from Africa."

TJ didn't know whether to wring her neck, shout at her to get out of here, or throw himself between her and a man on the brink of self-destruction. He didn't know what the colonel was doing here, but he knew his arrival wasn't the action of the rational man he knew and admired. "Mara, Jim's back at Cleo's. Go find him, why don't you?"

"The tabloids call you two an item," the colonel said casually, flinging down the cigarette and rubbing it out with his foot. "How do you like sleeping with a traitor, Miss Simon? I trusted McCloud with my life, and he shot me in the back."

"He did no such thing!" The indignation in Mara's voice would have made a more timid man wince. "*I* told him to turn those papers over. They were tearing him apart. He hoped they would prove your innocence. But you're not so innocent, are you?"

Oh, shit, TJ thought. Now all hell would break loose. The colonel despised having his authority challenged.

Quietly TJ edged through the bushes at the bottom of the dune to the beach side, hoping to put himself between Mara and a dangerous man behaving erratically. "Why are you here, Colonel?" he called, letting Martin know he was close and available, hoping to distract him from Mara.

"You were like the son I never had, TJ." Martin's voice changed from belligerent to weary. "I love my daughters, but they don't understand. I thought you did."

The gaping wound inside TJ tore wider at this admission. He should have made more effort to listen when the colonel talked, to understand what made him tick. Maybe Martin had had some problem that they could have talked out and resolved. Maybe the reason he didn't have relationships was because he was incapable of communicating with anyone but dead people. Maybe he'd lived inside his head for so long, he didn't know how to listen to others.

"I didn't read most of the material, Martin," TJ called, making a last-ditch effort to understand. "I'm not a military expert, so I gave it to a man I trusted, hoping the truth wouldn't be buried in government red tape."

He could hear Mara breathing in the shrubbery at the base of the hill, and a trickle of fear slithered down his gullet. He was torn between grabbing her and running, and staying to hear what the colonel obviously needed to say.

As if hearing his unspoken fear, Mara whispered, "I have a black belt in karate, but I didn't know whether to take him out or not."

TJ hugged her pragmatism close to his heart. She knew how to take care of herself—and the baby. "Just don't get between us until I work this out, okay?"

He waited for her whispered agreement before he would act.

"I'm safe here. Just take care of yourself, all right?"

Accepting this as her way of agreeing, TJ challenged Martin. "I'd hoped that the evidence in those boxes would clear your name, Colonel."

"You should have given me a chance to explain." The man on the hill sounded sad and disapproving. "I had my reasons. You should have known that."

Fighting off the adrenaline that demanded he protect Mara first, TJ positioned himself between her and Martin, shielding her with his bulk. Right now his major concern was the colonel. The man never talked about his feelings. Something was definitely off-kilter.

But TJ wasn't listening to logic. He was listening to random sounds, hoping Mara was moving away.

"I did know that, Colonel. That's why I gave the boxes to Roger." Instinct screamed warnings, but TJ couldn't see any obvious threats. Martin didn't appear to be armed.

He couldn't take any chances. Keeping to the bushes, he crept farther up the dune.

"Hey, Colonel Martin," Mara shouted, covering the rustle of TJ's movement. "I've got wine back at the inn. I'll introduce you to Glynis Everett and my PR people. We'll tell your story to the press, let the world hear your side."

The colonel snorted and lit another cigarette. "Interesting female you've hooked up with, McCloud. A little fantasy to hide the reality?"

No doubt about it—the colonel was a menace to himself and to others. Still hidden, TJ searched Martin's silhouette for signs of firearms. "Mara's my reality, sir. She's right. If you have a story to tell, she's in the best position to do it."

"My story won't play well in the press," the colonel said in resignation. "I didn't do it for profit. I'm not guilty of all the crimes they'd like to pin on me, but I *am* guilty. Do a job well and unrewarded for thirty years, slip up once, and I'm a condemned man."

Warning sirens clamored in TJ's head. Lowering himself to all fours, he crawled out of the cover of shrubbery. Sand shifted and crumbled beneath his fingers. "I'm sure you did what you thought best at the time." TJ even believed what he was saying. The colonel he knew was an honorable man.

The man at the top of the hill wasn't the colonel he knew.

"I just wanted you to know the truth."

From where he was positioned, TJ could see the colonel tossing a ball between his hands, and he froze as he recognized the grenade. *Mara! Get Mara out of here.*

"Milo Turkosevic is my mother's uncle," the colonel announced without warning.

Oh shit. TJ tried not to slide back down the hill. Milo Turkosevic—the war criminal who'd allowed untold hundreds of women and children to be raped or killed because they were a different religion from his. He really hadn't wanted to hear that. "I suppose he said he was fighting for his country?" TJ couldn't resist asking. Stupid thing to say to a man with a grenade in his hands, but this was the kind of heated discussion he and the colonel used to share, and he needed time to think. Could he run back down the hill, grab Mara, and haul her to safety? Or should he stop the colonel?

"In war, you do what you have to do. I did it in 'Nam. War is about principles and strategy, not about people."

"War is about rich people getting richer and powerful people holding on to power," TJ replied with scorn. "We were there as *peacekeepers.*"

Mara, get out of here, his mind screamed. The colonel could only harm himself—if she would run.

"I know. I regret what I did, and I'll pay the price," Martin said, as if they were discussing world news over a beer. "I just wanted you to know why I did it. I knew about the protection scam, the graft that freed prisoners for a price. I'd gathered the evidence to put them out of business—until Milo got arrested. He swore he was innocent, swore he would leave the country, and instead of arresting the profiteers, I used them to free Milo. He was family, and I believed him. You've got to believe in *something.*"

TJ heard Martin's desperation and couldn't answer it. He'd protected the colonel for weeks because he'd believed he was a friend. He didn't know what he would have done if Martin had been one of his family.

The colonel took his silence as condemnation. "I thought you'd understand, even if no one else would. Better get out of here, McCloud. Take your movie star with you. I won't dishonor my family any longer."

"TJ!"

He heard Mara's cry of alarm, knew she understood as well as he did. He couldn't let the colonel do it. He'd spent seventeen years in hell for his failure to prevent Brad's death. His life wouldn't be worth living if he couldn't at least attempt to stop another friend from becoming a grisly statistic.

"You aren't dishonoring anyone," TJ shouted back. Somehow he had to find the words that always failed him. He had to talk Martin out of this.

Scrambling to his feet, he advanced up the hill. "You'll devastate your family if you pull that pin. Have you ever known anyone who committed suicide? Do you have any idea what havoc suicide wreaks on the people left behind? You'll destroy your daughters, your wife, rob them of their happiness for the rest of their lives. They'll go to their graves wondering if there was anything they could have done to stop you. The burden of guilt will cripple them more than the dishonor you fear."

"They'll be glad to see the last of me," the colonel countered. "The press hounds them night and day. They're afraid to step out the door. Get back from here, McCloud. I've made up my mind, and you won't change it. I don't mind taking you out with me if I have to." The colonel hefted the grenade in the light of the pale moon.

"TJ, don't!" Mara screamed from the safety of Cleo's side of the dune. TJ prayed she was going for help.

This time, he was mature enough to see the danger and act on it. Without another thought, TJ vaulted toward the colonel.

Martin crumpled beneath TJ's tackle. TJ's shirt seams ripped as he wrestled with the older man, straining to grasp the grenade. TJ knew he was larger, but Martin was trained in hand-to-hand combat. The colonel locked him in a hold that toppled TJ to the sand. Grappling for a stronger position, TJ twisted, but the colonel held him in a viselike grip. They rolled down the hill, toward the beach and away from Mara. Her screams of terror echoed in his ears.

Punching TJ in the throat with his elbow, the colonel freed his hand and pulled the pin from the grenade.

Three seconds to live.

TJ fought as he never had before. He wasn't a fighter by nature, but he wanted to live. He wouldn't leave Mara with the vision of his bloody body sprayed in pieces across the sand. And he wouldn't let the damned colonel die either.

Two seconds.

Pinning the colonel's arm against the sand, TJ grasped the hand holding the grenade. Martin struggled, but TJ was stronger. Determinedly he peeled the colonel's fingers off the weapon. Bones cracked, and with a cry of pain the colonel released his hold on the deadly ball.

One second.

TJ flung the grenade as far and as hard as he could in the direction of the deserted beach. The explosion spewed sand across the night sky, and the weakened dune rumbled.

Beneath him, Martin continued struggling, and TJ was forced to return his attention to the colonel by applying pressure across his windpipe.

"Dammit, Colonel!" he shouted, still shaken by the nearness of death. "Do you have any idea what that could have done to Sandy? To your kids? Have you ever lived with the suicide of someone you loved?"

The colonel quit struggling to gasp for air.

"Death ends it all! You'd never have another chance to explain what you did or why you did it. Think about Nicole and Michelle, spending the rest of their lives believing their father didn't love them enough to live for them."

Breathing heavily, Martin lay still. The night of Brad's death flamed across TJ's memory as strongly as if it had been yesterday. Shaking, he released the colonel's throat. "I didn't think you the kind of man to take the coward's way out."

Beneath him, the man he'd thought of as a father let out a choking sound. The colonel shook his head, unable to reply.

"Do you have any idea what it would have done to *me* if you'd died like this?" TJ asked, his voice cracking as grief and terror spilled through his reserve. "You're the father I've never really had. I'd carry the guilt of your death forever. All you had to do was confess you made the wrong decision, give up your commission, and retire, and your family would have loved you and respected you. And you chose to ruin all of us instead? Are you out of your mind?"

"Maybe." The colonel's voice was raw and raspy. "I couldn't bear the shame."

"Bear it," TJ said gruffly. "Pay the price of your wrong decision. Just don't make others pay it for you."

"I hate it when you're right," Martin whispered.

Sagging with relief, TJ rolled over, listening to the sound of Mara scrambling toward them. He needed her in his arms right now, needed to feel life again after this close brush with death.

The sand shifted as he started to stand.

With a slow rumble of thunder and a cloud of dust, the excavation above them collapsed in on itself. A surprised scream drowned out the crashing tide.

Mara!

Panic instantly replaced triumph. Leaving the colonel nursing his crippled hand, TJ raced up the cascading dune, a litany of prayers escaping his lips. *Please, Lord, save Mara. I'll give up my job and go to Hollywood and be her houseboy and bodyguard. I'll raise the baby by myself. I'll do anything you like. Just make her safe.*

Mara's moan whispered from beneath an avalanche of loosened sand.

No! Please, not Mara!

Heart rate escalating, TJ tripped and slid headfirst into the shrubbery. Sand covered the waist-high wax myrtles. Scrambling for footholds, he half crawled, half tumbled through the debris, screaming Mara's name.

He heard shouts in the distance, but the shattering sound of Mara's moan obliterated all else.

"Mara, I'm coming. Where are you? Talk to me." He slithered through broken sticks and briars, seeking the source of the sound.

"The baby," he heard her whisper. "I'm losing my baby, TJ." Her voice was thick with tears and panic.

Sickened, he crawled in the direction of her pale face outlined against a backdrop of half-buried palmettos. "I'm here, Mara. Just hold on."

"I'm bleeding, TJ," she whispered.

"It's okay. Everything will be okay. Just hold on. I'll get you out of here." He didn't know what he was saying. His mouth was moving faster than his brain. He simply had the overwhelming urge to paint the world bright for the woman he loved, the woman who had suffered far too much to suffer more.

"I love you, TJ," she murmured as he lifted her in his arms. "Take care of my baby." Trusting in him, she lost consciousness.

THIRTY-ONE

"Pacing the floor won't help," Clay advised, grimacing at the coffee he sipped from the paper cup.

"Standing still won't, either." TJ crossed to the window overlooking the hospital parking lot. The wild ride back to town in the limo had told him Mara and the baby needed more help than he could provide. The town ambulance had taken Mara straight to Charleston. They hadn't let him ride with her. He'd flown here with Clay, vivid images of Mara doubled up in agony branding every nerve and synapse.

The knifelike anguish successfully dried his tears. He would never forgive himself if he lost Mara now, just when her life was really beginning—just as he was coming to understand what it meant to love someone.

As if reading his mind, Clay spoke quietly. "It's not your fault, TJ. You couldn't know the dune would collapse."

"I could have at least considered it." He didn't want to be relieved of the guilt. He needed to hurt as much as he'd hurt Mara. More. He deserved whatever punishment God wreaked on him for taking her life in his hands, risking it for a man who probably didn't deserve it.

"I gave the police the colonel's phone number so they could notify his family. Should I call and warn them?" Clay voiced his concern in the only manner the McClouds understood, in practicalities.

TJ shrugged. Who was he to give out advice on family

matters? "Do what feels best. I'll talk to them later. I'm not leaving here until I see Mara."

For the first time in years, Clay's cynicism slipped, and sympathy reached his voice. "She'll be okay, TJ. Mara's a fighter."

TJ clenched his teeth and nodded curtly. The prickles behind his eyelids were harder to combat now. Clay didn't know what was at stake here.

Mara had begged him to take care of her baby. *She wanted to keep it.*

So did he. If only they could save the baby, they'd be fine. They could work things out. He wouldn't let anything bad happen to Mara and his child. He knew people. Modern medicine worked miracles.

Relief spilled through him when a nurse finally appeared in the doorway. "Mr. McCloud? Miss Simon is asking for you."

TJ left his brother to his own pursuits. The entire movie crew would turn up shortly. He needed to see Mara first. Clinging to desperate hope, he didn't dare question the nurse. His whole life lodged in his throat as he walked the interminable hospital corridor.

Mara seemed to be sleeping, covered by white hospital sheets, wearing one of those abominable green hospital gowns, her curls spilling across a nearly flat pillow. He needed to bring one of her fluffy pillows here, and a bright red teddy bear. He wished the gift shop had been open. He remembered clearly the night she'd cooed over that ridiculous bear in a toy store window. He'd bought it to give to her for her seventeenth birthday—and then Brad had died.

So many things he hadn't done, and now it was too late. TJ sat down on the bed's edge and lifted the pale hand lying on the covers. Mara's eyes opened instantly, green and bright with tears.

"I lost the baby, TJ." A fat tear slid from her eye and down her temple. "Our beautiful baby. I'm so sorry, TJ." A sob racked her throat, halting her words.

Pain sliced his heart in two, and the tears he'd been holding back dripped down TJ's cheeks. He grappled for words, a task more difficult than fighting the colonel for both their lives. "I'm sorry, Mara."

"How could I even think I didn't want her?" she whispered. "Everything I've ever wanted has turned out wrong. I was terrified I couldn't do the mother thing right. But how could I even have dreamed of giving up our little girl?"

TJ cracked. Tears pouring down his face, he tugged her into his arms and wept against her neck. Knowing she needed him to be strong, he fought for control, but the only words he could find were hopeless. "It's my fault. I should have gotten you away from there—"

She shook her head against his shoulder. "You can't shoulder the blame for the world, TJ." She hiccuped on a sob. "The doctor said that losing it this easily meant I would have lost it anyway, that something wasn't quite right. It's not your fault."

He held her tighter, and took a deep breath to fight back tears. They'd lost a little girl, maybe one with Mara's laughter and loving eyes. Placing blame didn't ease the agony of loss. He still couldn't find the right words to comfort her. Her tears were soaking his shirt. He could only hold her in his arms and rock her.

"Did you save your friend? Is he all right?" she whispered through her tears, wrapping her arms around him as if to offer him the comfort he wanted to give her.

A subject he could handle. "My *friend*," TJ replied in a hollow voice. "I'm lousy at picking friends. Yeah, he's got a couple of cracked fingers, but he'll live. Don't waste time worrying about him. He could have cost me you. He cost us a *child*."

"Tim, don't do this to yourself," she murmured, fading away on whatever drugs they'd given her. "This is just the way it was meant to be. It's not our call."

He didn't have enough faith to believe that. He'd acted on fury, not logic, and lost what he'd wanted most in this world. He wanted to tell her how much he loved her, how much pain the loss of their child caused him, but the words stuck on his tongue as her eyes closed.

She was alive, no thanks to him. He shouldn't ask for more.

Gently he laid Mara against her pillow and watched over her until she breathed evenly in slumber.

Mara woke to the light of a streetlamp on her pillow and the clatter of dishes in the hospital corridor. No clock gave her the time, but the window was dark. What on earth did these people do at this hour to make such a racket?

Then the events of last night flooded back, and she sought frantically for TJ to tell her she'd only dreamed the last hours.

In the darkness, she sensed the room's emptiness. Alone. Again. She'd been given the chance to bring life and hope into the future, and she'd wished it away.

Tears slipped from beneath her eyelids. As if waiting for that signal, a sob caught in her chest, and a wail of anguish emerged. Weeping, Mara buried her face in the pillow to hide her pain, as she'd learned to do long ago.

She didn't know how long she cried before the familiar scent of her favorite pillow seeped through her misery. Seeking anything to distract her, Mara blinked away tears and searched the darkness.

Cuddling the fluffy pillow, she groped for the bedside light, pushing it on just as a nurse's aide cheerfully burst into the room.

"Good morning!" the woman called, pushing back the ugly curtains to reveal fuzzy halos of light over a parking lot. "Are you up to washing on your own, or would you like some help?"

The light illuminated a castle of familiar items stacked around the bed. Awed by the attention to detail, Mara could only stare instead of answering. Someone had neatly arranged all her beloved family photos on the nightstand. A selection of her favorite books rested within reach on the bedside table. A multicolored array of roses and baby's breath filled the top of the dresser—someone must have woken up the florist in the middle of the night for those.

And beside the roses sat a bright red-and-blue patchwork teddy bear with an impish, lopsided grin. Adorable blue button eyes gleamed back at her, and she bit her finger rather than cry again.

She wasn't alone.

She couldn't stop the tears, but these were healing tears. TJ had done this.

No one else in her life had ever cared enough to give her what she needed. Other people only cared about what she could do for them. They told her she was being foolish when she wanted teddy bears or bright red lipstick.

TJ *understood.*

For the first time in years, she trusted someone enough to trust her own instincts. TJ loved her. She'd lost their baby, and he still loved her. That kind of unswerving devotion seemed a miracle to her.

"I'll wash," she murmured. "Would you hand me the bear?"

The nurse smiled and moved the stuffed creature. "This one looks as if it was made with love. That's hand stitching on there."

Mara clasped it in her arms and rested her cheek on its round head—not a baby, but a promise. She could bear the loss if she had someone to help her through it. Maybe asking for help wasn't such a bad thing, after all. Maybe they could help each other.

Something torn and ragged inside her soul began to mend. She hadn't lost herself this time. She might even have found what had been lost long ago. It had been so very long since love had touched her. . . .

With the car packed and nowhere to go, TJ stopped at the hospital on his way to the airport. He'd called the hospital several times this morning, but Mara's line was always busy. He'd checked with the nurse's station to be sure she was all right, then finished clearing out his office and gathering his scattered belongings.

Reporters hounded his every step. He had no desire to tell them what had happened. Dodging them seemed the easier alternative. His security guards blocked the press from the B&B while he picked up his duffel bag. He'd slipped out the back way and locked himself in his office before they discovered he'd escaped. Then he'd pried open the back alley door to get to his car after he'd seen Roger Curtis parking his carcass at the front.

TJ had all his notes on the dig site, but he'd have to write an inconclusive report.

He didn't give a damn about his report.

Walking out of the hospital elevator onto Mara's floor, TJ heard the laughter and loud voices before he entered the corridor. At the sight of Glynis Everett and Ian chuckling over something outside Mara's door, and a host of crew members laughing around them, TJ halted. He could hear Constantina chattering excitedly in Italian from the room, and more voices attempting to override her.

Mara didn't need his company.

Feeling let down, TJ turned in the direction of the waiting room. The nurse had said they would release her today. They had no reason to keep her. It wasn't as if doctors could do anything to replace the baby.

He should be happy she was taking this so well. After her pleas last night, he'd feared she might suffer an episode of depression, but she seemed to be coming through this with flying colors.

"Timid Tim, there you are!"

TJ rolled his eyes and didn't bother looking to see who'd just stepped off the elevator. He could hear the concern behind Jared's insult.

"You're being mean, Superman. Shut up." Cleo.

TJ almost smiled at the image of Cleo coming to his defense, sort of like a bantam rooster protecting a hawk.

"How's Mara?" she demanded, confronting him with hands on hips and no preliminaries.

"Having a party." TJ gestured in the direction of the noise. "I thought you were planning on staying in Miami longer."

"Clay called last night. We figured if you didn't need us, the beach might. You did quite a job on it, Timothy Jerk." Jared slammed him on the back and sneaked in a squeeze of sympathy.

The beach. TJ hadn't given it a second thought. He'd simply checked the cottage after he'd returned from his second trip to Charleston, verified he'd left everything where it belonged, and crept out before dawn. He'd given up sleeping for the duration. Too many nightmares. "They were going to bulldoze the dune anyway," he replied with a shrug.

Cleo watched him with curiosity before the noise down the hall distracted her. "Looks like we're not needed here. Let's go home and let Mara have her rest."

Her dry tone didn't escape TJ's notice, but he didn't call her on it. No one knew about the baby, unless Mara had told them. Cleo and Jared's baby would have had a cousin almost the same age. . . .

He wouldn't go there. "I was headed for the airport. Reporters are still crawling all over the place, and I'm not inclined to give them what they want. What did you do with the kids?"

"Left them with Cleo's sister for a few days." Jared draped his arm around his wife's shoulders. "We thought a second honeymoon was called for before Junior becomes a problem."

Cleo attempted to poke him in the ribs with her elbow, but Jared dodged the jab.

"They had to call off the bulldozer," she said. "Water is filling the hole at high tide, and they've declared it unsafe. It's your chance to see if you missed anything. . . ." Her voice trailed off, her questioning gaze inquiring about his intentions.

TJ glanced down the hall at the crowd of movie stars, then back to Jared and Cleo, looking like the happiest couple in the world. He preferred to run and hide, to take the next plane to parts unknown, to drive people away before they did something inexplicably hurtful, or he hurt them. Those were his usual tactics. They'd served him well in the past.

Maybe not this time.

He doubted he could hurt himself or Mara much worse. Why not go for broke and stay to see what developed? He could handle newspaper reporters. The worst that could happen would be Mara going back to her job and ignoring him, or calling him a jerk and breaking his nose. That might even make him feel better.

"All right, let's see what the tide's washed in." Turning on his heel, TJ stalked toward the elevator.

"You are covered in bruises," Constantina clucked as she fluttered around the bedroom at the B&B, putting things away. "You should be in bed, resting."

Mara hugged the teddy bear and shrugged. "Bruises don't hurt any worse standing up." The hollowness inside her did, but she wasn't about to share a memory that belonged to her and TJ alone.

She'd hoped TJ would come to see her, or be here waiting when she arrived, but given the crowds hovering solicitously, she couldn't blame him for disappearing. As much as she'd worked to gain this kind of attention, she'd learned it didn't provide the fulfillment she sought. Hordes of people did not equate hordes of friends.

But the patchwork bear told her she was loved.

It was just a stupid bear. She shouldn't place that much hope on it, but she let optimism rule. Even if he didn't realize it, TJ loved her. All the glamour in the world couldn't replace the satisfaction of that insight. Instead of distrusting her feelings, as she had the last time he'd turned his back and walked away, this time she had to act on them. She just wished she knew how. Looks had been her fallback position for years, but TJ knew her too well for disguises to work. Beauty might be power in some circles, but power would never make her happy. She needed love for that. She needed TJ.

She couldn't ask Irving or Sid or Aunt Miriam or any of the consultants and staff she had at her beck and call to intervene and bring TJ to her. This was her life, her decision, and for once she must be brave and do it all on her own.

The idea of relying solely on herself for something so important as pinning down TJ terrified her. She'd prefer to have a consensus of opinion that she was doing the right thing. But she was learning everyone had their own agenda, and those agendas weren't always what was best for her. She'd married Irving because her family advised it. She'd married Sid because all her so-called friends had told her it was a good idea—so she could help them get jobs. Only she could judge what *she* really needed, and it was high time she had confidence enough to put herself first.

TJ trusted her judgment. He hadn't told her she was better off marrying him. He hadn't ordered her to give up her career or to keep the baby. He hadn't even blamed her for staying when she should have fled—at the cost of their child.

Maybe he didn't trust her judgment anymore, but she had to find out.

"Tell Jim to bring the car around," Mara instructed Constantina.

Hugging the bear for reassurance, Mara inched gingerly down the stairs. She ached in places she didn't know could ache. She wasn't at all certain she was doing the right thing. What if TJ had acted on guilt and not real love? Was she fantasizing again?

The bugaboo of insecurity would never leave her, but if she thought too hard, she'd never act, never accomplish anything at all. Better to be a fool who tried rather than one who didn't. Had she gone to TJ after Brad's funeral, her entire life might have been different. And his.

"To the island, Jim," she ordered, easing into the backseat as her driver held the door. She waited until he'd taken his seat before adding, "And thank you for everything you did the other night. It was above and beyond the call of duty to take Colonel Martin to the hospital and watch over him until the police arrived."

"The man had his fingers broken. Had to take him to the hospital," Jim scoffed. "It was Dr. McCloud who got you into town. I thought this old car would go airborne, the way he drove it. Nearly ran over his brother."

"Clay? He was there, too?" Seemed she'd missed all the excitement.

"Stole someone's motorcycle. Guess he got worried when we tore out of town like that. He wanted to fly you to Charleston in his helicopter, but it only has one seat, and Dr. McCloud insisted he could get you to town faster."

Thank goodness at least one McCloud brother had sense. If she'd woken up lying on the floor of a vibrating helicopter, she'd probably have leapt out in terror. The image of TJ driving recklessly into town while she lay bleeding and unconscious beside him brought more tears to her eyes. She'd put that poor man through hell.

"You still deserve a bonus," she asserted. "I told the reporters you were the one who brought the colonel in." Which helped keep TJ's part in the drama quiet. The colonel's family didn't need to hear the details of that night. "I know this car has some miles on it, but the company doesn't have enough cash for anything else. I'll have the title transferred as soon as I can reach the lawyers."

Jim slammed on the brake, gaped at her in the rearview mirror, shook his head, and eased back to speed again. "I've never owned a car like this. I could start my own business with this baby. You're a crazy woman, for certain, but I thank you."

She *was* a crazy woman. Now that TJ wasn't tied to her by the baby, maybe he wouldn't want a mentally ill woman who shouldn't have kids. She really ought to think these things through better, but she couldn't. She had to know what TJ felt. She needed it spelled out in clear terms before she could proceed further. "Well, if this film doesn't get made under budget, you may have to use the car to earn a living. I want to make certain everyone lands on their feet if that happens."

"You'll do it, Miss Simon," Jim said with assurance. "Crazy people get things done."

She smiled at that. Maybe it did take a crazy person to do what she had done. What she wanted to do.

She knew what she wanted to do. For the first time in her life, she had a goal, and it was all hers and no one else's. Her heart raced excitedly at the endless possibilities. If TJ didn't want her . . . well, she'd figure it out. Now that she'd found herself, she would desperately try not to lose sight of who she was again. She didn't need TJ to tell her what to do. She just needed him in her life. Friends were too precious to throw away.

When they arrived at the place where the dune had been, they discovered a dozen cars and trucks parked in the sand. The remnants of the giant sand mound lingered in the rough terrain, spilling across bushes and palmettos. A peacock surveyed the company from the branches of a wax myrtle sticking out of the sand, occasionally squawking and spreading his tailfeathers.

"Wonder what they taste like roasted," Jim mused, opening the car door for Mara and helping her as if she were a fragile piece of porcelain.

"I'd only try if I wanted to find out what *I* tasted like roasted. Cleo doesn't take lightly to people messing with her pets."

Jim snorted and followed her across the rough path trampled in the sand. Beneath the shade of an oak twisted by ocean winds, she shook off his helping hand and gazed into the glare off the water. The tide was out, the sun was behind her at this hour, but the blue sky and waves were dazzling.

Despite the glare, she could see the crowd on the beach clearly. TJ wasn't among them. Disappointment flooded through her. Had he left, then? As he had before, as he always did?

She couldn't bear it if he had. All the confidence she'd been feeling drained away. She'd revealed her innermost secrets, and he'd chosen to reject her. Or he'd stupidly decided she was better off without him. Or—

Sand flew up out of the hole the crowd stood around.

She recognized the muscled arms wielding that shovel.

With determination, and the stuffed bear in her arms, Mara slipped and slid down the remains of the dune to greet the crowd turning their attention to her.

She didn't even know if they recognized her without her sunglasses, hairpiece, and heels, and she didn't care.

TJ was down in that hole, and she wanted him out here where he could see her.

THIRTY-TWO

"Company, Tim," Cleo called softly from above.

With sweat pouring through the grime covering his bare chest and arms, TJ wiped his forehead and glanced upward, but he couldn't see anyone. He'd warned people to stand back. He didn't want anyone else harmed by dangerous excavations.

Carting a bucket of artifacts, he crawled up the ladder he'd laid on the gradual slope carved from the blast area. There had damned well better not be any more reporters hanging around, or he was likely to stuff them down the hole and bury them.

The instant he stood on the beach, TJ saw Mara, and his heart performed a leap that would have done credit to an Olympic ski jumper.

She wore a wide-brimmed, swooping hat to shade her face, but he could still see the bruise on her cheek from the fall she'd taken. She hadn't covered it with makeup. Her hair fell in a long braid down her back. A gauzy, ankle-length dress floated around her legs and clung to her curves, and he would have thought her an angel except for the red and blue bear in her arms. She was hugging it as if she would never let it go.

She was more beautiful than any woman he knew, and a dangerous combination of fragility and strength he didn't know how to cope with. He stood there gaping, aware of his filth and stink and wishing he could run straight into the ocean before greeting her.

"Hercules instead of the Hulk?" she suggested, sauntering closer, appraising his bare chest blatantly.

A corner of TJ's mouth cocked as he returned her stare. "Anne of Green Gables? Or Scarlett O'Hara?"

She laughed, a melodious laugh that struck him in so many places, he couldn't think straight. Reckless urges swept through him, but he didn't dare act on any of them. Nothing had been settled between them, might never be settled, and he damned well wouldn't try in front of an audience. Still, he couldn't resist brushing his grimy finger under her hat brim and lifting it to see her better. The look in her eyes knocked the breath out of him.

"I honestly don't know," she admitted, sounding as breathless as he felt. "I'm trying it on for size, looking for what fits. Do you like it?"

"You don't want to hear my reply in front of company. I thought you were supposed to be resting."

She beamed up at him, understanding his growl better than he did. "Chasing me off, McCloud? I won't go. What are you doing here?"

Patsy Amara Simonetti had the staying power of a snapping turtle when she applied her mind to it. A thrill shot straight to his groin, but TJ covered it with practicalities. "Digging up the remains of two German soldiers." Clasping her hand firmly in his, he led her away from the excavation.

Surprise and alarm crossed her expressive features as she glanced back to the contents of the canvas spread across the sand. "Have you called the mayor yet?"

"The mayor?" Cleo eased nearer now that they'd left personal topics for one of interest to her.

TJ watched Mara glance uneasily at the crowd closing in. "You found something at the courthouse," he said for her, drawing her to him so he could feel the life pulsing through her and know that she was safe and sound.

She nodded. "Sort of. I had a bit of a tiff with the mayor outside the courthouse, and went back in to dig around some more. I think you'd better call him." She rummaged through her purse and produced her cell phone, handing it to TJ.

He glanced at Cleo and Jared. Jared had given up trying to help and was sitting on the beach, shirt off, barefoot, sketching a design in the wet sand—a design remarkably like a U-boat. His artistic brother might not be much of a history buff, but he listened when people talked. He knew what was happening here. Cleo stood near him, watching everything and everyone, poised like a deer to flee at the slightest danger. Both of them watched TJ with expectation.

"I can't hide it, Cleo," he apologized in advance. "No matter who they were or what they represented, there are two men down there. Their families deserve to know what happened, and they deserve a proper burial. I can't judge their politics or beliefs, just their remains."

"It's the living I worry about," Cleo replied, "but you're right, it does no good to cover up the truth. Call him."

A buzz murmured through the crowd of townsfolk and movie crew. Word had spread rapidly that morning after Ed had poked into the hole blown loose by the grenade. The bones sticking out of the edge of the crater had sent Ed scurrying to Jared and Cleo. After he'd called all his bar cronies, the news had spread by osmosis. Realizing the grenade had uncovered the remainder of the skeletons he'd been searching for in the dune, TJ had set up the excavation. One of Mara's cameramen was recording the event, even though he had no idea what was going on.

"Don't bother about the call, TJ," Mara said softly, glancing in the direction of the demolished dune. "The mayor's here, with his mother."

"You want to tell me what this is all about before I say something I shouldn't?" he muttered for her ears alone.

"I can only guess, and my imagination may be more vivid than reality." She stepped closer, so they could talk softly. "I'd heard the mayor's father was German and that he'd bought a lot of land in town. I checked some of the deeds to property the mayor's family owns, and much of it was purchased in the early days of the war in the name of Schmidt. Then I checked the records office. The mayor's father changed his name from Schmidt to his wife's maiden name of Bridgeton during the war. The mayor's mother is the one with the old local origins."

Hastily pulling on the shirt he'd doffed earlier but not taking time to button it, TJ regarded the frail elderly woman in summer white heels, flowered dress, and blue-white hair approaching, and didn't want to be here for this. "Couldn't we just slip down the beach and let this play out without us?"

Mara dug her fingers into his arm. "I'm going to teach you to hang around instead of running off, Timothy John. This has the makings of a wonderful story. I hope there's a romance in it. I've got this idea for a screenplay. . . ."

TJ rolled his eyes and remained planted where she held him. Having someone to keep him on an even keel was a new and not entirely unpleasant sensation.

The mayor and his mother gazed in dismay at the skeletons carefully laid out on tarps from TJ's gear. He'd boxed the bits of buttons and shoes and other remnants that made the skeletons come alive, but his curiosity hadn't allowed him to hide the bones. He'd wanted to know that he had them all. The intellectual challenge had overcome his grasp of human nature, as usual. He'd been working this damned job too long.

The mayor shot TJ and Mara a weary, angry look. "You couldn't leave it alone, could you? What good does it do to dig up a sixty-year-old story?"

"Are you the one who trashed my office and the dig and left those messages?" TJ asked in incredulity, remembering the cut fences and the vandal skulking in the darkness and running for a motorboat on the other side of the jetty. Surely the mayor was too old for those antics.

"I left the messages," Mrs. Bridgeton said defiantly. "You had no right to unearth the dead or harm my family with something of no concern to you."

"It was a U-boat, just like I told you," Ed shouted jubilantly. "I'm not crazy. They landed right here, got themselves killed. Your daddy wasn't a half-bad sort for all his highfalutin ways. He knew they was coming, didn't he? I knew he came out here for more than hunting. He's a war hero!"

The mayor blinked in disbelief at this take on things, but the murmurs of excitement rumbling through the crowd caused him to look around and take stock before speaking.

"I vote we go back to the house and break out the cold drinks," Jared shouted, jumping to his feet and catching Cleo's arm. "It's not every day we get to toast a hero."

TJ gave his brother credit for knowing how to woo an audience without even trying. The crowd cheered at the promise of free drinks—even the nonalcoholic kind. Less apt to engage in unwarranted enthusiasm, Clay hung back, helping TJ cover the remains while the others traipsed to the house, chattering excitedly.

"Come along, Mayor, Mrs. Bridgeton." Mara took their arms and led them toward the boardwalk rather than the shortcut through the demolished dune that the others were taking. "Tell me the story, and I'll get my people to put the right spin on it."

With the skeletons protected against the tide and scavengers, Clay fell into step beside TJ, dragging up the rear behind Mara and her captives. "You said those guys were shot," he whispered. "Did the lady do it?"

"I wouldn't put anything past women," TJ grumbled, "but I don't imagine this one did. My money is on the mayor's daddy."

"So why keep it a secret all these years? He's a hero, saving the country from Germans during wartime. I didn't even know Germans landed in this country."

"According to the books Ed gave me, the Germans trained crews of kids who'd been raised or schooled in the U.S. but were loyal to the German cause. If you want to believe those books, the Germans manned some of their U-boats with guns and money and English-speaking crews. They dropped operatives up and down the coast. They hoped to blend with the crowds and blow up centers of transportation like Grand Central Station, causing chaos—except some got caught by observant citizens and ratted on the others."

Clay whistled. "So if those are Nazi bones back there, they could have been terrorists. What the devil would they blow up out here?"

TJ shrugged. "Parris Island? It's a huge training camp today, and I suppose it might have been one back then, too. But if that's what they are, I don't know how they figured to blend in here in a rural area where everyone knows everyone."

They reached the benched lookout area of the boardwalk, where Mara assisted Mrs. Bridgeton in taking a seat. TJ admired the way she handled the obviously nervous mayor and his mother, smoothing the way with words and smiles and promises. He couldn't do that in a million years. He didn't think the shy teenager he'd once known could have, either. Mara had come a long way since those days. She didn't need him anymore. He couldn't imagine how he could ask her to stay. What could he offer that she could possibly want?

"Clay, fetch some drinks from the house and let Mrs. Bridgeton catch her breath," Mara ordered. "Tell the others we'll be right up."

Clay cocked an eyebrow at the command, but with an insouciant swagger he strode up the boardwalk toward the main house.

"I could never get Clay to do anything I told him," TJ commented, wiping his face with a handkerchief and wishing he'd thrown himself in the ocean while he had the chance. His shirt was sticking to his back.

"That's because you never expected him to listen," Mara whispered back.

"My husband did what he thought was right," Mrs. Bridgeton asserted, her gaze challenging them.

"Now, Mama, you don't have to say anything. This isn't a courtroom, and everyone concerned is long dead." The rotund mayor pulled out his handkerchief and nervously mopped his neck.

TJ leaned against the railing, crossed his arms, and watched a pelican circling the cottage. "He knew the U-boat was landing, so he must have known someone on it," he concluded aloud.

"His cousin," Mrs. Bridgeton declared stoutly. "Friedrich wanted no part of it, but his cousin came anyway. They'd gone to school together. They were a close family. But Friedrich married me and didn't want to go back to Germany."

Mara curled her cool fingers around TJ's grimy arm, and he realized how tense he was. He relaxed and inhaled her fresh jasmine scent.

"So the boat landed, unloaded two spies, one of them the cousin, and your husband met them." The Germans would have been executed had they been caught, as most of the other U-boat commandos had been. Some had just spent a great deal of time in prison, though, their lives spared by incompetence or family connections or for giving evidence against their comrades. These men weren't offered the opportunity.

"He shot them," Mrs. Bridgeton whispered. "His cousin wanted him to bring them into town, introduce them as part of the family, take them to the military base to show them around. Friedrich couldn't do it."

TJ didn't comment but looked at the mayor, waiting for the rest of the story. There usually had been a great deal of money in the hands of the other terrorists arrested. They hadn't planned on starving while on these expeditions.

The mayor loosened his tie. "I was just a kid. I thought my daddy was a hero, and I wanted to help him fight Germans. I heard him arguing with Mama, and I sneaked out to follow him. I was big enough to row out here on my own."

Clay clattered back over the boardwalk bearing buckets of ice and cold drinks. "Water, soft drink, or lemonade?"

"Water will be fine, dear. Thank you very much. Dear Cleo is fortunate to have such a wonderful family." Mrs. Bridgeton didn't look at TJ as she said that.

"Am I supposed to go to my room now and let the adults talk?" Clay asked when the silence lengthened.

"That would be nice," TJ agreed solemnly. Clay would be easing up on thirty by now, so TJ supposed he'd have to stop thinking of him as his baby brother, but the urge to harass didn't go away.

Mara swatted TJ with her hat, then pointed at a bench in the corner. Clay dropped to the seat and swigged his soft drink, leaning his elbows back on the rail and watching as if they were a TV show.

"Did you arrive in time?" TJ asked the mayor, keeping an eye on the crowd milling in Jared's yard, knowing the curious wouldn't stay away much longer.

"He was digging the grave by the time I got there. The island was larger then. That area was covered in oaks. The beach has moved over the years, and hurricanes have swept away most of the trees. I couldn't have found the place again had I wanted."

TJ nodded and sipped from his bottle. When neither the mayor nor his mother continued, he pried a little deeper. "Did you let him know you were there?"

The mayor shrugged uncomfortably. "I was a kid and terrified of my father. That's the way things were back then. I knew they were Germans. I'd heard the shots. But the sight—" He broke off and stared into the distance. "I was glad I didn't have to go off to war. I ran back to my rowboat and rowed home to Mama. I heard them arguing later that night."

"Friedrich kept their money," Mrs. Bridgeton answered before TJ could ask. "I don't know where he hid it, never knew how much it was. But every so often, when he discovered a piece of land for sale, he invested some of it. I imagine the money was all gone by the time he died."

She fumbled in her handbag and produced a little black book crumbling around the edges. She handed it to TJ, but Clay was instantly on his feet, looking over TJ's shoulder.

"I don't speak German, but I think the letters in there are probably abbreviations of German words. I can't make head nor tail of them, never could. But I can read dollar signs. Friedrich had it on him the day he died."

Mara leaned against TJ's arm and traced her fingers over the fragile pages. "Lists of land he bought?" she suggested.

The mayor cleared his throat, drawing their attention. "I apologize for the trouble I've caused you. If you still need the office, my rental company will renew your lease. I will admit I encouraged a few overeager hoodlums by telling them there might be pirate gold in your office in hopes they'd scare you off. I didn't want my father's action to become public knowledge, and I thought keeping it secret was in my family's best interest. I can see now that it's better not to hide the truth. Mother and I have talked about it, and we've decided to donate the proceeds of the sale of the remaining land to a public park out here. It seems the only fitting thing to do."

Clay looked up with interest. "You'll have to buy out the people who own the beach property, won't you?"

The mayor glanced uncomfortably toward the happy party in Cleo's backyard. "They won't all have to sell. Most of the land to the east of here is occupied by trailers and fishing shacks whose owners will be happy to have the money."

Mara, meanwhile, was considering the old notebook in TJ's hand. "A mystery," she murmured. "Some of that money might still be hidden somewhere."

Right there and then, TJ decided it was time to answer a few questions of his own before opening up a whole new can of worms. He had all he needed for his report—no need to share it with the crowd drifting in their direction.

Catching Mara's elbow, he returned the book to the mayor and steered her toward the cottage. "Write your story later. We need to talk."

She widened her eyes at him. "Why, do tell, Timothy John. What can we possibly have to talk about?"

He still didn't know whether to strangle her or hug her, but he wasn't doing either while covered in filth. "Books and bones and babies," he told her curtly, half dragging her across the sand. "Not necessarily in that order."

"You can't make me talk," she warned jovially.

"Oh, yes, I can." Out of sight of the rest of the party, TJ scooped her up and carried her across the cottage porch, shoving open the unlocked door with his shoulder and kicking it closed behind him.

Only when he had her completely to himself did he dare lean over and kiss her.

THIRTY-THREE

Mara eagerly inhaled the scent that was TJ and threw herself into the kiss with all her wounded heart and soul. She could never replace what was lost, but TJ's desperate hunger washed over her like a soothing balm. She might be reading far more into his kiss than she deserved. She was very good at fooling herself. But this was TJ, and she would trust him far more than she trusted herself.

She spread her palms across his back, reveling in his strength as he held her. Instantly he lowered her to her feet. With a dazed look on his face, he shoved a hand through his hair and stared down at her.

"I stink. I've got to take a shower. Anyway, we can't do this. Wait here. Don't go, or I warn you, I'll hunt you down." He jogged up the stairs, taking them two at a time.

Mara couldn't follow at that pace. As he'd reminded her, she wasn't in any condition to be thinking of an act that might create another child.

The idea of TJ and the shower, however . . . that was all about living. She'd vowed to live her life to the fullest, and so she would, one day at a time. She wanted to take TJ with her on that journey into the future. She wanted to show him how much she loved him, how beautiful life could be—if he would let her.

She prayed he would give her a chance to share thousands of showers and sunrises and sunsets. Gripping the windowsill, she stared out at the surf lapping the beach outside the cottage. The few years of a human lifetime were grains of sand in the face of the eternity out there.

Vowing not to waste another moment fearing the future because of past heartbreaks, she swallowed her uncertainty and listened for the sound of the shower shutting off.

By the time TJ clattered down the stairs, dressed in a blue button-down short-sleeve shirt and khaki shorts, Mara had ice water in tumblers creating wet spots on the navy tablecloth she'd spread over the porch rail, and a bouquet of sea oats waving from an empty blue wine bottle. She could set a scene anywhere. She smiled at TJ's stunned look.

"I'm good at this, you know. I designed the set on that jetty." She gestured toward the ugly gray rocks now covered in what appeared to be sand, sea oats, and waving palmettos.

TJ grabbed a glass of ice water and gulped half the contents. Firmly setting it down on the railing, he met her questioning gaze. "I still want to marry you."

Mara laughed. She couldn't help it. The man must be close to six foot six and over two hundred pounds, and he looked as if he'd just volunteered to climb down an active volcano. He didn't look any more pleasant at her laughter.

Before he could stalk off in a snit, Mara leapt from the rail to throw herself into his arms. He caught her, as she'd known he would. TJ had excellent reflexes, which was good, given her precipitous tendencies. "I love you, Timothy John McCloud. I love you, adore you, and I want to spend my life with you, but we have one or two problems."

His arms closed around her, and joy swept through her at his instant acceptance. TJ wasn't one to hesitate, ponder, or calculate her worth. She snuggled there, with his chin resting on top of her head as if nothing could separate them.

"No, we don't," he assured her. "Last night I cursed myself for not telling you how I felt, and I'm not letting you go until you understand. I love you. I've loved you since you were a skinny kid following me around, singing *Doo-wah-diddy-diddy* off-key, and I love you even more now and probably more tomorrow. I don't want to lose you."

She needed those words so badly, she thought she'd soak them up before they emerged from his mouth. Flattened against TJ's hard body, she was whole. It was the most exhilarating sensation she'd ever experienced. She didn't interfere with his declaration. Couldn't. She just meekly nodded and let him ramble.

"I'm not good at words or feelings, never learned what to say when. I'm more comfortable with old bones that can't talk." He ran his hands down her back, keeping her nestled against him. "But I can say things to you that I could never say to anyone else. I love you, whether you look like a librarian or a starlet or Scarlett. You bring terrifying things out in me, but I'm more alive when I'm with you. The other night—" His voice broke. "Don't make me try to explain how I felt that night when I thought I could lose you—that the world could lose you. You bring life to everyone you touch."

She heard his tears, knew how painful this was for a man so courageous and honorable he would risk his life to save another's. She cupped his face and pressed a kiss to the side of his mouth. "You don't have to tell me, TJ. I know. I'll always know. Whatever you feel, I feel. It's frightening, but we're old enough to deal with it this time."

He directed the kiss more firmly, inciting her to passions they couldn't explore yet. Before they went too far, he moved back a step and took a deep breath. "I love you, and I don't know what the hell to do about it, but I'm not letting you get away again."

"We could go inside for a start," she suggested, with a slight gesture toward the crowd at Jared's. "We're not completely out of sight."

Glaring at the party going on above them, TJ tugged her into the dim light of the front room and carefully seated her on the sagging sofa. "I don't have a house to take you to. I don't have a glamorous life to offer. I had a call this morning from the state police in New York in the wake of all these news stories. They're offering me a steady contract, but I haven't given them an answer. I can rebuild my independent contracting business without the feds, but that means traveling."

"Sit down, TJ, you're making me dizzy. It's like watching a Ping-Pong ball when you pace like that."

He flopped onto a slatted wooden rocking chair across from her. He clenched the arms of the rocker, then ran a nervous hand through his still-damp hair. His crooked eyebrow quirked in an expression more doubtful than questioning, but Mara didn't underestimate the intellect behind that expression for a minute.

She'd intimidated the Intimidator with weapons he hadn't learned how to handle.

"I have to finish this film," she told him while he gathered his forces and regrouped. He'd march right over her if she didn't take the initiative. Maybe she'd needed these years of experience to learn how to handle a man like TJ, so she didn't become the doormat her mother had been. "A lot of people's jobs are at stake if Sid keeps the company, and I won't let that happen."

"Let me take care of Sid," he suggested hopefully. "Any man who doesn't appreciate what he has in you ought to be flushed down the sewer."

"You aren't listening." Unable to stay away from him any longer, Mara got up from the couch, planted her knees on either side of one muscled thigh, settled her butt on his knee, and dug her elbows into his shoulders. Staring into her breasts shut him up. "I learned from Irving, and the second time around I married someone who liked what I had to say and how I handled business. Sid *appreciated* me. He just thought he could shut me up in the closet when he didn't need me. *I* took care of that. You don't need to."

TJ scowled and locked his hands around the chair arms rather than her. "He's still too stupid to live. I'm not. What do you need me for?"

She pressed a kiss to his nose, then licked it. He bucked in the seat but refused to grab her. She wiggled her rear on his knee, and her Wonderbra-less chest nearly rested on his. "I don't need you for your money or your connections, TJ. Are you going to listen or do I have to munch your ears?"

He took a long time thinking about it. She narrowed her eyes at him, and he relented. "You'd better talk quickly," he muttered, "because the position we're in right now is dragging my brain southward."

She chuckled and returned to the couch. "Despite all his faults, I learned from Sid. I know how to hire good people. I learned I hate being management. I like designing sets, and I love working on the scripts, but let's face it, I'm a creative flake and not executive material."

"You're organized, efficient, hardworking, and far more logical than anyone else I've seen out there. You're damned good executive material."

Mara adored TJ's loyalty, but sometimes his hormones made him just a little dense. "Just because I have the brains to do it doesn't mean I *want* to do it," she corrected. "I can do anything I damned well want to do, but all I've ever done was what I *had* to do."

She waited for that to sink in before continuing. "If I *have* to, I'll run the studio, but I don't *want* to. I need the money to pay for around-the-clock nursing for my mother, but if I bring her to live with me, then I won't need so much. Or if I live somewhere else besides L.A., I'll have enough to pay for both nursing care and my own home. Life is about choices."

She watched TJ's Adam's apple bob up and down as he absorbed all the implications of her words. The man wasn't slow by a long shot. He just needed time to grapple with his place in the scheme of things.

"What do you *want* to do?" he asked carefully.

She beamed at him, her heart swelling with joy and pride. She got up and planted herself in TJ's lap properly this time. Wrapping her arms around his shoulders, feeling his instant arousal, she nibbled on his ear. "I want to write screenplays," she whispered against the ear she nibbled. "And maybe sometimes design sets. I want to make a home for you, TJ, and take care of you. You need someone to look after you."

"Take care of *me*?" he asked incredulously. "You want to—"

She bit his earlobe, and he shut up. "I can take care of you far better than you can take care of yourself. I can make a home for you. If the company makes money, I can pay for my mother's nursing care. She doesn't have to live with us, just somewhere I can visit. I don't know about children, though," she said with familiar sadness, but even that eased a little as TJ rocked her with his arms around her waist.

"I can afford you and your mother and anything else that comes along," he said, "unless you have a penchant for expensive jewelry and yachts and that kind of thing. But if I tell you I can take care of you, I figure you'll hit me."

She laughed into his shoulder. "Probably. I'm taking care of myself these days."

He nodded, as if that answered his question. "I'm fine with that. I want to hear you singing and laughing and throwing things at me. I want your arms around me, telling me I'm alive and real and not bad company."

She tightened her arms around him and kissed his whiskery cheek. "No finer company anywhere," she murmured.

"I don't know what to tell you about children. Until these past few days, I never thought about having them. I'm terrified I may be too much like my father and forget they're there, but I like the idea of having kids. If you want them, I figure you'll help me be a good father."

TJ stopped rocking to catch Mara's face between his hands. "But if what you're worried about is the future of your mind, don't. You're the sanest person I know. If you want children, we'll have them. Life doesn't come with guarantees."

She broke down and cried again, and let him rock her like a baby. Even the sound of a helicopter overhead didn't deter her, though her crying slowed as the rocker did.

A whistle and a splat hit the roof.

Mara's head jerked up as TJ shifted into instant alert.

Another whistle and a splat, followed by the low roar of the helicopter, then a hail of splats against the roof.

"Is the colonel bombing us?" she asked more in wonder than fear. TJ's arms gave her the courage she didn't naturally possess.

"Not from a helicopter."

Something suspiciously yellow and egglike slid down the side window exposed to the elements.

"What on earth?" Jarred out of her tears, Mara tried to peer out the window without leaving TJ's lap.

"Remember how I used to avoid Clay and Jared by sneaking out the back door and over the pool fence?" TJ inquired, carefully returning her to her feet so he could rise.

"Yeah, you said they were pests who would follow you everywhere." Mara cupped her hands and face against the window, trying to see what was happening up there.

"Every time I escaped them, they conspired to find ways of annoying the devil out of me when I returned." TJ opened the door to the porch and leaned over the rail for the water hose on the side of the house.

Mara stood safely in the doorway, listening to the helicopter overhead, eyes widening as TJ turned on the faucet. Normal people would use it to clear the egg dripping down the window. There was nothing normal about a McCloud. "TJ, you really shouldn't—"

He did. Turning the knob on full force, pulling the

trigger of the hose nozzle, he shot a steady blast of water at the occupants of the small helicopter as it passed near the porch.

Mara heard the shouts, closed her eyes, and listened for the helicopter's crash. Instead, it ducked and dodged and sped out of range.

Laughter bubbled up from deep inside her. "That's insane, TJ," she cried. "You could have killed them."

"Nah, Clay has excellent reflexes." He shut off the nozzle and, looking both professional and satisfied, turned to admire her standing in the doorway. "They'd only have landed to see if I was still alive if I hadn't come out. I saved their hides and an expensive machine. There's not enough beach for a safe landing."

"What were they throwing at the roof?" Mara could barely keep from diving into TJ's arms again. He stood there looking so fearless and confident with his hands shoved into his pockets and love smiling from his eyes. From the looks of the stream of visitors heading this way, she didn't think they'd have time for kisses. Maybe later. At the thought of a lifetime of laters, she beamed with joy.

That rocked his expression a little, but returning her smile with a heartwarming one of his own, TJ shrugged. "Cleo's rubber eggs, apparently with the latest addition of a whistle. And when there weren't enough of those, they resorted to the real thing." He indicated the slime sliding down the porch rail.

"Your brothers might be more of a problem than my mother," she said solemnly as the helicopter hovered over a distant landing field.

"My *mother* will be more of a problem than yours," he asserted. "My brothers are just icing on the cake. Before Cleo gets down here and starts ribbing me, are you going to marry me and be the boring wife of a forensic anthropologist?"

"I'll never be boring, but I'll be your wife," Mara

agreed, loving the way his grin twisted wryly at her correction. "But I sure hope you take that New York job and not one down here. I need my espresso."

"I think that can be arranged," he said with complete gravity before leaning over to retrieve one of the rubber eggs from beneath a wicker chair, swinging around unexpectedly, and flinging it with the strength of a seasoned pitcher at the familiar reporter leading the procession.

Roger Curtis ducked, and the rubber egg splatted the beaming mayor.

"Works for me." Tugging Mara from the porch, TJ ventured out to meet the townsfolk in his newly acquired status of a man engaged to the most beautiful woman in the world.

EPILOGUE

"Saying farewell to your Hollywood days?" TJ asked, propping his tuxedo-clad shoulder against a corner of the balcony overlooking the wedding reception in the B&B's lobby. Below, Mara's film crew mingled with family and townspeople to the rousing notes of a local band.

He kept his expression deliberately impassive as he watched Mara instead of the party. Leaning on the rail beside him, she wore some kind of frothy, sheer gold fabric over a figure-hugging gold silk sheath. TJ definitely noticed what she wore these days because he never knew what she had on underneath. This outfit had a perfectly respectable heart-shaped neckline, but he had glimpsed bare skin in that keyhole opening between her breasts.

"I won't miss Hollywood." Turning to lean against the rail and study him through too-perceptive cat eyes, she raised an eyebrow in a fashion remarkably similar to his own. "No more playing the starlet and flapping eyelashes to pry money out of deep pockets. Unless you have other ideas?"

She was taunting him, TJ realized. She knew he wasn't like her other husbands and wouldn't use her that way. It might take a little time until he could unbend and tease her back, but her laughing look reminded him that she understood his caution.

It was a matter of trust, he decided. He trusted Mara not to walk out if he said the wrong thing or if he got wrapped up in his world and forgot to be human occasionally. "People will think you're crazy for giving up Hollywood for a snow-covered burg in New York," he said.

Mara laughed. Crossing her arms under her breasts, she drew his gaze to a part of her anatomy he'd refrained from touching until she'd fully healed. He was afraid he'd start drooling if he looked too hard.

"Can't see yourself wielding a shovel in a postage-stamp-size yard, McCloud?"

TJ grinned at the obnoxious little-girl tone she adopted for old times' sake. He never wanted her to cry again, and he was a little anxious about his ability to make her happy, but Mara would always be Mara, and he loved her that way. "Albany has a Starbucks and a newsstand. If that's all you require, I can handle snow. It's no heavier than sand."

Mara snuggled closer, compelling TJ to wrap his arm around her. They'd been celibate these last two weeks while they planned the wedding. Touching the softness of her bare shoulder, inhaling the flowery aroma of her perfume, was testing his limits now. Even his limited imagination could envision the night ahead in Technicolor detail. A familiar heaviness settled in his groin, and he adjusted his tux discreetly. Making love with Mara was something to look forward to, but in these last weeks he'd learned just having her within reach to hug and laugh with was special. The bond between them was so strong that he could almost hear her thinking.

"I'll choose snow over Hollywood any day," she said without hesitation. "Will you curl up in front of the fire with me?"

"Every night." He gripped her tighter, knowing with this woman by his side, he gave up nothing but gained a dream. "I'll come home and you can read to me what you've written that day and I'll applaud heartily."

Mara laughed. "No, you won't. You'll tell me it's melodramatic garbage, but that's okay. I can live with criticism. I'm glad the lawyer suggested I form a consortium to buy out Sid. It will be nice having a real life again."

"Not to mention an automatic buyer for your scripts," he added gravely.

She stuck her tongue out at him. "The scripts have to be good or the films won't sell."

He cocked an eyebrow at her. "Did I say I doubted you?"

She kissed his cheek and loosened his tie. "No, but you just want to get in my bed and will say anything to get there."

"You have a problem with that?" As the music below changed to a slow tune, TJ wrapped his arms around Mara and led her into a dance step. Her smile of delight at his impromptu action was so devastating, he almost swept her into his arms and carried her off right then and there. He'd never understood that a simple thing like dancing could delight a woman. He needed to invest some time in learning what else made Mara happy. Teddy bears and dancing. Maybe flowers? Moonlight. He bet she'd like moonlight. He'd dance with her in the moonlight tonight.

Swaying easily in his arms, Mara chuckled at the memory of an earlier incident. "I can't believe your mother tracked down the colonel and scolded him. She's probably scared him into writing his memoirs and nominating you for sainthood for saving his life. I think she's terrorized half the journalists in the crowd into believing you're a hero."

"I *am* her favorite," he replied solemnly, although a smile tugged the corners of his mouth.

Glancing over the railing as they swung past, she lifted her eyebrows questioningly. "Which is why Clay and Jared are over there in the corner with their heads together?"

"Who needs kids when I have brothers?" TJ asked, halting their dance to check over the rail again. Grimacing at the sight below, he reached down to pick up a shield he'd unwired from the suit of armor in Katy's collection of antiques. He set it in place just as the first rubber egg whistled upward, splatting nicely against the tarnished metal.

Mara looked startled, then glowered. "Why, those little brats—"

TJ lifted a basket he'd hidden behind the post before she could rush down the stairs and scalp his brothers. "Fresh off the production line. Knowing Jared, I expected this. Introducing Cleo's toy at our reception is no doubt his idea of good advertising. I'd aim for the punch bowl next to Clay, if I were you."

Mara's whole face lit with such delight that paralysis nearly set in. TJ caught the next whistling egg just in time.

She'd never had a real childhood. It made him happy to offer her one.

Grabbing a handful of the spongy eggs TJ held out to her, Mara barraged the group below, hitting the punch bowl, the leftover wedding cake, Ian's cell phone, and her Aunt Miriam's tiara.

Without further ado, TJ dropped the shield, grabbed Mara's wicked right arm, and tugged her toward the back stairs. "Now!" he shouted.

Under cover of screams of laughter from below, TJ and Mara raced for the safety of the yacht waiting in the harbor, ready to set sail for the first night of the rest of their lives.

Read on for an excerpt from
Patricia Rice's
next historical romance

HER MAGIC TOUCH,

featuring Ewen Ives and Felicity Malcolm.
Coming from Signet in
August 2003.

Sheltering from the storm in an inn at a port just inside of Scotland where he expected to catch a ship to Edinburgh, Ewen Ives, fourth in succession to the title of Earl of Ives and Wystan, kicked a chair out from under the table to allow his unexpected guest to sit. The tavern wench in Ewen's lap bussed his cheek and leaped to fetch a clean tankard for the newcomer.

Aidan Dougal looked more like an Ives than any of the Ives, although he had no claim to any branch on the family tree. Browner and brawnier than his tall, swarthy relations, bearing a more prominent proboscis, he carried the certain stamp of aristocracy despite his plebian appearance. He settled his lengthy frame into the seat offered, crossed his boots at the ankle, and observed the twin serving girls eagerly filling pitchers and tankards at the behest of his laughing "cousin."

"I'm on my way south and thought to quench my thirst," Aidan said. "I thought the family had ordered you to stay put in Northumberland for a while, to oversee the mine and canal. Your boots must have wandering soles."

Ewen hooted in laughter, and the serving maids dimpled at the sound of a handsome man enjoying himself.

Accepting a tankard of ale from one twin, Aidan ignored her inviting smile and threw back a hefty swallow. With a toss of her glossy curls, the maid turned back to Ewen, who rewarded her with a broad grin and a pat on the hip.

"He's an ogre who eats beauties like you. Fetch us a bite to eat, will you? Looks like the storm has blown away my ship, and we'll be lingering a while." Ewen patted the second maid on her ample bottom so she wouldn't sulk, and sent both of them out of the private drawing room.

Sprawled in his chair like lord of all he surveyed, Aidan quaffed his ale and regarded Ewen from beneath a lifted eyebrow. "You have a way with the lasses."

"They have their way with me," Ewen returned. "All they ask is a little attention and a kind word. You should try it some time."

Aidan grunted, set down his mug, crossed his arms over his broad chest, and rocked back in his chair. "They cost too much for the likes of me. I've a mind to find one who will be a helpmate, not a drain on my pocket."

That subject veered too uncomfortably close to one Ewen was avoiding, so he sipped his ale in lieu of answer.

As usual, his damnable interfering relation blithely disregarded his silence. "I hear you promised to fund the rebuilding of the village that flooded when the canal lock gave way last winter."

Aidan had heard correctly. Ewen had borrowed against everything he owned to restore the village, and still, it hadn't been enough. And the first bank payment was coming due. He'd never been burdened with responsibility, and he didn't like it now, but he would do what had to be done. "It was my lock gear that gave way," Ewen said, shrugging.

"But the canal belongs to more than you." Aidan eyed

him shrewdly. "All the investors should have pitched in for repairs. It's not as if you have funds to throw about."

"Not that it's any of your concern, but I have expectation of income," Ewen said carelessly, as if coins spilled from his pockets as he walked. People tended to accept his wilder statements at face value if he said them with bravado. "The other investors are family men and cannot spare the coin."

"The other investors are hoarding their cash and letting you take the fall. Even if that mine turns a profit this year, it won't be enough to rebuild a village."

Ewen hid his pain with a broad smile. "Well, that's what banks are for, isn't it?" Of course, banks liked to have their money back within a reasonable amount of time, and his time was running out.

"There's some who say that is what marriage is for."

The conversation had taken a decidedly uncomfortable shift. "I never saw it that way," he said stiffly.

One of the twins returned with a heaping platter of sliced bacon and eggs. Setting it on the table, she leaned her generous bosom against Ewen's shoulder. Absently, he rewarded her by circling her waist with his arm. She ran her fingers through his hair, loosening the ribbon of his queue. When she tried to sit on his lap again, Ewen handed her their empty pitcher. "Later," he murmured. Right now he had more important things on his mind—like avoiding the web Aidan was spinning.

The maid pouted, trailed her fingers through his shirt lacing, and tickled his chest hair. Impatiently, Ewen brushed aside her marauding fingers.

Touching yesterday's whiskers, he reached for his coat where it lay across a chair. A razor that didn't require soap and water danced through his mind. He rummaged for a pencil lead and a wadded piece of paper in his pocket. Pulling them out, he began to scribble a design instead of helping himself to the eggs steaming in front of him.

Aidan snorted as the maid sauntered away. "Marriage has its purposes," he said, continuing the conversation

Ewen had already forgotten. "Are you so comely you've never felt the itch without a woman about to scratch it?"

Truth to tell, Ewen had never had a problem *finding* women. Quite the contrary. He couldn't get rid of them. Women had been set on snaring him from an early age, although he could see no good reason why. He had no home, no fortune, and little interest in either. But he did enjoy women.

"It's not scratching the itch that's the problem," he admitted, "but avoiding a noose around the neck afterward. I like each woman for a different reason, and no one woman has it all. Marriage isn't natural for my sort."

"Then take your pick from wealthy ones, and your money problems are solved," Aidan said cheerfully.

Ewen spooned eggs on his plate and shook his head. "I can't abide the clingy twits of society or demanding ladies who require constant attention. If I must marry, I prefer an experienced woman who will go her own way while I travel about on my own business." That's what he would prefer. He feared that wasn't what he would get.

"Sounds as if you have someone in mind," Aidan suggested, partaking heartily of his fare.

Dammit all, the man could pry words from the speechless. Avoiding answering, Ewen glanced through the window at a yacht bobbing in the harbor. The ship he'd hoped to catch hadn't arrived yet. He wondered where that one was headed. He longed to be on any ship at all, heading for anywhere but where he must.

Although the mines he supervised were close to the family estate in Wystan, he'd avoided the family's usual port in Northumberland. Having had word from his brother Dunstan that some of his wife Leila's relations would be arriving shortly, Ewen had chosen to slip away to a more northerly port across the border in Scotland. He figured it simpler if he avoided family and argument until he was properly betrothed.

"There's a widow in Edinburgh, daughter of a wealthy Cit," he offered up to Aidan's insatiable curiosity. "We've dallied before, and she's made her interest clear. If I explain what I need, she'll be happy to exchange some of her wealth for my name and position, such as they are."

And for a ball around his leg and a noose around his neck as well. Despite her clever mind, he feared Harriet Dinwiddie would not understand his wandering ways. Like her merchant father, she held on to what was hers.

But it was that, or debtor's prison in a month if he could not find the funds to make the bank payment.

The musical tones of feminine voices penetrating the door of the parlor distracted Ewen from his thoughts.

In the past, he might have stepped to the door to investigate the rising argument in the hall. Women traveling alone were an oddity, and often appreciative of male assistance. But now he was practically a married man and didn't have the right to flirt.

"We'll pay well," rang clearly from the lobby beyond the door.

Even through the closed door, Ewen recognized something familiar in the distress underlying the woman's brash declaration. Ignoring the instinct to help, he reached for his fork. It was his damnable instinct to fix things that had him in this position in the first place.

A second female murmured something indistinguishable. Even Aidan was watching the door with interest now.

"I ain't takin' two runaway females anywheres," a wrathful male replied.

"Do we look like runaways? How *dare* you, sir!"

"I'll lay odds they're runaways," Aidan murmured, slapping a coin on the table.

The amount wasn't enough to interest Ewen in the wager. "Let 'em run away, then. Didn't you ever run away as a lad?"

"This isn't a fancy lane between mansions in Surrey. That's a rough road out there. They'll be robbed the instant they set foot on it."

"Go save them, then. I haven't the time," Ewen said, attempting to dig into his cold eggs.

"If you won't rent them to us, we'll buy the cart and horses." A calm voice overruled the agitated shouts of the driver and the termagant. "How much are they worth?"

"Ten pounds!"

Ewen choked on his mouthful. If they were talking about the wagon outside the window, the woman would do better to make the cheat pay *her* for taking those broken-down, hay-burning nags off his hands.

"Two pounds, and you'll include the reins and harness," the soft-spoken woman offered.

The gentle timbre of her aristocratic accent struck Ewen's ear as oddly familiar, but he shook his head. Impossible.

"That's theft, it is! Nine pounds, and not a farthing less."

"Felicity, take it," the louder of the two said. "It's our only chance."

"Three pounds, and you'll include the feed," the soft voice demanded with authority, ignoring the frantic one.

"Who do you think you're dealing with, girl? Some high muckety-muck what can afford to throw away a man's wages? Eight pounds or I'm leaving without ye."

Ewen caught himself holding his breath, waiting for the soft-spoken woman to call the thief's bluff. He exchanged a glance with Aidan, who leaned nonchalantly against the wall, arms crossed, listening. The coin he'd wagered sparkled on the table.

They were runaways. Young and unprotected and obviously of good birth. And they were about to risk their few coins on a cart and horse that would no doubt leave them stranded in a robber's haven.

He must be daft to even consider intervening, yet he scraped back his chair with resignation, and rose before the loud female could cinch the deal over the clever one's head. Had she called the clever one Felicity? How many Felicitys could there be in this world?

Dunstan had been expecting visitors from his wife's

Malcolm family. Dunstan lived a day's journey south of here.

With a sick feeling in the pit of his stomach, Ewen strode to the door as Aidan looked on knowingly.

"Then leave, sir, for I'll offer no more," the soft-voiced one declared.

"Felicity!" the loud one wailed. "We *need* that cart."

"I'll be off then," the cart owner said smugly.

With a sigh of inevitability, Ewen jerked open the door.

On the other side stood the two blue-eyed, golden-haired Malcolms that Dunstan was expecting back in Northumberland.

His sisters by marriage.

Spoiled little witches who invaded Iveses' lives like pestilent locusts. It was always an ill omen when they appeared on a man's doorstep.

Look for t[illegible]es
fr[illegible]

ALMOST PERFECT

C[illegible]toonist Ja[illegible]aughs. So he ren[illegible] a sec[illegible] fall to unblock his creative juices—and falls for Cleo Alyssum, his reluctant landlady. Cleo has more important things to do than to chat with the sexy, impossibly bullheaded hunk living in her guesthouse. Yet somehow Jared and his devilish charm inch their way into her life. Will Cleo open her heart to a man who falls short of her expectations? After all, it wasn't her intention to fall for someone who is almost perfect. . . .

NOBODY'S ANGEL

Adrian Quinn trusts no one. Four years in prison will do that to a man—especially if he's innocent. Somebody owes Adrian the truth, and his late partner's ex—a spoiled society wife—is the first person he'll look to. Faith Nicholls escaped her two-timing husband right after he shattered her girlish dreams. Left with nothing, Faith has made a fresh start in a quiet place where nobody knows her name . . . until Adrian Quinn stalks into town, dredging up dangerous secrets—and awakening smoldering passions. . . .